Age of Heroes: The Witch Hunter's Gauntlet

By

B. A. Schulte

Thanks to Mom, Dad, Jessica, Andrea, Whitney, and Amy for putting up with me.
Special thanks to Karen, the Empress of Editors and to James, the King of Covers.

Prologue

Alexander Nero Jr. was not a fan of the cold. Standing on a barren, wind-swept ice cliff on Ellesmore Island, deep inside the Arctic Circle, would normally fall very low on his to-do list. But this remote and frigid island happened to be the home of one of the most heavily protected magical vaults in the world. And he intended to rob it.

The crafty old wizards of the Sorcerors' Guild had used their best spells to hide and booby-trap the vault. They even managed to turn it invisible and untouchable. The charms could only be broken if the vault was damaged, and since no one could see or touch it, the wizards thought it would remain undisturbed forever.

But they didn't know Alexander Nero.

He activated his specially designed goggles. His vision warbled for a second until suddenly a steel door set in a block of stone appeared before him. The vault hung in the air just over the edge of cliff, exactly where his late father's notes said it would be.

Nero picked up a chunk of ice and flung it at the door. The ice passed through the steel door as if it wasn't even there. He could see the vault, but he still couldn't touch it.

He had a plan for that. According to his sources, there was one law of physics that those old wizards had forgotten about, and he had brought along one of Nero Industries' latest creations to take advantage of that fact. He signaled his men to start it up.

There was only one person who stood in his way now.

He had a plan for her too.

Chapter 1

Cookies of Doom

Five minutes ago fourteen-year-old Samantha Hathaway became the most wanted criminal in the world.

The impossible had happened. The most magically secure vault on Earth had been violently breached. Droplets of lava sizzled in the Arctic snow around the shattered remains of the vault's stone guardian. The once invisible and untouchable steel door had been torn off at the hinges and tossed several yards away.

More troubling than the loss of the vault's dangerous contents was the fact that not a drop of magic had been used in the robbery. Only the Hathaway family was known to have the skill and knowledge necessary to pull off a feat of this magnitude. As the last surviving Hathaway, Sam immediately jumped to the top of the suspects list.

Sam had no clue that powerful and secret forces from around the globe were zeroing in on her. At the moment she was busy scrubbing a particularly stubborn smudge of burnt oatmeal off of a cookie sheet. A smudge she had been working on for nearly fifteen minutes now.

"Sparky! What are you doing?"

Sam had been working at the Cookie Emporium in Presley, Illinois's tiny one-story mall for the last five weeks now. In that time, her co-worker Alison had only referred to her as Sparky because every time Sam took off her hairnet her frizzy auburn hair would sprout out wildly, making her look a bit like she had been struck by lightning. Fortunately Alison didn't bother to talk to her much.

In all fairness, Sam didn't really feel like talking to Alison either. Sam and Alison hadn't traveled in the same circles since third grade. If it wasn't for the fact that they each needed a minimum-wage-paying low-stress job to earn a little cash before the start of freshmen year, they probably could have gone on blissfully ignoring each other until graduation.

"What's wrong?" Sam asked, letting the cookie sheet slip under the water.

"Can't you smell that?" Alison asked.

Sam sniffed around. She caught a hint of burning peanut butter.

"Oh, no."

She darted past the smirking Alison. Her heart pounded in her ears as she slipped on a pair of oven mitts and reached into the oven, hoping beyond hope that the cookies were still okay.

The sheet of burnt peanut butter and macadamia nut cookies was another tragic victim of the Sam Curse, her unfailing ability to mess up even the simplest of tasks.

"That makes over twelve dozen now, doesn't it?" Alison asked. It was no secret that she was scheming to get rid of Sam so that her friend Chloe could take her job and they could spend the summer gossiping and flirting with the boys across the hall at the Sports Corner.

"What is going on back here?" asked Susan Ferris, the frazzled manager of the Cookie Emporium, as she hustled into the kitchen.

"She did it again."

"Oh, Sammy."

Sam understood Susan's disappointment and confusion. After all, how hard is it to pop a dozen prepackaged fast-food-style frozen cookies into the preset oven for fourteen minutes without burning them?

"Okay, you know what?" Susan began. The wheels of her mind were clearly spinning extra hard this time. "Maybe baking isn't for everyone. Why don't you grab the register? Alison can bake another batch of peanut butter and macadamia nuts before we run out."

"Why do I get the sweaty, nasty job? I didn't burn anything," Alison whined. Alison lived for register duty, because it was the best way for her to spy on the rest of the mall.

"Fine," Susan said throwing on one of the spare aprons. "I will bake the cookies and finish the dishes. Alison, you take the register. Try to steer people towards the oatmeal raisin cookies. We have plenty of those. Sam, why don't you get the Windex and go out and clean the glass? There are finger smudges all over the display case."

Alison smugly grabbed the Windex and a rag off the rack and made a big show of handing them over to Sam.

As it turned out, the display case was absolutely filthy. Little kid fingerprints were everywhere. It was nice to think that she wasn't just doing busywork.

"Having fun?" Alison asked from behind the register.

"Yes, quite," Sam said through gritted teeth as she scraped off a nasty smudge--some sort of cheese, from the looks of it.

"That's good," said a sickly sweet voice from behind her. "You know, you are very lucky. Most people spend years and have to go to college to find their future career path, but you have already found yours."

Sam spun around. "Hello, Courtney."

Courtney Cho always found time in her busy day as queen bee to make sure that Sam knew she was inferior in every way. Sam had become Courtney's favorite punching bag the day she moved into Courtney's old room in the small apartment the Cho family lived in before Mr. Cho was promoted to head engineer at Nero Industrial Heating and Cooling. Ever since then Courtney looked at Sam and her godparents as the old poorer version of her own family--and took every opportunity to remind Sam of that fact.

Of course, Courtney wasn't aware that Sam's parents had died saving the world or that Courtney, her family, and all the pretty pop stars she worships would be enslaved or worse right now if not for the sacrifices of the Hathaway family. But Sam wasn't allowed to tell anyone about that, not that she knew much to tell, or that anyone would believe her if she did.

"What do you want, Courtney?" Sam asked in her most disinterested voice.

"Tsk, tsk. What kind of customer service is that?" Courtney shook her head. "I might have to tell your manager about that."

"Go for it."

"Ah," Courtney said in mock concern. "Do we not like our pathetic little job?"

"Do you really have nothing better to do than bother me today?"

"I was shopping, nitwit." Courtney held up her shopping bags. "The Hole just got in Monica Summers's new line."

Sam could not care less.

"Do you know what your problem is?" Courtney asked in her patented condescending way.

"At the moment?"

"Very funny." Courtney brushed Sam's sarcasm off with a wave of her hand. "You have no-"

Sam waited for her to make whatever hurtful comment she wanted. She had her mental list of comebacks ready.

But Courtney didn't finish. In fact, she didn't even finish not finishing her sentence. Her mouth remained frozen in mid speech.

Sam stared at her for a moment, almost impressed that she could hold that expression for so long. She stepped closer and noticed that Courtney's face didn't seem to be moving at all; she wasn't even breathing.

"Uh, Alison?" Sam began as she turned to check and make sure that Alison was seeing this too.

Alison was turned away from Sam, restocking napkins.

"Hello? Alison?"

Sam watched her for a moment and realized she wasn't moving either. She was frozen in mid-reach.

Sam's heart was racing now.

"Susan?" Sam yelled at the back room.

No one answered.

Sam whipped around, looking in every direction. Everywhere she looked people had stopped cold.

"What is going on?" she yelled.

Sparks of panic zipped through her body. She wanted to run, fast, in any direction. But she had no idea where.

"This had better be some kind of prank," Sam said to the Courtney statue.

She suddenly remembered that she had the bottle of glass cleaner in her hand.

"Prepare to get wet," she said, pointing the bottle right in Courtney's face. She waited half a second and pulled the trigger. The spray hit Courtney in the face, but there was no reaction from her frozen features.

"Okay," Sam said. "Last chance."

Sam unscrewed the head of the bottle and poured the entire contents into Courtney's shopping bag. Courtney still didn't react. If this was all a prank she was really taking it to an extreme; Sam had just destroyed a few hundred dollars' worth of clothes.

It occurred to Sam that maybe time had stopped, like in one of those old black and white sci-fi television shows she watched late at night when all the talk shows were over.

Over Courtney's shoulder Sam could see that the fountain in the mall's center was still running. During her time at Cookie Emporium, she had somehow trained her ears to block out the constant gurgling of the fountain, the bad mechanical music of those stupid little plastic horses kids can ride for a quarter, and the annoying vending machines that say the same three phrases over and over again like people were going to buy stuff just because the machine was trying to have a conversation with them. But now all those sounds were flooding back.

So time hadn't stopped. That was good. She could never stay awake long enough to find out how the people on the TV show got out of it. On the other hand, everyone was still frozen, which was very weird and very bad. She needed to find help.

She made a mad dash for the nearest doors, the glass double doors that led from the food court out to the parking lot. Dodging the frozen people with their Sbarro trays, she craned her neck looking for signs of movement outside.

"So, you're just going to abandon these people and save yourself. Why does that not surprise me?"

Sam stopped and spun around on the spot. Two men in robes stood next to the still unmoving Courtney.

Her first thought was that these guys must have come from the comic book store down the hall. Occasionally people came out of that store dressed as hobbits or Stormtroopers or whatever. But usually they were teenagers with bad skin and were pretty harmless. Sometimes they were even kind of fun. There was one particularly cute guy who actually made for a very passable Captain Jack Sparrow. These guys seemed more extreme, and their robes didn't look like they came from Wal-Mart's Halloween section. The taller of the two men had unruly gray hair with a few stubborn patches of brown mixed in and a weather-beaten face.

The younger man looked to be in his late twenties; his long, dirty-blond hair was intricately braided in strands that tied in the back.

"Who are you?" Sam asked. "What's going on?"

The older man smiled at her, a smile that radiated contempt and fiendish glee.

"Hold it right there, Miss Hathaway. There is nowhere for you to run," the younger man said. He held his right hand up, palm open, towards Sam.

"What are you doing, the Jedi mind trick?" Sam asked.

Faint blue sparks leapt between the young man's fingers.

"Uh, okay. That's interesting," Sam said. Her eyes darted around the food court looking for any signs of help or escape.

"Personally I'd like to see you make a run for it. How far do you think you'd get?" the older man said as he flexed the fingers on his right hand menacingly.

Nothing was making sense to Sam. Every fiber of her being was telling her to run, but as far as she knew these two guys were the only other non-frozen people in the whole world. On the other hand, they were extremely weird people, and one of them had sparks dancing between his fingers.

"Okay, stop. Rewind," Sam tried to act calm. "What is going on? Who are you? How are you moving? How am I moving? Why are they not moving? What is the deal with your hand?"

"Oh, sorry," the younger man said. He reached into his robe with his non-sparking hand and pulled out a silver medallion. It looked like the badge sheriffs wore in old Westerns, except instead of a star it had a triangular symbol that curved a bit at the corners set inside a circle.

With a flick of his hand, the blue energy coiling around his fingers shot out, wrapping itself around Sam's wrists like a pair of handcuffs.

"I'm Deputy Crispin Colver, of the International Sorcerers' Guild Magical Enforcement Squad. This is Chief Constable Horatio Albion. You are under arrest."

Chapter 2

Mall Security Gets An Upgrade

Sam's brain was shorting out. She was trapped in a mall with a bunch of time-frozen people and two seriously weird guys in robes who were trying to arrest her. Two guys who claimed to be from some organization with 'magical' in the title — which, judging by her new transparent blue energy handcuffs, seemed more likely than she would have believed thirty seconds ago.

Sam knew magic existed, of course. Her parents had told her that there were real witches and wizards in the world. They had also told her that most of them were nice normal people that liked to live separately from the rest of the world. She remembered her parents mentioning the International Sorcerers Guild too; they were some sort of police force in charge of keeping the magical community a secret from the rest of the world. This was the first time she had ever actually encountered magic, though, and so far she didn't care for it much.

"I cannot express to you how much I have no idea what you are talking about," Sam said. Her mind was racing uncontrollably. "Just tell me what is going on."

"I really have no interest in playing this game with you, Miss Hathaway," Chief Constable Albion snarled. "You are going to prison and we are recovering the Lantern of the Blue Flame. The Judicial Council may go easy on you if you tell us where it is now."

"I don't believe you read Samantha her rights, Chief Constable."

The two robed men startled at the voice. An African-American man and a pale redheaded young woman with lots of freckles approached them. They each wore black suits and sunglasses. They looked like stereotypical Secret Service-type government agents, but Sam was willing to take that over freaky guys in robes any day.

"Are you all right, Samantha?" the woman asked.

"I don't even know. Please, what is going on?" Sam asked, hoping that the nice-looking woman could explain why her entire world went completely crazy in the last few minutes.

The female agent pulled a badge out of her pocket. It was a badge Sam remembered well. When she was nine and a pillar of glittering white light erased her grandfather's house with her parents inside a dozen men with similar badges arrived to tell her that her life would never be the same again.

"I'm Agent Rosenberg," the woman said. "This is Agent Sampson. We're from the Bureau of Extraordinary Affairs. We handle delicate matters of a paranormal or otherwise unusual nature. We're going to straighten this all out, okay?"

Sam was well past her limit for weirdness today. She wanted some straight answers. "Paranormal or otherwise unusual?"

Agent Rosenberg nodded, a big smile spread across her face. "The three 'M's. Magic, monsters, and mad scientists."

"Miss Hathaway is in our custody Agent Sampson. We will be taking her back with us," Albion snapped. "She broke into a secured top-level vault, stole an extremely powerful artifact, and desecrated the tomb of an ISG council chairman."

Sam was willing to admit that she was completely in the dark on this situation, but she was fairly certain she had not done any of those things.

"We are aware of the charges," Agent Sampson said in a calm, controlled voice. "Your boss informed our office of them just minutes ago. He also agreed that Samantha Hathaway is clearly within our jurisdiction and that your organization is to cooperate in the investigation."

Agent Rosenberg handed Constable Albion a very official-looking document. Sam didn't know exactly what official orders looked like, especially the magical kind, but the glowing purple seal on the back was a dead giveaway.

"Investigation!" Albion exploded as he broke the seal and quickly read the document. "Bureaucratic fools. We all know she is guilty. You can't possibly believe you will get away with this. The Hathaway family may have gotten away with crimes against the magical community in the past due to the sentimentality of certain members of the Council, but even they cannot over look the evidence in this case. Or the theft of such a dangerous weapon."

"And what evidence is that?" Agent Rosenberg asked politely.

A smug, victorious grin spread across Chief Constable Albion's face as he withdrew a glittery silver box from his robe. It looked like an elaborate jewelry box with images flashing on every side like tiny movie screens stuck on fast-forward. Without a single word he opened the box.

"Samantha, don't move!" Agent Rosenberg yelled.

Everything went white.

He had blinded her with some magical flash of light. Sam was sure of it. She could be blind for the rest of her life.

Then the whiteness blew away.

It wasn't white light at all. It was snow.

As the snow cleared, Sam found herself on the edge of an icy cliff overlooking the ocean. Large chunks of ice smashed violently against the jagged rocks below. Instinctively Sam huddled over for warmth, doing her best to wrap her still magically cuffed arms around her self, and backed away from the edge.

"Samantha, stop," Agent Rosenberg's voice cut through the wail of the wind.

Sam looked up to see the others standing exactly where they had been standing in the food court. None of them seemed the slightest bit worried that they were perched on the edge of a cliff in the middle of frozen nowhere. In fact, Deputy Colver was stifling a laugh.

That's when Sam realized she wasn't cold. Not even a little bit. She couldn't even feel the wind swirling the snow around her. Cautiously she straightened up.

"I know it looks like we are in the Arctic right now, but we're not," Agent Rosenberg said.

"Arctic?" Sam was very confused.

"We are still in the mall. Honest." Agent Rosenberg laughed a little. "Can't you smell it?"

Sam had been too concerned with all the snow around to worry about the smell. She took a deep breath. The familiar scent of pizza, egg rolls, grease, and stale pop flooded her nose.

Agent Rosenberg waved her arms. "This is not real. It is called a glamour; sort of like a magical hologram."

Chief Constable Albion cleared his throat loudly.

"It is a security recording." His angry eyes fixed on Sam. "Of your theft."

"Of her alleged theft," Agent Sampson corrected.

"Whatever," Agent Rosenberg said dismissively. Both Albion and Sampson took offense. She pressed on anyway. "You can't see it, but we are still standing in the food court so you don't want to move around too much and run into a table or a person."

Sam nodded in agreement.

She casually pushed her right foot forward, gently kicking at a chunk of ice. Her foot passed right through it. She pulled it back quickly.

"The evidence speaks for itself," Chief Constable Albion said gesturing to something behind Sam.

Sam spun on the spot to see four people she somehow hadn't noticed before. They were all dressed head to toe in thick, puffy, black cold-weather gear, complete with fancy goggles. Four sets of sled dogs played in the snow behind them. Two of the guys (she assumed they were guys, even though it was impossible to tell with all the impressive Discovery Channel-level gear they had on) were anchoring a machine to the ground.

"Can they see us?"

"No," Agent Rosenberg said reassuringly. "They are part of the recording."

"Sort of a Ghost of Christmas Past kinda thing?" Sam asked.

Agent Rosenberg chuckled. "Sure, that's a good way to look at it. Although this happened less than an hour ago."

"What is that machine?" It looked like some sort of futuristic laser cannon, and it was being aimed right at her.

"As if you don't know," Chief Constable Albion said.

"It is an electromagnet," Agent Rosenberg explained. "Although I've never seen one this small with so much power."

"What does it do?"

"You'll see."

The other two Arctic adventurers trudged up to the cliff's edge. Sam could have reached out and touched them-- if they were solid, of course. It was an awkward feeling being so close to someone who didn't know you were there.

Even though they wore winter masks and goggles that completely hid their faces, up close the differences between the two were startlingly obvious. She mentally nicknamed the taller one Big Guy. He was well over six feet tall and had the V shape of a professional wrestler, although the puffy coat probably added a bit. The smaller one was about her height and skinnier than the others.

Most likely a teenager, Sam thought.

"Wait! You think this is me don't you?" she asked Chief Constable Albion.

"We know it is you," he said matter-of-factly.

"That's insane!"

"Let's just keep watching," Agent Rosenberg said calmly.

The Fake Sam adjusted her goggles. They were clearly far more impressive than Sam had originally thought. The lenses changed colors and little mechanisms wiggled and whirred on the sides. Sam didn't know what any of that meant, but the goggles were obviously meant for more than just protection from the elements.

Sam jumped as Fake Sam bent down and picked up the very chunk of ice she had earlier tried to kick. Fake Sam flung the ice over the cliff, watching as it tumbled all the way down to the ocean below. Satisfied Fake Sam and Big Guy stepped away from the edge and Fake Sam gave the electromagnet guys a thumbs-up.

The magnet hummed to life. It was pointed at the edge of the cliff, facing a vast emptiness. Sam had no idea what they thought they were going to attract.

A few seconds of nothing passed. Then the whole machine began to shake with slight vibrations at first, followed by violent thrashing as it tried to leap right off the cliff. The anchors struggled to hold it in place.

The air began to wiggle and wave like heat lines on a hot summer highway. With a loud pop the wavy air vanished, revealing a train car-sized block of roughly chiseled granite with a large steel door similar to a bank vault. The block hovered in the air just a couple feet from the cliff.

"The Vault of the Blue Flame," Agent Rosenberg said as if it was something important Sam was supposed to know about.

Before she could ask any questions Sam noticed that the great steel door was vibrating wildly. Cracks cobwebbed their way across the face of the stone as the door strained against its hinges. The next thing she knew a dark gray mass rushed toward her, and her ears ached with the squeal of twisting metal followed by a loud crunch.

The steel door flew right through her body, leaving her stunned and staring into a dark vault.

"Whoa!"

Sam turned around to find that the door had completely smashed the electromagnet. Bits of scattered machinery glittered across the ice and snow. The guys operating the magnet had run for safety just in time and were now slinking back to survey the damage.

Agent Sampson chuckled. "The fabled Vault of the Blue Flame, one of the ISG's most secure secrets, cracked in under a minute. You might have tried something a little more creative than just an invisibility charm."

"We did," Chief Constable Albion said darkly.

A series of loud thumps drew Sam's attention. The thumps came from inside the dark vault and they were getting louder. Something in the darkness emitted a deep gargled growl like gravel in a mixer.

A large stone gargoyle leaped out of the vault, slamming onto the icy ground in front of Big Guy and Fake Sam. The gargoyle slashed at Fake Sam with its clawed hand, knocking her to the ground. Fake Sam rolled away from the gargoyle until the stone beast pinned her to the ground between its talon-like toes. Flames erupted from the gargoyle's gaping mouth and poured down on Fake Sam.

Sam didn't even know that gargoyles could breathe fire. Then again, she didn't know that stone gargoyles could walk around either. It looked like her fake counterpart was also quite surprised. Fake Sam tried desperately to pat out the flames on her winter gear.

The gargoyle raised up its hand to squash Fake Sam when Big Guy leaped onto its back. It tried to shake him off, but Big

Guy had looped his left arm over the creature's wing, anchoring him in place. He brought his free hand up to his face.

Sam couldn't believe it; Big Guy had a grenade and he pulled the ring out with his teeth like an action-movie star. Despite the fact that it was still spitting flames, Big Guy jammed the grenade into the gargoyle's mouth before jumping free. The creature staggered back, clawing desperately at its head. Its stony hands were too large to fit between its long jagged teeth.

Big Guy threw himself onto Fake Sam just as the gargoyle's head exploded. Pieces of stone flew everywhere. The remains of the beast's body fell in a heap on the ice.

Big Guy rolled Fake Sam over the ice smothering the flames. Her coat was still smoking as she stood up. She gave the gargoyle's body a powerful kick, snapping off the left wing. Satisfied, Fake Sam faced the vault once again as if daring it to try something else.

The vault obliged with a torrent of molten lava accompanied by a green mist with a very angry face. Even though Sam knew she was watching a recording she felt the mist creature looking at her. She took an instinctive step backward smacking into something behind her--most likely a table, judging by the sounds of toppling and splashing soda cups behind her. Fake Sam, however, didn't waver at all. As the lava approached she stood her ground, calmly removing her right glove to reveal a large gaudy ring, an opal set in silver. Fake Sam then produced a digital recorder from her pocket.

"Excelsior," spoke a recorded man's voice.

The ring turned a vivid purple. In an instant the lava and mist evaporated. The face looked very disappointed as it faded away.

"That ring is only worn by members of the ISG High Council," Chief Constable Albion interjected. "Councilman Tobias Longfellow's tomb was found defiled three months ago."

"Eww." So far everything Fake Sam had gone through was pretty impressive to Sam, but wearing a dead guy's ring was beyond gross.

Sam figured "Excelsior" must have been the literal magic word that, along with the ring, disabled the vault's traps because Fake Sam and Big Guy marched directly into the vault without any hesitation. The interior of the vault was no longer dark. A beautiful blue light flickered within. The light grew brighter until Fake Sam emerged carrying a gorgeous ancient Chinese lantern. Blue flames danced majestically inside the delicate lantern.

One of the guys from the magnet rushed up to Fake Sam with a small crate. As Fake Sam carefully lowered the lantern into the crate and closed the top a whooping noise caught Sam's attention. A black cargo helicopter was approaching.

In a flash the scene disappeared, shrinking back into the elegant box in Chief Constable Albion's hand.

"I believe you know what happens from here," Albion said.

Sam shook her head. She had no idea whatsoever.

"That was quite the show Albion," Agent Sampson said. "But what makes you believe that Samantha here was involved in any way?"

Albion blew a long burst of frustration out his nose before he spoke. "We also found several hairs at the crime scene. We immediately scryed for their owner, which led us to her. There is no doubt that she is our thief."

"According to the information provided by your superiors, the thieves struck less than an hour ago," Agent Sampson said matter-of-factly. "How could she have possibly traveled all the way from the Arctic to Illinois in that amount of time?"

"That is something I am very interested to find out. No doubt she had access to some form of transportation that the BEA has not seen fit to inform us about," Albion said with an angry sneer.

"Sam, were you in the Arctic at anytime today?" Agent Rosenberg asked.

"What? No," Sam said. She could barely get to the mall on time for work; how was she supposed to get to the North Pole?

"Can anyone verify that?"

What a ridiculous question, Sam thought.

"I got to work two and a half hours ago. You can check." Sam raised her cuffed hands to point at the Cookie Emporium.

"Lies."

"The Arctic to the Presley Mall in an hour? That would be pretty impressive." Agent Rosenberg pointed a finger at Albion. "How long did it take you to get here?"

Albion just sneered in response.

Agent Rosenberg turned to Colver. "I think we can remove those cuffs now."

"She is still a prisoner."

"She is a suspect," Agent Rosenberg corrected. "And a pretty unlikely one at the moment."

"We found her hair inside the vault. You cannot deny this. You know the Hathaways' history of sneaking into places where they do not belong."

"I also know that the Hathaways acquired a number of enemies over the years, within both the magical and non-magical communities. Does it not seem likely to you that someone is trying to use her family's rather famous history to frame Samantha in order to cover their own crime?" Agent Sampson asked.

"Nonsense!" Constable Albion shouted. A tiny dribble of saliva flew out of the corner of his mouth. "You just want the lantern for yourselves."

"Your own superiors have agreed to let us take her into custody, for her own protection," Agent Sampson said. "If you have a problem with that then I suggest you speak to them. I would hate for this situation to turn into an unfortunate incident. An unfortunate incident that some people might mistakenly believe was caused by an overzealous ISG agent who was transferring his pent-up jealousy of an old rival onto an innocent teenage girl."

"Ridiculous," Albion spat.

Agent Sampson shrugged. "It doesn't matter, really. Orders are orders. And yours are to turn her over to us."

"Oh, don't forget to remove the handcuffs," Agent Rosenberg added with a playful snap of her fingers.

Colver snapped his fingers and the blue energy around Sam's wrists disappeared.

"Thanks," Sam said to Agent Rosenberg. She rubbed her wrists happy to be free.

For a second Albion looked like he was ready for a fight. He looked at the two smug agents and then at his wide-eyed young partner. He sighed angrily.

"I am going to have a long talk with my superiors, and if that lantern falls into the wrong hands in the meantime, the outcome will be on your head," Albion said with grim certainty.

Deputy Colver withdrew a silver pocket watch from his robes. "One minute left."

"I'll be seeing you again soon." Albion pointed an angry finger at Sam as he and Colver walked away towards the rear exit by the movie theater.

"What is happening?" Sam asked.

"Wait a moment." Agent Rosenberg held up her hand to pause Sam.

A moment later Sam was struck by the sudden sounds of people moving and talking again. Everyone was going about their business as if nothing had happened. A few people gave the agents curious looks, but no one seemed too surprised they were standing there.

"Time-stopper watches freeze selected targets for ten to twenty minutes. Only members of the ISG Enforcement Squad get them," Agent Sampson said before Sam could even ask. "And no, you can't have one."

"Ow! What's wrong with my eyes?" Courtney yelled somewhere behind Sam. "Hey! How did you get over there?"

Sam spun around to find Courtney marching straight at her, the shopping bag swinging from her clenched fist while she rubbed her eyes with her other hand.

"You can't just walk away from me like that. I should let your boss know how you treat customers." She flashed her evilest grin as she tossed her long, silky black hair over her shoulder.

"You are still not a customer," Sam replied dryly.

"Not now, that's for sure. You know what? I think I'll go tell your boss that right now," Courtney's eyes turned from Sam to the two agents standing next to her. "Uh, wait. Who are these people?"

Agent Sampson produced a badge from his pocket. "Agent Sampson, Agent Rosenberg, FBI."

The badge was in fact an FBI badge. Or at least it looked like one to Sam. She wondered how many other badges he was carrying.

Courtney's mouth fell open in pure rapture. "Are you under arrest?"

Sam looked at Agent Rosenberg, who gave the faintest of shrugs and somehow managed to smile with just her eyes.

"Yep. I'm heading to jail. Probably won't see you for a while," Sam said.

"Really? What did you do?"

"I stole this lantern thing. Turned out to be really important. I probably shouldn't have done that," Sam said as casually as she could muster.

"I knew you were a loser, but I never figured you were a thief too. You're going to jail--that's awesome!" Courtney was shaking with joy.

She whipped out her cell phone. "I am so going to tell everyone."

Courtney dashed off with her cell phone glued to her ear.

"Okay, everyone she's ever met will know I'm going to jail. Which is going to make me the most famous person in town in, like, ten minutes," Sam said.

"Come on, we need to get you home. We already contacted your godparents and they are waiting for us," Agent Rosenberg, said putting her hand on Sam's shoulder.

Sam's heart sank into her stomach. Hadn't she ruined her godparents' lives enough already? There had to be some way out of this.

"Wait, I don't get off work for another three hours."

"That's all right, I'll clear everything up with your boss," Agent Sampson, said waving his FBI badge.

Chapter 3

Slow Ride Down Memory Lane

During the seemingly endless car ride to Sam's apartment her mind was racing with questions about her parents. She knew that her parents had lived very interesting lives before she was born. Her father had been an archaeologist and her mother had been an anthropologist. They had traveled the world together studying ancient cultures, digging up old pots, and hunting for mythical hidden treasures, some of which that had actual magical powers.

They had also saved the world on two separate occasions. In college her parents defeated a world-hungry sorceror named Cervantes. According to her mother, Sam's parents might never have fallen in love if they hadn't had to work together to defeat him. Sam was six when she first heard the story, and it always sounded like some sort of fantastic romantic fairy tale to her.

The second time they saved the world turned out to be far less romantic. Sam was nine at the time and her parents had toned down their globetrotting lifestyle to do the whole family thing. One day her dad got the idea to donate some of her late grandfather's artifacts to a museum, so they took a rare trip to Hathaway Manor in New Jersey, which was so full of the family's discoveries and inventions it was practically a museum itself. But when they got there they discovered that someone had broken into the mansion. Her parents called the BEA and rushed into the house. Twenty minutes later, the entire house was destroyed in a flash of light. The BEA agents arrived some time later to find Sam sitting alone in the car staring at the hole in the ground that used to be her life.

The entire matter was classified top secret, but they assured her that her parents had somehow saved the lives of everyone on Earth, and then they swore her to secrecy about the BEA, her parents' adventures, and everything she knew about magic, which was pratically nothing anyway. The day she lost her parents was the first and last time she had met a BEA agent, until today.

Now this Albion guy showed up from who-knows-where accusing Sam of stealing something she had never even heard of and claiming that her family was a bunch of thieves. She wasn't about to let him get away with that.

It was time to start asking some questions.

"So is anyone going to tell me why that, uh, warlock I guess, was so angry with me?"

"They prefer wizard. Or sorcerer," Agent Rosenberg answered from the passenger seat. "And Albion is always angry. He's a fossil from the old days. The poor guy really should retire."

Agent Sampson cleared his throat in a serious manner. "Chief Constable Albion is a great man and was one of the International Sorcerers Guild's best field agents in his day. He banished the strangling fungus back to Monster Island, and he cleared all the ghost pirates out of Hong Kong."

"That's interesting, and a little frightening," Sam said. "But why is he coming after me?"

"The Lantern of the Blue Flame."

"But what is it?" Sam asked.

The agents exchanged a brief unreadable look before Agent Sampson returned his attention to the road.

"It's a very dangerous magical object that had been missing for two thousand years, long enough that most people believed that it never existed in the first place. But a tenacious few kept obsessively searching for it, including Albion. It was the Holy Grail of lost artifacts--except, of course, for the actual Holy Grail. But in 1974 your grandfather, Dr. Samuel Hathaway Sr., found it hidden in a secret chamber in the tomb of Emperor Qin, the first emperor of China."

Agent Rosenberg twisted in her seat so she could look directly at Sam.

"Now, Sam, we want you to know that you will not get in any trouble for this. Do you know where the Lantern of the Blue Flame is?" she asked sincerely.

Sam couldn't believe it. In less than ten minutes these people had gone from defending her to accusing her.

"What? I have never stolen anything in my life." This was a lie and she knew it. But she also didn't figure that swiping Mary Johnson's pink-haired Bratz doll when she was seven really counted in this situation.

"We are not accusing you of stealing. After all, the lantern was loaned to the ISG by your grandfather as a gesture of goodwill, so technically it still belongs to your family," Agent Rosenberg said.

"But it is an immensely powerful magical object," Agent Sampson added. "It is important that it be turned over to the BEA for protection."

"I don't have it," Sam said in her fiercest tone. "But if I did, what could it do?"

The agents shared a look.

"If you don't have it, then you don't need to worry about that," Agent Rosenberg said.

"Uh huh." Sam was starting to get the picture. They were friendly with her as long as they thought she had something they wanted, but they weren't willing to explain what that something really was. She was going to have to try a different strategy. "So if I had stolen this lantern what would have happened to me?"

"You'd be on your way to an ISG maximum security prison right now. And you would remain there until you turned over the lantern," Agent Sampson said bluntly.

"But I don't have it."

"Then you'd be there for a long time," Agent Sampson said darkly.

"Why is everyone so sure I stole this thing anyway?" It didn't make any sense to her. Clearly these people knew nothing about her. If they did they would know that she was way too uncoordinated to be a baker, let alone a safecracker.

"The hairs they found inside the vault," Agent Rosenberg explained. Sam noticed that Agent Rosenberg was studying her closely, trying to gauge her reaction. "They scryed them, sort of a magical DNA test, and found out they were yours."

"How is that possible?" Sam asked.

"That is something we are going to find out," Agent Rosenberg said. "Our best guess is that someone is trying to frame you. After all, the Hathaway name is enough to get you convicted by half of the magical community. Your grandfather embarrassed them by finding the Lantern of the Blue Flame and your parents embarrassed them by saving them from Prince Cervantes. Honestly, this couldn't have happened at a worse time."

"Why is that?"

Agent Rosenberg looked to Agent Sampson for permission. He shrugged, which she took as approval. "Relations with the Sorcerer's Guild have been strained more than usual lately."

"How come?"

"Hard to say exactly. They've always been nervous about science. They don't understand it, and people tend to fear what they don't understand," Agent Sampson said. "They have tried to slow us down before. I'm sure you've heard of the Dark Ages. This could lead to another war."

"That isn't going to happen," Agent Rosenberg said, shaking her head. "Nobody wants that. Right now all we have to worry about is finding and returning the Lantern of the Blue Flame."

Sam realized that despite how nice they were being to her she was still a suspect to them; in fact according to Agent Rosenberg she was the primary suspect. It was even possible that all of that war talk was just their way of trying to scare her into turning over the stolen lantern. She wondered how her life could have gotten so complicated in less than an hour. It wasn't fair at all.

Sam was so deep in thought that she was startled when the car stopped outside her apartment building.

"We're here."

Sam followed Agent Sampson up the steps to her apartment on the third floor. Agent Rosenberg followed behind her, pinning her in just in case she decided to make a run for it. Agent Sampson only managed to knock on the door once before Sam's godmother tore it open.

"Oh, Sammy," Helen said, wrapping her arms around her. Helen Robinson was barely an inch taller than Sam. She was very skinny, always wore her hair up in a frazzled unkempt bun. Helen was an anthropologist like Sam's mom, they had been college friends, but once she took guardianship of Sam she settled down to give Sam a normal life. There was very little for an anthropologist to do in Illinois, so she had become a secretary for a local temp agency.

"Are you alright, princess?" Harold asked when Sam finally untangled herself from Helen. Harold Robinson was a civil engineer specializing in bridge construction. Since Presley, Illinois already had all the bridges it needed, Harold took a job as a teacher at the local community college.

"I'm fine, I guess." Sam said. She kept waiting for the day when Harold realized she was too old to be called 'princess'.

Harold awkwardly shook each of the agents' hands in turn. "Thank you for bringing her home, uh, officers."

"Yes," Helen said squeezing Sam's hand. "Thank heavens you got to her before the GSI."

"ISG," Agent Rosenberg corrected. "And we didn't. But they've agreed to let her go for now."

Helen instantly wrapped a protective arm around Sam's shoulders. "For now? What can we do to keep her safe?"

"I believe I have a solution for that," said a mysterious new voice from the kitchen. The voice belonged to a man in a drab brown suit.

The man handed Sam a brochure with the words MILLER'S GROVE ACADEMY emblazoned above a picturesque private school.

Harold spoke up. "Sam, this is Vice Principal Luis Hernandez. He's been waiting for you."

"It is a great pleasure to meet you Miss Hathaway," he said, shaking her free hand. "I understand you've had quite a day. I come bearing good news. You have been accepted into Miller's Grove Academy for the Exceptionally Gifted and Talented."

Sam and the Robinsons sat on one side of the kitchen table and Vice Principal Luis Hernandez sat on the other.

"Miller's Grove Academy rests on the eastern shore of Lake Laverne across from Futuro University, in beautiful Miller's Grove, California. The university, founded forty-three years ago by Dean Alistair Futuro, has produced many of the world's foremost scientists, scholars, and business leaders. The university will share many of its facilities and faculty with Miller's Grove Academy. And Miller's Grove students will be given priority consideration for university enrollment." Vice Principal Hernandez handed Harold another brochure.

"It is the goal of Miller's Grove Academy to provide a learning environment that fosters the development of a wide range of uniquely gifted and talented students."

"Gifted and talented how?" Sam asked. She knew for certain that she didn't fit into either of those groups.

"All of our students are the best of the best in their particular fields. In some cases that includes special skills that might otherwise be ignored or overlooked by other schools," the Vice Principal answered vaguely.

"Special skills like what? Reciting all the state capitols in fifty seconds? Tap dancing? Magic?" Sam asked. She had no intention of going anywhere near any magical people.

Agent Rosenberg burst into laughter in the living room.

"Uh, no. Dean Futuro takes a very dim view of the magical community. Besides, they have their own schools," Vice Principal Hernandez said, sweeping the idea away with his right hand. "No, we have recruited students with particularly high aptitudes in all subjects from math and science, art and dance, to ancient Mayan rituals and what I believe are referred to as 'extreme' level sports. I even recently interviewed an interesting young man who won the Gameco National Video Game Championship."

"So how did I get put on this list?" Sam asked.

"Sam," Helen cut in. "You are one of the most talented young women I have ever met. And you deserve the best education available."

Sam squirmed the way she did anytime someone complimented her.

"Actually you've been on the list since before you were even born," Vice Principal Hernandez said with a gleam of fanlike devotion in his eyes. "Your grandfather was one of the school's founders. All of your expenses will be covered. The main stipulation in his will was that the school be completed in time for his first grandchild to attend."

He kept talking, but Sam tuned him out. She couldn't help it. This school was starting to sound like the one the X-Men went to. She had no doubt Miller's Grove would be full of mutants, just not the cool Hugh Jackman kind.

Vice Principal Hernandez was excitedly pointing at something on the map of the school. Sam figured she had better start paying attention again.

"As you can see, one of the residence halls was named in his honor."

Sam found the building on the map. Hathaway Hall was one of four identical dorms. All four were linked together by a dining hall in the middle.

"So, this is where I would be living?" Sam asked. She brushed the letters of her name with her index finger.

"No, I'm afraid not. Hathaway Hall and McQueen Hall are both boys' dorms. The girls' buildings are Cooper Hall and Rosalyn Hall," Vice Principal Hernandez said pointing them out.

It was kind of nice to think that her grandfather had been looking out for her even though he died before she was even born. It did seem like an odd request though. Something else bothered her too.

"It took you fourteen years to build a school?" she asked.

"Sixteen, actually. Our Board of Regents has very exacting standards."

"By all expenses, does that include books, food, and what about uniforms?" Harold asked.

"I'm not wearing a uniform," Sam said as adamantly as possible. She crossed her arms and her legs to show just how adamant she was.

"We do not have uniforms. It is the belief of our founders that uniforms would stifle our student's creativity and individuality." Vice Principal Hernandez cleared his throat. "Miller's Grove Academy also proudly offers the highest security of any school in the nation. I don't believe it was a coincidence that this incident happened today. It seems likely that someone is trying to prevent Samantha from getting to school."

Harold and Helen shared a look. Sam knew exactly what they were thinking. Mr. Hernandez certainly knew how to push their buttons. If they thought this school was the only place she was going to be safe there was no way Sam was getting out of it. She was going to have to do something drastic.

She stuck out her bottom lip slightly and turned her big pleading eyes on Helen. It wasn't hard to do. The tears that welled up on her lower eyelids were very real. Judging by the tears in her own eyes, Helen got the signal.

"Mr. Hernandez," Helen began politely as she shuffled all the brochures and papers into a neat pile. "We would like to thank you for coming today, and for presenting Sam with this amazing opportunity. I'm sure you understand that a decision like this takes a little time. We have your number here somewhere, and we will give you a call soon with Sam's decision."

Harold took the cue from his wife and stood up to shake Mr. Hernandez's hand. "It was a pleasure to meet you, Mr. Hernandez."

But Vice Principal Hernandez didn't stand up to shake Harold's hand.

"I understand that today has been particularly stressful and I wish we could have met under better circumstances, but there is one more matter we need to discuss," he said sternly.

Harold pulled his hand back. His smile quickly faded from his face. "And what is that, Mr. Hernandez?"

Agents Sampson and Rosenberg walked in from the living room and stood next to the table.

"Miller's Grove University also has one of the highest security vaults in the country. It would be the perfect place to keep the Lantern of the Blue Flame," Vice Principal Hernandez said with a toothy smile.

Sam leapt out of her chair so fast it startled everyone at the table. Even Agent Sampson made a reflexive reach for his vest pocket before realizing that she wasn't a threat. He earned himself some very nasty looks from Helen and Harold for that mistake.

"I don't have your stupid lantern. I don't even know what it is. If it means so much to you, you should go look for it. Leave me alone."

"I think you should go now," Harold said firmly.

"Sam has already assured us that she doesn't know anything about the lantern," Agent Rosenberg said, clearly trying to smooth over the situation.

"Miss Hathaway, I apologize. Clearly I was given bad information," Vice Principal Hernandez rose to his feet.

Sam turned away from the three strangers in her dining room. Who were they to come out of nowhere and accuse her of stealing things she had never even heard of? She was so angry her legs were shaking. Helen hugged her even tighter.

"Mr. Hernandez, we have your information. If Sam chooses to attend your school we will contact you." His voice left no doubt that the conversation was over.

"Very well," Vice Principal Hernandez said lifting his briefcase. "I hope you won't hold my little mistake against the academy."

"Good day," Agent Sampson said as he followed Vice Principal Hernandez to the door.

"I hope to see you there, Sam," Agent Rosenberg said sweetly. She gave Sam a cheerful little wave as she headed for the door. "Nice place you have here Mr. and Mrs. Robinson. Sorry for the hassle."

"Thank you," Helen said, more by reflex than anything else.

Harold closed the door behind them.

"Sam, I…" Helen began, but Sam was halfway to her room before she could finish.

Sam shut the door and locked it before throwing herself on the bed. She doubted quite highly if anyone she knew had ever had such a strange day. No one that was still alive anyway.

Without even knowing why, she burst into tears. She pulled in Mr. Hopscotch, her teddy bear that her father had made on the day she was born so that they would always be the same age, and she hugged him like she hadn't hugged him in years.

Poor Mr. Hopscotch. He only got this kind of attention when things went bad. She hugged him even tighter.

For some bizarre reason, it is difficult to tell time while crying. Sam felt like she cried for over an hour, but it was likely far less than that, because she doubted Helen would wait that long before coming to check on her. When Sam finally ran out of tears she rolled out of bed and grabbed her Kleenex box while purposely avoiding looking up at her vanity mirror. It was weird how her body only let her cry for so long before her nose completely filled with snot. It was either a design flaw, or a safety feature to keep her from crying forever. Either way, it was unbelievably gross.

"They want me to go to some freaky school, Mr. Hopscotch," Sam told the bear. He took the news with a smile. He always did.

If Vice Principal Hernandez was any indication of the type of people there, this was definitely not a school she wanted to go to. But her grandfather apparently thought she would. She wondered how her parents would feel about it. They had to have known about it, and she understood why they never told her; they were probably waiting until she was older. Still, someone should have maybe waited to ask her what she wanted.

Maybe I could get a refund, Sam thought. Sam could use that money to pick her own college in a few years. She could also give some of it to Helen and Harold to help out, and maybe buy a car.

Her nose was finally empty, so she set the Kleenex box back down on her bureau next to her parent's picture. She had built a small memorial to her parents with a few items she collected before the rest of their stuff was put into storage. Her mother's favorite music box and the mancala game they used to play every Sunday sat on one side across from four ornate snow globes of the Sphinx, the Great Pyramid, the Statue of Liberty, and the Eiffel Tower her father gave her when she was very young as promises of vacation spots they would visit one day.

She wound up the music box and watched as the tiny ballerina danced to the tune her mother had used to sing her to sleep as a child.

"Do you know what kind of kids go to private schools?" Sam asked Mr. Hopscotch.

"I'll tell you," she said, setting him down gently on the bed. "Rich kids, supersmart kids, and troublemakers whose parents don't want to deal with them anymore. Does that sound like a group of people you would like to hang out with?"

Mr. Hopscotch just kept smiling.

"Well, sure. You would. You get along with everyone. Everybody loves you."

Sam kissed him on the forehead.

As she lifted her head she saw Sara Berlin smiling at her from her poster on the wall. Sam had to plumb the depths of the internet to find this particular poster of Sara Berlin from her very first concert, but it was worth it.

"You don't even go to high school. You probably have a whole army of personal tutors. I don't suppose you could spare one?" she asked the poster. "It would certainly help a lot."

The poster did not answer back.

"Oh, sorry about that rich kids comment."

Sara Berlin was a self-made millionaire. Her mother was a kindergarten teacher and her father was a baker. She didn't have a family name to live up to. She got to make her own way in the world.

Sam had the Hathaway name hanging over her. How many people at Miller's Grove Academy would know that her parents saved the world, or that her grandfather was a brilliant scientist and adventurer? And how on Earth could anyone expect her to live up to a legacy like that?

No, she really didn't need to go to a school where everyone would know exactly how much she was letting the family name down. She was much better off at her current school where she was just another nobody. Her mind was made up.

She slowly opened the door. She half expected her godmother to be camped out in the hallway. Sam tiptoed towards the kitchen, stepping carefully to avoid the tattling squeaky floorboard at the end of the hall.

"I'm just saying it is an amazing opportunity for her."

"But only if she wants to go. We can't make her go."

Sam crept closer to hear the conversation better. Somebody was nervously tapping a foot on the floor.

"If Samuel and Joanne were here, they would want her to go."

"We don't know that, Harold. We don't what they would want at all," Helen said, sadness lacing her words.

"I know. I know."

A chair was pulled across the floor as someone either stood up or sat down.

"This may be one of the few links to her parents she has left." Harold said. "Besides, it could really open doors for her. I don't need to tell you that we haven't exactly built much of a college fund. So unless we let her use up all of her inheritance, I don't know how we're going to pay for everything."

Sam's heart sank. Again she was reminded of how much trouble she had caused the Robinsons, how much she had taken from them while they had done nothing but give to her. It was bad enough that she had cost them their careers, but now she was causing money problems and almost getting arrested.

She was a delinquent. Her reign of destruction had to end. It was time to give something back.

Sam stepped into the kitchen. Helen and Harold startled at her presence. Helen looked like she had been crying. She was about to say something when Sam took a deep breath and went for it.

"I want to go to Miller's Grove Academy."

Chapter 4

Baldorag Castle

Baldorag Castle was a gothic nightmare of slick black stone built deep inside the crevice of an otherwise completely uninteresting mountain in the heart of the Swiss Alps. The castle was built so deep into the mountain that it only received one hour of sunlight a day. It would take the most skillful mountaineer in the world to find and reach the castle.

Fortunately Alexander Nero had a helicopter and a map.

Snow that had been untouched by humans for over a decade whipped through the air as the helicopter touched down on a rocky ledge near the castle.

"Everyone remember where we parked," Nero quipped as he climbed out of the helicopter.

"Good one, sir," Commander Carlson, Head of Nero Industries Security and Nero's personal bodyguard, said as he gently removed the box containing the lantern from the helicopter.

"Thank you, Carlson."

Nero couldn't think of anyone else with whom he would rather have traveled to the Arctic, robbed a magical vault, and fought off a fire-breathing gargoyle statue come to life. Nero was still a little annoyed that Commander Carlson got all the fun of fighting the gargoyle, but it had been necessary to maintain his disguise as the weak and frail Samantha Hathaway.

He comforted himself with the thought that his plan was nearing completion. It had taken three years and a sizable portion of his late father's fortune to learn the location and password of the Vault of the Blue Flame from a very corrupt and indebted member of the ISG and then obtain the correct ring on the black market from a rather unpleasant hunchback. Not to mention the two years it had taken to develop his goggles--which not only corrected for light refraction enabling him to see magically invisible objects, but were also equipped with infrared, X-ray, microscopic, and a half-dozen other forms of vision. He figured he could make a second fortune selling them out of the backs of comic books.

On a personal vanity note there was also the matter of his hair--which, to is mother's great concern, had turned completely white by his fourteenth birthday. Still, it was a small price to pay to complete his father's work and regain the family honor.

Thanks to Constable Albion's recent failure to arrest Samantha Hathaway, he was forced to switch to Plan B. Plan B was a brilliant plan, as all of Nero's plans were, but it was slower than Plan A.

Ah well, he thought to himself. If taking over the world was easy, someone else would have done it by now.

Nero shook his head in disbelief. Two mountain peaks away, people were skiing and drinking hot chocolate in cute little lodges, completely unaware of this grand old castle and the historic battle that was fought within. As they entered the great crack in the mountain, Nero rolled the dial on his trusty goggles to night vision mode. Everything went ghostly green.

"Sir, I would strongly prefer it if we brought along some of the men," Carlson said anxiously as followed Nero into the darkness.

"We have the lantern," Nero said reassuringly.

The sound of their boots crunching over the pebble-strewn ground filled the narrow space between the castle walls and the mountain. Two of the castle's four towers had caved in untold years ago. A third was leaning against the mountain wall, ready to crumble at any moment. No one had even bothered to close the front gate when the castle was abandoned for the last time.

A thick layer of ice coated every surface inside the castle. Nero signaled to Carlson to step around the remains of a long wooden dinner table that had cracked in half under the strain of its icy cocoon.

Something fluttered in the corner of Nero's goggles-- a moving shadow that vanished around a corner.

"Sir," Carlson said sternly. With the box in his hands he was ill prepared for a fight.

"Do not drop the box," Nero ordered as he stepped into the Great Hall.

The Great Hall had seen better days. The west wall had collapsed under the weight of one of the crumbled towers. Broken bits of furniture lay in heaps under an inch of ice and debris. But

Nero was more interested in the ceiling, mostly because it was moving. Hundreds of bats clung to the ceiling. They appeared as a massive wriggling green blanket in his goggles.

Squeeee.

A cloud of startled bats dove on Nero and Commander Carlson.

"Open the box," Nero yelled as he covered his head with his hands.

The light from the box bathed the entire room in a bright glow. It was so bright he had to rip his goggles off, which was not a smart thing to do in a room full of angry bats. Cowering from the bats' attack, Nero yanked his right glove off and lifted the Lantern of the Blue Flame out of the box.

"Necro Retondo," he yelled.

Tendrils of blue fire whipped out of the lantern and writhed across the floor until they rose into the air as a small blue tornado of flames. Bits of dust ascended from the ice into the swirling vortex. Soon the dust particles began to take shape. As the blue flames spun faster and faster Nero could make out the vague shape of a man inside the tornado. Fortunately, the flames seemed to scare the bats away.

With one final burst of light, the flames retreated into the lantern, leaving behind the figure of a man with his right hand stretched out as if he was holding something up in the air to study it.

"-shall die!" the man yelled in a feral rage.

He clutched at the air a few times, trying to grasp whatever it was he had been holding. A low guttural growl of confusion and anger escaped his throat as he frantically scanned the room. The light from the lantern revealed the man to be in his early twenties. He had long bright red hair and handsome features. He was also naked.

His rage-filled eyes fixed on Nero and Commander Carlson. His lips curled back to reveal long white fangs.

"Who are you?" he demanded in a kingly fashion.

"I am Alexander Sebastian Nero Jr., your new master," Nero said, getting to his feet and brushing the ice off his expensive thermal pants.

The man laughed, long and deep, like a man who hadn't laughed in years.

"Normally I throw the small ones back. But today…" the man said with a toothy grin.

"Sit," Nero commanded.

The man sat down on the icy floor. His head whipped around, stunned by his own actions. His muscles strained as he struggled to stand back up but could not. He growled some more.

Nero smiled politely. "I think you can call off your little friends now, if you please."

The man squinted in disapproval, but he couldn't stop himself. He waved his right hand and a hundred glittering specks of red light flew from his fingers, streaking into the mass of flapping wings. A second later the floor was littered with hundreds of little dead bat bodies.

"I see. You possess the Lantern of the Blue Flame," the man said, staring at the lantern. "So, apparently I died."

"Yes."

He took a long breathe. "How long?"

"Almost twenty years," Nero answered.

The man's eyes widened. "Elizabeth?"

"If you behave I might tell you about her sometime."

"I see." The man nodded curtly. His fingers flexed with an aching desire to strangle Nero, but his eyes never wavered from the lantern. It had a power over him that he could never break.

"I have a job for you," Nero said.

"You hold the lantern," he said, gesturing to the icy floor on which he sat. "I have no choice."

"Oh, I think you will like this job. It involves destroying those who once opposed you and eliminating the daughter of your killer," Nero said.

A twisted smile crept across the man's face.

"But you will have to work by my time table," Nero said. "And you will need some clothes."

"I agree to your conditions."

"Good," Nero said, extending his hand. "Then rise, Cervantes; we're on a tight schedule. I have to get ready for school."

Nero had to admit that Miller's Grove, California was a brilliant hiding place for a school for extraordinarily talented weirdos. Anyone passing through would think this was just another random mountain town built from the American Small Town Starter Kit. Throw up a Wal-Mart over there, a one-story mall over here, maybe a McDonald's or two, add a bowling alley or skating rink for good measure, and top it off with a pinch of small town charm.

The school itself was built on the edge of town. It was surrounded by a thick forest. A single road connected the school to the town. The words "KNOWLEDGE IS POWER" were written above the main gate in steel lettering.

As Nero stepped out of the rented minivan in the school's giant parking lot, he caught a glimpse of himself in the door's mirror. He ran his hand through his recently dyed hair and sighed. It had been a simple trick to hack into Miller's Grove Academy's student registry and find a freshman to impersonate. The real student had recently left the country when his mother was unexpectedly offered a high-paying job at a Nero Industries facility in Japan.

"The things we do to save the world," Nero said to himself as he watched the flock of students meander towards the auditorium.

"What was that, sir?" Commander Carlson asked from inside the van.

"Nothing. This could take a little longer than I originally thought," Nero said.

"We'll be ready at a moment's notice, sir."

"I'm sure you will," Nero said as he closed the van door.

"Have fun at school, sir," Carson called from the driver's-side window.

Without turning around to give Commander Carlson the satisfaction, Nero rolled his eyes to himself and kept walking toward the large blue domed auditorium next to the administrative building. The ultra-modern auditorium was constructed of thousands of hexagonal sound-amplifying panels, making it look like a giant blue beehive. In contrast the administrative building,

Merriweather Hall, housing the faculty offices, meeting rooms, and official entrance to the academy, was built to resemble a 16th-Century Renaissance-style mansion. There was even ivy growing up the walls and curled around the white columns already.

Students were frantically rechecking their information packets, so Nero did the same, even though he knew that all the students were suppose to meet at the auditorium for orientation. He did his best to shuffle along and look confused and anxious like the students around him. It seemed Plan B was going to take more patience than he had originally thought, but it was still preferable to Plan C.

Three guards stood watch over the passing students. Each wore a dark blue campus security uniform and carried a state-of-the-art Nero Industries electro-static stun gun. They were very handy weapons capable of temporarily stunning a person from fifty yards away. Nero guessed the guards were all college students picking up extra cash or credit.

As the crowd funneled into the auditorium, it was forced to part around a lone tall black marble statue of a smiling elderly man in a graduation-style mortarboard and gown who held the world in his outstretched right hand. Upon closer examination, he appeared to be squeezing the world. The craftsmanship was really very exquisite. Nero didn't need to read the plaque below to know that this was a statue of Dr. Alistair Futuro, one of the titans of the secret scientific world. Nero decided that he might have to steal the statue later if he had the time.

As one, the crowd of students suddenly stopped in their tracks. People were staring and pointing at a helicopter that came swooping over the school buildings. It hovered momentarily over the crowd, and someone inside waved, causing the collected students to cheer. Then the helicopter moved on and settled on the helipad behind Merriweather Hall.

Pangs of annoyance shot through Nero. It should be him in that helicopter looking down on the rabble. But it was important for him to pretend to be just another part of the herd. So he'd play along, for now.

The crowd surged towards the auditorium doors again. Nero flashed his fake ID at the security guard and went inside. He picked a seat near the middle where he could keep an eye on everyone. The auditorium was nearly full when he saw Samantha Hathaway enter.

Chapter 5

Orientation

Sam found an empty seat near the back of the auditorium. She had to squeeze past three people to get there. She hated being late. It made her feel like everyone was watching her--usually because everyone was--but Helen had insisted on taking pictures of Sam in front of the main gate, by the doors, by the bushes, under the WELCOME STUDENTS banner, and even by the creepy statue outside. Thankfully, Harold finally convinced Helen that they had to leave Sam alone so they could drop off her stuff in her dorm room. Sam figured Harold would end up doing most of the hauling, while Helen would be busy taking pictures of every square inch of Sam's new room.

The auditorium was awash with a thousand excited voices. The stage was empty except for a podium and a couple of chairs. As the anticipation grew, the idle chatter dulled down to nothing more than a sea of whispers.

Finally two people stepped out on stage and approached the podium. One of them was Vice Principal Hernandez. The other was a tall black woman in a crisp light blue suit. She had a wide toothy smile and her hair was pulled back in a tight bun. She nodded contentedly as she took the microphone.

"Good morning, students," she said in a cheerful tone. "I am Principal Martha Shepherd. This is Vice Principal Luis Hernandez. Welcome to Miller's Grove Academy."

Mr. Hernandez gave a curt little nod of his head to the crowd of students before sitting down in one of the chairs on stage.

"This is an exciting time for all of us. You are the first group of students to pass through these halls. You will be the standard for all other students who follow. And we are the first faculty and staff to teach at Miller's Grove Academy. We will be travelers on this grand new adventure together," Principal Shepherd said.

"While many of you will be with us for several years, sadly you seniors will only be here for a single year. In that time we shall try our best to get to know each and every one of you and make sure you are fully prepared for the big wide world beyond-"

Thump. Thump.

Principal Shepherd turned from the crowd to face the source of the thumping noise coming from somewhere offstage. Sam swore she saw the Principal frown for a split second before returning to her big toothy grin.

"And now, I would like to introduce you all to our, uh, benefactor and the Dean of Futuro University, Dr. Alistair Futuro," she said as she stepped away from the podium.

The whispering stopped the instant Dean Futuro appeared on stage.

Sam had never seen anything like this man before. Dean Futuro had to be over ninety years old, possibly a hundred. He was horribly hunched over, relying on a cane to move around. The cane was slim and black; it sparkled with many gems and made a surprisingly loud thump on the stage as he approached the podium. His dark blue suit hung loosely on his skinny body. Sam had never seen a suit jacket with tails in real life. Combined with the top hat that sat atop his wispy white hair, he reminded Sam of a circus ringmaster or an elderly, broken-down Willy Wonka. Although, judging by his beaklike nose and beady dark eyes, she doubted he had ever been nearly as nice as Gene Wilder or as gorgeous as Johnny Depp.

Principal Shepherd clearly didn't know what to do. Part of her seemed to want to help Dean Futuro somehow and part of her wanted to stay as far away from him as possible. In the end she just wound up standing there with her arms out--ready to catch him if he fell--and then sat down when he reached the podium safely.

Dean Alistair Futuro surveyed the silent crowd from under his wooly white eyebrows. No one made a sound.

"Look at the person on your left," he said in a cold, commanding voice. Sam looked to her left, as did a surprising number of the other students. "Now look to your right. One or both of these people will not make it to graduation."

A murmur of disbelief and anger roiled around the auditorium. Sam saw one dark-haired boy three rows away who was smiling and nodding happily as he looked around at the other shocked students as if counting to himself which students were destined to dropout. He locked eyes with Sam. He smiled even bigger as he pointed at her and waggled his eyebrows. Sam looked away.

"You have been told that you are here because you are special, that you are exceptionally talented in some manner. You need to be aware that everyone in the world is talented in some way and that you in fact are not special. All you are, every one of you, is lucky. Lucky that we started this new school and needed a few warm bodies to fill it. From this point on, the world will not be beating a path to your door. From here on out you must fend for yourselves."

Heads turned and mouths fell open across the room. As far as orientation speeches went it had to be the worst--not that Sam knew any others to compare it to, but still, it had to be way down the list. Sam half expected someone to get up and storm out. No one did, though.

Slowly, a stunned Principal Shepherd got up from her chair. "Uh yes, thank you Dean…"

Dean Futuro waved her off with his cane. Principal Shepherd sat back down, looking like a scolded child.

Dean Futuro continued. "I must also remind you that Academy students are not allowed to prowl around on University property without faculty supervision. I insist on the strictest of security and anyone found skulking about will be dealt with harshly. That is all."

The auditorium was utterly silent except for the thumping of Dean Futuro's cane on hard wood as he turned and slowly walked away. No one seemed to breathe again until he had finally disappeared offstage.

Sure, he was massively creepy and severely overdramatic, but he had raised an interesting point in his extremely brief speech. Everyone else in the room had been selected to be here because they were good at something, supergood, but Sam was here because her family had been good at things. Sam suddenly realized that she was officially the least talented person in the room. She often felt this way, but it was entirely different to know it for sure.

"Yes, thank you, Dean Futuro, those certainly were, uh, inspiring words," Principal Shepherd said, now back at the podium.

"I want to assure all of you that we are here to help you become the leaders of tomorrow. Over the next few months I am sure there will be many things we will learn from each other, and I want you all to know that you are welcome to come to me, Vice Principal Hernandez, or your Resident Advisors about any questions, concerns, or problems you may have," she said, eliciting a new batch of giggles and whispers from the crowd.

As frighteningly overcheery as Principal Shepherd was, Vice Principal Hernandez was the exact opposite. His unwavering steel gaze made sure that everyone in the room knew to stay away from his office at all costs. Sam figured she would have to be on fire and missing three of her four limbs before she approached Vice Principal Hernandez for help.

"Now then, I suspect that you are all excited to check out your rooms, unpack, and meet your new roommates. As you all, no doubt, have already discovered, your dorm assignments and class schedules are included in your information packets; as well as a map of campus, but if you have any questions please do not be shy in asking. Now if you will all kindly file out of the auditorium in an orderly fashion we can all get settled in," Principal Shepherd said cheerfully.

Sam trudged along with the crowd until she got outside. The annoying boy who had locked eyes with her was standing in the middle of the stream of kids waiting for her. He had a confident smirk that made her hate him immediately.

"I guess they'll let just anyone in here," he said.

"What is your deal?" she asked coldly.

"Rude. I see you're living up to your side of the family's reputation." His smile grew. He knew he had just thrown her for a loop.

"What do you know about my family?" she demanded.

"More than you do, cuz," he said. "I'm Zack McQueen."

Sam didn't know much about the McQueens other than that they hated the Hathaways so much that they cut off all contact with her mother and never bothered to check on Sam after her parents died. She didn't need to know anything else.

"Maybe I'll fill you in a little sometime," he said. "If you last long enough."

He slipped into the crowd, leaving Sam confused and standing in people's way.

Sam looked at the packet in her hands. The third page had a map and had her room number on it, but she couldn't dare pull the map out in front of all the supersmart kids and let them know that she was lost. She casually made her way over to a bench next to a clump of perfectly manicured bushes away from the other students. Sam held the packet loosely and at a downward angle so that the first few pages appeared to accidentally slip out and fall onto the bench. She made a big show of being annoyed as she scooped up the loose pages, but she kept the map on the top of the pile so she could study it in secret as she collected the rest of the pages.

"Smile for the camera!"

She looked up to find two boys with a microphone and a video camera peering at her.

"What the heck are you doing?" she asked.

"Hi, I'm Sick," the taller of the two boys, and the one with the microphone, said. "This is Wrong. We're looking for people to interview for our new show. Would you mind answering a few questions?"

The other boy, Wrong, which almost certainly was not his real name, held the camera. He was also bopping along to some song playing through the earbuds of his iPod. Sam couldn't tell if he was disinterested, rude, or just really good at multi-tasking.

"What show?"

"Oh, we are starting a new show for the school's television station. *The Sick and Wrong Show*," Sick said with a big dopey grin.

"Ah, well, that's pretty cool then. When will it be on?" Sam asked.

"We haven't really set that up yet," Sick admitted with a shrug. "We need to put together our demo tape first. So you can be the first person immortalized on our show. Ready?"

Normally Sam would have passed on their offer in an instant. She really didn't need to embarrass herself on television. But it occurred to her that maybe this would be a good chance to introduce herself to the rest of the school.

After all, you get bonus cool points just for being on TV, right?

"All right, ask away," Sam said, hoping for the best.

Sick looked almost surprised for a moment, as if no one had ever agreed to be interviewed by him before. Wrong steadied the camera on his shoulder while Sick thrust the microphone at Sam.

"Okay then, uh, what is your name?" Sick asked.

"Oh, I'm Sam, Samantha Hathaway." She stopped, not sure what to say next. But she kept her smile glued on.

"Right, uh, so tell us about yourself, Sam," Sick said, clearly searching for questions. "Where are you from?"

"Presley, Illinois," Sam answered. She nervously brushed her hair behind her right ear.

"So, Dean Alistair Futuro, pompous windbag, or creepy undead loser?" Sick asked.

Sam smiled as she thought about that. "Are those my only options? I'd have to go with creepy undead loser."

"And what talent or gift has brought you to this fine establishment where your gift or talent is meaningless and you must fend for yourself?" Sick asked.

"I don't really know," Sam answered honestly. "Nothing really."

"Good for you. You might be the only one here who isn't hobbled by their own greatness," Sick said matter-of-factly. "Well, let's get to know you better. Any hobbies? Juicy gossip? Nasty break up stories?"

"Getting a little personal, aren't we, camera boy?" a girl said next to Sam.

Sam hadn't even known the girl was there until she spoke. She was a slim and tall African-American girl with her hair pulled back in long intricate braids that instantly made Sam jealous.

Sick made a great show of bowing as he spoke. "I humbly beg your pardon for any offense."

"Um, that's fine." Sam said.

"You are too kind." Sick turned his microphone on the new girl. "Would you like to be interviewed for our show too?"

"Check it out," Wrong said, pointing over Sam's shoulder.

A crowd of very excited students formed around the doors to the auditorium. Four very serious-looking campus security guards came out and shooed the students back, making room for someone.

"It's Tiffany Summers!" Sick yelled.

It actually was Tiffany Summers, the younger sister of mega pop star Monica Summers. No doubt she was the one that arrived in the helicopter.

"Why is she here?" Sam asked. "I honestly thought I was the least talented person here. All she does is ride her sister's coattails. Just because her sister can sing doesn't mean she-"

Before Sam could finish her sentence Sick and Wrong took off towards the crowd, camera and microphone ready.

"Well, that got rid of those guys anyway," the girl said, holding out her hand. "I'm Tasha, by the way. Or Natasha Beaumont if you're really formal. Never Nat."

Sam shook her hand. "Sam. Samantha Hathaway. Nice to meet you. Which dorm is yours?"

"Cooper Hall. You?"

"Really? Me too, that's great," Sam said excitedly. "You wouldn't happen to know how to get there, would you?"

Tasha laughed. "I think so. It should be three buildings down and two over. Follow me."

The first building they passed reminded Sam of a Greek temple, with its tall white columns; a statue of a woman in a toga wearing a war helmet with an owl on her right shoulder and a spear in her left hand stood guard in front as if the building could be attacked at any moment.

"This might be the weirdest place I've ever been," Sam said.

"Oh I know," Tasha said, pointing at a steel and glass building where every window was actually a transparent TV screen displaying a different famous painting. "I wasn't really big on the whole private school thing, but it is already way cooler than the school back home. Plus it means I don't have to work at my parents' store after class anymore."

"What kind of store?" Sam asked.

"They own a lumberyard back in Madrigal, Louisiana, where I'm from. It's the biggest lumberyard in the area. It serves three whole counties. Oh, and it is the most boring place on Earth."

The girls laughed.

"So I take it you don't plan on following in the family business?" Sam asked.

"I don't know," she said. "Right now I'm just focusing on my gymnastics."

"Going for that Olympic gold?" Sam asked seriously.

"Anything could happen," Tasha replied, flicking a stray braid out of her face. "How about you? Your parents pushing you towards anything?"

Sam hated questions like this. Her answer always made people act different toward her.

"Not really, no. My parents died when I was nine." There was the look of pity she knew so well. "My dad was an archaeologist and my mom was an anthropologist, but personally I don't really find the idea of digging up a bunch of old pots that much fun."

"I'm sorry. That must be rough." Tasha's eyes kept looking past Sam, not sure if it was safe to look at her.

"It is, but my godparents are pretty great." Sam had learned over the years that this was the perfect response. Letting people know that she was part of a semi-normal family structure put people at ease.

"That's good. 'Family is family,' as Grammy Beaumont would say." Tasha said.

"I suppose so. They are the only real family I have left. Both of my parents were only children and my dad's parents died before I was born."

"What about your mom's parents?" Tasha asked.

"Long story," Sam said.

Tasha nodded her head in acknowledgement. And just like that, the topic was dropped. Which was good, because Sam wasn't sure how she felt about this newly found cousin and didn't want to talk about it.

"That's not all bad. I have, like, six aunts and uncles on one side, two on the other. Twenty-one cousins last I counted." She looked at the ground for just a split second as if she was still counting. "Plus one brother."

"Must be nice around Christmas time. Lots of presents."

Sam imagined Tasha at one of those large family Christmases like in the TV commercials, with a big Christmas tree loaded with decorations, little kids sneaking away to shake the presents, and everyone retelling stories of Christmases past. It sure beat Sam, Helen, and Harold sitting around the apartment looking at their two-foot-tall plastic tree that came out of the box with the lights and decorations already attached.

"Are you kidding?" Tasha burst out. "More than thirty people trapped in a house with only two bathrooms. That is no one's idea of a good time."

Sam laughed. They had reached the dormitories.

Cooper Hall and Rosalyn Hall were on the east side of the complex. The two boys' halls were on the west side, with the communal dining hall and lounge in the middle. The four dorms were identical, as far as Sam could tell. Each one was five stories tall and built of large red bricks. The cafeteria building was only one story high, but it was a stylish building lined with large bay windows.

They were going to have to weave their way through the buzzing swarm of students in various stages of moving in and parents saying their tearful goodbyes.

"I'm in room 320," Tasha said. "How about you?"

Sam checked her packet. "314."

"Practically neighbors," Tasha said. "It would have been funny if we'd wound up in the same room."

"I know." Sam considered. "You're the only person I know here."

"Likewise," Tasha said. "Of course, we just got here."

"Good point."

"I suppose we should head up to see our new roomies," Tasha said. "Besides, my parents are probably waiting for me to say goodbye again."

Sam knew that Helen and Harold would have already left. They had flights to catch. But maybe she would run into her roommate's family. That could be fun.

Sam tugged on the door handle. The door wouldn't budge.

"You need your card," Tasha said. "In your packet."

Tasha swiped her card through the slot next to the door, and the door unlocked with a loud buzz.

"Like living in a hotel," Sam said walking through the door.

"Hmm." Tasha did not seem nearly as impressed. "I bet that thing keeps records of every time we open the door. So they can check on when we get in at night."

That had not occurred to Sam, but it made sense. "I suppose so. They would probably get majorly sued if someone's kid disappeared and they hadn't been keeping watch."

"I guess so." Tasha eyed her keycard suspiciously.

Fortunately the dorms had elevators, so they could get to the third floor in no time.

They stepped out off the elevator into a wall of noise. Girls and parents were running everywhere, carrying boxes, TV sets, computers, reading lamps, and other essentials.

One of the girls in the room closest to the elevator was freaking out that she couldn't find her favorite pair of shoes. Her very bored-looking father assured her that if she hadn't brought them, he would send them to her. She didn't seem at all satisfied with that answer, and she made sure everyone knew it by stomping her feet and sighing loudly and often.

"You don't suppose it is going to be like this every day, do you?" Sam asked.

"Nah," Tasha replied. "Once the parents are gone it will get really wild."

Sam smiled at that, though inside she sort of worried if she would ever get a decent night's sleep here. As an only child, she was not used to living with people who stayed up past Letterman. She needed quiet when she went to bed.

They reached Sam's room first.

"I guess this is my stop," Sam said.

Looking at her new door, she realized she was going to have to get one of those dry erase boards to write little amusing messages on, like in college movies.

She swung the door open.

"Whoa. What the heck is that?" Tasha asked loudly.

Sam was curious as well.

Inside her room there were two beds, two squat bookshelves that doubled as nightstands, and two desks, just like the brochure said. She had studied the layout of her future room many times to figure out exactly what to pack. But what caught her eye first was something that she was pretty sure was never mentioned in the brochure.

A large metal ring stood on one side of the room. A string of wires was wrapped around the ring, which in itself appeared to be made from random bits of machine parts. She recognized a couple of motherboards, most of a transformer box, and half of a toaster among the parts. Attached to the bottom of the ring by a thick black cord and a thin silver wire was a control panel with a number of buttons, dials, and blinking lights.

All in all it appeared to be a leftover piece of scenery from some cheesy low-budget black and white sci-fi movie. Maybe her roommate was a major science nerd, or a filmmaker, or one of those abstract artists who made sculptures from pieces of trash. If Sam got to choose she would go with artist. She figured an artist roommate would be a lot of fun.

Sam looked around the rest of the room for more clues. The left side, which she assumed was her side, was empty except for the furniture and the boxes of her clothes and other belongings that sat next to the bed where Helen and Harold had left them. Her roommate had clearly moved in already. The closet door was open and stuffed with clothes. Her bookshelf was full of books already. Mostly physics books, including *A Brief History of Time* and *Quantum Theory and Practice*, which put a damper on Sam's artist idea.

There was even an Albert Einstein poster on the wall, the famous one where he is sticking his tongue out at someone.

"What kind of nerd queen are you living with?" Tasha asked.

"I can only imagine," Sam said, shaking her head. She was imagining someone with uneven pigtails and thick glasses, perhaps someone not too different from a young Helen.

"Hi, my name's Zoey," said a voice from behind them.

Chapter 6

Roomies

Sam hadn't heard anyone enter the room and now, after being in her new dorm room for less than five minutes, she had already insulted her roommate. Sometimes Sam was surprised by just how easily she could get her freakishly oversized foot into her mouth. It was really quite a talent.

Sam and Tasha both turned slowly to face whatever well-deserved wraith her new roommate was about to unleash.

She was an interesting sight. Sam couldn't help but notice that she was an extremely pretty Indian girl, like movie-star pretty, and she clearly had an eccentric fashion sense. Her long, gorgeous hair was raven-black with a streak of blue down one side and a streak of bright pink down the other, which matched her bright pink skirt. She had on a baggy black T-shirt, red-and-white striped leggings, and thick-heeled boots that made her an inch taller than Sam.

"Hi, I'm Sam. Uh, Samantha. Hathaway. Your roommate," Sam said, truly hoping that Zoey didn't take offense to her and Tasha's earlier comments.

"And I'm Tasha. I live down the hall," Tasha said pointing at the hallway.

"Good to meet you. I'm Zoey, like I said. Zoey Dalal." She curtsied. "I hope I didn't take up too much room."

"No, no. Everything seems fine," Sam said. "We were just wondering what that giant ring was?"

"Oh, that's my senior project," Zoey said matter-of-factly.

Sam didn't even know there was a senior project, and certainly had no plans to start on it in her freshman year. She was only taking the basic classes this semester anyway, until she figured out what she wanted to do with her life. So far her options seemed to be cookie baker and bum.

"That's very impressive," Sam said. "What does it-?"

"I don't suppose you're going to have any spare room in your closet, will you?" Zoey asked. She walked over to the unpacked boxes on her bed.

"I don't know." Sam really had no idea how much closet space she was going to need. She had never been much for fashion, really, especially on the Robinsons' dime, but she had brought enough clothes for a whole year.

"That's all right." Zoey stuffed one of the remaining boxes under her bed.

"Oh, no," Tasha said, poking her head into the hallway. "My parents must be waiting to say goodbye to me. My dad is standing in the hallway like a goon."

"Nat!" a deep voice called.

"He saw me. I'd better go," Tasha said, smirking. "Talk to you later."

Tasha stepped into the crowded hallway nearly running into a girl carrying an astronaut helmet.

"So, your parents didn't stick around to help you unpack, huh?" Sam asked Zoey in the hopes of sustaining conversation.

"Nope, they are out of the country," Zoey said while casually tossing socks into the top drawer of her dresser.

Sam realized that she should start unpacking too.

"How about your folks? They seemed to be in a hurry this morning," Zoey asked while sniffing a sock to make sure it was clean.

"Helen and Harold are my godparents actually," Sam said as she ripped the tape off of her first box; the one labeled SAM'S STUFF SUPER IMPORTANT.

"I didn't think you looked much like them." Zoey examined the pair of green and pink socks in her hand like she had never seen them before. "Do these look right to you?"

They deserve to be burned immediately.

Sam figured that was an impolite response so she chose something more diplomatic.

"Interesting."

"Gag me with a spoon," Zoey said and tossed them out the window.

"Whoa."

"I'm sure they will be found by some nice chipmunk and keep him warm," Zoey said.

The balled up pair of socks came flying back in through the window, landing on Zoey's bed.

Zoey and Sam exchanged looks.

"I guess the chipmunk didn't like them," Sam said with a shrug.

"Guess not."

The girls peered out the window.

Three floors below them a boy with shaggy brown hair was brushing leaves off of his pants. Apparently he had driven his yellow moped into the bushes right below their window.

Most likely because a pair of socks mysteriously fell on his head, Sam thought.

"Lose something?" he called up.

Sam picked up the socks and waved them out the window. "She didn't like them."

"Neither do I," he said.

He pulled his moped back upright. Only now did Sam notice the massive anime collection sprawled across the sidewalk next to an overturned box.

"Sorry about that."

"Huh?"

"Your cartoons," she said pointing.

He looked down at the DVDs around his feet as if he had forgotten they were there. "Not a problem."

He set the box right side up and started scooping up the DVDs.

Zoey leaned out the window. "I'm Zoey, by the way. This is Samantha."

"Sam," she corrected automatically.

"Howdy. I'm...," he held up one finger. "Wait, I know this. Lucas. I'm Lucas."

"Sure about that?" Zoey asked.

"Pretty sure." He haphazardly crammed the DVDs into the box. More than once, a DVD fell out and he had to pick it up again.

"Lucas Horatio Fry, get a move on," said a woman's voice in a distinctly mom-ish way.

"See, I was right. Lucas." He sat the full box on the back of his moped.

The girls couldn't help but laugh.

A woman in her mid-forties, almost certainly his mother, walked up to him, carrying a clothes hamper.

"Do you expect your father to carry everything himself?" she asked in an unpleasant tone. She looked from him up to the girls. "He'll have to talk to you later. He's in Hathaway Hall. Room 312."

"Mom!"

"Now come on, we have a lot to move," she said to Lucas.

Lucas hung his head in utter embarrassment. He hopped on his moped.

"Well, say goodbye," his mother urged playfully.

"Goodbye, ladies," he called up as he started his moped.

"'Ladies.' Aren't we the smooth talker?"

"Mother!"

Zoey snatched the socks away from Sam.

"Oh, I bet we never see him again." She smiled as she tossed the socks into her dresser drawer.

"I am so glad my godparents left early. I guarantee they would find a way to embarrass me five times worse than that," Sam said, heading back to her side of the room to keep unpacking. She distinctly remembered the time Helen dropped her off at her first boy/girl party and wouldn't leave until she got all the other kids' parents' names and phone numbers in case something happened.

"So do you get along with the godparents well?"

Sam reached into her box and picked up her most valuable item in the world: Mr. Hopscotch. She sat him down on the bed where she could see him at all times, just in case Zoey decided to keep hurling things out the window.

"We get along fine. They were just in a hurry to get back to the airport. My godmother, Helen, is an anthropologist. When I decided to come to school here she called her old professor and got a job on a dig down in Peru. Harold, my godfather, designs bridges. He's on his way to Australia. They both have flights out of LAX tonight," Sam said.

"Super-neat," Zoey said, folding up a pair of purple jeans.

"You wouldn't think so if you had to ride all the way here from Illinois in a Ford Escort loaded with three people's luggage." Sam shuddered. There were few things on Earth as boring as driving across the vast flatness of Nebraska.

"Do you have a little brother?" Zoey asked.

Sam shook her head.

"Don't complain to me about cross-country trips until you've spent thirteen hours in the back seat with a ten-year-old boy." Zoey shivered dramatically. "The smells. I can't even describe them."

Sam had to chuckle at that. She had always wondered what it would be like to have a sibling. But somehow she never factored a smelly little brother into her fantasies.

"Fire in the hole! Fire in the hole!"

A tall blonde girl in overalls ran past their doorway shouting at the top of her lungs.

"Get down people!" she yelled from down the hall.

Three sparkling red bolts zipped past the door.

There was a great deal of yelling and banging from the hallway. Sam and Zoey rushed to the doorway.

Another red firework flew by. Someone's mother shrieked as she flattened herself against the wall, barely getting out of the rocket's path in time.

"Stellar," Zoey said, her eyes widening with excitement.

Cheers and applause filled the hallway, followed quickly by loud, angry parental shouting. Most of the girls in the hall ducked back into their rooms to spare the firework launcher the humiliation of a public chewing out. Sam and Zoey went back to their unpacking.

"Until just now, I thought this place was going to be insanely boring," Sam said.

"Hopefully we'll get almost blown up every day," Zoey agreed.

Looking around, Sam noticed that Zoey's desk was just as empty as hers.

"You didn't bring a computer?" she asked.

"Bah, computers are for morons," Zoey said, tapping her right temple. "I got everything I need up here."

Sam didn't know how to respond to that.

"I'm kidding. I just couldn't bring mine with me. I have to settle for one of the school's loaners. You?"

"Same here," Sam said. She opened her closet to find it surprisingly spacious for a dorm room. If she left her sweaters and other winter stuff in boxes under her bed, she would have enough room for all of her clothes.

Someone tapped on the doorframe.

"Knock, knock," Tasha said. "How would you like to meet the 'rents?"

Mr. Beaumont was a tall, muscular man who looked like he would be perfectly at home on a football field, except he had a wise, professorlike face. Mrs. Beaumont looked very much like an older version of Tasha. She was also tall, although not nearly as tall as Mr. Beaumont, and she had long, lean arms and legs. She had probably been a gymnast as a kid, just like Tasha.

"Mom, Dad, this is Zoey and Sam."

"Hello," Zoey said, extending her hand to shake each of theirs in turn.

"Hi." Taking her cue from Zoey, Sam extended her hand as well.

"I expect you girls to keep my little Nat out of trouble, now," Mr. Beaumont said, shaking Sam's hand. He gave her a little nod and a smile.

"It's a pleasure to meet you both," Mrs. Beaumont added.

"Likewise," Sam and Zoey said together.

"Jinx, you owe me a soda," Zoey blurted quickly.

Mrs. Beaumont tapped her husband on the arm. "It looks like the other parents are heading out. We should give these girls some time to get settled in."

"Goodbye, pumpkin." Mr. Beaumont gave Tasha a quick hug, which she pretended to find annoying.

"Have fun, girls," Mrs. Beaumont said with a wink as she and her husband stepped into the elevator.

Once the elevator doors closed, Tasha turned her questioning eyes on Sam and Zoey.

"So, what did you think of my parents?"

"They're keepers," Zoey said with an enthusiastic thumbs-up.

Sam nodded in agreement, trying to stick to the rules of Jinx, which meant that she was not allowed to speak again until she bought Zoey a soda. She hoped there was a vending machine nearby.

"Come on," Tasha said, checking the time on her cell phone. "The RA is holding a meeting in three minutes."

The three girls joined the others who were filing their way into the recreation lounge at the end of the hallway.

From the brochure Sam knew that each floor had its own Resident Advisor; a girl, or boy for the boys' dorms, from the college who volunteered to live in the academy dorms to help students adjust to their new school, settle disputes between roommates, and generally just be a big sister or brother to the new students. It seemed like a lot of work to Sam, especially for someone who was taking college classes.

"Welcome, welcome," a familiar voice beckoned. "I am your Resident Advisor, in case you hadn't guessed. My name is Amy Rosenberg."

Agent Rosenberg gave Sam a little wink before going on to explain to the girls the rules of the dorm and her personal hopes for the coming year.

Lucas' arms hung lifelessly at his sides, clearly indicating that he was finished hugging, but his mother held on for several more seconds.

"Let the boy go," his father said lovingly.

Lucas wiggled free of her loosening grip.

"You can call me any time, day or night," his mom said, holding back tears.

"Gotcha," Lucas said holding up his brand new cell phone.

"Tell your mysterious new roommate that we are sorry we missed him," his mother said.

"I will."

Lucas waved goodbye to his parents. His mother kept waving until his parents reached the parking lot. He dug out his key card and zipped inside the building. He hoped nobody saw him standing there waving to his mommy like a little kid.

She was right about his roommate being mysterious, though. According to his parents, his roommate had already moved in his stuff before they got there. Lucas had snooped around his new roommate's belongings a bit for clues about his personality. He had a brand new extremely expensive computer that could run circles around Lucas' machine, a globe sat on his desk, and a map of the world hung over his bed labeled PLANET NATCH.

When Lucas finally got back up to his floor, the elevator doors opened to reveal a cheering crowd in the hallway.

"Kill him," someone yelled. A chorus of voices agreed.

Lucas looked over a shorter boy's shoulder to see what everyone was so excited about.

Two robots were locked in battle.

More specifically, a two-foot long mechanical scorpion was dueling with a miniature monster truck with a snapping dragon's head in the front and a swinging wreaking ball for a tail. Judging by the way the side of the dragon's head had been scarred and one of the scorpion's claws had been crushed Lucas had missed some serious action.

The scorpion snapped its remaining working claw at the dragon's studded rubber tires, causing the dragon to back away. When the scorpion charged forward, the dragon spun around quickly, striking the scorpion with its wreaking-ball tail. The ball crushed the scorpion's already crushed claw even further.

But the scorpion had a tail of its own. A thick blue fluid shot out of the tail, covering half of the dragon, including the tail. The fluid weighed the ball down too much for the dragon to swing it anymore. As the fluid dried, it became sticky, slowing the dragon down.

"Watch it," a tall boy in a football jersey shouted as the dragon backed up toward him.

As a whole the crowd had to keep moving around to make room for the dragon robot, which was running scared now. The dragon found itself pinned between the wall and a beanbag chair someone hadn't put away yet. Cheers and laughter rose as the scorpion closed in for the final showdown.

The dragon wasn't going down without a fight, though. It snapped its jaws at the approaching scorpion and caught its tail in mid-strike. The dragon began lashing back and forth, dragging the helpless scorpion around.

But just as it looked like the dragon was going to rip the scorpion's tail off, its head erupted with the sticky blue fluid. The fluid rolled down the dragon's neck shorting out the robot. The fight was over.

"Loser," one boy yelled.

"Your robot fu is weak," yelled another.

With the battle over, the crowd quickly broke apart and went back to unpacking.

"I think I might have got him if it wasn't for that stupid beanbag chair," said a disheartened voice behind Lucas.

Lucas turned just in time to see that the speaker had come out of the dorm room next to his. He was a bit pudgy around the middle, and his shoulders drooped a bit. He had a radio controller in his hand.

"That isn't your chair, is it?" the boy asked, a bit annoyed.

"Uh, no," Lucas answered. "I'm Lucas. I'm in room 312, right next to yours."

"Ah, you're the one with the massive TV I saw earlier. Very nice. I'm Jerry. Jerry Little," he said, stooping down to pick up his robot.

"So did you build these?" Lucas asked excitedly.

"No," Jerry scoffed. "I couldn't put a toaster back together if my life depended on it. But Esteban, the guy who did build them, challenged me to a match. It seemed like a lot of fun. Too bad I'm really bad at it."

The scorpion robot scurried down the hall. The boys walked along behind it.

"Well, it was your first time and you were fighting the guy who built the things," Lucas said kindly.

Jerry just shrugged in response.

Lucas noticed that the radio controller had a small screen in the middle that gave the operator the robot's view from the little camera mounted on top. That would explain why he never saw either of the operators in the hallway; they had been controlling their machines from their dorm rooms. It looked like a lot of fun.

"So where does Esteban live?" Lucas asked, but just then he stumbled across the answer.

They had reached the only closed door in the hall, other than the bathroom, of course. But this door was different from all the others; it was solid steel. There was an eye slot in the middle of the door much like a dungeon door would have, and a doggie door at the bottom just big enough for the robots to slip inside.

Jerry pushed his robot in through the flap.

"The controller too," came a muffled voice through the door.

"I know, I know," Jerry said, slipping the controller through the flap. "Maybe we can have a rematch sometime."

"Sure thing," the muffled voice said.

"And that would be Esteban," Jerry said with raised eyebrows as he and Lucas walked back to their rooms.

"When did you meet him?" Lucas asked.

"I still haven't," Jerry said as he stopped next to the door to his room. "I was dared by my roommate to knock on the door. He had that door specially installed, I guess. He sent the robots out to greet me."

"So you haven't seen him?"

"Nope. And I don't think we ever will," Jerry said wistfully. "There are cameras in every classroom of the school and he is tapped into all of them. He says that he plans to take all of his classes from his room."

"Well, that's weird beyond weird." Lucas suddenly imagined Esteban as one of those six hundred pound guys who need the fire department to come cut a hole in the wall so they can get out of their house.

"You think that's weird? You haven't met your roommate yet, have you?" Jerry asked with a grin.

"No," Lucas answered slowly. "Why?"

"No reason. I'd better let you get to that," Jerry said slipping into his room.

"Later."

He wasn't sure if Jerry was setting him up or not so he decided to peek into his room before entering.

"People of Earth! Kneel before the might of Natch, Emperor Supreme. Give me your lives, your wealth, and your pizza rolls." A black-haired boy sat in a high-backed office chair, hoisting a globe in the air like a trophy.

"Ahem," Lucas said to announce his presence.

"Who goes there?" the boy asked angrily. "Identify yourself."

"I'm Lucas Fry, your roommate. I'm-"

"Yes, I know," the boy said, clasping his hands together under his nose. "The big-screen TV and boxes upon boxes of video games were a dead give away. You're the guy who won the Gameco National Video Game Championship this summer."

Lucas still hadn't gotten used to the fame his championship win had given him. Granted, he was only famous within the gamer community, but it was still embarrassing.

"So you are a gamer?" Lucas asked.

"Not really."

"Okay. And you are?"

"Natch," the boy said proudly. "Future Emperor Supreme of Earth and all points beyond."

"Okay," Lucas said slowly. "Is Natch your first or last name?"

"Neither. Both."

"Right." Lucas decided to try a different angle. "So I'm sure you've guessed that I was invited here after my big victory." In fact, his tuition was mostly paid off as long as he tested video games after class three times a week in Dr. Zhang's lab. "What brought you here?"

"I'm going to take over the world," Natch said matter-of-factly as he sat down his globe.

"Sounds time-consuming." Lucas tore open the box holding his stash of *Pizza Guy* comic books. "Say, when you take over the world, can I have Australia?"

"Hmm." He really seemed to be thinking it over. "How about New Zealand?"

"Deal," Lucas said flipping through his comics. He hoped the local bookstore carried all of his favorite titles.

"By the way," Natch said slyly. "Which of those girls were you hitting on?"

Lucas felt his ears burn with embarrassment.

"What? I wasn't- Were you watching me?"

"Not on purpose." Natch got up from his chair and pointed out the window. "I noticed you had a lot of heavy boxes that still needed to be moved and you would likely ask for my help, so I hid until you were finished. I was sitting on that bench right outside the cafeteria when you were hit by the sock."

Lucas suddenly realized he could see the girls' dorm from his window. Counting up from the bottom, he found the girls' window. Unfortunately, it was too far away to really see anything.

"Here you go."

Natch handed him a pair of binoculars.

"Uh, why do you have these?" Lucas asked, taking the binoculars.

"Always be prepared," Natch said with extreme smugness.

"Thanks." Lucas was beginning to think that sharing a room with a would-be world-conquering super-villain was going to take a little getting used to.

At first the only thing he could see in the room was Albert Einstein sticking his tongue out at him. Finally he spotted her standing with her back to the window, running her hand through her hair. She was talking to someone, probably her roommate.

Now he just had to figure out how to talk to her without sounding like a complete moron.

He had a better chance of flying to the moon.

Chapter 7

And So It Begins…

The horrible day had finally come. It was time for class.

Unfortunately she failed to factor in the fact that she now shared a bathroom with thirty-nine other girls. By not brushing her teeth or blow-drying her hair, she was able to make it to class three minutes late.

Her first class of the day was English with Professor Woolf. It seemed survivable enough, although she had to read fifty pages by Wednesday. The best part of the class was that Tasha and Zoey had it too. Unfortunately Zoey did not have biology next so Sam and Tasha headed over to Montgomery Hall without her.

They made sure they got seats next to each other at one of the many tables in the room just in case this was a class where you had lab partners.

As the other students filed in, she spotted Lucas and waved to him automatically. Tasha looked at her in surprise. Sam had surprised herself.

Fortunately, Lucas waved back and made a direct line to her table.

"How's it going, Samantha and friend?" Lucas asked as he sat down.

"This is Tasha," Sam said, pointing to the still visibly shocked Tasha.

"Hello," Tasha said scrutinizing Lucas. "How do you two know each other?"

"Oh, we go back a long ways. All the way to two days ago when I was nearly killed by a falling pair of socks," he said.

"Really?" Tasha asked, her eyebrows raised to their fullest height.

"Well, they were specially designed attack socks," Sam said, surprised at her own wittiness.

"I see," Tasha said approvingly. She flashed Sam a look that clearly meant they were going to a have nice juicy talk about this later.

"Hey, Lucas," a boy with untidy hair said as he sat down in the fourth and last seat at their table.

"Oh, hey," Lucas said a bit surprised. "I didn't realize you had this class too. This is Samantha and Tasha."

Lucas bobbed his head expectantly a few times.

"And this is Jerry," he said finally.

"Oh sorry," Jerry said looking down at the table.

"That's okay, Jerry," Tasha said. "But one of you had better be good at biology."

"Not it," Lucas called quickly.

Tasha giggled.

"Good morning, ladies and gentlemen."

Assuming Sam's schedule wasn't lying, that would be Professor Laurie Walsh. At least she looked like a proper professor. She seemed to be in her late fifties, and wore her hair back in a bun. Her lab coat disguised whatever fashion sense she had, but her sensible shoes indicated she was a very serious woman.

"I see a lot of unenthusiastic faces out there. I would like to guarantee that by the end of the year this will be your favorite class, but I think we both know this is just isn't going to happen," she said with amazing bluntness.

"But I promise we will all get through this. Step one: I hope you like the people you are sitting with, because they are now your lab partners for the rest of the year."

There were a couple of groans and sighs of complaint among the class. Sam and Tasha smiled at each other, happy with their cleverness.

"Now then, show of hands; is anyone here planning on a future in biology?"

One hand went up. It belonged to Leslie Chang, the girl Sam saw carrying the astronaut's helmet the other day. At their first hall meeting Agent Rosenberg, as the hall's RA, had everyone introduce themselves to the group. It turned out Leslie's mother was an astronaut and Leslie had dreams of being the person to find microscopic life on Mars.

"Okay," Professor Walsh said, a bit discouraged. "How about something medical or veterinary-related? Maybe pharmaceutical or genetics-related?"

More hands went up this time.

"Well then, this is an important class for all of you. And it can be helpful for the rest of you too," she said enthusiastically. "Honest."

The class was still unimpressed.

Professor Walsh slumped against her desk.

"Okay. You don't believe me. I wasn't going to do this so soon, but it looks like we could all use a shot in the arm," the professor said as she gestured for everyone to stand up. "We're going on a field trip."

There are few school-related words that can energize and excite the average student to the point of clapping and cheering, especially after they outgrow recess, but Professor Walsh had found them.

"Let's go," she said, checking her watch. "Bring your books; we probably won't make it back before class is over."

Sam noticed she was the only one at her table who had even taken their book out of their backpack. She stuffed it back in, grateful that she only had to carry three books around today.

"Where do you think we are going?" Lucas asked as they joined the throng of students pouring out of the classroom.

"Dairy Queen?" Tasha offered.

"Nice, but hardly biology related," Sam said.

"You've clearly never been in the back room before."

"All right, cross Dairy Queen off my list of places to eat," Sam said, disgusted.

Professor Walsh led the class out the building and across the quad. As they walked along the lake towards the college side, the guessing became more and more extreme. Someone squealed with excitement.

Up ahead were the school's stables. Four absolutely gorgeous horses stood in the pens outside. Two American Paint horses and two chestnut brown Arabian horses stood proudly by the fence, watching the students with curious eyes. Several of the girls rushed ahead of Professor Walsh to coo over the horses. Sam would have happily joined them, except out of the corner of her eye she caught Tasha rolling her eyes and Lucas shaking his head and she didn't want to look like a silly horse-obsessed girl in front of her new friends.

"Girls, please. We are heading this way," Professor Walsh said gently.

The girls groaned with disappointment, but they followed the professor into the building next to the stables. Sam understood their disappointment and made a mental note to come back here in her free time. She had never ridden a horse, and the idea of mixing the Sam Curse with a thousand pound animal seemed colossally dangerous, but she really wanted to try it.

The building that Professor Walsh led them into was different from the others Sam had seen on campus so far. This one was more sterile. The walls were all pearly white with shiny metal trim. Three men in lab coats met them in the lobby.

"Hello, Professor Walsh. Giving the tour a little early, huh?" one of the lab-coated men asked.

"Desperate times, Dr. Anderson," the professor answered.

"Have fun," he said with a chuckle. "You kids are in for a treat."

Professor Walsh led the students through several sets of doors and down two or three hallways. Sam wasn't sure she could find her way back out if she had to. Finally the professor stopped and let the students gather in a large room with yet another set of double doors.

"Okay, class, we are currently on university property so please be on your best behavior. I must ask that you not touch anything, especially the glass. We don't want you disturbing the animals any more than necessary."

Sam and Tasha exchanged excited looks. Who knew what kind of animals they could have hidden in this place?

Professor Walsh pulled a card from her pocket and swiped it through the slot.

With a loud buzz, the doors unlocked.

"Single file, now," she said holding the left door open for the class.

"Wow," someone ahead of Sam exclaimed.

They were right to wow. On either side of the hallway were glass enclosures with various animals in simulations of their natural habitats. Miller's Grove had its own zoo. Sam couldn't believe it. This certainly wasn't in any of the brochures she saw. But it really should be.

"Miller's Grove University takes in endangered animals from all over the world to study in order to preserve their health and hopefully return them to the wild some day," Professor Walsh said, slipping into tour guide mode.

"Meet the triplets," she said as the students rushed to the glass.

Three large pandas stared back at the students. Two of the pandas sat happily chewing on bamboo stalks. The third was splashing playfully in the small pond in their enclosure.

"They're so cool," Leslie whispered.

"I know," Sam whispered back.

For just an instant Sam thought she saw Lucas' reflection in the glass looking at her instead of the pandas. It could just have easily been her imagination. Before she could tell for sure he looked away.

"Technically the Chinese government doesn't know we have them, so let's keep this quiet, huh?"

Everyone laughed, but Sam wasn't sure Professor Walsh was joking.

Next to the giant pandas was a forestlike enclosure housing at least six very large turtles.

"Oooh, look at these," a girl whose name Sam didn't know cooed, pointing at a pen full of colorful birds.

Just like that, the group broke apart as students ran to different enclosures. Professor Walsh didn't seem to mind; in fact, she seemed quite pleased to see her students enthusiastic about something. She walked from enclosure to enclosure, sprinkling trivia.

"Check these out," Lucas said, pointing at a different pen.

"They look like penguins," Tasha said.

Sam had to agree. The black and white birds were waddling around on a pebbly beach. Then, one by one they dove into the water. They shot through the water like cute little torpedoes spiraling and swirling around one another.

"Hmm. According to the sign they are Great Auks," Lucas said.

"Still look like penguins to me," Tasha said stubbornly.

"No freaking way," a boy shouted loudly from five pens downs.

The entire class turned to look at him. He was pointing excitedly at the glass; his mouth hung open foolishly.

"I believe Mr. Cutler has discovered one of our special guests," Professor Walsh said, nearly bursting with pride. "Come. Gather 'round."

Sam and the others crowded in around the glass as best they could. Annoyingly, Jerry and Tasha were squished in so close behind her she could barely breathe.

Four large vaguely wolfish creatures were lying in the grass. They could have been some sort of dog, except the black tiger stripes on their hindquarters made Sam think maybe they were closer to the cat family.

"These are some of the last known Tasmanian Tigers in the world. They were housed at a private zoo in New Zealand for many years before coming here three years ago," Professor Walsh said.

"But aren't they extinct?" the boy who found them asked.

"Do they look extinct?" Professor Walsh asked joyfully.

Everyone was pushing and shoving each other aside to get a better look. Jerry was literally breathing down Sam's neck. It took a lot of self-control to keep her from elbowing him in the stomach.

"Oh, duh!" Tasha loudly slapped her forehead. She dug in her pocket and pulled out a cell phone. "I am so getting a picture of this."

Suddenly everyone else who had a camera phone was doing the same thing.

"Students, please," Professor Walsh said in a strict tone. "Photos are absolutely forbidden. I cannot stress that enough. We must protect these animals, not exploit them. Anyone who takes a picture will have their phone destroyed and will be immediately expelled."

"Do you know how much I could get for a picture of a live Tasmanian Tiger?" Tasha said sadly as she put her phone away.

Apparently everyone else had the same idea as they grumpily put their phones away, although by the way a few of them clutched their phones Sam figured they were more concerned about their phones' safety than being expelled.

"I can make it up to you," Professor Walsh said. "Our next stop is everyone's absolute favorite part of the tour."

"What could possibly be better than extinct Tasmanian Tigers?" Lucas whispered.

"Unicorns?" Tasha guessed.

"Oh, wait," Lucas said excitedly. "Maybe they've got dinosaurs."

"Where would they get dinosaurs?" Jerry asked.

"The Natural History building has a fossil collection," an eavesdropping girl Sam didn't know said. "My mom is a paleontology professor at the university."

"Maybe they cloned some," Lucas offered. "Like that movie."

"That'd be so awesome," Jerry said.

The whispering and speculation came to an end when they reached the next enclosure. Professor Walsh carefully stood in front of the little plaque below the glass.

"Can anyone tell me what these are?" she asked.

Ten of the weirdest birds Sam had ever seen were waddling around inside their pen. The birds were about three feet tall and had gray feathers with a white tail. They were ridiculously fat birds like turkeys, but with larger beaks and smaller wings. It was highly unlikely these things could fly.

Two of the larger birds were pecking apart a chunk of watermelon.

"No! Freaking! Way!" a boy to Sam's left said in complete amazement.

"So anyone have a guess?" Professor Walsh asked.

"Dodo birds," the boy said; his hand over his mouth as if he was afraid to say the words.

"Exactly right."

Everyone pressed closer to the glass. Eight different people were crushed up against Sam, but she didn't care. As long as no one blocked her view she was fine. She could always breathe later.

"In 1657 Dr. Johannes De Groot trapped a few pairs of the birds on the island of Mauritius and brought them back to Europe, where he raised and studied them. A few decades later the dodo bird was declared extinct and the De Groot family fell on hard times, so the birds were sold to Count Darius Elwood, a British adventurer and collector of bizarre oddities. We only recently acquired the birds when the last of the Elwood family passed away. Sadly, they are not capable of surviving in the wild, but we hope to find them a suitable environment some day."

No one paid the slightest attention to Professor Walsh. Everyone was fighting for position to view the ridiculous birds waddling around on their tiny legs. They were so awkwardly built Sam could see why they wouldn't survive in the wild anymore; they would be easy prey for any predator.

Half an hour passed before Sam realized class was over. She only had twenty-seven minutes left to grab lunch before History class. After sprinting across campus and choking down a double cheeseburger in an unladylike, but world-record-setting, time, Sam made it to History class with a whole minute to spare.

Unfortunately History class was a total bust, something made all the more painfully clear thanks to her amazing biology class. Professor Spitz was quite possibly the most boring human being alive. Robots had more emotion than this guy, and not just those fancy new Japanese robots that look like kids and flight attendants and other creepy things, but those little Roomba vacuuming robots.

But that wasn't even the worst part. Sam had dealt with boring teachers before. But a little posse of five girls kept flashing nasty looks at Sam and whispering and laughing about something all class long.

After that came Latin, where Ms. Gaunt wouldn't let them speak English--which was a lot of fun for Sam who didn't know a single word in Latin and only took the class because it was a dead language and she wouldn't have to learn the words for automobiles, airports, computers, or other things made after the fall of Rome. After flipping through the book, though, it turned out that, while the language might be a little easier due to the lack of words, it was going to get really boring talking about farming and gladiators all the time. She was determined to stick it out, though; she knew it was exactly the type of class her parents would want her to take.

She couldn't help but notice two girls that kept looking at her. Sam had no idea why she was drawing so much attention lately. Finally one of them leaned over and asked, "Are you the girl who said that Tiffany Summers was a pathetic no-talent wannabe?"

Sam was stunned by the question. It took her a second to remember that she had.

"How do you know about that?"

"It is her," the girl said to her friend. "Rock on. Someone had to be brave enough to say it."

"Yeah," her friend chimed in. "You're a hero."

"What are you talking about?" Sam was thoroughly confused, but did not like where this was going.

"It is so lame how everyone is pretending to be such big fans of her just because she is sort of famous," the second girl said.

"Seriously, I don't know what you are talking about. How do you know what I said about her?"

"The video," the first girl said. "On the school's home page. Haven't you seen it?"

"Oh no. Those idiots."

"Somebody made a video about all the new students on the first day. But you were the best," the first girl said.

She didn't even realize Sick and Wrong had recorded her saying those things. At least it couldn't have been up very long.

"Do you think Tiffany Summers has seen it?" she asked.

"Oh yeah," the second girl said. "Her lawyers already made the school take it down. My roommate Serena is part of her little posse." She rolled her eyes at that last part.

Sam guessed the girls in her earlier class were part of the posse too. Just great. It was her first day and already she had ticked off one of the most popular girls in school. Her best hope was to lay low and hope that Tiffany's posse would move on.

Chapter 8

Worst. Lunch. Ever.

By the third week of classes Sam had fallen into a nice little routine, but today a thunderstorm had rolled in just in time to drench her on her way to lunch, destroying the last shreds of excitement Sam felt about going to class that day. She had already had more homework in the last three weeks than she had ever had in two months at her old school. The fourth draft of her validating-her-existence paper was due in two days. So far, no one had written a paper that met with Professor Woolf's approval.

To top it all off, that morning she had discovered that the art class she took because she thought it would be a fun and easy class was full of people who were actually really, really supergood at art. One of the kids already had a full-scale exhibit of his work in a Manhattan art gallery. Sure, she later found out from a purple-haired girl who called herself Celestial that the boy's mother owned the gallery, but still, his work was pretty impressive. His people actually looked like people.

The truly amazing part was that all of these amazing artists considered her a hero for telling Tiffany Summers that she was a poser. It didn't seem to matter to them that Sam hadn't actually meant to take a stand or anything. Sam was just grateful to have a class free from torment; she didn't know exactly what the Tiffany fans in her Latin class were saying about her, but the pointing and giggling was getting old.

But it was lunchtime and her spirits were rising as she ran from building to building trying to avoid the rain as much as possible. Doc Frost and a crowd of upperclassmen in rain slickers holding beakers and rain gauges stood in her way. One of them pulled a small eyedropper out of her pocket and squeezed a single red drop into a large puddle. The spot where the drop hit turned to ice. Ice crystals spread out and froze the entire puddle.

This did not seem to surprise the rain-slicker people at all, although two of them were feverishly jotting down notes.

"Uh oh. Scenario nine, scenario nine!" one of them yelled. "It's not stopping."

The ice spread out to neighboring puddles. Soon there was a sheet of ice the size of a kiddie pool in the otherwise warm and rainy quad, a sheet of ice that was rapidly expanding towards Sam.

"Quickly now, quickly," Doc Frost urged. "Formula seven."

Frantically the girl who first froze the puddle pulled out another eyedropper, this time with green liquid, and squeezed two drops onto the ice. The ice shuddered a little bit and suddenly vanished in a big burst of steam.

"Yes!" they all shouted together while trading high fives.

"Well done," Doc Frost said with a strong dose of relief in his voice.

Sam decided to stay away from that area for a while, which meant she had to cross a larger puddle. She psyched herself up, resituated her backpack, and leapt.

She looked back at the puddle, impressed with her defeat of the Sam Curse. Suddenly she felt a hand pushing on the small of her back. With a surprised high-pitched yelp, she fell face-first into the puddle.

"Good going there, cuz," Zack said snidely behind her.

Sam picked herself up to the laughter of Zack's idiot friends.

Her entire front was soaked. Thankfully, her homework was safe in her backpack. She did her best to squeeze the water out of her shirt, which was pretty pointless in the rain.

"And they really think *you* stole the Lantern of the Blue Flame?" With a flash of his trademark cocky smile he turned and headed into the Student Lounge, his trio of idiots in tow.

Sam stopped in mid-squeeze. Zack knew about the Lantern of the Blue Flame. When she thought about it, she shouldn't have been surprised. The McQueens and the Hathaways had been rivals in all things weird, mythical, and scientific for generations. Zack would have grown up knowing everything there was to know about things like the Lantern.

The life Sam would have had if her parents hadn't died.

Now fully depressed and standing in the rain, Sam decided to go inside and see if she could drown her sorrows in chocolate pudding. The instant Sam entered the cafeteria someone flapped a flyer in her face.

"Vote for Sherry Hoyle," the flyer waver said with great enthusiasm.

"Vote for her for what?" Sam took the flyer just to get it out of her face.

"Student Council President," the flyer waver said with a roll of his eyes that clearly meant that he thought Sam must have been living under a rock.

"Vote for Sherry Hoyle," he said to the people coming in behind Sam. She was clearly no longer important to him.

Not more than a second later another flyer was thrust into her hand. This one wanted her to vote for a Milton Hubble.

Every wall in the cafeteria was covered with posters of smiling faces asking for her vote. She counted at least twenty different people running for Student Council President and another forty running for Treasurer and Secretary and various other offices.

Since everyone running was a senior, and it was only the third week of class, Sam felt really unprepared to pick a candidate. But according to the wall of posters, she had four whole weeks until the election to think about it. She hoped someone would try to buy her vote with food or cold hard cash.

She was harassed twice in the food line by kids with flyers and once by Sherry Hoyle herself, shaking hands and promising to make sweeping changes. Sam assured Sherry she had her vote, and Sherry wandered down the line to harass other hungry students. After filling her tray, Sam scanned the cafeteria for her friends.

Zoey desperately waved Sam to hurry over. She was sitting at their usual table with Lucas, Jerry, and Lucas' roommate Natch, who all seemed to be engaged in a heated debate that was boring Zoey to tears.

"The building is fine, assuming they don't figure how to use the swipe cards." Natch was waving his fork around as he spoke. A macaroni noodle flew off and landed on Jerry's shirt, but he didn't seem to notice. "But we'd be separated from the main food source. We'd be stuck living on vending machines."

"We could probably come up with some way to slide down onto the roof without touching the ground," Lucas said before taking a bite of his cheeseburger.

Zoey caught Sam's eyes, silently begging for help.

"What's up, guys?" Sam asked as she sat down next to Zoey.

"They're figuring out what to do in the event of a zombie attack on the school," Zoey said with intense disinterest.

"Right," Sam said, trying not to be too insulting to the boys. Her dripping pants were making little puddles under the table.

Lucas put down his cheeseburger. "Natch here likes to make sure any place he lives is as zombie-proof as possible."

"Hey, when the roaming undead come to feast upon our brains I don't want to be caught unprepared," Natch said with complete sincerity.

"Thanks a lot," Zoey said twisting her spaghetti around her fork. "There goes my appetite."

"Hey, in a zombie situation it is every man for himself," Natch said unapologetically.

"I would so be zombie food," Jerry mumbled as he speared a kernel of corn with his fork.

Sam felt a strong need to change the subject.

"What is with the army of flyer wavers?"

"Apparently people are taking this election very seriously," Zoey said, hopping on the new topic.

"I see that. But we barely know anyone here yet," Sam said. She wasn't prepared to call shaking hands with Sherry Hoyle in a lunch line officially knowing her.

"It doesn't matter," Natch said. "It's all about establishing yourself. This whole school is one big crazy Darwinian experiment, and the smart people are picking out their places in it."

"Oh great, now you got him started," Lucas said slumping down in his chair.

"Think about it; most schools usually have two or three top athletes, smartest nerds, most popular girls, whatever, who compete to be the big dog. But this place collected bunches of those kids from other schools all over the country. There are four quarterbacks in our dorm alone. There are going to be massive power struggles to prove who is the best of the best."

"Well, I think the title of most popular girl is already taken," Zoey said, pointing to the far end of the cafeteria where Tiffany Summers and her groupies were sitting.

Sam watched as Zack not-so-gently pushed another boy aside and sat down next to Tiffany. An unholy alliance was forming over there. Her life was about to get infinitely more difficult.

"Well, that's not good," Zoey said, clearly reading Sam's thoughts.

"I know." Sam hoped that the shiver going up her spine was due to her being completely soaked.

She knew it wasn't.

"Do you really think she is still after you?" Lucas asked.

"Maybe not her, but someone wrote LOSER thirty-seven times on our door this morning," Sam said. It only took her a second to wipe them off the dry erase board, but it was not a fun way to start the day.

"Bummer," Lucas said between bites.

"I cannot believe that Tiffany and Zack are friends." Sam rested her head in her hands.

"Why not? It is a strategically beneficial relationship," Natch said in that condescending voice of his. "He gets to hang with the popular girl and she gets to jump-start her failing career with a live performance in fabulous Las Vegas."

Sam was not connecting the dots on that one.

"What are talking about?" she asked.

Natch set his fork down on his tray. "Well, his parents do own the Camelot casino in Las Vegas. I'm sure Zack can sweet-talk them into letting her perform there."

Sam was dumbfounded.

This must have been obvious to anyone looking at her because Lucas said, "You didn't know that? Aren't they family? I mean I know you're not close or anything. But I think if I had a relative anywhere in my family tree that owned a casino I'd be all over it."

"But how would you know, if you didn't know?" Jerry asked, pulling himself away from his butterscotch pudding.

"Good point," Zoey added. "Besides it isn't like he goes around bragging about it like a normal person would. Or at least I haven't heard about it. How did you know?"

"The Camelot is where they held the Gameco National Video Game Championship," Lucas said. He seemed to sink a little lower in his seat as he said it.

"Wait a minute," Zoey said, pointing sharply across the cafeteria at Zack. "He was a finalist at a competition held in his parent's own casino?"

"I'm surprised he didn't win," Natch said flatly.

"Thanks a lot." Lucas looked up and to the side the way some people do when they are trying to remember something. "I don't think he cheated. He is actually pretty good."

"Yeah, didn't he actually beat you twice last night?" Natch asked with a mischievous look on his face.

Sam couldn't believe her ears. "Have you been hanging out with Zack?"

Lucas held his hands up in surrender as he spoke. "Listen. I know you don't get along with your cousin. I don't like him either. But my parents couldn't afford for me to come here, so to pay off part of my tuition I have to let Dr. Zhang hook electrodes to my head while I battle Zack on *Hyper-Urban Assault* for some sort of crazy psychological study about how video games affect eye-hand coordination and strategic planning and problem solving and blabbity blah blah blah. So me, Zack, and a couple other people play games after class a couple times a week."

"You could have told me that before," Sam said. She would have understood.

"Yeah well, it is a little embarrassing. Plus, I am actually getting bored of video games, which is really traumatic for me," he said. His mouth smiled, but his eyes didn't.

"Tired of smooshing poor innocent turtles and storming the castle to rescue the princess?" Zoey asked playfully.

"You haven't played a video game in a while have you?" Lucas asked in an accusatory tone.

"I don't really have the time. Oh-" Zoey yelled angrily as she jumped out of her seat, rubbing her shin. "What was that?"

A two-foot tall robot with outstretched Frankenstein-style arms and tank-tread wheels rolled out from under the table.

"Feed me," the robot said in a creepy buzzy robot voice.

"Hey Esteban," Natch said.

"Hey Natch," the robot buzzed.

"What is that?" Zoey asked. She seemed more curious than angry now.

The small camera mounted where the robot's head should be swiveled to look at her.

"Hello Zoey Dalal, my name is Esteban Ruiz. Pleased to meet you." The robot tipped forward slightly as if bowing. "Sorry for bumping into you."

"Uh, hello, Esteban," she said examining the camera closely. "That is quite all right."

"You two have a nice chat. I'll be right back," Natch said as he got up and headed back to the buffet line.

Zoey squatted down to have a better look at the robot. She poked at the robot's left arm. Sam zoned out when Zoey started asking very technical-sounding questions about how the robot was built.

"Ah, young love," Lucas said sarcastically. "When girl meets robot."

Sam couldn't help but laugh at that.

"Do you know this Esteban fellow?" Sam asked in her mock-concerned-mom voice. "Is he a fine upstanding young gentleman?"

"Sort of," Lucas answered seriously. "He lives on my floor, but he has never come out of his room as far as I know."

"Never?"

"Nope."

"So you've never seen him?"

"Correct."

"I wonder how he goes to the bathroom," Jerry said, annoyingly interrupting Sam and Lucas' fun back and forth.

"We are eating here, man," Lucas said to Jerry as he carelessly tossed his fork down on the table in annoyance.

"Sorry," Jerry said sheepishly and went back to eating his pudding.

But something had just occurred to Sam.

"So if he doesn't ever leave his room, he must not go to classes."

"Right," Lucas said.

"So how does he know Zoey?"

Lucas put both of his hands up to cover the sides of his mouth.

"He knows everyone," he said quietly. "He's a computer nerd. He hacked into the school's systems and read everyone's files. And he's tapped into all the cameras."

"That's creepy and probably illegal," she said. "And he can read lips?"

"We don't know. But why risk it?"

She put her hands up to her mouth just like Lucas. "How do you know he's done all this?"

"Natch," Lucas said with a nod of his head. "He's been using Esteban to look up information on everyone. And he bribed him to not tell me his real name."

"Wow, major paranoia," she said. "But he knows everything that's in our files?"

"That is correct, Samantha Diane Hathaway of Presley, Illinois, daughter of Drs. Samuel and Joanne Hathaway, born April 1, in Menlo Park, New Jersey," Lucas said with a sly look.

"That is so creepy," she blurted out. "What else do you know about me?"

"Nothing, really," he said defensively.

She could tell from his face that he knew he had done something wrong, not just that he had said something wrong, but that he had actually done something so stalkerishly creepy that she might jump up from the table and never talk to him again. But in reality she was wondering exactly what her file said. It could have useful information on her parents or the stupid Lantern of the Blue Flame that everyone wanted so badly.

"Uh, listen," Lucas said hurriedly. "I'll tell you anything you want to know to make us even. My middle name is Horatio. I don't know how to swim. Uh, I'm from Riverside, Iowa. When I was eight I took all the clothes off of my sister's Barbie doll because I was curious. I-"

"It's okay," Sam said, cutting him off. "Well, maybe not the Barbie part, that is kind of sad. But I'm not mad."

He let out a long breath and slumped back into his seat, more relieved than anyone she had ever seen.

"Do you think I could get a copy of this file?" she asked.

The relief drained from his face to be replaced with suspicion.

"Why? Don't you already know everything about you?" he asked.

"You would think so, wouldn't you? Not that there is much to know," she said as nonchalantly as she could.

"Oh, I'm sure there are a lot of interesting things to know about you," he said casting his eyes down on the table.

Did he know more than he was letting on? Or was he just trying to be nice? Sam couldn't tell. She needed to see what was in her file.

"I don't know about that," she said, attempting to change the subject for now. "I really can't compete with the video game champion of the universe."

Lucas actually blushed.

"I am never going to live that down am I?"

"Never. Besides, it probably made you the coolest guy in Riverside, Iowa."

"First off, Riverside is too small to be the home of anyone that anyone else would think is cool. Secondly, I think you are the first person to include me and cool in the same sentence." He had such a dopey smile on his face.

"Hey, you guys should really check this out," Zoey said. She had taken the front panel off of her little robot friend and was examining the wires and gears inside.

"Ah, naked robot," Lucas said, covering his eyes.

Jerry snorted just as he put a spoonful of pudding in his mouth. A good deal of it oozed out the corners. He reached for a wad of napkins to wipe it off.

"Well, that's disgusting," Natch said as he returned with a loaded tray of food that smelled five times better than the food they had been eating.

"What is that?" Sam asked.

"Coriander and pepper-crusted Yellowfin Tuna over Nicoise salad," Natch said with just a touch of snootiness.

"Where did you find that?" Lucas asked, looking sadly at the remains of his cheeseburger.

"I have my sources." Natch sat the tray down on the robot's outstretched arms.

He put the front panel back on the robot, which earned him a sulking pout from Zoey.

"Your little friend has to go now," he said.

"Goodbye, Zoey," the robot buzzed.

"Goodbye, robot," she said, patting the robot on the camera that served as its head.

The little robot weaved its way through the cafeteria. Most people were happy to get out of the way, but one athletic-looking boy stole the apple off the tray. The robot's head camera turned and looked at the boy for a moment before rolling on. Sam looked up at the security cameras on the ceiling again and could have sworn she saw one turn ever so slightly to watch the boy head back to his table.

"Oh, he is going to pay for that," Lucas said.

"What do you think Esteban will do to him?" Sam asked. There was no telling how much damage a master hacker could do to a person's life.

"Who knows, maybe he'll just change his grades or something," Lucas said.

"Or he could add his name to the FBI's Most Wanted list," Natch said happily.

"That is horrible."

Natch just shrugged and opened his can of Mountain Dew.

"No, this is horrible."

Natch stood up and poured the can of soda on Sam's head.

"NO, I WILL NOT GO OUT WITH YOU, YOU LOSER," he yelled at the top of his lungs as he shook the last drops of soda onto her head.

She sat there dripping for several moments in complete and utter shock. She was too surprised to even yell at him. Slowly the world around her began to filter into her brain.

The entire cafeteria was laughing and pointing at her. Lucas was cussing Natch out, and Zoey threw her unopened pint of chocolate milk at him. For his part Natch was having a ball, doing a little victory dance for the crowd as he walked over to Tiffany and Zack's table, where he was met with a round of applause. The only person who seemed unfazed was Jerry, who just watched the whole scene with a silent wide-eyed stare.

"I can't believe he did that," Zoey said angrily. She stole the unopened milk off of Natch's tray to replace the one she had just thrown.

"I can," Lucas said glumly. "He's all power crazy. He's just trying to suck up to the popular people."

Sam took another look at Natch and his new friends. The only person not laughing was Tiffany, who kept eyeing Natch suspiciously. Sam thought for sure Tiffany would order her followers to pounce on him at any second, but after a few exchanges with Zack, she nodded her head and waved for Natch to sit down.

"I can't believe she let him in," Sam said.

"He's a jerk. They are jerks. They have a lot in common." Zoey said succinctly.

Sam was very inclined to agree--about the jerk part, anyway.

"Wow. That was harsh. Please tell me you got all that." Sick and Wrong approached the table. Wrong had his video camera trained on Sam. He gave Sick a thumbs-up sign.

"Are you guys ever not filming?" Lucas asked.

"Professor Ramirez, the faculty advisor to MGTV, suggested that if we could prove we could cover a news story like the Student Body President election we might be able to get our own show. But then we stumbled across this story-"

He was cut off by a roar of laughter from Tiffany's table.

Zack was doing a pantomime routine that looked a lot like Sam falling in the puddle. Sam was glad she couldn't hear what anyone at that table was saying. Sick snapped his fingers and motioned for Wrong to film Zack's act.

"Get out of here, you vultures," Tasha commanded.

Tasha appeared out of nowhere with her traditional lunchtime snack: a gigantic 120-ounce cup of soda. If Sam had to get up for gymnastics practice at four in the morning, she would be a caffeine junky too.

"Shoo. Go."

Sick and Wrong exchanged a fearful look and scurried off to film Tiffany's table.

"I am so sorry," Lucas said, reaching across the table to hand Sam his napkin. "I am so going to chew him out back in our room."

"It's fine. I guess," Sam said doing her best to blot the Mountain Dew out of her hair.

Just then the bell rang.

"Come on," Tasha said placing her hand on Sam's shoulder. "We should get there early so you can wash up."

"That's right you want to be all squeaky-clean for your beat-down next period." Zack had snuck up behind her.

She fought back the urge to punch him in his big gloating face.

"Speaking of beat-downs," Lucas chimed in. "I hope you've been practicing Hyper-Urban Assault. I'd at least like some sort of a challenge."

"Don't worry about that, my new friend Natch told me all about those cheat codes of yours. I think our next match will be a bit more fair." Zack flashed his trademark smile and walked away in triumph.

Zoey spun in her chair to face Lucas. "You cheat!"

"No," Lucas said offended. "Never. Well, not in a real game. Never against Zack."

"Uh-huh," Zoey said playfully.

"I am going to kill Natch," Lucas said sitting back and crossing his arms, his eyes squinting a bit.

"Maybe we'll do it for you," Tasha flexed her fingers menacingly.

"He is in our gym class next period," Sam explained. The problem was that Zack was also in their gym class. Never mind the fact that it seemed patently unfair to put freshmen and sophomores in the same gym class; it was just torture to put Sam and her super-well-trained competitive cousin in the same class.

Tasha rubbed her hands together. "This is going to be sweet."

Sam wasn't so sure. Zack spent every single gym class purposely hitting whichever type of ball they were playing with at her because he knew she couldn't catch or hit it back. Even when they were on the same team, he would pass her the basketball just so she could miss the shot or have it stolen from her. The only thing that saved her from complete embarrassment was that Natch nearly always stopped a game in the middle by contesting that he successfully stole first base or that he was not going to run track because he was not going to run around in circles just because a fat man with a whistle told him to.

Sam had never looked forward to a gym class less in her life, which was really saying something.

Chapter 9

Gym Class in Wartime

The one small upside to gym class was that it gave Sam the chance to quickly wash the Mountain Dew out of her hair before class started. Of course, that meant that she was stuck with wet hair for the rest of the day and that she would frizz out like crazy. But she didn't smell like stale soda and puddle water anymore, so that was a plus.

"To those who are about to die, we salute you," Tasha said. If that was supposed to be reassuring or inspiring Sam didn't see how.

The Roundhouse was a decent-sized gym with enough room for a basketball court, a weight room, a number of racquetball courts, a martial arts dojo, a dance studio, a climbing wall, and multi-purpose areas currently set up for volleyball and cheer squad rehearsals as well as a room with wall-to-wall floor mats for gymnastics practice. The whole area was surrounded with a six-lane track and enclosed under a multicolored glass dome.

Sam couldn't decide what she thought of Coach Powers as easily as she could her other teachers. He seemed generally nice, but he was even more of a gung ho sports nut than her old gym teacher, Coach Walters. But unlike Coach Walters, it turned out Coach Powers had been a football star, a fact that he managed to work into nearly every speech. He played a few years at Notre Dame and was on his way to the NFL until he suffered some sort of injury that ruined his career.

The only real problem she had with Coach Powers was that he was too dedicated to his job. Coach Walters had been a jerk, but it usually worked out in Sam's favor. Coach Walters turned his gym class into thinly veiled extra practice times for the baseball, basketball, and football teams and had little interest in everyone else, so most of the time Sam was allowed to spend gym class just walking the track. Coach Powers made sure everyone was participating in class, whether they wanted to be or not.

"'Are you ready for your beat-down?'" Tasha asked in her best Zack impression.

Sam was incredibly grateful that Tasha found all of this funny. Tasha was easily one of the best athletes in the class; they almost always wound up on the same team, and they hardly ever won. It really wasn't fair to her.

They lined up with the other students and waited for Coach Powers to arrive. Zack and Natch were getting along like old friends.

"Figured out how to weenie your way out of playing today yet, Natch?" Tasha yelled at them.

The smile instantly vanished from Natch's face as the rest of the class laughed and nodded.

"Calm down, calm down," Coach Powers said as he strode across the gym floor. He had a netted bag of red balls over his shoulder.

Sam's heart skipped a beat.

"All right class, thanks to the rain and the cold we will be having gym class inside today. You're rather lucky; this is about the only school left in California where you can still play…," he paused for dramatic effect as he pulled one of the red balls out of the bag. "Dodgeball."

Apparently a huge smile had sprung up on her face because people were looking at her like she was deranged. She did her best to suppress it.

"All right. Blue team, you have the north side; gold team, you get the south."

Their gym shirts were reversible, with one side being blue and the other gold. Since Coach Powers always split the teams based on colors, everyone could plan ahead. Miraculously, the teams remained fairly even at twenty each. Natch wore the blue side of his shirt for the first time today.

Sam took a spot near the front line, where Coach Powers had placed five red balls. Zack was fidgeting with excitement. He pointed at Sam and then made a slashing motion across his throat. He was getting way too into this, but more importantly, HE WAS GOING DOWN.

Coach Powers blew the whistle, and the teams charged the central line. Three of the balls went to the blue team. One of them went to Zack and he immediately threw it at Sam. Sam was more than ready; she always charged the front line to draw the eager throwers. A shoulder roll to the right and the ball whizzed by harmlessly.

Zack cursed quietly and Sam gave him a little wink.

"Not that easy, cuz."

Whatever witty response he had was lost when he had to dodge a ball aimed at his head.

There were more athletes on the blue team. A lot of the guys apparently didn't feel manly in gold, and most of the girls in their class liked the gold. But that meant that Sabrina, the captain of the softball team; Rebecca, the award-winning swimmer; and Tasha were all on Sam's team.

The blue team was falling into a classic pattern of aiming for the perceived best players on the gold team. This gave Sam the opportunity to run around freely and collect stray balls for the best throwers. After the first ten minutes, most of the boys on Sam's team were out and sitting on the sidelines looking depressed.

Obviously Tasha's old school played dodgeball, because she was a pro. She even knew to aim for people's legs to decrease the odds of them catching the ball.

For her part, Sam made for a great target. She brazenly strutted along the centerline basically begging for the blue team to hit her. Not that any of them could.

Tasha caught a ball, taking the big football player that Natch had been using as shield out of the game. Even before he could walk off the court, Tasha whipped the ball back across and caught Natch in the side of the head.

"Ow," he howled as he fell to the floor.

"Out," Coach Powers yelled with joy.

Natch skulked off the court to join the others on the sidelines.

The teams shrank rapidly. The blue team finally started aiming for Sam due to a lack of more reasonable targets. Three balls zeroed in on her at the same time. Sam had to lean back and jump Matrix-style to avoid all three.

"Hey," Sabrina yelled. She was nursing her right shoulder where one of the balls Sam had dodged had hit her.

As she walked off the court she gave her boyfriend Derek, who was on the blue team and had thrown that particular ball, such a nasty look that he just stopped moving and let a ball hit him.

"Idiot," Zack yelled at him as he sheepishly walked off the court.

Zack was getting really vicious now. He caught a ball thrown at him and hurled it with a savage grunt, catching Tasha in the leg.

"Ha ha," he yelled through gritted teeth.

Rebecca saw her chance and threw a ball at his gloating head, but he reached out and caught it. As Rebecca walked off the court, Sam found herself in a very familiar position. She was the lone survivor of her team. There were five members of the blue team left, including Zack, and there was only one ball left on her side of the court. Not that it mattered much. She was at the part where her mad dodgeball skills always failed her. She could run and dodge and taunt like no one else, but sadly, she could not catch or throw to save her life.

"Come on, Sam," Tasha yelled from the sidelines.

"Get 'em," Sabrina chimed in.

Sam reached for the one ball on her side and suddenly three red balls flew at her. She picked up the ball just in time to use it as a shield, deflecting the ball headed straight at her. By dropping to the floor she let the other two soar over her.

"Rock on, Sam," Tasha yelled.

Now the only armed member of the blue team was Zack.

"Come and get me," he said as he did a little dance.

"That's not sportsmanlike behavior, McQueen," Coach Powers shouted.

"Sorry, Spaceman," Zack replied.

"Watch it, McQueen."

Sam didn't think being called "Spaceman" was very insulting, although it seemed a bit random.

"Sam, Sam, Sam," Tasha started chanting. Soon the rest of the red team was chanting along with her, and even Derek was chanting from the blue team's side, no doubt due to another nasty look from Sabrina.

Sam knew they were just being nice, but she really didn't need the pressure right now.

Zack was busy spinning the ball on his finger.

The chanting continued.

She was running out of options. She either had to throw the ball, which would probably be caught, let Zack hit her, or stand there until class was over. There was no way she was letting Zack tag her out. She reached back and prepared to throw. But just then Zack threw his ball. Sam didn't have enough time to bring her ball up to block, so she let it slip from her fingers and jumped sideways out of the way.

The ball barely slipped by, but she jumped so awkwardly that she couldn't bring her feet back under her to land, and she fell flat on her back.

All five of the balls were now on her side of the court.

The chanting grew even louder. Zack was laughing and pumping his fist in the air. Sam really had no other choice now. She couldn't just stand there for the next thirty-seven minutes. She picked up a ball and felt the weight of it in her hands. She had slightly better aim when she threw underhanded, and she walked up to the line to cut the distance between them.

He stood there ready to catch it.

"Sam, Sam, Sam," the chanted continued.

She reached back and-

DEENT DEENT DEENT.

Alarm sirens went off throughout the building.

Coach Powers rushed out into the middle of the court.

"Everyone. Everyone stay calm," he said to the assembled students who had rushed off of the sideline benches.

"Is it a fire?" someone asked. "Shouldn't we be going outside?"

"That is not the fire alarm," he answered. "It is best that we just stay here until-"

He was cut off by the sounds of the big metal double doors located all around the building flying open. Suddenly a dozen campus security guards appeared; all of them had their stun guns drawn.

"Everyone stay calm," Coach Powers repeated. "This is all a part of the standard drill, I assure you."

"Drill for what?" Derek asked.

"I'm sure it is nothing to worry about," Coach Powers said. He sounded a bit annoyed. "Dean Futuro doesn't like uninvited guests showing up on school grounds. Those alarms sound when certain people show up without calling first."

Sam was very curious to know who these "certain people" were, but before she could ask, two of the security officers stepped up to Coach Powers.

"We need two of your students. Hathaway and McQueen," the guard said.

He clearly didn't know to whom the names belonged because Sam and Zack were standing a foot away and he didn't even look at them.

Coach Powers stood silently for a second. "All right. Hathaway, McQueen, you're up. The rest of you hit the showers. And someone please turn that alarm off."

Sam looked back at Tasha, who had a very concerned look on her face. Sam shrugged and frowned a little bit; she had no idea what was going on. Zack didn't seem too worried, but maybe he was just trying to look calmer than he really was to freak Sam out even more.

Sam followed the guards out of the gym. The good news was that the rain had stopped, but a biting wind had set in, chilling her to the bone. If only they would have given her a few minutes to change out of her gym clothes.
If Zack was cold he didn't show it. In fact, he was perfectly content as he climbed into the back of the guards' little golf-cartlike vehicle.

Sam and Zack sat silently in the back seat together all the way across campus, around Lake Laverne, and through the college grounds. They finally stopped outside of a large, authoritative-looking building with tiny windows and dead vines still clinging to its walls. They were bustled up through a sparsely decorated marble lobby, past a rather bored-looking secretary, and through a set of large oak doors into the office of Dean Alistair Futuro himself.

He squinted at them, his eyes slowly scanning from Sam to Zack and back again.

The guards silently stepped back to guard the door.

Sam looked around in wonder. The office was exceptionally large, with a marble floor and no windows. Instead of windows, the walls were lined with large television screens showing scenes from different places around the world ranging from a tropical jungle to a windy mountaintop to the street in front of the Eiffel Tower. Sam couldn't tell for sure, but it looked like they were live images. She also couldn't decide if Dean Futuro's desk was comically large or if he was comically small.

But it was the other people in the room who really drew her attention. Sitting in one of the plump leather chairs in front of Dean Futuro's desk was Agent Sampson, and sitting across from him was Constable Albion. From the looks of it, Sam would wager good money that the two men spent the last several minutes staring angrily at each other.

"There she is," Constable Albion said, rising from his chair. "The girl who unleashed the beast upon us."

Before she knew what was happening, Sam was floating in the air, her arms and legs pinned by some unseen force, while alarms were going off all around her again.

The two guards drew their stun guns, but Agent Sampson was fastest on the draw. He withdrew some sort of fancy ray gun from the breast pocket of his suit and had it trained on Albion's hands in no time. It was only now that Sam realized that Albion's hands were glowing a dull yellow.

"Albion, would you kindly stop floating my students around my office and setting off my magic detectors," Dean Futuro said calmly. "You may not have realized this, but they are quite annoying."

"You are harboring a felon here, Futuro," Albion said.

"And you are about to get zapped like you wouldn't believe," Dean Futuro said as he steepled his fingers.

The glowing stopped and Sam fell to the floor. She just barely got her footing in time to not fall flat on her face. Zack cracked a bit of a smile, but Sam was terrified. She didn't know what was going on or why Constable Albion had come back into her life; but, no doubt, it had something to do with some magical doodad she supposedly had stolen or some other crazy thing she had never even heard of before.

"So what did I do now?" Sam asked.

"The resurrection of a known murderer leading to the deaths of twenty-three wizards and witches, resulting in the siring of at least fifteen new vampires," Albion rattled off in rapid-fire police speech.

Every eye in the room was on Sam. Even Zack seemed a bit shocked and maybe even a little impressed.

"What?" Sam squeaked out, completely dumbfounded.

Agent Sampson slipped his ray gun back into his pocket and turned in his chair to face Sam. "It appears Prince Cervantes has returned."

"Returned!" Albion shouted. His nostrils were flaring wildly. "He did not simply return. No one, not even Cervantes could return from death. He was brought back. Brought back by her."

Sam's eyes locked on the yellow tipped finger that was pointing accusingly at her.

"You have no basis for that accusation. In fact, we have sufficient evidence that Ms. Hathaway never left Presley, Illinois all summer and has stayed on school grounds the entire semester," Agent Sampson said.

Sam's life seemed pretty dull when described out loud like that.

"Evidence." Albion spat the word out. "You think I don't know that you can alter pictures with your computers? We are not as naive as you think."

"You didn't know about my magic detectors," Dean Futuro said.

"How much more of your trickery do you expect the ISG to put up with, Futuro?" Albion clinched his fist and it seemed to Sam that he would have liked nothing better than to punch the frail old man as hard as he possibly could. But he was greatly outnumbered and knew it. He slowly sat back down, but his glare could freeze lava.

"Listen, is anyone going to tell us why we are here?" Zack asked. Apparently now that Constable Albion was somewhat subdued, Zack's insanely overdeveloped confidence was rearing its ugly head again.

"You are here, Mr. McQueen," Dean Futuro began, "because the ISG has lost control of the magical community and needs someone else to blame for their inadequacies."

He shifted his gaze to Albion--who was about ready to explode, from the looks of him.

Agent Sampson quickly interjected. "Prince Cervantes—or, quite possibly, someone who has assumed the alias of Prince Cervantes--has begun terrorizing the magical communities of Europe and Africa. There has even been one unconfirmed Cervantes sighting in Japan."

"But my parents killed Cervantes," Sam said. She wasn't sure if and how a vampire could come back from the dead.

"Yes, they did," Agent Sampson said in a serious tone. "That is why we need to talk to you, both of you."

"What have you done with the Lantern of the Blue Flame?" Albion snarled. His eyes were wild, and he was snorting through his nose.

Dean Futuro smiled as he typed away on the laptop on his desk. He actually smiled. It was the single creepiest thing Sam had ever seen in her life. Judging by the way the wrinkles on his face ran away from his smile rather than with it, Sam figured he must not smile much.

"What is so special about this thingy?" Sam asked. She was so tired of being out of the loop.

Zack snorted in amusement.

"You don't know what it does?"

"No, and no one will tell me!"

"It brings people back from the dead," Agent Sampson said.

Well, that didn't seem possible.

"It does what?"

"Roughly three thousand years ago, the Great Dragons of China left this realm for the Transcendental Spheres," Agent Sampson explained. "Before they left, one of them, a blue Spirit Dragon, lit a lantern with its breath, the breath of Eternal Life. The Lantern of the Blue Flame, as it came to be known, allowed anyone who was in possession of it to bring people or animals back to life. It also gave the possessor complete control over the things he or she brought back."

"Zombie armies," Zack said excitedly.

"Yes," Agent Sampson said dismissively. "That is why it was so fortunate that the Lantern disappeared and also why it was so sought after over the centuries. It was assumed to be lost forever until Dr. Samuel Hathaway, Sr. found it."

"And then the fool turned it over to the ISG," Dean Futuro mumbled from behind his computer screen.

"Only after several years of the ISG petitioning the BEA for the return of a priceless relic that clearly belonged to us in the first place," Albion snapped.

"Finders keepers," the old man replied. It was strange to see someone so old acting so childish.

"Anyway," Agent Sampson said, steering the conversation back on course. "The lantern is one of the extremely few items on this planet that could resurrect a slain vampire. That is why we were so concerned when it was stolen four months ago."

"Who would want to resurrect a vampire wizard?" Sam asked.

"Two names spring to mind." Albion bared his teeth in a nasty self-righteous grin. "Hathaway and McQueen."

Sam had more than enough of this. "Why do you people keep thinking I would steal this thing?"

"Because your names are scary to them," Dean Futuro said, cutting off both Agent Sampson and Constable Albion. "The Hathaways and McQueens have been the premier names in relic acquisition for generations. If anyone was going to steal the Lantern of the Blue Flame from a high-security magical vault, it would have to be someone from either of those two families, especially after the death of that fraud and opportunist Alexander Nero Sr. No one else has embarrassed the ISG quite as thoroughly. Isn't that right, Albion?"

Albion huffed and looked away.

Dean Futuro hit a button on his computer, and the screen showing a shot of the Eiffel Tower turned into a shot of an icy windblown cliff overlooking an ocean somewhere.

"Does that look familiar to anyone?" Dean Futuro asked, pointing his cane at the screen.

Sam nodded. She wasn't likely to forget that cliff anytime soon.

"Ellesmere Island," Zack said.

"Very good, Mr. McQueen," Dean Futuro said with genuine praise.

"How about this?"

One of the screens behind Dean Futuro changed from a shot of a tropical beach to some unknown, dark, stone-walled room with what appeared to be hundreds of dead bats all over the frost-covered floor.

"Baldorag Castle I presume," Zack said, all smart-alecky.

"Correct again."

Albion jumped to his feet and slammed his fist on the dean's desk.

"This is insufferable. You claim to be an ally, and yet you spy on us-"

"Unlike you with your silly crystal balls, oracle pools, and mind reading?" Dean Futuro interrupted.

"What about your secret magic detectors?"

"To make up for your invisibility and memory-altering spells."

"Which are necessary to protect ourselves from your small-minded bigotry."

"Gentlemen," Agent Sampson said sternly. "We have to focus here."

Albion let out another strained sigh.

"Very well," he said in what seemed to be a physically draining attempt to appear calm. "Have your machines revealed the identity of the thief?"

"No," Dean Futuro said. "Unfortunately, I overestimated your ability to maintain security on an abandoned castle. My wanderwindow just reached the castle."

"Wanderwindow?" Sam asked.

"A cloud of flying nanobots with cameras that I can remotely control," Dean Futuro rattled off quickly as he tapped on his computer and the image on the screen shifted. It came to rest on a corner of the icy room. Sam wasn't exactly sure what she was looking at, but there seemed to be a person-sized hole in the ice.

"The armor is gone."

"Stop wasting my time," Albion shouted. "Where is the Witch Hunter's Gauntlet?"

Sam ran her hand through her hair. When were they going to realize that she didn't know anything and just leave her alone?

"Miss Hathaway, Mr. McQueen, do either of you know the present location of the Witch Hunter's Gauntlet?" Dean Futuro asked.

"Nope," Zack said quickly. "And I would like to point out that I am a minor, and any further questions you have should wait until my parents and lawyers are present."

"I don't even know what it is," Sam said. Her shoulders drooped.

Agent Sampson cleared his throat. "The Witch Hunter's Gauntlet, also known as the Gauntlet of Gilgamesh, Brace of Hercules, Hand of Guan Yu, or simply the Hero Glove is a very-"

"Very powerful magically doohickey that you aren't going to tell me anything about, because if I don't have it then I don't need to know what it can do," Sam said with a burst of sarcastic bravery that bubbled up from somewhere deep inside.

"More lies!" Albion screamed. "We know that Joanne Hathaway used the gauntlet to destroy Prince Cervantes. You have been hiding its location ever since. I have an official proclamation from the International Sorcerers' Guild demanding that you turn over the Witch Hunter's Gauntlet to us immediately."

He pulled a piece of parchment from his robes and unrolled it on Dean Futuro's desk. Someone with amazing handwriting had painstakingly written the document in large, looping letters.

"Please remove that dirty piece of animal hide from my desk," Dean Futuro said, twitching his nose as if the parchment smelled.

Agent Sampson delicately picked up the document and read it thoroughly.

"Believe me, Constable Albion, the BEA wants Cervantes dealt with as much as the ISG. If we had knowledge of the gauntlet's location, we would make it available to our allies. But it was never in our possession," Agent Sampson said in a very sincere-sounding tone.

"Isn't that very convenient for the BEA," Albion said with acid dripping from every word. "The vault containing the Lantern of the Blue Flame was burglarized by someone with highly detailed information about magical vaults and access to very sophisticated technology. Then someone uses the lantern to resurrect the greatest threat the magical world has faced in over a century-"

"Second greatest," Dean Futuro interjected.

Albion nodded. "Too right. The second greatest, thanks to your science."

Dean Futuro smiled back.

"And do not think it has escaped our notice that Cervantes has only struck magical targets," Albion said accusatorially.

"What are you suggesting?" Agent Sampson asked in the sternest tone Sam had heard yet.

"It just seems odd, doesn't it?" Albion asked in a fake calm voice. "Last time Cervantes struck multiple targets among both of our communities. However, this time he has focused solely on us. And we all know that, if Cervantes was resurrected by the Lantern of the Blue Flame, he has no choice but to act out the orders of his master. It would seem his master is purposely neglecting to attack the BEA, perhaps because he works for the BEA."

Sam wouldn't have thought it possible for this situation to get more uncomfortable, but apparently she was wrong--very, very wrong. It looked like the war that Agent Sampson and Agent Rosenberg had mentioned was just a few minutes away.

"An observant person might draw the conclusion that the BEA is purposely undermining the ISG in order to mount an attack on the magical community."

"Never," Agent Sampson said, calmly but firmly.

"Then provide us with the necessary weapon to defend ourselves," Albion said. "Or we may have to cancel this useless alliance and retrieve our rightful property."

"Bring it on," Dean Futuro said. The old man drummed the top of his cane with his fingers.

"Gentlemen, please. We all have the same enemy," Agent Sampson said. "We should be focusing our efforts on finding ways to track and destroy Cervantes. Without the Witch Hunter's Gauntlet, we are going to have to work together."

"You can't handle one little vampire?" Zack asked in his oh-so-special condescending way. "Some wizard."

Alarms clanged as Albion's hands flared green.

"This is insufferable," Albion growled. "Theft. Desecration. Murder. And all you have to offer is mockery and lies. That war you wanted fifty years ago, Alistair? You just might live to see it after all."

Albion tucked his arms back into his robe and stormed out of the office.

"Escort him off school grounds, gentlemen," Dean Futuro said to the guards. There was no trace of worry or regret in his voice.

"You may have single-handedly set human/magi relations back by centuries, Dean Futuro." Agent Sampson pinched the bridge of his nose and hung his head.

"Ah, Albion's all talk. Two-thirds of the Sorcerer's Council would have to vote to go to war, which they would never be foolish enough to do," Dean Futuro said happily.

"You had better hope not," Agent Sampson said.

Dean Futuro brushed Agent Sampson's comments aside. He leaned in to get a better look at Sam and Zack. "As for you two, if either of you knows where the gauntlet is, which I am sure you do, I would advise you to use it as soon as possible."

His eyes flicked over their heads for a moment and he frowned. "More unwanted company."

Sam turned around at the sound of the office doors creaking open. She noticed for the first time that there was a screen above the door showing an image of the room outside. Principal Shepherd marched into the office, her heels clicking on the marble floor.

"Dean Futuro, what right do you have to take my students out of class?" She crossed her arms and pursed her lips.

"None at all," he answered. "But my guest here…"

Agent Sampson stood up and presented a badge. "Agent Sampson, BEA."

"BEA? What could you possibly need to see these two students about? Why was I not notified of this?"

"A family matter, ma'am," Agent Sampson said. "Pertaining to a possible inheritance-"

She cut him off. "Agent Sampson, is it? I would think that the BEA would be well aware that when dealing with minors any questions you have should be asked with the child's parents' or guardians' knowledge and consent."

"Of course, ma'am," Agent Sampson said sheepishly.

"Good." She touched both Sam and Zack on the shoulders. "We shall be going, then."

She steered them out of the office.

"Don't worry; I will contact your parents immediately about this. Dean Futuro has greatly overstepped his bounds here," she said as they stepped out of the building.

Agent Rosenberg and some nervous-looking college boy who Sam assumed to be Zack's Resident Advisor stood outside next to a pair of the golf-cartlike vehicles the security officers used.

"Now, I need to go back and have a few words with the Dean. Your Advisors will take you back to your dorms." She added as an afterthought. "Oh yes, and you have been granted excused absences for the classes you missed."

Zack strutted over to his RA's cart. He winked at Sam as the cart sped away.

"Come on kid, let's roll," Agent Rosenberg said jovially as she started up their cart.

It was still windy and wet and miserable, so Sam happily climbed into the cart. Agent Rosenberg was surprisingly quiet on the way back to the dorm. Maybe she just didn't want to risk someone overhearing her in Agent mode instead of Residential Advisor mode.

Sam's mind was racing for what seemed the hundredth time in just the last few weeks. Instead of just being accused of stealing something, she was now accused of hiding something that could save lives. Oh, and it could lead to a war if she didn't hand it over soon.

She couldn't shake the nagging fact that Zack knew more than she did, probably a lot more. There was a good chance he even knew where this gauntlet thing was hidden. Sam knew that her mother didn't get along with her family; but with Sam's parents dead, there weren't any Hathaways left to protect the thing. Sam was only nine at the time, and Harold and Helen, though good people, were not equipped to defend something from wizards and vampires and evil scientists. Maybe the gauntlet had gone back to the McQueens for safekeeping.

It was an intriguing theory. On the one hand, it would let Sam off the hook; but on the other, it would also give Zack one more thing to be cocky about.

Not to mention the fact that it put all of the McQueens in danger, if true.

"All right, we're here. Home sweet home," Agent Rosenberg said when they reached the dorm entrance. "I need to take the cart back, unless you need to talk."

"No, I'm fine." It seemed unlikely that Agent Rosenberg would suddenly give her any useful information. Sam stepped out of the cart.

"All right then, here's my spare card."

Sam took the card and waved goodbye to Agent Rosenberg as she putted away on her little cart.

It wasn't until she was in the elevator that Sam remembered that her clothes were still in her gym locker. She had one more class that day, but she decided she had earned a mental health break and was going to go to her room, change into something comfortable, hit the vending machine for some chips, and just watch a little TV. She hadn't actually watched much TV since classes started and figured her shows were feeling neglected.

Zoey would still be in class for a while so Sam had the room all to herself; the only sign of Zoey's presence was her messy bed.

After a quick wardrobe change, the great quarter hunt began. By scrounging through her backpack, her desk, the gap between her night table and the wall, and yesterday's pants she managed to find a dollar seventy-five. She needed one more quarter to buy her super-nutritious dinner, so she decided to see if Zoey had left any change lying around on her side of the room. Sam could pay her back later.

When she walked around Zoey's bed, she saw it. Outside of the window was a floating metal ball. A metal ball with a bright little red light on it that was targeting her.

Chapter 10

Everyone Hates A Good Riddle

Sam had never seen anything like it. The little round robot was just hovering there outside her window. The tiny helicopter propeller was spinning so fast that she could barely see it above the little baseball-sized spherical body of the robot or whatever it was.

Sam jumped back and squealed a little when a tiny robot arm unfolded from the sphere and tapped on the windowpane.

The little red light seemed to be looking right at her. It actually looked like it was pleading with her to let it inside. She wasn't sure why, but she found herself reaching for the latch. The robot bobbed up and down appreciatively. Or at least that's what it looked like to Sam.

She opened the window, and the little robot zipped right past her and landed on her desk between her borrowed laptop and her sphinx snow globe. The propeller stopped and the blades folded up and slid back into the body of the sphere. Sam stood there for several long minutes, staring at the little red light that was staring right back at her.

She rummaged through her backpack for a pen. Very gently she poked the sphere. It rolled back a little, but otherwise nothing happened.

But then she saw two odd blue ovals under the slot where the little robot arm was hidden. Next to the top oval were the letters SDH, and next to the lower oval were the letters ASN. She poked the lower oval with her pen again and the ball rolled over.

If the robot was going to attack, she figured it would have by now so she took an extra-deep breath, held it, and picked up the metal ball. It was smooth to the touch and very cold from being outside in the wind and rain. She turned it over in her hands.

She had no idea who or what ASN was, but she did know an SDH: Samantha Diane Hathaway.

The blue oval was roughly the size and shape of a person's thumb, so she pressed her thumb against the blue plate. The oval lit up and the little red staring light turned green. Something sharp poked her thumb.

She yelped and sat the ball back down on her desk. But it was no longer just a ball. Four little legs poked out of the bottom of the robot, stabilizing it on her desk. A bright green light shot out of the robot right into Sam's face, nearly blinding her.

"Hello, Samantha," a familiar voice said.

Instantly her knees buckled and she found herself on the floor. Tears were streaming from her eyes so uncontrollably that she couldn't see anything but blurry colors, and she so desperately wanted to see right now.

"I realize this might be quite a surprise for you," the voice said.

"No! Wait," she pleaded as she rubbed her eyes. Her face was completely wet now.

She dabbed her eyes with the bottom corner of her bedspread. Steeling herself against any new tears, she looked back up at the green flickering image of her father.

The fully three-dimensional hologram of her father stood completely still. His eyes locked in a gaze over her head. He looked kind of worried and kind of tired.

Sam was so excited by the fact that her father was standing in her room that it took a while for it to sink in that he was not moving.

She must have paused him when she said "wait" earlier.

"Oh, no." She stood up to address the hologram. "Restart. Unpause. Go. Speak. Play."

The flickering image began to move again.

"I don't know how old you will be when this message reaches you. I hope you are old enough to understand that we love you more than anything, and if we left you it was because we had no choice. I also hope you are old enough to handle this. Harold, Helen, if you are seeing this before Sam is ready I trust you to make the right decision."

He stopped and absentmindedly looked at his watch the way he always did when he was trying to think of the perfect thing to say.

"Samantha, since you are seeing this message two things must have happened. Your mother and I have passed on and the BEA has issued an Alpha Level Threat warning. The last time that happened was when the vampire prince, Cervantes, uncovered the Witch Hunter's Gauntlet and set out to destroy the world. Your mother stopped him, and the time may have come for you to do the same sort of thing.

"You see I am going to link this little whirlybot your grandfather invented up to the Bureau of Extraordinary Affairs' database. Unfortunately honey, due to your family's history, the BEA will be keeping tabs on you for the rest of your life. This robot is programmed to find you if the Witch Hunter's Gauntlet is ever needed again."

Sam sat down on the end of her bed.

"The gauntlet is rightfully yours, and it will be your responsibility to find it and find the right person to wear it. For security's sake, the gauntlet is hidden where only you will be able to find it."

He stood up a little straighter, as if preparing to give a big important speech.

"Take your oldest friend to the place where the four monuments of endless winter meet and a Pendragon's weapon waits."

Sam sat there dumbfounded. She had absolutely no idea what that meant.

"It's time," a mysterious voice said. Her father turned his head to look at the unseen speaker.

A gigantic dopey smile spread across her father's face.

"Well, apparently you are on your way. They just took your mother into the delivery room. I can't wait to meet you," he paused for a moment. "Goodbye, honey. Remember, we love you and have faith in you."

The hologram vanished. Sam sat in silence, wondering how she could play the message again, when the robot sparked and popped until a puff of smoke wafted out the top. Sam decided it must have been one of those "this message will self-destruct" things.

"Wow, Obi-Wan Kenobi, you're our only hope." Zoey sat up in her bed.

Sam leapt to her feet.

"What are you doing here?" she yelled in surprise.

"I live here," Zoey said indignantly. She wiggled her way out of the mound of covers.

"Yes, you do. Sorry. I thought you were out," Sam scrambled for words.

"I don't have a class this period, so I usually come back and take a nap," Zoey said apologetically.

"How much did you hear?"

"The whole thing," Zoey said, shrugging her way out of her twisted cocoon of a bedspread. "I was going to tell you I was here, but then the hologram popped up and you started crying and…"

"Sorry about that."

"It's fine. I understand, really. It is hard to lose your family," Zoey said. She climbed out of bed.

"Is your family still out of the country?" Sam asked. She felt a little bad for not asking before. She didn't even know what country they were visiting.

"What? Yes. Was that really your dad?"

"Yup," Sam said, bracing for the inevitable flood of questions.

"That was a pretty awesome hologram." Zoey picked up the sphere. "This is really amazing. Your grandfather built this?"

That was not one of the questions she was prepared for.

"Apparently," Sam said. She didn't know anything more than what the hologram said.

"Did he say something about a vampire?"

"Yeah, yeah he did." Sam thought it over for a moment. It looked like this crazy stuff wasn't going to go away anytime soon. Maybe it was time to see if it would cost her a new friend. "Do you believe in unicorns?"

Zoey gave her a look that clearly showed that she thought Sam was crazy but was too considerate to say so.

Sam explained everything she knew about the ISG and BEA and Cervantes and all the other crazy stuff. It didn't take long, since she knew very little, and Zoey just sat there and absorbed it all.

"So, you're, like, supposed to save the world or something?" Zoey asked, as if it was a real question and not a joke or a completely insane idea.

"No," Sam said automatically. It was an absurd idea. That couldn't be what her father meant. Could it? "Well, maybe."

"Hmm, that seems like an important thing to know." Zoey put the sphere back down. "I mean, if I was suppose to save the world I would like to know."

"I am not saving the world," Sam said, more adamantly this time. It was a ridiculous idea. Will Smith saves the world. James Bond saves the world. Joanne and Samuel Hathaway Jr. save the world. Samantha Hathaway watches TV.

"Well, you just said that witches and vampires are real and that the witches believe that you have this fancy glove that can defeat the vampires." It seemed even more ridiculous when Zoey explained it. "And if you don't find this glove and give it to them they will declare war on us. Is this going to be a fun super-happy war?"

"No."

"Then I think you're saving the world, Sam," Zoey said with a nod.

"Nuts."

Zoey sat down next to her and put her hand on her shoulder.

They sat there for what felt like hours.

"So, have you figured out your dad's clue yet?" Zoey asked.

"Nope."

Zoey patted her shoulder again.

Just as Sam began to wonder just how long she could sit there in silence, someone knocked on the door. Zoey jumped up and rushed to the door. Sam understood; it was an awkward situation, and anything that could break it was welcome.

Tasha practically leapt on Zoey when the door opened.

"Did you hear. Did you hear?" Tasha shouted as she jumped up and down in excitement.

Zoey watched Tasha jump a few more times before responding, "I'm going to go with a 'no'."

"They just put up posters all over campus," Tasha said. "They're holding a Halloween Masquerade Ball."

Sam and Zoey stared at her in silence.

"On Halloween," Tasha added nervously.

"Figured that, yeah," Zoey said.

"Okay, I am sensing that you are not nearly as excited about this as I am," Tasha said, a little crestfallen.

"It's just that school Halloween parties are pretty lame. At least at my school," Zoey said.

"Mine too," Sam chimed in. She had vivid memories of standing around the middle school cafeteria in a Hermione Granger costume drinking a terribly watered-down orange drink as her World Cultures teacher, Mrs. Wong, acting as DJ, played *Monster Mash* over and over for an hour. That was not something she was interested in repeating.

"First of all, it is not a Halloween party, it is a Masquerade Ball. And second of all, hello, have you seen this school?" Tasha exclaimed. "Yesterday in my chemistry class we created a glowing purple goo that eats through glass. A third of the students here have million-dollar trust funds. There are dodo birds ten minutes from here. This ball is going to be completely insane."

Tasha had a good point. This school did not shy away from extremes, and it was insanely well funded. Sam imagined this dance looking like the school dances in the movies. Movie dances always had professional DJs with strobe lights and disco balls or live bands. Everyone came in elaborate outfits that cost more than most people's cars and the dances were professionally choreographed. If the Masquerade Ball turned out to be even half as cool as Sam imagined, it was going to be simply amazing.

Too bad she couldn't go.

There was no way she could justify doing something as fun as going to a dance now that she had a war to stop. There was no telling how many people could get hurt if she didn't figure out her father's riddle.

It was so massively unfair.

"Who are you going to ask?" Zoey asked Tasha.

"Uh, no one. He has to ask me."

"Okay, fine, Miss Last Century, who do you want to ask you?" Zoey pried.

"Wouldn't you like to know?" Tasha said with raised eyebrows.

"I would, that's why I asked," Zoey said. "Of course, we know who Sam wants to ask her."

"What?" Sam said. All of her thoughts of war fell away. How could they know whom she wanted to go to the dance with? She didn't know whom she wanted to go with. Or did she?

"Who?"

"Please." Zoey brushed her question aside. "The real question is who am I going to go with?"

"Oooh, oooh," Tasha said shaking with excitement. "I know the perfect guy. His name is John. He's on the gymnastics team. He's a master of the uneven bars."

Zoey shook her head. "I'm not really comfortable with a guy who's more flexible than I am."

Zoey and Tasha ran through a list of boys for Zoey to take to the dance. Sam nodded along and laughed at the right times, but her mind was busy replaying her father's message over and over. If she didn't crack it soon, the world as they knew it could be destroyed by Halloween.

Nero had to take his headphones off. He couldn't stand listening to them pick out their dates anymore. Besides, he was recording the entire conversation; his computer would listen for any important keywords and alert him later. It was a simple but effective program.

Finally, after endless weeks of listening to inane teenage girl prattle, Nero sifted out the mother lode of information.

It had been a simple trick to sneak into her room the first week of class and plant the bug. He hid the tiny transmitter in Samantha's laptop so he could listen to her conversations everywhere she took her computer, which it turned out was practically everywhere except the bathroom. It also allowed him to monitor her emails and web surfing. She wasted a surprising amount of time on pointless social networking sites.

"'Take your oldest friend to the place where the four monuments of endless winter meet and a Pendragon's weapon waits'," Nero repeated to himself.

It looked like he was heading back into the cold. But where?

Clearly the clues where not meant to be taken literally. There was no such thing as an endless winter. Even perpetually frozen places like the Arctic or the tops of mountains experienced all four seasons.

There was a good chance that he wouldn't have to go anywhere cold at all. The clue referred to four monuments of endless winter. They could be scattered across the globe.

And then it hit him. He knew what the four monuments were. It was so obvious. Now all he had to figure out was where they met.

He also knew what the Pendragon's weapon was, but again he didn't know where it was waiting. No one did. If anyone did know they would be the King of England right now. So that clue had to be a metaphor.

He tabled that problem for now and put his mind to work on the first part of the riddle.

Nero called up Samantha's file on his computer. Her first friend was Tabitha Crenshaw. They had play dates together when they were four. But they hadn't seen each other since they were five. Samantha had had few friends growing up because the Hathaways moved around so much. But even when she finally settled down in Presley she had made very few close friends. This had made it easy for him to get her dimwitted co-worker at the Cookie Emporium to collect a few hairs from Samantha's hair net so he could make a voodoo doll of her. But now, her lack of a social life was proving very inconvenient for him.

Maybe he was thinking about this the wrong way. The hologram was made just before she was born. There was no way her father could have known who her oldest friend was going to be.

It was possible then that the clue did not refer to a particular person. It could be a magical lock, like a kiss-of-true-love spell, that wouldn't require a specific person to do the kissing as long as their love was true. Magical spells of that sort could be very subjective. The riddle might not refer to Samantha's first friend after all. It could refer to the friend she had had for the longest period of time, or a friend she held in her heart more deeply and longer than any others, or it could literally refer to her oldest friend by age.

Nero was somewhat impressed with Samuel Hathaway's riddle-making ability. But there wasn't a riddle on Earth that Nero couldn't crack in time, but time was not his friend. The fastest way to solve this riddle would be to get Samantha to solve it for him.

There was no telling how long that could take so he decided that a little incentive might speed up the process.

He grabbed his phone.

"Hello, Master Nero," Cervantes said on the other end of the phone, the sound of rushing wind threatening to drown out his voice.

"Where are you?" Nero asked.

"Ulan Bator."

"That is wonderful news," Nero said. Still, it is a long trip from Mongolia to California, even as the vampire flies and every minute wasted was another minute Sam would sit around not solving the riddle for him.

"I need you to come to California now."

"On my way."

Tossing the phone aside, he flipped through his latest acquisition--a copy of *Advanced Hexology*, the textbook for the highest Hex class offered at the California Institute of Magic. Calmag jealously horded their teachings from competing magic schools and especially from the non-magic world, but they couldn't stop a few angry and desperate dropouts from selling their old books to Nero. Over the last several weeks he had pored through four years of Calmag's curriculum.

All of their precious secrets were now his.

Chapter 11

When the Search Engine Breaks Down

Sam woke up with a mission.

She had spent the last several days trying to decipher her father's clue with absolutely no luck. Google was absolutely no help, and she couldn't find anything in the library that seemed remotely helpful. Not that she had really expected it to be that easy, but it would have been nice.

Her homework had taken a substantial hit recently; it was pretty difficult to write a ten-page paper about the communist undertones of *Death of a Salesman* while trying to stop a war. It also didn't help that the Sam Curse had caused her brand-new computer to crash twice in the last two days either. But the second computer crash had given her a brilliant idea, one that required Lucas' help.

Today the only class they had together was Physics with Doc Frost. It was going to be tough to find a quiet time to talk to him in private. Doc Frost's classes were always the most fun.

On the first day of class, Doc Frost took them outside to watch the launch of a ten-foot-tall rocket. It exploded on the launch pad, raining bits of metal all over the field and setting Sharon Foster's clipboard on fire. But that was still pretty cool. A few weeks later they got to remote-pilot miniature submarines around the lake. It was Sam's favorite, and yet most difficult, class.

Sam got to class early to catch Lucas before class started, but unfortunately, he walked in mere seconds before the bell rang. He slumped into his chair at the table next to hers. There were dark circles under his eyes; and his hair was a mess, like he forgot to comb it after showering.

"Long day?" Sam asked.

He shook his head. "Natch would not let me sleep last night. He refuses to accept that I am better than him at, well, anything. So we were playing *Mario Kart* for six hours last night."

Natch. What a jerk. It was a shame that Lucas had to live with him for a whole year.

"Why don't you just tell him you don't want to play?"

"Oh, but it is so much fun to see the look on his face when he loses. Again and again and again." His smile was downright devilish. But in a good way.

"Hello, class," Doc Frost said as he took his usual place behind the lab table at the front.

Doc Frost was in his late sixties, but he still spiked his short white hair and he wore an odd set of glasses with tinted lenses that changed colors randomly. Over the last few weeks, Sam had come to notice that he only had three different white lab coats. She could tell because each of them had distinct stains and burn marks.

Once the class quieted down, he continued. "Today we are heading out to the testing range for another field experiment. So bring your goggles."

The class moaned a bit as they got up. It was great to get to go outside for class, but not when it was fifty degrees outside. Fall was proving to be especially cold this year. Fortunately, Sam was adjusting to life in the mountains and brought along her coat. Lucas, apparently, was not adjusting as well. His short-sleeved shirt and faded jeans were not nearly as cozy as her fluffy pink coat.

"Freaking cold," he muttered as they stepped out into the chilly wind.

"Doesn't it get this cold back in Iowa?" She had spent the last several years in Illinois, which was right next door. She had suffered through the same winter storms as he had, just a day later.

"Yes, but this is California," Lucas said, rubbing his arms for warmth. "I came out here expecting beaches and sun."

"The beach is somewhere that way." She pointed west.

"Thanks a bunch."

"Watch your wallet, Lucas," Sharon Foster yelled from ten people away.

Naturally everyone's head turned to look at Lucas and Sam. Most of them chuckled, so Sam knew that they had heard the stories about her. Lucas's confused glances revealed that he had not.

"What?" he asked patting down his pocket.

"Yeah," Sam started slowly. "Someone has been spreading the rumor that I got into Miller's Grove because I am the best orphan pickpocket in Chicago."

"Natch!" he said through grit teeth.

"Natch? Why would he have done it?"

"I don't know. It just seems like something he would do," he said with a shrug.

"I'm pretty sure it was one of Tiffany's minions actually," Sam said.

They marched along with the rest of the class to the grassy field behind the physics building. Three large burnt patches of grass on the field stood as testaments to failed experiments. On the opposite side of the field sat a flatbed truck parked on the grass. A large white sheet covered something big and boxy in the back of the truck.

The class formed a loose semicircle around the truck.

"Ladies and gentlemen," Doc Frost said in a booming voice. "Prepare to have your lives forever changed."

Doc Frost grabbed one end of the sheet and gave a quick tug to reveal a large, square machine with a big pulsing yellow light in the middle. It was certainly science fiction and all that, but to Sam it was just a big confusing mess.

"Neat," Lucas whispered in her ear.

"This is a fully functional portable ion generator. We just recently got it working properly. It is the most powerful portable generator in the world."

Another chorus of yawns ensued. Sam wasn't sure if it really counted as portable if it had to be hauled around on the back of a truck. That kind of seemed like cheating with the definition of portable.

"But this is not what I wanted to show you." He stepped behind the machine and returned carrying a black plastic saucer that was attached to the generator by a long silver cable. It reminded Sam of the cheap round sled Helen bought for her the first winter after she came to stay with them. Except this sled had all sorts of high-tech circuits and lights and foot straps.

"What the heck is that?" Felix asked rudely.

"This is what I wanted to show you." Doc Frost set the saucer down on the ground, as giddy as a toddler, and excitedly stepped back from the saucer. He bit his lower lip as his finger slowly crept next to a green button on the generator.

"Here we go."

He pressed the button.

Nothing happened.

Sam looked from the saucer to Doc Frost. He didn't seem bothered by the fact that nothing was happening. A chorus of oohs and aahs drew her attention back to the saucer on the ground. Except it wasn't on the ground any more.

The underside of the board had turned a bright blue while it hovered an inch off the ground. Slowly the saucer rose higher and higher in the air. Soon it was a foot off the ground, then two feet.

"You invented a hoverboard," Lucas exclaimed.

The rest of the class applauded.

Doc Frost waved the clapping down.

"Not completely," Doc Frost said. "First we need to get it to stop exploding."

Everyone took a giant step back.

He laughed. "I'm kidding. We have haven't blown one of these up in weeks."

"Can I ride it?"

"How does it work?"

Felix and Sharon had asked their questions at exactly the same time.

"Simply put, it works on the principle of polar repulsion," Doc Frost began. "Just like when you push the positive ends of two magnets together and they resist and push away from each other. They already use this principle on high-speed trains in Japan. The train and the track are both positively charged and therefore repel each other, allowing the train to hover above the track. This board is charged to repel against the very Earth itself. The real trick is generating enough power to keep the board in the air."

Doc Frost tugged on the extension cord. The board wobbled in the air. "So for now the board has to be tethered to the ground."

He seemed more disappointed by this than he should have been.

"Now, I believe someone wanted to go for a ride."

Everyone's hand went in the air. Even Sam raised her hand, although she was very afraid of falling off or breaking the board. Doc Frost eyeballed the eager students for a moment. He was clearly enjoying toying with them.

"Mr. Manning," he said finally. "I believe you are our resident skateboard expert."

"Yes," Felix said, pumping his fist in the air.

The rest of the class gently moaned their disappointment. Sam wasn't sure if she was more disappointed about not being picked or about Felix being picked. She had to admit it made sense, though. He was an egotistical jerk, but he was also an X-Games champion.

Felix stepped up to the hoverboard.

"Uh, how do I do this?" The board was two feet off the ground now.

"Just step up onto the board, get your shoes into the bindings," Doc Frost said, less than confidently.

"Okay," Felix said warily.

He lifted his right foot up and slowly slid it over the board. The second he lowered it onto the board it tipped and his foot slid right off. He tried it three more times, but the board just wouldn't stay level long enough for him to step up onto the hoverboard.

"Okay, that doesn't seem to work," Doc Frost said. He slapped the red button on the generator. The board dropped instantly onto the grass.

Felix stepped onto the grounded board. He slipped his shoes into the bindings and stood there stuck to the board.

"Let's try this again," Doc Frost said, turning on the generator.

Everyone watched silently as the bottom of the board lit up and the board started to rise. Felix was obviously trying to stay as still as possible, but even so, the hoverboard wobbled slightly.

"Steady, steady," Doc Frost coached. He kept a close eye on the board.

Finally the board hung in the air consistently at about a foot and a half off the ground.

"Very good," Doc Frost said excitedly. "Now let's see if you can move around a bit. There are sensors hooked up to the footpads. If you lean forward the board should go forward, lean back to slow down, right to turn right, left to go left. Simple."

"How do I go higher?" Felix asked.

"Oh, we'll worry about that later," Doc Frost answered. "Let's just see if you can move around at this height."

Felix leaned forward and the front of the board dipped down a little, but it also started moving forward. He glided across the grass field.

Everyone cheered.

He leaned back, and the board slowed down and eventually stopped. Suddenly he leaned forward with all his weight and the hoverboard took off. He whooped with excitement as he shot across the field, pulling more and more cord behind him.

"Not so fast," Doc Frost yelled after him. "Remember you don't have any friction with the ground to slow you down."

"How fast can it go?" Lucas asked.

"No idea," Doc Frost answered, keeping his eyes on Felix.

After making a few practice circles, Felix was swerving and looping around the field as if he were surfing on an invisible wave--although one time he looped around too fast and nearly choked himself with the extension cord. He was starting to get really cocky now, rocking the board back and forth, dancing in the air.

"Give other people a chance," Lucas yelled in a half-friendly, half-impatient tone.

Felix responded with a rude hand gesture.

"Bring it on back," Doc Frost said, his finger resting next to the power button.

Felix hovered back to the truck at high speed. He leaned back and stopped immediately.

"That was the coolest thing ever," he said as he freed his shoes from the bindings and jumped off the board.

Doc Frost hit the stop button, and the board fell lifelessly to the ground.

Lucas went next, followed by Carla and two other students before class ran out. Doc Frost made his apologies to everyone who didn't get a ride. The hoverboard was going back to the lab, but if he could arrange another field test they might get a shot. Otherwise everyone was going to have to wait a few years for the boards to show up in stores. Apparently there was a lot of safety testing to do first.

Lucas remembered he was cold as they walked back to the building to grab their books. Not surprisingly, he had forgotten all about it while sky surfing. Fortunately this was their last class for the day, so there was no need to hurry back.

"Seriously, that was insanely cool," he said while rubbing his arms for warmth.

"It looked cool. I bet they'll be really expensive." Sam knew she would never be able to afford one.

"That's true," he agreed glumly.

They were the last ones back to the empty classroom; apparently everyone else was afraid Sam would steal their stuff. She examined her book closely just to make sure no one had done anything unfriendly to it. The last time she left a book unattended, someone had glued all the pages together with nail polish.

"This will be another fun thing to tell Natch that he missed," Lucas said with a devious sneer.

"He doesn't take Physics, he doesn't take English, and he doesn't take Math. What does he take?" she asked.

"I have no idea." Lucas shrugged his shoulders. "He hides everything. I've never seen any of his schoolbooks. He does his homework at the library or something."

Somebody must have thought to pack an Ultimate Frisbee disk in their backpack, because a twenty-person game had broken out on the quad already.

"Maybe he takes classes at the university." She didn't like the idea that Natch could be that much smarter than she, or at least farther along in school than she. "Zoey takes some science classes across the lake."

"Really? That's impressive. The only thing I go to MHU for is to let Dr. Zhang hook electrodes to my head."

Sam had had mixed results with her two trips to the college side. The dodos were awesome, but being hauled into Dean Futuro's office most certainly was not.

"I, uh," Lucas said.

And that was all he said.

"You, uh, what?" Sam asked jokingly.

But from the look on his face Lucas took her mimicking as an insult instead of the gentle kidding she intended.

"Never mind," he said looking at the sidewalk.

"No I'm sorry, what did you have to say?" she asked softly.

"It's not important."

They walked in silence for a while. He kept his eyes on the sidewalk as they walked. He slammed his fist into his right leg twice.

"So do you know what you're going to be for Halloween?" he asked. He had perked back up.

"No. I hadn't really thought about it. It really crept up on me though. Time flies so fast here. There's just so much new stuff to get used to," she said. It was true, too. Maybe she should get a calendar so she could keep track of time better.

"Me either," he said. "We have a few weeks to decide, though, I guess."

"Yeah," she said.

Zoey and Tasha were super excited for the dance. Sam figured she would be to if she didn't have more important things to worry about right now.

"Wow, that's right I needed to ask you something?"

"Yeah?" His voice went a little higher than usual. His eyes locked onto hers.

"Yeah. I need to talk to your friend Esteban."

"Oh, Esteban. Sure, we can do that," he said. His eyes darted away from hers. He fumbled in his pocket a bit and pulled out his swipe card. "I've got the magic key to get you in."

It was weird. She hadn't really thought about it before, but she had never been inside Hathaway Hall. She was strangely nervous as Lucas swiped them in and they rode the elevator up.

The building was designed exactly like Cooper Hall, but it had an odd smell. When the elevator doors opened on Lucas's floor it struck her just how different the hallways looked. None of the guys had decorated their doors. Every single door on Sam's hall had photos or construction paper decorations or something on them.

Then again, no one on Sam's hall had a metal dungeon door like the one in this hallway.

"Guess which room is Esteban's."

The guys in the hall didn't give her a second look as they scurried about.

"Everyone's getting ready for the big game tonight," Lucas explained.

The Miller's Grove Fighting Martians were playing the Newport Prep Neanderthals. Apparently it was a big deal.

Lucas banged on the metal door.

"Esteban, are you home?"

"Of course, I'm home. Where else would I be?" a voice from beyond the door said.

"The bathroom maybe. You do go to the bathroom, right?"

"What do you want?" Esteban asked.

"Sam needs to ask you something," he said, gesturing for her to speak to the door.

"Hi, Esteban. We met earlier, sort of. You were a robot at the time. I have a favor to ask," she said, feeling completely ridiculous.

"Sure thing, Samantha Hathaway," Esteban said through the door.

"Can you, uh, access the university's computer systems?" she asked. Lucas gave her a surprised look.

"Already in. What do you need?"

"Nothing sneaky," she said. "Just any files they have on me. And anything related to the, uh, Witch Hunter's Gauntlet or monuments of endless winter."

Lucas looked at her like she was nuts. So did a boy walking back from the bathroom. Sam didn't care. She needed answers fast.

"Not a problem. But my services are not free," the voice said.

Of course not. He was a friend of Natch's, after all.

"Lucas? Go away for a minute," the voice said.

"Um, really?"

"This is private Lucas," Esteban said.

Lucas raised his hands and stepped back. "No problem."

Sam stood there by the door in silence for a moment. Lucas stood several doors down, waiting.

"So what do you need, Esteban?" she asked.

"Can you get me a date to the dance with Zoey?" Esteban asked so quietly through the door that she could barely hear him.

"Zoey?"

"Yes."

"I'll try," she said. She had never played matchmaker before. It could be fun. Zoey didn't have a date yet. Then again, she knew nothing about Esteban. "No promises, though."

"Thank you," he said.

Chapter 12

We Have Spirit, Yes We Do

If Sam was going to talk Zoey into going to the Halloween dance with Esteban, she was going to have to go to the last place she had ever expected to go: a football game.

Fortunately, Lucas agreed to go to the game with her. He even had a pair of plastic blue and gold pompoms. He had one clipped to the back of his Miller's Grove Academy Fighting Martians hat, and supposedly he bought the other one to give to his older sister over Christmas, although it seemed unlikely she would be all that excited about a pom-pom from her little brother's school.

Sam decided not to argue with that story. She really wanted him to go to the game with her, and insulting him didn't seem like a good way to make that happen. So she took the extra pom-pom and rushed back to her room to get her blue sweater and yellow scarf.

Lucas met her outside her dorm in a thick gray coat.

"Are you ready for some football?" he asked in a loud deep voice.

"I guess," she said.

Zoey was already at the game. Once Sam saw the stadium, she realized it was going to be a lot more difficult to find Zoey in this crowd than she originally thought. It didn't help that it took nearly twenty minutes for them to buy two sodas, two hot dogs, and some extra cheesy nachos. Lucas volunteered to carry it all.

Lucas scanned the thousand or so cheering people in the stands. "So, where do you think she would camp out?"

"No idea." There were way too many people here.

"Who is she sitting with? Maybe we can find them."

"Nobody, as far as I know. I told her I wasn't going and Tasha has practice or something."

"Well, that will make this a bit more difficult," Lucas said. "Okay, that side has an awful lot of 'KILL THE MARTIANS' banners, so I'm guessing that is the opposing team's fan section. Let's look over here."

Picking their way through the hungry crowd on their way to the stands, Sam couldn't help but notice that these people were way more into this game than she was. Everyone was decked out in Miller's Grove Fighting Martians apparel. It was a sea of blue and gold.

And who were all these people? Apparently nearly everyone's parents must have flown in to watch this game. Sam couldn't imagine Helen and Harold flying all the way back just to watch a football game.

"Just the two of you? How cozy. How sad." Zack stepped in front Lucas.

"Go away Zack," Lucas said.

"Wow, that really hurts," Zack said, sniffing back a fake tear. "That looks like quite the handful there."

He swiped at the poorly balanced food in Lucas' arms. Lucas twisted out of the way so fast one of the hot dogs rolled off, taking a big glob of nacho cheese with it.

"You're buying us a new hot dog, Zack," Lucas said, kicking the cheesy mess at him.

"Tell you what," Zack kicked the hot dog at Sam, missing her by half an inch. "If there are any leftovers in the skybox, I'll have them sent down to you."

Sam couldn't help herself. "What skybox?"

Zack smiled that smile of his. "Tiffany Summers's ultra-exclusive skybox. Complete with its own private bathrooms, wifi, satellite TV, and catered buffet."

"So no one will actually bother to watch the game. Brilliant," Lucas said.

"Well, duh," Zack said. "Did I mention that a bunch of her Hollywood friends showed up to not watch the game? In fact, I'd better get back up there; the redhead from *Teenage Wasteland* is waiting for me."

"Selena Marsh?" Lucas asked, failing to hide his admiration.

"That's it, Selena. Thanks a lot."

A cheer rose out of the stadium and spread across the crowd in line for snacks.

"Well, sounds like they scored again. Way to go, Coach Spaceman," Zack said with a smirk. "Well, I've clearly got much better people waiting for me, so I'm out of here."

Nothing would have made Sam happier than to fling the remaining hot dog at his smug head as he strutted away, but it was Lucas's hot dog, so she restrained herself.

"Let's just find our seats," Lucas said, a bit dejected.

"Do you really think a bunch of celebrities are here?" she asked as she dodged around food-laden football fans.

"Probably. Tiffany has to have some friends somewhere, right?" Lucas kept fighting his way through the crowd to the stairs leading to the stands.

They stopped at the base of the stands. From here they could see the field. Someone had spent an insane amount of money on this football field. After all, how many high school football stadiums had better grass than a golf course, or jumbotrons? On the screen she saw Coach Powers chewing out one of the players.

"Found her."

They found Zoey in the exact center of the stands. She had a thick, fuzzy zebra-striped coat on and a blue and gold blanket across her legs. There was a two-liter bottle of Diet Pepsi on her right side, and a huge tray of nachos in her lap. But more surprising than her preparedness was her company. Jerry, Sick, and Wrong were huddled together for warmth next to her. It was the first time Sam had ever seen Wrong without a video camera in his hand, but he still had the earbuds in.

"How's it going, guys?" Lucas asked, taking a seat on the opposite side of Zoey from them. He left enough room for Sam.

"So cold," Sick whined through chattering teeth.

"Man up, ladies," Zoey yelled.

"Wow, how's it going, Zoey?" Sam asked sitting down next to her on the cold, cold steel bleachers.

"We're up fourteen to six. Neanderthal punks couldn't make a field goal. Losers," she said incredibly loudly.

"I see," Sam said, grabbing a nacho. "So you remember the whole riddle thing? The one we got in that message recently. Anyway, I figured out someone who might be able to help-"

"Get 'em. Smash 'em. Don't let him get away, you pansies," Zoey yelled at the players.

"But he wants something in return." Sam checked to make sure Lucas and the boys weren't listening.

"Uh-huh," Zoey said flatly, her eyes never looking away from the field.

"He wants to go to the dance with you," Sam said quietly.

This got Zoey's attention.

"Who does?"

"Esteban," she whispered.

"Who's that?"

"The guy with the robots."

"Oh, Robot Boy. Sure. But I thought he never leaves his room," she said.

"I guess he is willing to make an exception for you," Sam said, raising her eyebrows encouragingly.

"Wow." Zoey thought that over. "Wait, what was he like?"

"I don't know. I talked to him through a door."

"Through a door?"

"Yeah."

"Quirky," Zoey said. "Did he say what kind of costume he was going to wear?"

"No, why?"

"Just to see if I want to find a matching one or something. I already picked mine out, though."

"I'm sure that will be fine. He probably-"

She was cut off by the sudden tones of "The Imperial March" from *Star Wars*. Sick rummaged around in his pocket until he found his phone.

"Speak to me."

He looked over at Sam.

"Yeah, she's right here."

Sam smiled at him inquisitively, but he looked away.

"Okay."

He crammed the phone back into his pocket without saying another word.

Everyone except Wrong was looking at Sick expectantly. It hadn't escaped anyone's attention that he was talking about Sam. She wanted to know who would have called him asking about her.

Pretty much everyone she knew and liked was sitting less than five feet away.

"So Sick," Lucas started, a trace of concern and a wee bit of annoyance in his voice. "What was that about?"

"Shh," he replied, his eyes still locked forward. "I don't want to miss the show."

Before anyone could ask, "What show?" the gigantic plasma screen flashed from a shot of the spiraling football in mid flight to a close-up of Tiffany Summers's gigantic, smiling face. Her mouth was at least four feet wide; if she wanted, she could chomp down and swallow Sam whole. Every molecule of Sam's body was telling her to run and hide.

Slowly the camera pulled back from Tiffany to reveal a room full of pretty people laughing and bopping along to music. Half of the Disney Channel's prime-time lineup was in there, along with Tiffany, Zack, and the rest of their usual posse. The camera followed Tiffany around as she flitted about the celebrities like a hummingbird determined to drink the nectar of every flower in the world's most exclusive botanical center. As she drank up the fame, she got bouncier and more erratic.

Tiffany was tugging on the arm of a boy who played the youngest brother on Sam's favorite show. Tiffany was trying to get him to dance with her, but he clearly wasn't in it. Sam smiled a bit. But her smile faded just as quickly; behind them she spotted Natch picking over the hor d'oeuvres, and Sam finally realized what was happening.

It was Natch who had called Sick. He wanted to make sure she didn't miss Tiffany's little documentary about how cool she was. She didn't know why he had suddenly made it his goal in life to torment her; maybe it was the only way he could impress his cool new friends. She didn't care, and she wasn't going to give him the satisfaction.

Sam was on her feet in an instant, putting as much distance between her and the others as she could just in case they would try to convince her that it really wasn't so bad and she should stay-or, worse, if they decided to storm out with her. There was no reason for them to miss the rest of the game.

Besides, she wasn't exactly responding in the most mature way possible, and she didn't need a bunch of people tagging along drawing even more attention to her. As it was, she hoped that the annoyed people she stepped around just thought she was desperately rushing to the bathroom or something. It didn't matter what they thought, as long as they paid as little attention to her as possible.

She wasn't fast enough. A tidal wave of derisive laughter hit her from all directions. Ducking her head to avoid looking up at the giant TV screen, she pushed her way through the crowd.

Before she could reach the safety of the stairs, someone grabbed her right wrist and spun her around. Instinctively she curled her left hand into a fist and swung blindly at her attacker. She smacked Lucas right in the ear.

"Ow." He released her arm so he could rub his ear.

"I am so sorry," she said, yelling over the roaring laughter.

"That's okay," he said, still rubbing his ear. "My fault, I guess. But I had to stop you. Look at the screen."

"No. Why?"

She couldn't help herself. If Lucas was willing to risk her violent wrath to show her, she might as well take a look.

A giant Zack was hopping around on the furniture, air-guitaring to whatever music they were playing in the skybox. He certainly seemed to think he was cool. That was probably because he didn't realize that right below him, in big neon yellow letters, it read "STILL SLEEPS WITH HIS BABY BLANKIE."

Best of all, Zack had no idea that over a thousand people were laughing their heads off right now. Sam couldn't remember the last time she was so happy. She wrapped Lucas in a full-body hug.

"Thank you for stopping me!"

"No problem," he said, his arms pinned to his sides.

She released him. The camera had moved on, and Sam didn't want to miss whatever came next. It landed on Tiffany, who was dancing in a large cluster of other girls, although now she had red flaming eyes and cartoonish devil horns. The effect was amazing; the horns stayed in place no matter which way she turned or how fast she moved. She dragged a boy band member onto her little impromptu dance floor. Below him appeared the words "IS FIRING HIS AGENT FOR TALKING HIM INTO THIS."

Fresh laughter filled the stadium.

A puffy computer-generated thought balloon floated up from the head of one of Tiffany's friends. Instead of words, this balloon just had a shot of empty outer space. Several of the other girls got equally unflattering treatments, including a monkey tail and banners that read "STOLE HER LAST 3 BFF'S BOYFRIENDS," "DATED HER CHAUFFEUR FOR CONCERT TICKETS," and "DOESN'T KNOW HER BOYFRIEND HAS BEEN STOLEN."

Two panic-stricken girls ran up to Tiffany, pointing at the window. As one the crowd rushed to the window and saw themselves on the giant screen.

Sam got to see just a split second of Tiffany's rage before the screen went black. But it was a very satisfying split second. The screen switched back to a shot of the game, so Sam and Lucas started their long walk back to their seats.

"That was so weird," Sam said. "Do you think it was Natch?"

"I don't know," Lucas said after a few seconds. "I can't think of anyone else who would have done it. Esteban, maybe. He'd know how to do all the graphics stuff, anyway. A lot of students here probably do, but how many would be willing to get on her bad side like this? Besides, it seems like Natch's sense of humor."

"But why would he do it?"

"No idea. Maybe it is his way of saying he's sorry." Lucas paused. "Assuming he is capable of being sorry, or even realizing he did something wrong."

Sam had to laugh at that.

"Woo hoo!"

They made it back to their seats to find Zoey dancing on her seat, pointing at the field.

Someone in a blue uniform and gold helmet was running down the field with the football cradled in his arms. Three big guys in Neanderthal green were closing in on him. He spun out of the way of the first guy, who had actually caught up to him, and simply outran the other two.

The stadium exploded with joy.

Zoey jumped up and down and took Sam's hands to make her jump up and down with her.

"That was awesome," Zoey said sitting back down. "Want under my blanket?"

"Hey," Sick yelled. "You didn't let us share your blanket."

"You smell," Zoey said. "Now be quiet, they're kicking."

Sam tucked the blanket around her and set the nachos on her own lap cautiously, in case Zoey decided to jump up and dance again. But Zoey refrained from jumping this time and just screamed in excitement as the ball soared through the goal posts.

"Check that out," Lucas said, pointing at the cheerleaders who had now taken the field.

The cheerleaders had made a pyramid. An actual pyramid, like in the movies, or on ESPN. The girl on top back flipped off the pile and made a perfect Olympic-style landing.

"Awesome," Sick yelled.

"Amazing," Wrong said and started clapping.

Lucas, Jerry, and Sick joined in.

"Stupid boys," Zoey said under her breath.

"Hey now," Lucas said. "That's pretty impressive. Could you do that? I couldn't do that."

Zoey just rolled her eyes and chomped on a nacho.

"And to think they almost had to cancel the pyramid. A few of the girls suddenly disappeared. Went home or whatever. Couldn't hack it. But they got the alternates up to snuff in time," Sick said.

"You are scarily overinformed about the cheerleading squad there, Sick," Lucas said.

"We made a documentary about them recently. Didn't make it to TV," he said even before anyone asked. "But those girls are really amazing."

As if on cue, more girls started doing flips off the pyramid.

"My sister is in the band back home, so I got dragged to a lot of football games. Those cheerleaders never did anything like that. But then, there were only six of them," Lucas explained.

"Just six? How small was your school?" Zoey asked.

"Decent-sized, I think. There were over three hundred in my class. But being a cheerleader was not a smart social move at our school."

"They were all mean?" Sam asked.

"No, they were all extremely nice actually. They had to be to put up with all the half eaten hot dogs that got thrown at them," he said, mimicking tossing a hot dog.

"Wow, at my old school the cheerleaders were the top of the social ladder," Zoey said. "It would have been so much fun to throw food at them."

"If either of you girls is still looking for a Halloween costume, I highly suggest the tried-and-true cheerleader uniform. They have a few spares," Sick said with an innocent look on his face.

"Yeah, thanks," Zoey said, obviously not buying Sick's innocent act.

"I'm going to be a bumblebee," Jerry volunteered out of nowhere.

"Have you come up with a good costume yet, Sam?" Lucas asked.

"No," she answered shortly. She didn't feel like telling him that she probably wasn't going to the dance. It would just raise questions she couldn't answer. "What are you going as?"

"Oh, I don't know. I was thinking I would find out what other people are going as first," he said.

Zoey put her hands to silence them. "I am trying to watch the game. You can deal with all this dance stuff later."

The rest of the game went by quickly for Sam. She didn't know the rules, so she just cheered when everyone else cheered and booed when everyone else booed.

But eventually the cheering enthusiasm died down. The Fighting Martians were up 38 to 6 with less than ten minutes of game time left. Even Zoey was looking a little bored. Plus they had eaten all the nachos. Wrong had started drinking the Diet Pepsi right out of the bottle, and no one wanted to drink it after him.

Zoey yawned. "You want to head out early? Beat the crowd?"

"Sure. Maybe we can run by Lucas's dorm and see Esteban," Sam offered. She thought maybe he would open the door for Zoey, and that was something worth seeing.

"Hey if you're leaving, I'm leaving too," Lucas said.

"And you call yourself a fan?" Sick said to Zoey.

"I'm a fan who wants to get to bed," she said, folding up her blanket.

"Crybabies," Sick said with his nose in the air.

"You could at least leave us the blanket," Jerry said hopefully.

"The blanket is only for people who do not insult me. Have fun freezing, boys," she said with a cocky tilt of her head.

Lucas led the way out of the crowd and back to the stairs.

"This was a lot easier without all these people here," Zoey said after hitting the fourth person in the head with her blanket.

"How early did you get here?" Lucas asked.

"About ten minutes after class."

Once they made it out of the stands, they were free and clear. Everyone else was patiently waiting for the inevitable victory, or hitting the snack bar for their last-minute snacks.

But when they made it out of the stadium onto campus, Sam suddenly felt very lonely. Campus was vaguely unnerving in the dark without any people around. Other than the streetlights, the only lights came from dorm windows several blocks away.

Suddenly a large cheer rose up from the stadium. Strangely, it made Sam feel even lonelier.

"That was the visitors' side. They must have scored," Zoey said in disappointment. "It was probably just a kick."

Zoey checked over her shoulder a few times as they walked, just waiting for another cheer. They were between the Chemistry building and Architectural building when Sam saw something odd. A shadow was moving among the other shadows. She only saw it for a moment, but it looked very much like a person.

"Did anyone else see that?" Sam stopped in place instantly and pointed at the bushes where the shadow had vanished.

"See what?" Lucas asked.

"First off I am not crazy." It seemed important to put that out there right away. "But there is a shadow hiding over there."

Both Lucas and Zoey stared at her like she was crazy, even though she had just explained that she wasn't.

"A shadow is hiding in the dark over there?" Lucas asked.

"Yes," she said. "The shadow of a person."

"Well, that's a little different," Lucas said. He scooped up a rock from the ground and flung it into the bushes.

The rock crashed through the bushes and skittered across the sidewalk.

"I was really hoping to hit someone," Lucas said. "I figured it was Natch or one of Zack's friends."

"I don't know about Zack, but I'd certainly like to be your friend," a mysterious female voice from behind them said.

Sam turned to find herself staring down three senior cheerleaders in full uniform, each one blonder than the girl next to her. It was hard to imagine that Sam hadn't noticed them coming; the gold in their uniforms sparkled under the streetlights. But their eyes were weird. They seemed to look through her instead of at her, but not in the snobby kind of way she was used to.

The snobby way would have been way less spooky.

"Who are you?" Lucas asked.

"We're your biggest fans, Lucas Fry, Video Game Champion of the world," the blondest cheerleader said.

"That's National Champion actually," he said while blushing.

"Close enough," the cheerleader said, taking several long-legged steps closer.

"Shouldn't you be at the game?" Zoey asked.

"There's more important things in life than football," one of the other cheerleaders said. Her friends giggled.

"How's it going, Samantha? Or do you prefer Sam?" the girl on the left asked.

"We are kind of busy right now."

"Oh, not too busy for us. We're going to be the best of friends." One of the cheerleaders grabbed her by the shoulder. It felt cold, even through the sweater.

"Lay off cheer girl," Zoey said. One of the cheerleaders had her by the wrist.

Sam looked over at Lucas. A cheerleader had him by the arm as well, but he didn't seem very concerned about it, unless he smiled and blushed a lot when he was concerned.

But then in an instant his smile fell away and his eyes doubled in size.

"Uh, uh, uh," he babbled to the smiling cheerleader in front of him.

"What is it, sweetie?"

"I should be going now. Yes, definitely must be going now." His eyes were huge and fixated on a point behind the cheerleader.

Sam followed his gaze. All six of them were standing outside of the Architectural building, which had gigantic tinted windows in the entranceway. In the dark like this, they reflected everything around them perfectly.

Except the cheerleaders.

Sam stifled her urge to scream.

"We really do have somewhere to be. People are waiting for us," Sam said, her survival instinct finally kicking in.

"Oh, but we're on our way to a party," the vampire cheerleader said in a sugary sweet tone.

"Well, we don't want to go to your stupid jock party," Zoey said, trying to wriggle her hand free.

"That's good. Because you weren't invited." Slowly the cheerleader smiled wider and wider, baring her teeth. She laughed as her fangs grew out.

The other cheerleaders joined her, both in the laughing and the growing of fangs.

"That's, that's a cool trick," Lucas squeaked out.

"Can I eat the weird girl?" Zoey's cheerleader asked.

"Go for it. We only have to turn Sammy here."

Sam didn't like that. She didn't want to spend the rest of eternity as a fourteen-year-old vampire. She needed a plan.

Just then Lucas screamed like a six-year-old girl, frantically slapped the cheerleader holding him until she let him go, and took off running at full speed across the yard. Apparently the vampires were just as surprised by his cowardly childish maneuver as Sam, because she felt the hand on her shoulder slacken just a bit.

"Run, Zoey, run," she yelled as she slipped out of the cheerleader's grip and ran after Lucas.

She looked back over her shoulder to see Zoey right on her heels; and the vampires were right on hers.

"We need to find help," Sam yelled ahead to Lucas. She suddenly wondered where Agent Rosenberg was right now. Probably at the game.

And that's when an arrow flew past Sam's head.

"Why are vampires shooting arrows at us?" Zoey yelled behind her.

"I don't know."

"Where were they hiding them?"

"I don't know."

"This way," Lucas yelled to them. He was holding open a door to the Physics building.

Sam and Zoey ran inside. Lucas followed them in.

"Now what?" Zoey asked.

"Those are real vampire cheerleaders," Lucas said, wide-eyed.

"Yes."

"That is so cool."

Zoey stamped her foot on the marble floor. The sound echoed up and down the hall. "Excuse me, but those real-life vampires are trying to eat us. They are real, right?"

"Very," Sam said.

"Then maybe we should find a place to hide."

"Help me hold this door," Lucas said, bracing his back against the door.

Crash.

One of the vampires leapt through a window.

"Hello, kiddies," she said.

Sam, Zoey, and Lucas screamed in unison as they ran down the hall. As they ran, it occurred to Sam that the vampires were only after her. Maybe if she stopped running, Zoey and Lucas could get away.

A door swung open ahead of them.

"This way," Doc Frost called from the door.

The three of them ran inside, and Doc Frost slammed the door closed.

Doc Frost had a very impressive laboratory. Sam couldn't even guess what all the machines in here did, but the sheer number of them was impressive enough. But what really stood out was the car frame in the middle of all the machines. It looked like a car with the doors and hood and trunk and several other things missing, including the wheels. But where the tires should be were four hoverboards, and in place of the engine was a portable generator lying on its side.

"Vampires!" Zoey yelled between huge gulps of air.

"I see. That would explain all the screaming." Doc Frost stroked his chin.

"No, there really are vampires," Sam said.

"Cheerleader vampires," Lucas added.

"Oh, I believe you," Doc Frost said. "I just don't have anything good for dealing with vampires."

Thump. Thump. Thump.

Someone was pounding on the double doors. Pounding so hard the metal doors were beginning to buckle.

"Right." The gears were starting to spin in Doc Frost's head. "Lucas, grab that Perma-glue gun."

Lucas turned around. Behind him was a cart with a large oddly designed gun on top. Instead of a trigger it had a long metal plunger in the back.

"Now we're talking," Lucas said, holding the gun like some action hero.

"Quickly boy." Doc Frost waved him over to the door.

"Why does the boy get the gun?" Zoey asked.

Suddenly a fist punched through the gap between the doors.

"Never mind, just do it," Zoey said, ducking behind a workbench.

Lucas pointed the gun at the doors and shoved the plunger all the way in. A thick gray goop shot out of the gun all over the floor.

"What the heck," he said, wiping the goop off the end of the gun.

"No!" Doc Frost rushed towards him. "Don't touch it."

Lucas looked up in bewilderment as he tried to wipe the goop off onto his pants.

But before Doc Frost could reach him, the doors burst open. Two cheerleaders strutted into the lab with big fangy smiles on their faces.

"Party time."

Shuft.

An arrow poked through the nearest vampires' top, next to the big yellow M, and right through the heart. She crumbled into a pile of dust in a cheerleader uniform.

"Raaaah," the other cheerleader hissed as she spun around.

"Two down, one to go." A slim figure all in black and carrying a crossbow appeared in the hallway. She looked like a ninja assassin right out of a Japanese cartoon.

"Kinda skinny, aren't ya?" the vampire sneered.

With one high kick the crossbow flew out of the black figure's hand and skittered across the tiled floor. The ninja assassin, or whatever, dropped to the floor and swept the vampire's legs in one quick spin. She then pounced on the cheerleader, pinning the snarling girl to the floor.

"You would have made a pretty good cheerleader," the vampire said, snapping her jaws. "And you'll make a great vampire."

"Fat chance." The ninja pulled a wooden stake from some hidden pocket and drove it straight through the vampire's heart. She rose from the floor in a cloud of vampire dust.

"Very well done, Natasha," Doc Frost said.

"Thanks, Doctor Frost," Tasha said, unwrapping her ninja mask.

"Tasha?" Sam and Zoey asked in unison.

"Hey." She waved with one hand while brushing the dust off her ninja suit with the other.

"There were three of them," Zoey pointed out.

"I got the third one outside," Tasha said matter-of-factly. "We should go get the uniform before someone notices it."

"Uh, hello. Little problem here," Lucas said. His hands were stuck to his pants.

Doc Frost chuckled deeply. "That's Perma-glue. Dries in seconds. Strong as steel."

"What?" Lucas frantically tried to tug his hands free.

"Don't worry. I have a solvent back at the house that'll dissolve it right off. That's why we could never sell the stuff. No one wants a construction adhesive that can turn to soup if someone spills the wrong chemical on it."

Chapter 13

Freezerburn

Everyone crammed into Doc Frost's tiny car. Sam was a bit leery of the whole deal. What kind of nerd visits a teacher at their house?

But on the other hand, everyone whose opinion mattered to her was going with her.

Doc Frost's house was oddly normal. It was a conventional square two-story house in a quiet, sleepy neighborhood so far away from Miller's Grove Academy that Sam could almost believe that she was in a normal town somewhere. Then again, a lot of horror movies took place in quiet, normal houses in small towns, so it wasn't that reassuring.

Doc Frost pulled his car into the garage. It barely fit between the tarp-covered car on one side and the pile of old computers next to the door.

Two walls of the garage were nothing but shelf after shelf of machinery, random loose wires, and tools. There was a dusty plastic Santa with eight reindeer parked in a corner next to two boxes labeled LIGHTS and a dingy old lawn mower with solar panels attached to the handle.

"What's under the tarp?" Zoey asked.

"My candy apple red '66 Mustang convertible. My own personal pet project," Doc Frost said.

"Hello! Still glued here," Lucas whined from the back seat.

"Right, yes. Let's go save Lucas' hands," Doc Frost said, stepping out of the car. "The kitchen is right inside. You girls help yourselves to the refrigerator."

As far as Sam could tell, aside from the addition of a microwave, the kitchen hadn't changed since the 1950s. She could only imagine what the food in that ancient refrigerator was like.

"Okay, the solvent is in the basement. We're going to take this one step at a time."

Lucas had to stoop to walk down the stairs with his hands glued to his thighs. Doc Frost went first just in case he fell. "Right foot down. Good. Now the left one."

As soon as they disappeared down the stairs, Tasha threw open the refrigerator.

"Let's see what we got here. Orange juice, chocolate milk, half a watermelon, uh, mystery stew-"

"What is with you?" Zoey more shouted than asked.

"I'm hungry. Fighting vampires always makes me hungry. What's the big deal?" Tasha said as she rummaged through the crisper.

"That. That's it exactly. Why aren't you freaked out by the vampires? A normal person would be freaked out by vampires. I'm freaked out by the vampires."

"I grew up with vampires. Well, fighting vampires, actually. It's no big deal," Tasha said peeling the lid off off a yogurt container.

"Anyone know who those girls were?" Sam asked.

"Nope."

"No."

They stood there in quiet mourning for the girls they never knew.

Sam knew that it was a big school and that they were seniors and she was a freshman, so it was only natural that they had never crossed paths before, but she couldn't help feeling terrible that she didn't know anything about them.

"Are they connected to that Cervantes guy?" Zoey asked breaking the silence.

Tasha thrust the spoon back into her yogurt. "How do you know about Prince Cervantes?"

"Sam."

Way to rat me out, Zoey, Sam thought loudly.

"Sam, are you going around telling everybody about this?" Tasha asked angrily.

"No. I didn't tell you, did I? How do you know about him anyway?"

"I told you. I grew up with all of this. The Beaumonts have been monster hunters for generations," Tasha said matter-of-factly.

"Monsters? Like what?" Zoey asked.

"Oh, you know werewolves, zombies, mummies, wendigoes, yetis, all the things that go bump in the night. But mostly vampires. My parents were friends with Sam's parents, so they told me to watch out for her."

"You told me your parents owned a lumberyard," Sam said. Tasha was the first friend she had made at Miller's Grove. How much of that was based on a lie?

"They do," Tasha said, gesturing with her spoon. "It's a brilliant cover, don't you think?"

"I guess."

It actually was a brilliant cover for a bunch of vampire hunters. But Sam was still mad.

Zoey clapped her hands in triumph. "That's why you're always so tired. You stay up all night hunting vampires. So, are you like Sam's bodyguard?"

Tasha suddenly found something very interesting in her yogurt.

"Sort of."

"What?" Sam screamed.

"Yeah," Tasha said sheepishly. She studied the piece of mystery fruit on her spoon.

"Were you ever going to tell me?"

"I wasn't supposed to."

The muscles in Sam's arms and legs tightened with anger. She could probably bend steel in her bare hands right now. She almost wished she had a metal bar to practice on. Tasha must have picked up on this, because she took a small step backward and kept a watchful eye on Sam's hands.

Zoey stood there looking from Sam to Tasha and back to Sam. She could obviously feel the tension in the room. Fortunately, Doc Frost came clomping back up the stairs.

"He'll be all right. Turns out the solvent is a little stronger than I thought. It's safe on skin, but it dissolves pants. I'm going to go see if I have anything that might fit him." Judging by the way he smiled as he left the kitchen Doc Frost found the situation just as funny as Sam would have if she wasn't so mad.

"Aw, poor Lucas." Tasha said.

"I know," Sam said. Lucas was definitely getting the worst of it today.

"Maybe we should get him something to eat too," Zoey said, opening the refrigerator again.

"I'd like a turkey sandwich if he's got the stuff."

Zoey literally jumped and quickly hid behind the refrigerator door. But after the night they had just had, Sam couldn't blame her.

"Stop sneaking around," Zoey said between clenched teeth to Lucas's head, which had appeared at the bottom of the basement door.

"Sorry," Lucas said. "But you have to come down here."

"Yeah, not happening, Captain No-Pants," Tasha said.

"I'm serious," he said in a very serious tone. "And I still have most of my pants."

"Maybe Sam should check it out," Zoey said.

"Yeah, you go check it out," Tasha agreed.

"Will somebody please come down here?" Lucas asked in a highly agitated voice.

Tasha and Zoey gave Sam encouraging nods.

"Fine," Sam said. "But this better be worth it."

"It is," Lucas said, heading back down the stairs. "Doc Frost has got some seriously freaky stuff down here."

Sam slowly crept down the stairs. "Freakier than everything else we saw today? I mean, he's a little weird, but he's not some spooky mad scientist."

"Oh yeah?" Lucas asked when she reached the bottom.

The basement was fashioned into some sort of laboratory or workshop right out of an old science fiction movie. There were ray guns and robotic arms on the walls. Vials of colorful liquids bubbled and steamed on metal tables.

There was even a bulky 1950s-style robot in the middle of the room. Sam was suddenly flooded with memories of her grandfather's house. He always had the coolest, weirdest stuff.

And then she saw Lucas' pants. She couldn't hold back the laughter. There were two large holes in the thigh area where his hands had been stuck. She could see his pockets and the skin underneath. He just looked at her sternly until she stopped laughing, which took a monumental effort on her part.

"This is serious. The hoverboard thing is cool, but these things look deadly." He picked up a gun that definitely gave off a strong 'death ray' vibe.

"Be careful, you don't know what that does," Sam said.

He pulled the trigger.

A blue beam shot out of the gun and coated the basement ceiling with ice.

"Turn it off," Sam yelled. Doc Frost was definitely going to realize they were messing around with his gear if everything was covered in ice.

"Freeze ray. Awesome." He put the ray gun down.

"Stop messing with this stuff," Sam said.

"Okay, but look at this."

Lucas waved her over to an old rolltop desk stuck in the corner of the basement next to the washer and dryer. It was covered in old papers. Some of them were so old they had turned yellow and began to curl.

"Check it out," Lucas said, handing her a sketch.

The drawing was similar to those used by fashion designers. There was a generic male figure in different poses. A really ridiculous yellow and blue skintight costume was drawn on the figure.

The costume had a gun belt.

"Now look at this," Lucas said in a darker tone.

He handed her a FBI wanted poster of a man who easily could have been a younger Doc Frost in the same yellow and blue outfit as the sketch, except this costume included a mask.

"This can't be right," she said.

Lucas snatched the paper back from Sam and read out loud, "Elijah Frost, alias Freezerburn, wanted on charges of bank robbery, assault with a deadly weapon, resisting arrest-"

"Stop." Sam didn't want to hear any more.

"We have to get out of here," Lucas said. "Maybe tell Dean Futuro."

Sam would have bet a million dollars that Dean Futuro already knew all about Doc Frost's past.

"Okay, let's just get back upstairs. Put that back where you found it."

Lucas set the papers back down on the desk and closed the rolltop. Sam slowly backed away from the desk with her hands at her sides to make sure she didn't accidentally touch anything. Her back brushed against something hard and cold. She knew instantly that she had backed into the robot.

Now just step away before something bad happens.

"Kill all humans. Kill all humans," said a mechanical voice behind her ear.

Sam wasn't the slightest bit surprised.

"Massively uncool," Lucas said. He grabbed her hand and pulled her away from the robot.

She spun as he pulled her to him. The robot's head twisted around to look at them with its red glowing eyes.

"Kill all humans."

"Help!" Sam screamed at the top of her lungs.

The robot reached for them with one of its metal claws.

Lucas threw a pen at it. The pen bounced off harmlessly.

"Good going," Sam whispered.

Lucas grabbed the closest ray gun off the wall. He aimed at the robot and fired. A puff of green gas wafted out of the gun.

"What was that?"

"I don't know."

"Help!" Sam shouted again.

The robot took a step closer to them. It was a big clunky robot that rattled and whirred as it moved, but Sam figured it was also probably pretty strong.

"Split up," Lucas suggested. "I'll go this way, you head for the stairs."

Lucas ran past the robot just out of reach of its claw.

"Lucas, you're crazy."

"Go up the stairs. Get Doc Frost."

"It's still watching me."

Lucas frantically threw random bits of machinery at the robot. Slowly the robot's head rotated away from Sam and looked at Lucas.

"That's right, come and get me."

The robot's entire body swiveled to face Lucas.

Sam noticed that Lucas had pinned himself into a corner. With the robot's back turned, she slowly crept up behind it and snatched two guns off the nearby table. She stuffed the smaller one in her pocket. The big one had a crank on one side instead of a trigger. She pumped the crank as fast as she could. Instantly a pair of blades popped out of the end and began spinning like a fan.

Somehow the fan was spinning a thousand times faster than she was cranking. She did her best to aim at the robot, even though she didn't see how a strong gust of wind was going to stop such a heavy robot, but the force of the wind became too much for her, and she was thrown backward against the wall. She dropped the gun to the floor, where the blades chewed into the concrete for a few seconds before running out of steam.

"Oh, I've got a good one," Lucas yelled.

He was pointing a gun similar to the ice ray at the robot, but this one fired a red beam into the robot's face, melting it into a big sloppy frown. But the robot didn't seem to care about its melting face. It kept right on lurching its way toward Lucas.

Sam pulled the other gun out of her pocket. It didn't look like much. It had a skinny handle and two long thin prongs at the firing end.

Please be a laser or something.

She pulled the trigger.

Instantly her hands went to her ears and the gun fell to the floor, emitting a skull-piercing high-pitched noise that overrode all of her other senses.

When she finally recovered enough to open her eyes, she saw Lucas huddled in the corner with his hands over his ears as well. He had dropped his heat ray, just as she had dropped the gun she was holding. The robot's steel claws were inches away from his face.

She had killed Lucas!

"Robot stop."

The robot stopped instantly. Its heavy metal limbs swung lifelessly at its sides.

Doc Frost trotted down the basement stairs, a pair of brown slacks draped over one arm.

"Why didn't you just push the off button?" he asked as he swept past Sam.

"Now why didn't we think of that," Lucas said, standing up.

"It's a good thing you used the sonic disruptor or I never would have heard what was going on down here. This basement is practically soundproof. Good for working on experiments without arousing the neighbors. Not so good for meddling kids who like to pick fights with robots." He tossed the pants to Lucas. "Come upstairs, Miss Hathaway. We'll let the boy change in peace."

Back upstairs, Tasha and Zoey gave Sam extremely curious looks.

"So, what happened?" Zoey asked before taking a bite of her apple.

"Robot attack."

"Oh."

"Not that I don't enjoy having all of you here eating my food and breaking my equipment, but I sincerely hope we are through with the excitement for today," Doc Frost said, selecting an apple out of the basket on the counter.

"That depends on you," Lucas said from the basement door. "Step away from them."

Everyone in the kitchen was surprised by the forcefulness in his voice.

"Lucas, what-"

But Lucas cut Zoey off. "Step away from them, Freezerburn."

Doc Frost let out a sad, defeated sigh. "Lucas, listen-"

He stopped in mid sentence. Sam would have, too, if she had been the one staring down the barrel of Lucas' freeze ray.

Chapter 14

History 101

"Lucas, put down the ray gun," Tasha urged, stepping between Lucas and Doc Frost.

"You don't know what you're doing, Tasha," Lucas said.

"No, you don't know what you are doing," Tasha said back adamantly.

Sam couldn't believe this was happening. Being attacked by vampires and robots was one thing, but turning freeze rays on teachers was something else entirely.

Doc Frost stepped out from behind Tasha. He even put his hands up in the air.

"You've got me," he said playfully.

"What is going on?" Zoey asked, wide-eyed.

"Doc Frost is a super-villain," Lucas said way more seriously than Sam could ever imagine anyone outside of a cartoon saying.

Zoey burst out laughing. "What?"

He pulled the FBI wanted poster out of his pocket with his free hand and unfolded it for everyone to read. "See?"

"That's insane."

"No. It's quite true." Doc Frost shook his head and smiled with a twinkle in his eye. "I was a super-villain, or at least I thought I was. That was my intention anyway. But I was young and foolish. I even made a costume. Can you believe that?"

He took a bite of his apple and walked into the living room.

"Well, come on. If I'm going to tell you my sad little story, we might as well be comfortable."

Tasha followed Doc Frost into the living room. She looked back over her shoulder and gave a smile that told the others it was okay.

Zoey and Sam looked at each other and then to Lucas. He had lowered the freeze ray.

Sam decided to trust Tasha. She might have lied about, or technically neglected to reveal, who she really was, but Sam knew deep down that she had done it to protect her. And Sam knew a little about keeping secrets to protect people.

Lucas and Zoey followed her into the living room.

It was clear that Doc Frost lived alone and had very few guests. There was nothing more than a recliner pointed at an old TV set, a sofa used more for storage of half-read books and random papers than for sitting, and a wall-length bookcase haphazardly stuffed with books.

Tasha, Zoey, and Sam cleared off spots to sit on the couch. Doc Frost naturally sat in the recliner, and Lucas leaned against the wall and pouted.

"I was twenty-three years old, working on my post-graduate studies at MIT, and I had made the discovery of a lifetime." Doc Frost had a faraway look in his eyes. "I had found a way to project an energy beam capable of altering the vibrations of atoms. All temperature, as we understand it, is really the result of vibrating atoms. The faster they vibrate the hotter they are; the slower they vibrate the colder they are. I had invented the first freeze ray, and the first heat ray. I was on top of the world."

"So why didn't you just sell them?" Lucas asked snidely. "You would have been rich."

Doc Frost smiled a kind and patient smile.

"That was exactly my first thought too," he said. "But my supervising professor, Dr. Heinrich Markham, stole all the credit for my work. He was going to sell my designs for millions and completely cut me out. I didn't take it well.

"I destroyed every copy of my designs and took the two working prototypes. The school reported them stolen and suddenly I was a criminal. I went into hiding, cut off from my wife and baby daughter. All I had were my ray guns, which I couldn't even sell. I was desperate, and I had read a lot of comic books in my youth, so I put together a costume and robbed a bank."

Sam could see the pain in his eyes. Doc Frost was reliving what had to be the worst moments in his life. She wanted to tell him he could stop, but she knew how important it was to just let someone vent.

"The FBI arrested me two days later. The BEA covered up the entire event. It turns out a Cold War was brewing between the magical community and the scientific world and the last thing anyone needed was a madman in a flashy costume running around in public."

"Magical community?" Lucas asked in a small voice.

"You know, witches, wizards, the whole deal."

"So are we talking *Lord of the Rings*-style wizards, *Harry Potter*-style wizards, *Dungeon and Dragons*-style wizards, or what?" Lucas asked.

"Real-life wizards," Tasha said condescendingly.

Lucas crinkled his nose at her before turning to Doc Frost. "And they are at war with us?"

"Not exactly. And not with you," Doc Frost said in a reassuring voice. "For thousands of years *homo sapiens* and *homo magi*, regular people and magical people, have coexisted on this planet. But we have not always gotten along. They played tricks on us, we threw rocks at them, but for the most part the two societies lived together peacefully. Every now and then something would spark a fight between the two groups, and for the most part the magic people had the most power, but the normal people outnumbered them.

"Eventually the magical society went into hiding and the rest of the world forgot that magic was ever real, so everyone was happy. Until the Renaissance. With the dawn of modern science, we were finally catching up with them. A rogue band of wizards decided to stop our progress and a group of early scientists decided to fight back. When the dust settled, the good wizards and the good scientists made peace and agreed to maintain order while keeping everything secret from the rest of the world."

"And you're one of the good scientists maintaining order?" Sam asked.

Doc Frost pointed at Sam as if she had made a comment that reminded him of something. He got out of his chair and rummaged through his bookcase.

"The BEA offered me a choice. Fifty years in prison, or go to work for them."

"And what is the BEA?" Lucas asked. The freeze ray hung at his side, all but forgotten.

"The Bureau of Extraordinary Affairs," Tasha said brusquely. "A secret branch of the League of Nations established in 1920 by a small group of adventurers and inventors to protect humanity from the dangers of the extreme fringes of science and the supernatural. Keep up."

Lucas huffed and rolled his eyes.

Doc Frost produced a photo album from the bookcase. He flipped it open and handed it to Sam.

Sam studied the photo at the top of the page very carefully. Four men in their mid-twenties with wide, toothy smiles stood posed on the deck of boat. They looked like college buddies on a fishing trip. Sam recognized one of them as a younger Doc Frost and another as her grandfather.

Sam tilted the album so Zoey and Tasha could see the photo. "That's my grandfather, Samuel Hathaway, Sr."

Doc Frost pointed to the man standing behind her grandfather. "And that's Simon McQueen, your other grandfather. This is quite possibly the only photo of Samuel and Simon where they are both actually smiling instead of trying to kill each other."

Sam studied Simon's face. She had only heard his name mentioned once, and not fondly. He was tall and dark and broody. If they had been a boy band he would have been the bad boy of the group.

"What about this other guy?" Sam asked.

"That's Julius Nero. Alexander's father," Doc Frost said, as if that was supposed to mean something to her.

Julius Nero seemed to be the nerd of the group. He was short and skinny and had the thickest glasses she had ever seen on someone under fifty.

Wait a minute. Nero? Dean Futuro had mentioned the name Nero.

"Who is Julius Nero? And who's Alexander?"

Doc Frost tilted back in his chair and tapped his forehead with his fingertips. "Of course! You probably never met Alexander Nero. He and your father used to be the best of friends. We all thought they were going to be the next generation. Carry on our work. But over time they grew apart. Your father was more the adventurer type and Alexander turned his attentions to business.

He built a very successful pharmaceuticals corporation from his father's genetics research."

Sam hadn't met many of her parents' friends. She would have liked to have talked to him. He probably knew all sorts of crazy stories about her father that Harold and Helen didn't know. But Dean Futuro said that Alexander Nero was dead. That seemed to be a recurring theme in Sam's life.

"Anyway, it was a real honor to work for your grandfather," Doc Frost said earnestly. "Even though we never did get the tesseract technology to work properly."

"Tesseracts? Really?" Zoey perked up. She was as excited as Sam would have been if Doc Frost had said that Sara Berlin was coming to town. "How close did you get?"

"Impossible to say. But we managed to keep the universe from imploding, so that's a good thing."

"Uh, for the geek speak-impaired, what is a tesseract?" Tasha asked.

Zoey bounced up and down on the couch, so Doc Frost gestured for her to explain. "It's a pocket in space and time. Imagine a box where the inside is larger than the outside, except there is no box. You could put the entire contents of your closet inside this pocket and then close it down to the size of a grain of sand and carry it around with you."

"Awesome," Lucas said.

"Awesome indeed," Doc Frost said with a nod of his head. "But we could never find the right energy matrix to keep it from exploding. We blew up large chunks of the BEA's secret research and development island working on Samuel's project."

"It is so cool that you worked with my grandfather." Sam had so many questions for Doc Frost she didn't know where to start.

"He was a great and brilliant man. It was a shame we never got it to work. 'Hathaway's Folly' it was called. He took it hard. Practically gave up science all together." Doc Frost shrugged. "Of course, he did switch to archaeology in his later years, but if he hadn't then he never would have found the Lantern of the Blue Flame."

"The what of the what?" Lucas asked.

"Mystical lantern, lit by a dragon, brings people back to life," Sam said. It was nice to have an answer for once.

"Unfortunately," Tasha said heavily. "Someone stole the lantern and resurrected Prince Cervantes."

"Who is?" Lucas asked in great annoyance.

"A very powerful wizard turned vampire that was destroyed by Sam's mother and has now returned."

Lucas snapped his fingers. "And he is the one who sent the vampire cheerleaders after us."

"Most likely."

"And you're some sort of vampire hunter?" Lucas asked.

"Monster hunter." Tasha corrected with pride.

"So you're going to dust this Cervantes guy like you did the cheerleaders."

"No," Tasha said sharply.

"But isn't that what you do?" Lucas asked. "We could help."

"This isn't a movie," Tasha said harshly. "I'm sure you think vampire hunting is all sorts of fun. We'll just go charging in with wooden stakes and holy water and take him out."

"You didn't seem to have much difficulty with the pep squad," he said defensively.

"First of all, I've trained for this my whole life." She crossed her arms and stared him down. "Second of all, Cervantes is not a normal vampire. He is a vampire prince."

The room was silent for a few seconds.

"Yeah, uh, we don't know the difference," Zoey said.

Tasha smiled. But it was a small tense smile. "Okay. Vampire 101. In order to become a vampire you have to be bitten by a vampire. But Cervantes didn't do that. He was a very powerful wizard and was not willing to give up his powers."

She noticed that everyone was staring at her in confusion. "Right, important point, magic comes from a person's life force, so magical people lose their powers when they become vampires. The only way to get them back is to bite another magical person, but the magic wears off quickly. That's why magical children are taught by age six to conjure a ball of sunlight."

"Wait, go back. How did Cervantes become a vampire if he wasn't bitten by one?" Zoey asked while nervously chewing on her own hair.

Tasha bit her lower lip and stared at the floor.

"We don't know for sure. He is only the third person to actually pull it off. We're pretty sure it involves selling one's own soul."

"Who were the other two?" Lucas asked with squinty, interrogating eyes.

"The original vampire, whoever he or she was." Her voice dropped to a rushed whisper. "And Vlad the Impaler."

Judging from Lucas's sudden gasp and overall shocked and excited expression, he somehow knew this Vlad guy.

"Vlad the Impaler? You're serious?" His voice cracked.

"Very," Tasha said.

"So who is this Vlad the Employer?" Zoey asked.

"Vlad the Impaler," Lucas said, drawing out the last word. "Vlad Dracul. Dracula. As in, Count Dracula."

"No way," Zoey said, more impressed than shocked or scared.

Tasha nodded.

"Wow. Dracula was real?" Zoey asked.

"Is real."

"He's still alive, or undead, or whatever?" Zoey was way more impressed by this fact than Sam. "Have you met him?"

"No, and hopefully I never will. But even Dracula was just a normal - albeit completely insane - man before he became a vampire prince. Cervantes was a wizard. He found a loophole no one had ever imagined. Since he became a vampire without dying, he got to keep his powers, and he can drain the powers from other witches and wizards," Tasha said darkly.

"But if Sam's mom killed Cervantes, wouldn't he have lost his powers like other wizards?" Zoey asked before Sam had the chance.

"That's where the Lantern of the Blue Flame comes in. It can completely restore a person to their state just before they died, except for their soul, which is why using the lantern is so terribly wrong. It also gives the possessor of the lantern complete control over anyone or anything that has been resurrected by the flame."

Tasha nervously twirled one of her braids. "Except Cervantes already sold his soul a long time ago, so he probably doesn't even miss it."

Lucas scratched his head. "So let me get this straight. There is someone out there with his or her own pet wizard-vampire that can increase his power with every new victim. And on our side we have here the daughter of a couple of archaeologists, a monster hunter, and a retired super-villain. So what does that make you, Zoey? Alien? Robot? Alien robot?"

"Uh. No," Zoey said, a bit shocked and offended. Her eyes darted from person to person as if she was making sure that no one really thought she was an alien or a robot.

"I'm sorry. I'm new to all this. I've never dealt with vampires and tesseracts and giant mechanical grasshoppers before," Lucas said defensively.

"What giant mechanical grasshoppers?" Zoey asked.

"I don't know!" he yelled. "But I wouldn't rule them out at this point."

Sam could imagine how he felt. There was no way she would be able to handle all of this if she hadn't grown up with it. But there was no use freaking out about it either.

"Just calm down. There are no giant mechanical grasshoppers."

"Well, actually-," Doc Frost started. But when he saw the nasty looks Sam and the other girls were giving him, he stopped.

"Fine. No grasshoppers. I guess we already have enough problems," Lucas said, breathing heavily. "So this super-vampire guy is here in Miller's Grove?"

"Seems that way."

"Why?"

"Sam."

Everyone's attention turned to Sam. Sam was getting really tired of that reaction.

"Thanks, Tasha," she said coldly.

"What does he want with Sam?" Lucas asked, concerned and confused.

"The Witch Hunter's Gauntlet," Tasha said flatly.

"How do you know about that?" Sam asked. Although, considering Tasha was some sort of secret vampire-hunting ninja maybe she shouldn't have been surprised that Tasha knew about the supersecret magic gauntlet.

"We Beaumonts specialize in the supernatural. The Witch Hunter's Gauntlet is as supernatural as it gets," Tasha said.

"What is it?" Zoey asked.

"The Witch Hunter's Gauntlet, also known as the Gauntlet of Gilgamesh, the Brace of Hercules, the Hand of Guan Yu, or simply the Hero Glove was fashioned by Middle Eastern mystics thousands of years ago to grant magical powers to a non-magical person. Fight fire with fire. It draws on a user's personal strengths. Most people couldn't even use it if they tried. They wouldn't be strong enough. Their inner fears and doubts would overwhelm them. That is why it lies dormant for generations waiting for a new hero to rise. In the right hands it can grant great strength and power. Gilgamesh, Hercules, Mulan, Beowulf, Boudica, and many others were all great heroes who once wore the gauntlet. It turns up in every great Heroic Age."

"And this glove is what made them all so powerful?" Lucas asked.

"Partially," Tasha explained. "The glove draws from the user's inner strengths as well as their own perception of power, whether that is strength, speed, control over the weather, whatever. Fortunately, most of the people who wore the Hero Glove were unaware of its true potential. On the wrong hand, it could make someone nearly invincible."

"That thing has been missing for centuries," Doc Frost said abruptly. "Simon and Samuel used to argue about it all the time. They thought for sure one of them would find it and usher in a new Heroic Age. But like all forms of power, the glove must be earned and must be given up. It can take several generations for the glove to be found again."

"Sam's mother used it to destroy Cervantes twenty years ago," Tasha said with a Miss Know-it-All head bob.

Doc Frost's face lit up, making him look ten years younger. "They found it? That's amazing. Where is it?"

Zoey elbowed Sam gently in the ribs.

Sam didn't know if her parents would have wanted her to share the secret with this many people, but they were already involved. And Zoey already knew, and Tasha probably knew; she seemed to know everything else.

But most importantly, Sam didn't think she would be able to find the Witch Hunter's Gauntlet without a little help.

"I might know."

Sam told them all about the hologram and her father's riddle. They listened politely and quietly. Halfway through, Lucas sat down on the floor, holding his drooping head in his hands.

"No offense," Lucas said when she had finished. "But if your dad thought it was so important for you to find this Hero Glove and save the world, why did he have to make it so difficult?"

Sam had had the same thought at least a hundred times.

"He needed to be sure that Sam and only Sam would be able to crack the code and find the Hero Glove," Tasha answered logically.

"He could have at least given me clues I could figure out," Sam said.

Seriously, would that have been too much to ask? She screamed in her head.

"But he did," Doc Frost said. "Clearly your father designed this riddle specifically for you to solve. You just have to think about the clues from the right perspective."

Lucas raised his hand. "Uh, I think I know one of the clues."

He took a moment to bask in everyone's impressed stares. Sam let him. If he really had cracked part of the riddle, she would have been willing to stare at him in praise all night long.

"Well, spill it!" Zoey clearly was not as patient.

"'A Pendragon's weapon waits.' The only Pendragon I know of is Arthur Pendragon. King Arthur," He explained. "So the waiting weapon would be the sword Excalibur."

"Well done, lad." Doc Frost leaned back in his chair.

"Way to come through with the mythical reference," Zoey said excitedly.

"Well," he said with fake modesty. "You can't play *Battle for Camelot* for thirty-seven hours straight and not learn a little bit of Arthurian legend."

"Okay. Anyone know where Excalibur is waiting?" Zoey asked.

"No one knows where it is," Tasha said. "Or if they do, they aren't advertising the fact."

"Well, we do," Lucas said. "It's wherever the four monuments of endless winter meet."

"Thank you. That's very helpful," Zoey, Tasha, and Sam said in unison.

Sadly, no one else had any brilliant insights into the rest of the clues. Naturally everyone expected Sam to know who her oldest friend was, and refused to believe her when she said she didn't. Soon after, the living room was scattered with every book Doc Frost owned that had even the slightest reference to winter or monuments.

Zoey had copied down the riddle word for word and was racking her brain to find some sort of pattern or code in the message itself. She tried copying down every second, third, and fourth letter, she assigned numbers to each letter and then to each word, she wrote words backwards,   as well as a dozen other things Sam didn't really understand. All the while, Doc Frost kept trying to tell her that she was overthinking the problem. The answer was somewhere in Sam's mind. She just had to unlock it.

Out of the corner of her eye Sam watched as Lucas's head slowly slumped lower and lower until he turned the history book in front of him into a pillow. The adrenaline rush was wearing off, and everyone was crashing.

Doc Frost rubbed the corners of his tired, baggy eyes. "Okay, let's simplify this down to the most basic elements possible. Sam, I need you to think of any references your parents made to monuments. Any kinds of monuments."

Sam imagined that would be a tall order for anyone, let alone someone whose parents were globe-trotting archaeologists. She thought back over boring stories they told her about the Arc de Triumph or Hadrian's Wall. Now those boring stories were some of Sam's most treasured memories. To this day she still regretted never getting to hear the boring stories about the places in her snow globes.

"Oh, no way!" she yelled at the top of her lungs.

Lucas sat up with a start, a string of drool attaching his head to the book he was resting on, while everyone else stared at her like she was mad.

"I know what the monuments are," she clarified, speaking louder than she really meant to. "The Great Pyramid, the Statue of Liberty, the Eiffel Tower, and the Sphinx."

Her heart was pounding in her ears. She was more excited at this moment than she had ever been in her life. It had been so obvious all this time; she just wanted to slap herself.

"My dad gave me snow globes of all of them when I was a kid. He said we were going to visit them all some day."

"Someone get a map and a pen," Doc Frost ordered.

Quickly they unfolded a world map and Zoey drew little sketches representing the four monuments on their respective locations.

"Maybe," Zoey said to herself. She drew lines connecting the four spots. Unfortunately, the Sphinx and Great Pyramid were so close together that, instead of making a nice box with an X inside, it became a giant lopsided trapezoid.

"Maybe it's an arrow," Lucas said.

"Pointing which way?" Tasha asked.

"Good point," he said glumly.

"Maybe it is somewhere inside the trapezoid," Zoey offered.

"Well good, so we've narrowed it down to New York, Africa, Europe, or the Atlantic Ocean," Tasha said, annoyed.

Lucas snapped his fingers. "Atlantis."

"It is not in Atlantis," Tasha said.

Lucas crossed his arms and tilted his head. "Oh, and I suppose you know where Atlantis is."

"No. But how in the world is Sam supposed to find Atlantis?"

"I don't know. Magic?"

Doc Frost breathed out slowly and loudly. Tasha and Lucas took the hint and calmed down.

"If you recall, the clue says Sam has to go to the place where the monuments meet," he said.

"Maybe the Hero Glove is broken into four pieces and hidden at each of those places. That's how they would do it in a video game," Lucas offered.

"Maybe it meant the spot where the snow globes originally were," Zoey said.

"That can't be it," Sam said with great certainty. "We moved around a lot in those days and the snow globes were always in my room, and I think I would have noticed if Excalibur was in there."

"What if-"

There's no telling how long they would have kept up their wild guessing if there hadn't been a knock at the door.

Doc Frost answered it to find Agent Rosenberg standing there in her MGU sweatshirt and sweatpants. Sam hadn't seen anyone so mad in years.

"You are all past curfew."

Chapter 15

Ramifications

The next couples days were easily the most exciting Sam had had in years.

Sam was feeling so confident that the four of them—five, counting Doc Frost--would crack the riddle, stop Cervantes, and generally foil the plans of the unknown bad guy – who they had brilliantly nicknamed Bad Guy – that she thought she just might be able to go to the Halloween Dance after all. She started tossing around costume ideas in the back of her brain. In the last few years she had trick-or-treated as a penguin, Hermione Granger, and Pippi Longstocking, but she wanted something a little more grownup and fashion-forward for the big dance.

Since Sam had absolutely no idea how to do that, she decided to put herself in Zoey's capable hands; however, when she got to English class she found Zoey waiting with exciting, confusing news. Tasha had sent her a text message that consisted of nothing more than seven smiley faces. She hadn't responded to any of Zoey's pleas for more information.

So for now Sam was waiting with Zoey for Tasha to show up to class. A class Sam would probably have a solid B in if Professor Woolf didn't take so many points off for grammatical errors and typos. Sam imagined Professor Woolf as the type of person who pointed out punctuation and spelling errors in online chat rooms. Assuming anyone was foolish enough to chat with her.

Today was the day that Professor Woolf was going to hand back the midterm papers. Sam had pulled an all-nighter finishing her paper on *Treasure Island,* which she had actually really enjoyed even though she only picked the book because it had been made into a movie about a million times. The Muppet version was her favorite. She expected another C+ for her efforts.

Zoey clapped her hands together and pointed when she saw Tasha in the doorway. She reminded Sam of a little kid at the zoo for the first time.

Tasha sat down next to Sam, trying to pretend like nothing was going on, but she couldn't quite keep herself from smiling, and if she tried any harder she was likely to hurt herself.

"So?" Zoey asked dragging the word out.

"I have a date for the Halloween Ball," Tasha said.

"Uh-huh. With who?"

"Dave Schwartz." She sat back as if a great pressure had been released.

"Not bad." Zoey nodded approvingly.

That seemed like quite the understatement to Sam. Dave Schwartz was the Junior Captain of the gymnastics team. He was over six feet tall, with short blond hair that he gelled in that messy way boys do to make it look like they don't care about their hair. It looked good on him, though.

"When did he ask?"

"After practice this morning," Tasha said. "He asked me to help him put the mats away, and once everyone else was gone he asked."

"Just like that?" Zoey asked.

"Yep."

"No robots?" Zoey asked, half joking, half jealous.

"No." Tasha turned her gaze on Sam. "Has-"

But just then Professor Woolf entered the room. Everyone stopped talking and found a desk.

Sam noticed that she wasn't carrying a stack of graded papers. It looked like she would have to wait another day to get her C. Professor Woolf didn't walk over to her desk like normal, either. Instead she stood in front of the class, nervously folding and unfolding her hands.

"Class, I have the unfortunate duty of passing on some upsetting news."

Sam felt her heart drop in her chest.

"Three students, Mary Stevens, Joy Burkhart, and Beth Ringdale, were killed the other night in a tragic car accident."

No one spoke for several seconds. Professor Woolf took a steadying breath and continued.

"Some of you may have known the girls. All three were seniors and members of the varsity cheerleading squad. There will be a memorial held on Thursday on the East Lawn. Also, all classes are cancelled for the rest of the day. Dr. Wong and the rest of the school's psychology department will be available for any students who need to discuss their feelings on this sad day."

They ran back to the dorm the moment Professor Woolf let them out of class. Once they were safe in Sam and Zoey's room, Tasha explained that it was common practice to pass off vampire victims as the victims of mundane accidents, traffic accidents being the most popular. Sam couldn't help wondering if the parents of the three girls knew what had really happened to their daughters. After all, there weren't any bodies.

The days leading up to the memorial were uneventful. Even the students who didn't know the girls were respectfully subdued and thoughtful. The teachers seemed to go lighter on the homework as well. Sam also noticed that more people seemed to be wearing crosses around their necks. But whether this was as a sign of mourning or something else, she didn't know.

The actual memorial service was short and respectful. Principal Shepherd and the cheerleading coach said a few nice words about the girls. A pedestal was erected outside the football stadium, and the school was commissioning a statue in their honor.

Tiffany and her posse tried to turn the event into a fashion show by wearing the latest thing in funeral apparel. Fortunately, most of the student body was classier than that.

Sam couldn't go a minute without thinking about the girls and how their deaths had been because of her. Someone was trying to stop her from finding the Witch Hunter's Gauntlet. Whoever Bad Guy was, he or she didn't mind hurting innocent people to get to her.

What if they attacked someone close to her next time? Tasha might be able to take care of herself, but what about Zoey or Lucas? They didn't deserve to be a part of this. They didn't grow up training to fight monsters. They were just good people who had the misfortune of making friends with Sam.

She thought about leaving school. But she couldn't ask Helen or Harold to come home early. Besides, they were probably safer where they were. For now, Sam was going to have to stay at

Miller's Grove and trust that the BEA would do their best to keep everyone safe.

Sam decided the best thing she could do was turn into a hermit, or was it hermitess? Either way, she spent most of her time outside of class in her room, frantically Googling for any information she could find on the monuments in her snow globes.

Starting her new life of seclusion turned out to be easier than she had imagined. Tasha had redoubled her efforts to protect campus from vampires and other things that go bump in the night. She was living on Red Bull and four hours of sleep a night.

Zoey had also become incredibly busy recently working with Doc Frost on the hovercar. She was so excited about it that she even put off working on her big metal ring to spend most of her time down in the lab. Sam couldn't blame her; she would rather be working on the flying car too.

In fact, the only person who wouldn't leave her alone was Lucas. Every day after class he asked her if she wanted to play one of his hundreds of video games or watch one of his hundreds of cartoons. Fortunately she could use her dislike of Natch as a good excuse not to go to his room and her mountain of homework as a good reason to not let him visit her room. It just seemed safer if they weren't seen together.

She could still chat and play games with Lucas online without Bad Guy knowing about it, though. She could even beat him sometimes, unless he was letting her win, which was likely; he was a video game champion, after all; and seriously, nobody could possibly be that bad at Doodle Jump, especially not someone who had made it to the 256th level of Pac-Man. And, of course, she could still see him in class. Although even that was becoming more difficult with all the projects and lab assignments they were getting recently.

She had thought that maybe now that they were partners in trying to save the world, Doc Frost would go a little easier on them in the homework department. But apparently it was just as important that they compare the velocities of falling objects on Earth to those on Mars and Venus. Then on Thursday, Doc Frost announced that they were heading to the college to watch some sort of test.

He had arranged for a fleet of security golf carts to bus the class over to the Ballistics Testing Lab. Sam and Lucas shared a cart with Felix and Leroy.

"Do you think he's going to show us the, uh-" Lucas glanced at Felix and Leroy, who were busy having a paper ball fight with the cart next to them. "That special project of his?"

"Zoey calls it the Model T," Sam said.

"The Model T, huh? Kinda funny. Anyway, I bet he finally got it working."

"I don't think so. Last I heard it was still too heavy. Zoey probably would have told me if they had solved it."

She was pretty sure Zoey would have told her.

"How is Zoey? I haven't seen her in a while. I guess she's too cool to come eat lunch with us now." He batted away a stray paper wad.

"It is insane. She spends more time in the lab than I do in class. Sometimes she doesn't even get back until two in the morning." Sam wasn't sleeping well these days, so she always knew when Zoey got back.

"Even with that drill sergeant RA of yours?" Lucas asked. "She was all over us that night for being past curfew."

Amy certainly hadn't made any friends the night she busted them at Doc Frost's house. Sam understood it was part of Agent Rosenberg's job to protect her, but she had a feeling she would be a pretty strict Resident Advisor anyway. Not like Lucas' RA Jeff. Apparently he was in a band, so he was usually out later than any of the boys on their hall. It wasn't fair.

Speaking of unfair.

"Zoey got some sort of special GET OUT OF TROUBLE FREE CARD from Dean Futuro so she can work in the lab."

"Wow," he said, genuinely impressed. "She's still going to the Masquerade Ball though, right?"

"Um, yeah. Pretty sure." She thought about it for a moment. "Why?"

"Oh, I was just wondering," he said. "I just thought maybe-"

"Everybody out!" the driver yelled.

They had reached the Ballistics Testing Lab. It turned out to be a large airplane hangar with no windows or any interesting features at all. Doc Frost led them all into a small observation room that looked out onto the main testing range. Dozens of college students in white lab coats were scurrying around between a large metal wall that had been set up in the middle of the room and some sort of giant ray gun about twice the size of a UPS truck at the far end of the room. The multitude of burn marks on the walls and spiderwebbing cracks in the concrete floor told Sam that some seriously destructive testing had been done in this room.

And if Doc Frost's excitement was any clue, this was going to be particularly destructive.

She couldn't wait.

"Everyone take one, pass it along," he said as he set a cardboard box full of goggles down on the table. "Safety first, very important."

Lucas reached in and pulled out two pairs of goggles, handing the second pair to Sam with a questioning look. She understood why he found them so weird. They weren't the usual plastic safety goggles she was used to. These were ugly brown hard rubber goggles with dark lenses like the ones worn by the scientists waiting for the first atomic bomb to go off in those old grainy films. Lucas must have realized this too, since he was making explosion motions with his hands.

"This is going to be awesome," he whispered as he slipped the goggles on. He looked like a bug.

She put hers on, sure that she looked like a bug too.

"What exactly are we expecting to see?" Sharon asked eyeing her goggles suspiciously.

Doc Frost clapped his hands.

"Ah, that is a very good question."

He reached in his lab coat pocket and pulled out a shiny piece of metal slightly larger than a playing card.

"This is why we are here." He held the metal up for everyone to see. "A little composite metal created by Professor Larson. It is as light as aluminum and twice as strong as titanium. She calls it larsonite."

He waved the class over to the window.

"In fact, that is Professor Larson in the observation room on the other side. Everybody wave."

The whole class waved. Professor Larson and her college class waved back. They were far away, but Sam could tell they were all wearing the same bulky goggles.

"That wall down there is a foot-and-a-half thick slab of pure larsonite. So far it has proven highly resistant to every weapon we have thrown at it," he said excitedly. "So now Professor Larson thinks she has developed the ultimate indestructible metal. Meanwhile, Dr. Gupta has used one of my ion generators to build that ion cannon down there. In theory it is the most powerful gun on the planet, capable of blasting a hole through anything."

Doc Frost rubbed his hands together. "So what we have here is the fun part of science; the chance to put a theory to the test by blowing something up."

That seemed to perk up the class. Everyone pressed up against the glass.

"This is going to be so cool," Lucas whispered next to her.

A balding man Sam assumed to be Dr. Gupta was double-checking his machine. Finally he gave the thumbs-up sign. All of the lab coat people scurried out of the testing room, leaving just the metal wall and the giant ray gun.

"All of the last-minute checks are clear," Doc Frost announced. "The ion cannon is remote-controlled. We just have to wait for the power core to charge up. If all goes well, we should see quite the show in a little less than four minutes."

As if on cue, the whole class started chatting excitedly about what they were about to see, how bright it would be, if they were safe being this close, why people kept trying to build bigger and better weapons when there were more important problems in the world, and why they all had to wear such ugly, ugly goggles.

"Okay, be honest. How much do I look like a giant fly right now?" Lucas asked.

Sam laughed. "I thought the exact same thing earlier."

"If I hadn't already found a great Halloween costume I would think about borrowing a pair of these."

She couldn't help but be curious. "Whatchagonnabe?"

"Wow, slow down," he said. "I can't tell you. It would ruin the surprise."

"Oooh, a surprise. Tell me, tell me."

He sort of half-smiled as he ran his hand through his hair. "Well, that all kind of depends."

"On what?"

She wished she could see his eyes. But judging by the way he grit his teeth, she was guessing he had some bad news.

"It depends on if you… if you want, or would like, or might like, to go to the dance with me."

Suddenly she couldn't hear the rest of the class talking. For a horrifying moment, she thought maybe everyone had heard him ask and was waiting to see her respond. Maybe they all even knew he was going to ask and had just been waiting all this time. But then she realized she couldn't hear anything because her heart was pounding too loudly in her ears.

Soon the sounds of the class returned. No one seemed to know or care what she and Lucas were talking about.

Lucas was still staring – she was pretty sure he was staring – at her. His smile had drooped a little bit, and he was running his hand over his perfectly flat hair again.

"I didn't want to do that here," he said.

His smile was almost gone now. Sam knew she had to say something quick.

She couldn't believe it; her initial thought had been right. It was bad news. Wonderful news, but also terrible.

She was very confused.

Under different circumstances, she would have been thrilled. In fact, she was still thrilled. But she also knew she could not say yes. Bad Guy was still out there. She wouldn't be able to live with herself if something happened to Lucas because of her.

But she had no idea how to explain that at the moment.

His smile completely disappeared.

"I'm sorry," he said finally. "Let's just watch the test."

He turned to look out the window.

Sam grabbed him by the shoulder and spun him back around to look at her.

"It isn't you," she said, her mind racing. "I just don't like Halloween. Dressing up like ghosts to beg for candy? It's for kids. I wasn't planning to go the dance anyway. Not my kind of thing. It's more of a Tiffany 'look at me, look at me' kind of thing. I'd rather stay in my room. They're running a *Treehouse of Terror* marathon."

"I understand," he said flatly. "That's fine. I just thought that if you did want to go… It might have been fun. Whatever."

She couldn't tell how he really felt. His mouth wasn't giving her any signals.

"Thirty seconds!" Doc Frost announced.

"What do you think is going to happen, Doctor Frost?" Sharon asked.

"Well, we actually have a little pool going, so best case scenario it atomizes that slab of steel down there, puts a hole in the wall behind it, and I win fifty bucks," Doc Frost said adjusting his goggles.

"And the worst-case scenario?"

"The complete destruction of the universe."

"What?" Sharon asked. Everyone else turned in surprise. "Is that possible?"

"It is always possible," he said. "Mathematically unlikely, though. Twenty seconds people."

The class fell completely silent as everyone trained their eyes on the wall down below. Sam could hear Lucas breathing next to her. At least the universe ending would get her out of this situation.

It was a long twenty seconds.

Suddenly there was a burst of blue light that blotted out everything. But then, just as suddenly, it was gone and there was a giant smoking hole in the metal wall.

Everyone cheered except Sam. As soon as the cheering stopped, Sam turned to talk to Lucas, but he was already talking to Felix and Leroy about how amazingly cool the ion cannon was.

Sam rode back to class with Sharon.

When she got back to her room, she found three game challenges from Lucas on her Facebook page.

She did not respond.

Chapter 16

The Sam Situation

Three terrified civilians ran screaming from the flaming wreckage of the exploding tank, their arms flailing wildly as they ran from the crazy-eyed man with the rocket launcher.

Lucas switched from his rocket launcher to his flamethrower.

He lost three thousand points. Killing civilians was a big no-no. But Lucas didn't care about the score. He didn't care about much of anything except reducing Chicago to a pile of burning rubble.

The controller was sweaty in his hands. He had been playing Hyper-Urban Assault in the lounge for seven straight hours. After two hours people finally stopped watching; two hours after that, the room emptied out as everyone left to do homework or eat or whatever.

Lucas didn't care. He liked the privacy, and since he was the only person there, he could crank the volume up so loud that he could feel every explosion through the floor.

"Hey, where's the second controller?"

Natch and Jerry appeared on either side of him.

"No idea," Lucas lied. He had hidden it in the big potted plant in the corner hours ago.

"Uh huh," Natch said. "So considering you've been playing this game, a game which you recently claimed to be completely tired of, every night this week, I'm guessing the Sam situation did not go well."

"What Sam situation?" Jerry asked.

"Not important," Lucas muttered while reloading.

Jerry snapped his fingers. "You asked Samantha Hathaway to the dance!"

Lucas pushed a button and a city bus exploded. "Maybe."

"And she said 'no'?" Jerry asked. "Wow. That had to hurt."

"A bit, yes. Thanks for bringing it up."

A taxicab burst into flames.

"Do you have a date, Jerry?" Lucas asked already knowing the answer.

"No."

"How about you, Natch?"

Natch laughed. "Yeah, I'm going to waste my Halloween at a stupid dance."

"That's what I thought. At least I asked somebody. And FYI, she did not say 'no', she said she wasn't planning on going."

He paused the game to check the real-world damage he had caused. Jerry was staring at the floor, but Natch was smiling back at him like an idiot.

"What?" Lucas asked. Nothing good ever happened when Natch smiled liked that.

"Nothing. I'm just wondering why she lied. Besides sparing your feelings, of course. Like is she already going with someone else, waiting for someone else to ask her, or does she simply not want to go with you?"

Leave it to Natch to ruin his fun with the harsh light of reality.

"Well, she is very nice," Jerry offered.

"Exactly." Natch nodded. "But apparently not the kind of nice that would accept a friendly invitation to a dance over staying at home."

Lucas had thought of that already. In fact, he had thought of little else over the last few days. Maybe she thought that going to a dance together would somehow put a weird vibe on their friendship. Or maybe they just weren't as close of friends as he thought. Either way, he really didn't feel like talking about the most embarrassing moment of his life right now. But as usual, Natch was immune to other people's opinions and feelings.

"I could do a little sleuthing. See who she is really going with," Natch offered.

"I told you, she isn't going."

"Uh huh," Natch said with a maddeningly smug look on his face. "And why is that?"

"I don't know. She just said that she didn't want to go."

Natch nodded. "Sure, that makes sense. Girls hate dances."

Jerry snickered.

Lucas knew it was a weak story, but if he was willing to accept it, why couldn't Natch and Jerry?

"She thinks Halloween is dumb. Whatever. Leave it alone," he said, knowing that there was zero chance they were going to leave it alone.

"That's a shame," Natch said. "And after you spent two months' allowance on that costume to impress her."

"I did not- Wait, how do you know how much how I spent on my costume?"

"The receipt, duh."

But Lucas threw the receipt away, didn't he?

"Stop going through my trash, Natch. It's creepy."

Natch shrugged off the comment. "Did you tell her you were still going?"

"No. We haven't really talked about it since."

The truth was they had barely spoken about anything other than schoolwork all week. Between the game challenges, bumper stickers, and hilarious e-mail forwards he had sent her two dozen online messages in a vain attempt to act like nothing had changed. But when she did not respond after four days he realized he was probably coming off as a desperate geeky weirdo, so he stopped.

Natch smiled. "Okay, good, we can work with that. Here's what you do. Subtly drop the hint that you are going to egg teachers' houses with Jerry and me then we all show up at the dance and catch Sam with her date."

"I told you," Lucas said slowly, so that even someone as thick as Natch could understand. "She is not going. Neither am I."

"And I think it is really cute that you believe that, but we have to get serious here. This is war."

"No, it is a dance," Lucas corrected.

"Silence!" Natch yelled with a dismissive wave of his hand. "This is indeed war. And the key to any war is intelligence. We need information."

He pulled out his cell phone and started scrolling through his contacts list.

"I really don't think this is necessary, Natch," Lucas said hopelessly. Natch was too excited to be stopped now.

"You know," Jerry chimed in. "In the old days, if you liked a girl, you could just buy her from her parents for three chickens and a goat."

Lucas and Natch just stared at him.

"That is very romantic, Jerry," Lucas said.

Jerry sheepishly looked at the floor. "I'm just saying I could find three chickens and a goat."

"I'm sure you could," Natch said with mock encouragement.

"I don't need any goats, Jerry," Lucas said. "I just wanted to go to the dance. But a horror movie marathon is just as good."

Natch shook his head and sighed deeply. "No, no, no. You have to go or she wins."

"Wins what?"

"She just wins," Natch yelled. "She gets you to change your plans and waste that expensive costume you bought. You don't want to be the weird depressed guy that misses the party of the season."

Lucas was getting worried, because Natch was actually making sense, at least in a weird, crazy, paranoid sort of way, except he seemed to have forgotten something.

"Uh, didn't you just say you weren't going to the dance?"

"True. But I'm not trying to prove to some girl that I'm not some whiney loser stupidly pining away in the game room like a little kid."

Jerry got a good laugh out of that one.

Lucas' first impulse was to slug Natch, but he had never hit anyone before, and it seemed like a really bad time to start. Besides, Natch did kind of have a point.

Lucas didn't know much about girls, but he was pretty sure that you couldn't impress them by moping around and bombarding them with stupid online messages.

At that very moment, he vowed to stop wasting his time playing Hyper-Urban Assault and start being happy, charming, and outgoing. Or at least he was going to do his best to pretend he was all of those things.

Unfortunately, when Lucas made this great new life proclamation, he failed to factor in two important facts.

The first important fact was that he did not know very many girls. At least not well. With just over a week to go before the dance, there were very few girls left that did not already have dates lined up. And since he barely saw Zoey anymore, he turned his brand new happy charming self on Tasha, who he quickly discovered was already going to the Masquerade Ball with some guy from her gymnastics team.

The second important fact he failed to consider was that part of his tuition was waived because he had agreed to play Hyper-Urban Assault against Zack over and over again while Dr. Zhang studied him like a lab rat. So if he stopped playing he couldn't afford to stay, which would mean that he couldn't go to the dance. He was stuck.

So that Friday after class he made the long lonely trek to Miyamoto Hall on the university side of Lake Laverne.

"Welcome back, Mr. Fry. I trust you have been practicing," Dr. Zhang said, ushering Lucas over to the changing room.

"Yeah, a little."

"Ha." Zack emerged from his changing room in his biosensor suit.

As if it wasn't bad enough that Lucas and Zack, as well as a couple of very talented college students, had to play the same game over and over again, they also had to do it while wearing full-body suits that monitored their heart rates, reflexes, brain waves, and other medical information Lucas didn't understand. All he knew was that it was terribly uncomfortable and stupid-looking.

Zack turned his charming smile on Dr. Zhang. "Lucas here has been spending long hours practicing in the lounge."

Dr. Zhang nodded. "Good, good. More practice is always good. I noticed a fifteen-percent drop in Mr. Fry's response time over the last two weeks. Have you been ill recently, Mr. Fry?"

Zack laughed.

"No, I'm fine."

"Excellent. Today we are going to try a simple one-on-one scenario."

Those were Lucas' favorite. While he enjoyed thoroughly annihilating an entire army with his hovertank, it did not compare to the thrill of blasting Zack out of the sky. Dr. Zhang always let

Lucas and Zack duke it out in these one-on-one battles. It was the only way to keep them fair.

It took Lucas nearly twelve minutes to wriggle into the skintight suit and make sure each of the sensor pads was in its proper place, but when he finally stepped out of the changing room, Zack was still standing there with fake concern in his eyes.

"Are you sure you're okay, Lucas? I'd hate to mercilessly beat you again when you weren't at your peak gaming level."

"Don't worry about me." Lucas opened the door to his virtual reality pod. "Just try to give me a challenge for a change."

"That's the spirit. You know, Natch asked me to go easy on you today. Sure, most guys would be completely crushed if a girl turned them down in favor of going out with… well, no one. But I told him you were a fighter."

Zack climbed into his pod before Lucas could think of a good comeback.

As he climbed into his own pod, Lucas couldn't decide which was worse: that Natch had apparently gone around telling everyone about Sam turning him down or that Lucas had been dumb enough not to expect Natch to tell everyone about Sam turning him down. Either way, he was grateful to be sitting inside the virtual reality cockpit of a heavily armed combat vehicle.

The VR pod perfectly simulated the experience of actually being inside Hyper-Urban Assault, except better. While Hyper-Urban Assault boasted some of the best graphics on the market, the images inside the VR pod were completely realistic. Lucas honestly felt like he had been to Tokyo, Paris, Sydney, and a dozen other cities around the world.
Judging by the gondola gently floating by, he was in Venice this time.

He performed a quick systems check. Sometimes Dr. Zhang liked to switch off some of their weapons or damage their engines in order to see how they reacted. But according to his head-up display, the rocket launchers; dual machine guns; surface-to-air missiles; flamethrower; and, most importantly, the laser cannon, were all in perfect working order. It was hunting season.

He immediately spun the tank around and sped down a narrow alley, making sure to stay low between the buildings. Early on, Lucas had learned to zigzag and keep his eyes open. Zack loved to plant proximity mines and snipe people with his laser cannon.

Lucas checked his radar display, but there was no sign of Zack. Normally Lucas would hunt Zack down, but today he felt like having a little fun. After all, how many times was he likely to be driving a hovertank in a city where many of the streets were made out of water? He decided to take a pleasant little drive around town and draw Zack to him.

So he gunned the engine and sped out onto the street scattering the terrified virtual Venetians in front of him. He found the nearest bridge and made a hard right turn. He flew off the bridge and streaked along, skimming low across the water and forcing a particularly tall gondolier to jump off of his boat.

Lucas was having such a good time he almost didn't notice the gorgeous Renaissance church on his right explode. Instantly he went into fight mode. He spun his hovertank around to face Zack while simultaneously backing up into the sky in a zigzagging pattern.

The occasional machine gun round bounced off the side of his hovertank, but the laser blast missed him by several feet. Lucas fired back, but at the last moment Zack slid to the right, and Lucas' laser sizzled harmlessly into the water.

Zack's hovertank shot up into the air, matching Lucas' every zig and zag.

Rockets!

Two rockets were streaking right towards him. Instinctively he fired back, but he knew it was useless; Zack had already rolled his hovertank out of the line of fire. Lucas tried to do the same, but one of the rockets struck him on the right side.

His armor held, but he was now spinning out of control. In another second Zack's laser cannon would be recharged and ready to fire.

Zack had never played this aggressively face-to-face before. Lucas barely had time to think of a plan. Instead of fighting the spin, he turned into it and rolled his hovertank under a nearby bridge to buy himself a few moments of cover. But he suddenly realized a glaring flaw in his plan. His only hope was that Zack wouldn't figure it out.

He wasn't that lucky.

Zack fired his laser cannon at the bridge. The weight of the collapsing stone dragged Lucas' tank underwater. In less than a minute he was going to be buried at the bottom of a Venetian canal. He fired up the engine to full throttle and rocked the hovertank back and forth to try to break loose.

But the next thing he knew, his screens turned red as a barrage of laser and rocket fire obliterated his crippled vehicle.

The simulation was over.

He barely had time to take a few grateful deep breaths and remind himself that he was never really in any danger of drowning before the simulator reset.

Lucas found himself in a completely different city--Hong Kong, he guessed. Before he even had a chance to scope out the city he was under attack. He managed to fire off one blast from his laser cannon before exploding over the city.

He suffered the same defeat in Toronto, Sydney, Rio de Janeiro, Cairo, and a dozen other cities around the world before the VR pod finally powered down and the door slid open.

Lucas crawled out of the pod to find Dr. Zhang smiling at his computer.

"Mr. Fry, average survival time four minutes, twenty two seconds," Dr. Zhang announced.

Lucas saw the other players had finished too. Everyone except Zack was already out of their pods. Riko, Chris, Naomi, and Joe were furiously arguing over how each other had suddenly gotten so good.

Zack's pod opened.

"Mr. McQueen, average survival time four minutes, twenty-nine seconds."

"When did you learn to do that?" Zack demanded. "That was a dead-on shot from over a hundred yards."

"One hundred and fifty-four, to be exact," Dr. Zhang said. "Very impressive."

"I didn't make a hundred-and-fifty-four-yard shot," Lucas said, very confused.

"Quite right Mr. Fry. You did not. Mr. McQueen did. In a way." Dr. Zhang held up a computer chip roughly the size of a postage stamp. "In fact, in a way, each of you just defeated yourself. Congratulations; you are the first people in the world to be cloned. At least electronically."

"You copied our brains?" Lucas asked.

"Essentially, yes." Dr. Zhang flipped the blue chip like a coin. "In fact, this one is yours Mr. Fry."

Zack snorted. "Kind of small, isn't it?"

Dr. Zhang held up the red chip. "They are not exact copies, of course. Your personal thoughts, feelings, and memories are still safely locked inside your mind. These chips merely contain all of your gaming skills. Your responses, reflexes, intuition, and strategy."

"You made copies so we could fight ourselves?" Lucas asked, bewildered. It was certainly cool, but it also seemed like a big waste of time and money.

Dr. Zhang shook his head. "No. These chips will allow me to continue my research without human subjects."

Zack perked up at that. "Does that mean you won't need us anymore?"

"For now." Dr. Zhang said graciously. "I will need to call you back later for future experiments, but for now you are free to go."

"Yes!" Zack actually did a little happy dance.

Lucas was even happier to be free, but he thought it would be a little rude to celebrate right in front of Dr. Zhang, so he waited until they were outside to do his own happy dance.

"We're free!"

"Why do you care? All you're going to do is go back to your room and play games by yourself. Later, loser." Zack took off running for the dorms.

Lucas hung back to think about the truly weird night he had just had. It wasn't every day that he found out that his brain—or, at least, the useful part of his brain--had been copied onto a computer chip. He wondered if his scholarship was in trouble now that they didn't need him anymore.

The truly depressing part was that Zack was right. The very first thing Lucas thought to do with his newfound free time was to rush back to his room and get started on the brand new *Legend of Zelda* game he had been dying to play. On the long walk back to his dorm, he tried to think of something better to do. He couldn't go visit Samantha, Tasha was probably out on vampire patrol already, and he really didn't want to see Natch right now. Maybe Jerry was doing something fun.

When he reached his dorm, he was surprised to see someone sitting on the steps. At first he figured one of the guys had forgotten his swipe card, but none of the guys in his dorm had long, beautiful blonde hair.

There was a girl waiting for someone.

"Lucas?" She jumped to her feet. "Just the guy I was looking for."

Chapter 17

The Sick and Wrong Show

"There she is! Grab her!"

Before the elevator doors had opened completely, four hands reached in and roughly yanked Sam out.

"What is going on?" Sam asked.

"Never mind," Tasha said before clamping her hands over Sam's ears.

Zoey grabbed both of Sam's hands and pulled her down the hallway.

There was an insane level of excitement in the dorm that day. Sam hadn't seen the hall this chaotic since the day she moved in. Girls were literally jumping up and down in the hallway.

Sharon popped up in front of her. She was rapid-fire talking about something. All Sam could hear through Tasha's hands was a constant stream of high-pitched squealing.

Zoey rudely hip-checked Sharon out of the way.

"Sorry," Sam yelled as she was dragged into her dorm room.

Tasha finally let go of Sam's head when Zoey shut the door.

"So." Sam sat down on her bed. "Why are you kidnapping me?"

Zoey and Tasha just stood there looking at each other, urging the other to speak first.

"You're kind of freaking me out here," Sam said, breaking the silence.

"Sorry," Zoey said. "It is just that we have something to tell you, but we don't know how to tell you."

"Unless you already know. Do you already know?" Tasha asked.

"Do I already know what?" Sam asked, very frustrated. Had they jumped her just to play an extremely annoying round of Twenty Questions?

Tasha turned to Zoey. "She doesn't know."

"Is it Bad Guy-related?" Sam asked fearing the worst. "You have to tell me."

"No. It has nothing to do with Bad Guy," Tasha said.

"It could," Zoey added. "We can't know for sure."

"I really don't think so, Zoey."

"Seriously," Sam said as sternly as she could. "What is going on?"

Tasha and Zoey looked at each other again, but said nothing. Sam was about to scream.

Finally Zoey took a deep breath and started talking. "Okay, so you know how Sick and Wrong have been trying to get their own TV show?"

"Yeah." Sam already didn't like where this was going.

Tasha sat down at Sam's desk and spun the laptop to face Sam. The banner at the top read "THE SICK AND WRONG SHOW," and there was a picture of Sick and Wrong grinning like idiots while holding up a video window.

"Did you know your Internet was turned off?"

Of course she did. She was the one who had turned it off. It was the only way she could stop herself from responding to Lucas' messages.

"No. How weird."

Tasha gave her a look that told her that she knew Sam was lying, but was happy to play along for now and ask questions later.

"Anyway, Sick and Wrong apparently lost their patience and took their show online. Twenty minutes ago they e-mailed the entire school with a link to their first episode."

"Uh huh." Sam wasn't sure why this warranted the cloak-and-dagger treatment. She tried to remember all of the embarrassing things that had happened to her lately. Like three days ago when one of Tiffany's posse 'accidentally' spilled half a plate of spaghetti on her lap or the other day in Physics when she stepped on her very new, very expensive calculator. But lots of people had already seen those things happen. In fact, thanks to the

Sam Curse, most of her embarrassing moments happen in front of large audiences.

Besides, those things weren't really Internet-worthy. Seriously, there was no way that stepping on a calculator was going to compete with toilet-flushing cats or idiots trying to jump over speeding cars.

Unless…

"Did they film me in the shower or something?"

"No, no. Uh, you'll just have to see for yourself."

Tasha clicked the play button.

Sick's head filled the video window.

"Welcome, viewers. As you can see our site is still a work in progress. Wrong and I are currently working on the premiere episode of *Geek Wars*, which is coming soon, but for now we have a very special treat for you. The following is a sneak peek at our most recent rehearsal with a special surprise none of us saw coming. Enjoy."

The screen switched to two boys who were fighting with plastic swords outside of the dorms at night. But these were not just any swords; one had a yellow Jedi lightsaber, and the other had one of those weird curved blades from Star Trek. The kind used by the bumpy-headed Klingon guys.

"This fight is completely unrealistic," the Jedi boy said. "If this were a real lightsaber it would slice right through your stupid bat'leth."

"It sounds like someone is afraid to battle with a true warrior," the Klingon boy said.

The Jedi kid held out his right hand. "Ha! What makes you think a Jedi wouldn't just snatch your blade with the Force?"

"The same reason they never do that in the movies. They're too dumb."

The Jedi swung his sword, but the Klingon blocked it. Then the Klingon swung at the Jedi's head, but the boy ducked just in time. The Jedi smacked the Klingon in the shin with his sword.

"Ow," the Klingon boy yelled.

"Cut," Sick said from somewhere off camera. "You were supposed to jump Barry."

"He swung too early."

"I did not."

As the boys argued, the camera focused on a girl walking by in the background.

"It doesn't matter," Sick yelled. "Let's just try it again."

The camera stayed on the girl.

"Uh, Wrong, over here, please."

"Look. Is that who I think it is?" Wrong asked. The camera bobbed slightly as he spoke.

"Who?" Sick asked. "Oh. I think it is."

Sam had no idea who the girl was. It was too dark, plus she had on a baseball cap and seemed to purposely turn away from the boys as if she didn't want to be seen.

"Follow her," Sick ordered. "Stay down and keep quiet."

The camera followed her from a distance. Finally, she sat down on the steps outside of Hathaway Hall.

Sick and Wrong crouched down behind a bush. Wrong tried to brush a few branches out of the way to get a better look at the mystery girl.

"What is she doing?" Sick whispered.

The camera bounced as if Wrong had just shrugged.

The girl pulled the baseball cap off and set it down on the steps. As she tossed her hair a few times and strategically pulled it down over her shoulders, Sam finally caught a glimpse of her face.

It was Tiffany Summers.

She checked her watch and tapped her foot in annoyance.

Sam had never seen Tiffany go anywhere without her gaggle of fans. Something weird was going on.

"Someone's coming," Sick whispered.

Even in the dark Sam knew who it was.

"Lucas?" Tiffany bounced to her feet. "Just the guy I was looking for."

"Why?" he blurted out. "Er, can I help you?"

She brushed his arm. "I believe we can help each other. I heard that you are still looking for a date to the dance. So am I."

Lucas was truly stunned.

"You want to go to the dance with me?"

Tiffany giggled.

That sneaky little snake actually giggled!

"Yes."

"Um, that's cool, but why? I mean, why me?"

She leaned in and whispered something in his ear. A big dopey smile spread across his face. Sam wanted to shake the computer silly.

"Okay, it's a date," he said.

"Great." Tiffany looked over her shoulder as she walked away. "I can't wait."

Lucas watched her walk away with a dumb, bewildered look on his face. Finally he pulled out his swipe card and let himself into Hathaway Hall. At least, he did eventually, when he remembered it was a pull door, not a push door.

"Wow," Sick said. The camera turned to look at him. "Lucas Fry and Tiffany Summers. Wow. We have to get this online right-"

Tasha paused the video.

"Lucas turned to the Dark Side," she said.

It certainly seemed that way.

It had been so long since Tiffany had directly done anything to make her life miserable that Sam had actually thought that she had moved on. Apparently Tiffany was a lot more patient and diabolical than Sam had given her credit for. Sam already had one diabolical enemy out there; she really didn't need another one.

Sam had to get up and move. She paced around the room a few times as Tasha and Zoey watched silently. She found Mr. Hopscotch and hugged him tightly.

Now she knew why everyone was so excited. It wasn't every day you found out that a classmate was going to the big dance with a pop star, or at least the sister of one.

But why did it have to be Lucas? Was it possible that Tiffany really liked him? Had Lucas just been biding his time until he could trade up to a better group of friends like Natch did?

"He's a traitor," Zoey said, breaking the silence.

Sam really wanted to agree with her.

But part of her knew she didn't have the right. Lucas could dance with whomever he wanted. Tiffany was pretty, and popular, and maybe even nice to people who didn't insult her. Sam could see why most guys would have said yes.

But Lucas was supposed to be her friend, and Tiffany was sort of her enemy. She wasn't nearly as bad as Bad Guy, of course, but she was still pretty up there. Lucas should know that.

"I just can't believe it," Tasha said. "To be honest, I really thought he was going to ask you Sam."

Sam looked away. She couldn't tell them that he had. It would just raise too many questions about how she was purposely avoiding Lucas to protect him and how she had done it so well that she was probably going to lose one of her best friends. She clutched Mr. Hopscotch even tighter.

"You know what? He can do whatever he wants," she said.

"No way." Zoey stamped her foot. "Friends don't let friends date evil. We have to save him."

Sam cracked a small smile, but before she could ask Zoey how she planned to do that, someone burst through the door.

It was Zack.

"Howdy, cousin! I just heard the good news about your old friend Lucas." His fake sympathetic eyes landed on Mr. Hopscotch. "Aww, what a cute teddy bear. It is good to have a friend that can't runaway."

"Shut up!" Sam yelled.

He pulled a cell phone out of his pocket and snapped a picture of her. "Perfect. That one's going to be my new wallpaper."

"Get out!"

"I'd like to see you make me."

Tasha stepped up to him. "Fine by me."

Tasha had the same warrior look in her eyes that she had while fighting the vampire cheerleaders.

Zack took a step back. "Now, now, there's no reason to get violent."

Tasha didn't move a muscle; she just kept right on staring at him.

He put his cell phone away.

"It must be nice to have your own personal bodyguard. Although it doesn't really make up for not having any actual friends, now does it?"

"Out!" Tasha grabbed his right hand while Zoey grabbed his left, and together they dragged him out of the room.

Before the door closed Sam caught a glimpse of Amy Rosenberg standing in the hallway with her arms crossed and an extremely annoyed look on her face, although Sam couldn't tell if Amy was angry more as a BEA agent or as the RA. Either way, it just reinforced Zack's point. Amy and Tasha were both assigned to protect Sam. She might not even know Zoey if they weren't roommates. So the only actual friend she had made on her own was Lucas, and she had done a pretty good job of chasing him away.

She told herself it was for the best. Anyone connected to her was in danger.

But it still sucked.

If she ever figured out who Bad Guy was, she was going to punch him in the nose.

Badoop.

Sam recognized that badoop noise. Someone was IMing her. Her internet had only been back on for a few minutes and someone had already found her.

It had to be Lucas; she couldn't think of anyone else that would be trying to reach her right now.

But if it was Lucas, what was she going to say? She figured she would have to pretend to be happy for him, which would probably make her physically ill.

She could just leave. Or she could pretend she wasn't here to see the message.

Badoop.

She couldn't help herself; she looked to make sure it was Lucas.

It wasn't.

Jigawatt121 :   ur finally online.
Jigawatt121 :   hello? anyone home?
Saraberlinfan#1 :   who is this?
Jigawatt121 :   Esteban. DUH!
Saraberlinfan#1 :   hi Esteban. what's up?
Jigawatt121 :   I got the information u asked for.

It took Sam a full three seconds to realize what he was talking about. So much had happened since she had talked to Esteban. Everything had gone insane so fast.

Suddenly a file folder labeled WITCH HUNTER'S GAUNTLET popped up on her screen.

Jigawatt121 :   tadaa!
Saraberlinfan#1 :   wow. thanx a bunch. was it hard to find?
Jigawatt121 :   not if you know where to look. ☺

Saraberlinfan#1:   I hope it didn't take long.

Jigawatt121 :   it took longer than I expected. MGU has the most amazing computer security I've ever seen. Probably cuz a few dozen of the best hackers in the country go there.

Jigawatt121 :   u wouldn't believe some of the stuff I found while looking for ur files.

Jigawatt121 :   did u know the school is built on top of a thorium nuclear reactor?

Saraberlinfan#1:   No.

So the school was nuclear. That didn't seem like a good thing. Not surprising, but not good.

Jigawatt121 :   Dr. Lazslo is attempting to clone her own Woolly Mammoth.

Saraberlinfan#1:   neat.

Saraberlinfan#1:   I can't thank you enough. This is very helpful.

Jigawatt121 :   no prob. it was fun.

Jigawatt121 :   oh. I could not find your monuments to endless winter. lots of statues of winter scenes or winter spirits. but no endless winter.

Saraberlinfan#1:   that's okay. I figured that part out myself.

She decided to take a chance. Esteban seemed to know everything about everything anyway; she might as well put that to good use.

Saraberlinfan#1:   You don't happen to know of a place where The Eiffel Tower, Great Pyramid, The Statue of Liberty, and The Sphinx all meet do you?

Jigawatt121 :   ur kidding right?

Saraberlinfan#1:   its weird I know. It is a riddle in a game we're playing.

Jigawatt121 :   here you go.

A video window popped up on her screen labeled LIVE FROM ATOP THE STRATOSHERE.

And there they all were; all four monuments, live and in color.

In beautiful Las Vegas, Nevada.

She figured the Stratosphere had to be a very tall building, because she was looking down at about twenty different casinos along The Strip, but at the far end she could clearly see Lady Liberty, the Eiffel Tower, and a sphinx sitting ready to pounce next to a large shiny black pyramid with a bright beam of light shooting out the top. Nestled between those casinos was a large medieval castle.

A quick Google search revealed that it was the Camelot Hotel and Casino, which seemed to Sam like a very logical place to find King Arthur's sword. Finally something was going her way. It was amazing. All she needed now was to figure out who her oldest friend was and find a way to Vegas.

Simple.

And the faster she did it, the sooner she could get her life back.

Saraberlinfan#1:   thanks a bunch.

Jigawatt121 :   no, thank you. Zoey said yes. ttyl.

He signed off.

Three seconds later, Sam was completely lost to the rest of the world. She was diving deeply into the rich history and mythology of the Witch Hunter's Gauntlet. The file was filled with articles and reports from scholars and professors from all over the world who were tracking the gauntlet's story from stone tablets to modern day.

Sam barely even looked up when Zoey and Tasha returned. She nodded along as they told her about Amy chewing Zack out for bursting into a girl's room uninvited. She threatened to report him to Principal Shepherd unless he agreed to never step inside Cooper Hall again.

When they were finished, she returned to her computer. After a few minutes of silence, they asked her if something was wrong. She muttered something with the words "homework" and "late" in it and they nodded sympathetically and left her alone.

Sam found the earliest stories the most fascinating because they came with pictures of priceless ancient art. Most of the stories dealt with people defeating giant monsters, slaying gods, or smashing vast armies with their great power before being killed by their own greed or stupidity. Only a handful of truly great ones had been able to give up the power when their quests were over. Either way, the gauntlet would usually disappear for hundreds of years waiting to be found by the next hero.

That's when it hit her.

If the file was a rough timeline of all the people who supposedly had worn the gauntlet from King Gilgamesh until now, then the last person in the file would have to be her mother.

Sam scrolled all the way down to the bottom and there she was: Joanne Hathaway. The BEA had collected a novel's worth of information on her mother: everything from her birth certificate to her mysterious death. There was an equally long report on her father and even an embarrassing six-page report on Sam herself, including her travels with her parents and her school records from Presley.

It turned out her sixth-grade Social Studies teacher thought she suffered from a terminal case of shyness and her seventh-grade gym teacher thought she had an attitude problem. Apparently it never occurred to them that their classes were just boring.

Sam kept reading until her brain maxed out on information. So she went to class. On her way there, she discovered that something truly terrible had happened while she was busy.

Lucas was now the most popular person in school.

Well, technically the second most popular, after Tiffany.

Chapter 18

A Long Fifteen Minutes

It was practically impossible to find anyone who wasn't talking about Lucas and Tiffany going to the dance. Upperclassmen were high-fiving him in the hallways. There were even rumors that he was getting phone calls from Teen Vogue and Inside Edition asking for interviews, and a very excited Celestial told Sam that MTV was coming to film the dance. Celestial was searching for the perfect outfit that would ensure that she got on TV without looking like she purposely picked it out just to get on TV.

Sam couldn't wait until Biology to give Lucas a piece of her mind.

But Tasha beat her to it.

"Hello, Benedict Arnold," Tasha said the instant Lucas stepped into the classroom.

It looked for a second like he was seriously considering just turning around and running the other way. Instead he sheepishly walked over to their table and sat down avoiding Tasha's steely gaze the entire time.

"Uh, hi," he said with a small wave.

"Hi," Jerry said happily, unaware of the thick tension in the air.

After a few silent minutes passed, Lucas took a deep breath and said, "So I guess you're pretty mad at me, huh?"

"Mad?" Tasha asked extra-loudly. "Not at all. Surprised. Disappointed. Questioning your morals, intelligence, and cowardice, sure. But not mad."

He nodded. "I see. It is nice to have such good and supportive friends."

Tasha's eyes narrowed. "We are supportive. But what kind of friends would we be if we let you ruin your life like this?"

"Ruin my life? By going to one dance with a girl you don't like? A girl you have never even spoken to?"

"By being sucked into her superficial world. You know those people will only like you for the ten minutes it takes for her to get tired of you. And it is a Masquerade Ball, not a dance."

"Whoa, time out," Sam said, stretching out her arms across the table between them. She could not believe she was actually about to defend Lucas. "It is no big deal. Lucas can do whatever he wants. If he wants to date a rock star, who are we to judge?"

Tasha was still mad, but Lucas was clearly relieved. The truth was that Sam didn't want to feed his ego any more. It was better to let him think she didn't care what he was doing. She also didn't want Tasha to completely chase him away.

"Thank you," he said, leafing through his textbook. "It isn't like I'm a whole new person. Or a complete moron. But come on, I went from being a turned-down dateless wonder spending a depressing night egging houses with Natch to being asked out by a beautiful celebrity. That's the kind of story they make movies about!"

Off the top of her head Sam could think of at least six movies like that, although all of them were about a dorky girl who gets to go to the big dance with the most awesome guy in class. This seemed backwards and unfair.

"Right on!" Jerry raised his hand waiting for a high five.

Lucas shrugged, pretending to be embarrassed, before he slapped Jerry's hand.

Sam couldn't believe it. Not only was Lucas turning into a horrible phony, he was actually bragging about his date while simultaneously trying to make Sam feel guilty.
The whole pretending-to-not-care plan was going to be harder than she thought, but she managed a weak imitation of a polite smile. This was apparently the exact wrong thing to do because it made Lucas relax even more.

"So, Tasha," he started. "I guess I'll see you at the dance. Is Zoey going to be there? Or is she too cool for dances like Samantha here?"

"I never said I was-"

"What is Tiffany going to wear?"

One of the girls at the next table cut Sam off.

It was Rachel, someone Sam had sort of liked in that never-really-spoke-to-her-but-she-looked-nice kind of way. Now Sam wasn't so sure. Rachel looked at Lucas with wide, expectant eyes, as if he was about to reveal the secrets of the universe. The three other girls at her table were all smiles as well, just waiting for him to speak.

"Go on," Sam said. "Don't leave 'em waiting."

Lucas shrugged and turned to face Rachel's table.

"She's going to be Cleopatra."

The girls gasped in approval. One of them even wrote it down.

"She'll be gorgeous."

"Yeah," Lucas said, clearly enjoying being the center of attention. "I haven't actually seen the costume yet. She's in Italy right now being measured and all that by some fancy designer. I don't remember which one. It ends in an 'I'."

More gasps. More note taking.

"Thanks a bunch, Lucas," Rachel said before turning back to her table. "Okay, so we need to find Egyptian costumes to match. This is going to be so cool."

The girls immediately started tossing around ideas for gowns and headdresses and other Egyptian costume accessories. Lucas, realizing he wasn't the center of attention anymore, turned back to his own table. Sam just smiled at him.

"How about your costume?" she asked. "Don't tell me she's making you go as Caesar or, what's his name, Mark Antony."

"Nope. I had mine picked out a while ago when I thought… When I first decided I might need one."

"And? What is it?"

"Not telling." He crossed his arms and stuck his chin in the air. "If you're not going to go you don't get to see it."

"Dork," Tasha said. "Be that way. We won't tell you what our costumes are then either."

Lucas' eyes widened. "Wait, does that mean you are going to the dance now? That's great!"

Sam started to shake her head when someone kicked her leg. Hard. From Tasha's side of the table.

"You should see her costume," Tasha said, waggling her eyebrows.

Sam made a mental note to kill Tasha later. This was all going very badly very quickly. Tasha knew Sam didn't have a costume. She was playing some sort of game with Lucas, and Sam didn't want to be a part of it.

Suddenly the smile withered from Lucas' face.

"Who are you going with?"

Tasha tapped Sam's leg under the table again. Sam knew it was a secret signal, she just didn't know what it was supposed to mean. She and Tasha were going to have to have a conversation about their non-verbal communication.

"Um..."

"Are you saying that a girl isn't allowed to go to a ball without being forced to bring some stupid boy along?" Tasha said indignantly.

"So, no one," Lucas said smugly.

"I'm not going with anyone either," Jerry interjected quickly. "You could go with me if you want."

He looked so pathetically hopeful at that moment that Sam was truly temped to say yes, but that really wouldn't help her with the whole 'keeping her friends from being turned into vampires' thing.

"Thank you, Jerry," Sam said, thinking fast. "But I really don't think I'm going to go."

Tasha kicked her again.

"For the whole thing," she added quickly. "I might just show up for a little while. Make an appearance. Hang with my friends. See if MTV is really there. But I will probably see you there."

Sam hoped that response would keep her from getting kicked again.

Lucas furrowed his brow. "You're only coming for a little bit. What else do you have to do?"

Why was everyone suddenly so interested in Sam? Why couldn't they just let her do her thing? Now she was sinking deeper and deeper in a swamp of lies.

What else could she be doing on Halloween?

"I'm going trick-or-treating."

This seemed to surprise everyone at the table.

"Seriously?" Lucas asked. "Aren't you a little too old for trick-or-treating?"

"Can you ever be too old for free candy?"

Lucas thought about it for a moment. "I guess not. It is way better than Natch egging houses. But I'll save you a dance maybe? If you get back in time?"

"Um, sure. Maybe. If I get back in time."

"Well, I'm glad you worked that out," Professor Walsh said from directly behind Sam.

A quick glance around the room revealed that, just as she feared, everyone was staring at her. Now that she thought about it, she couldn't remember if she had heard anyone else in the class speaking for the last few minutes. Judging from the big goofy grins on everyone's faces, no one had been.

"Now that we've had our Teen Nick moment, can we return to class?" Professor Walsh asked.

Sam nodded.

"Good," Professor Walsh returned to the front of the class. "Everyone turn to page 254. Mitochondrial DNA."

Sam sank into her chair and didn't speak to or look at anyone for the rest of class. She was the first one out the door, with Tasha trailing right behind her. Once they were outside, Sam stomped over to a large elm tree just beginning to shed its red and golden leaves. It was not only gorgeous, it was far enough away from the sidewalk to make for a perfectly semisecluded place to chew someone out.

"What the heck was that?" Sam asked Tasha with her hands on her hips just to make sure Tasha knew she was serious.

"What?" Tasha asked innocently. "I am trying to save our friend Lucas, but you don't seem to want to help."

"Save him how? By making me look stupid?"

"You wouldn't have looked stupid if you had just gone along with my story."

"So you agree that I looked stupid?"

Tasha nodded her head. "Sorry."

Sam gave her the nastiest look she could.

Tasha giggled.

"Fine," Sam said, moving on. "How is lying about me having a costume going to save Lucas?"

"Oh, come on." Tasha rolled her eyes. "Did you see how excited Lucas was when I said you might be going to the ball? He clearly likes you. He probably would have asked you to go if Tiffany hadn't asked him first."

Sam looked away briefly.

Unfortunately it wasn't brief enough.

"Wait a minute. Did he already ask you? He did, didn't he?" Tasha's eyes were really big now.

"Sort of. Yes. A while ago," Sam admitted. It felt good to finally let the secret out.

"What?" Tasha whisper-yelled. "Why did you say 'no'? Lucas is fun. Plus you could have hung out with me and Zoey."

Sam didn't want to tell her the truth, and she didn't have a clever lie ready, so she just said nothing and looked shocked and sad.

"Poor Lucas," Tasha said, leaning against the tree. "All this time I thought you had waited for him to ask and he turned out to be too big a chicken to do it. I kind of feel bad now. Although he did agree to go with Tiffany, which is still really, really bad."

Sam nodded in agreement.

"So why don't we go find you a costume," Tasha said, springing away from the tree.

"When did I say I was going?" Sam asked.

Tasha's shoulders drooped. "You have to go."

Sam wanted to tell Tasha why she couldn't go. She really did. But how could she? How could she tell Tasha, the person whose job it was to protect her from monsters, that she was afraid to be friends with her friends because they might be killed by monsters?

It would be like telling Tasha that she had no faith in her. It would almost be like telling her that it was her fault Sam couldn't have fun.

"It is a dumb school dance. I think I'll live."

"Why do people keeping saying that? It is a Masquerade Ball." Tasha stomped her foot. "And if you don't go, I can't go."

"Why not?"

Tasha bit her lip. "Because I have to guard you. If Bad Guy finds out you are sitting up in your room all alone while everyone is busy at the big noisy ball what do you think he's going to do?

And trick-or-treating is out, I'm sorry. You probably shouldn't leave campus while Bad Guy and Cervantes are still loose."

Sam hadn't thought about that.

"I really don't want to guilt trip you, I just really want to go," Tasha said sincerely.

"No, I understand. Don't worry about it. I'll go. It'll be fun."

"Are you sure?"

"Yes," Sam said. "I really did want to go. I just didn't want to go alone to my first real dance. Or ball."

"Rock on. Now we just need to find you a costume."

"Yeah, that might be a little difficult two days before the ball. I'll get stuck with a giant bunny costume or something."

Tasha laughed. "I think you are forgetting that you sleep a mere five feet away from the greatest fashion collection in the entire school."

Twelve minutes later they were in Sam's room with Zoey's closet doors thrown wide open. They had explained the situation to her, and Zoey had already pulled out three blouses for Sam to try on.

"Oooh, how about this one." Zoey held up a black cutoff with a pink skull on the chest. "You could be a punk rocker."

"Hmm, we'll put that in the maybe pile." Sam tossed the shirt on Zoey's bed.

"How about a ballerina?" Zoey asked, holding up a pair of slippers.

"It's too cold out for that."

Zoey looked a little crushed. "Okay, you throw out an idea then."

"I don't know."

"Come on," Tasha prodded. "What do you want to be?"

Zoey held up a short red dress. "This'll get you some attention."

"I don't think I-"

"Hold that thought," Zoey said, carefully laying the dress down on her bed before rummaging through her closet some more. She pulled out a pair of red high heels and a silver purse too small to hold anything larger than a cell phone.

"We could bleach your hair, get some gaudy fake jewelry, and you could go as Tiffany. It would be hilarious."

"That's perfect," Tasha said.

"No," Sam said as forcefully as she could. "Absolutely not."

If Sam was going to dress up like someone famous she was going to dress up as someone respectable, like Sara Berlin. Besides, she sort of wanted something that people, namely Tiffany and her gang, couldn't make fun of. She needed a costume that wouldn't stand out too much.

"Okay," Zoey said a little disappointed. "Let's see, I have these big clunky boots and a ruffled shirt, if you want to be pirate."

Sam picked up one of the tall black boots.

"That's it!" She rushed over to her computer.

"Really?" Zoey asked, looking at the ruffled shirt with glee.

"Yes," Sam said, wiggling her mouse to wake up her computer. She went to her Witch Hunter's Gauntlet file and pulled up a newspaper article with a photograph. "Check it out."

Tasha and Zoey crowded in around her.

The photo was of several college students, including two girls in pirate costumes, being arrested by campus police.

"That's your godmother, isn't it?" Zoey asked pointing at one of the girls.

"Yep, that's Helen." Sam pointed at the other girl. "And that's my mom."

"She's gorgeous," Tasha said.

"I know." Sam zoomed out from the photo. "According to this 'Chicago Maroon Assistant Editor Joanne McQueen and Student Body Treasurer Helen Wilson, seen here dressed as Anne Bonny and Mary Read, were among the two dozen students arrested at last night's Halloween Ball after the celebration degenerated into a shameful barroom brawl.'"

"See, ball, not dance," Tasha said. "And wow, your mom started a fight."

"No," Sam said with a laugh. "My dad did. He was fighting with Zack's dad about something. This is the night my parents met."

"He got her arrested and she still went out with him?" Zoey asked.

"Apparently."

"So, you want to be a pirate, huh?" Zoey said stroking her chin. "Let's see what I can do."

After thirty minutes of digging through the closet and trying on clothes, Sam had a pretty descent pirate costume going. She had a white ruffled pirate shirt and a long blue coat with red trim and big gold buttons. The pants were ugly, baggy, and brown, but Sam had to admit that they did look pretty piratey, and she topped off the look with the tall black boots.

"You need a hat. And a sword," Zoey said, surveying her creation.

"Don't forget the eye patch and parrot," Tasha said making her best angry pirate face. "Aarrr."

"No parrot, no eye patch," Sam said. "No peg leg either."

"You're no fun."

Zoey checked her watch. "We've got an hour before the mall closes. And ten minutes before the city bus gets here."

"You memorized the bus schedule?" Tasha asked, impressed.

"Just to the mall. You've got five minutes to change, Sam."

Sam started to change when Tasha made big eyes at her. It took Sam a second to remember that she wasn't supposed to leave campus.

"I probably shouldn't go right now. If I'm going to go to the dance now then I have to get the first draft of my *The Grapes of Wrath* paper started," Sam said. Sadly it was true. She had actually put it off to give herself something to do during the dance.

"Okay, we'll go shop for you," Tasha said playfully. "If we have to."

"Thanks a bunch."

During the hour they were gone, Sam managed to write exactly three whole lines of what was supposed to be a seven-to-ten page paper on Steinbeck's crazy overuse of symbolism.

"Success!"

Zoey held up a cheap black tri-cornered hat with the skull and crossbones symbol on the side and a belt with a plastic sword and pistol.

Despite her better judgment, Sam was actually starting to look forward to this dance. For the third time.

Chapter 19

Best-Laid Plans

Sam stood alone in her room, checking herself in the mirror for the umpteenth time. She readjusted her hat, trying to figure out just how far to push it back to show off her hair without looking like she was trying to show off her hair. It was a delicate balance.

She checked the time.

Tasha and Zoey had left for the ball twenty minutes ago. They had agreed that Sam would make a more dramatic appearance if she arrived stylishly late, but Tasha had restricted her to twenty-five minutes. After that she was coming to get her.

Sam wasn't sure if that was part of Tasha trying to protect her, or if Tasha knew that without a deadline Sam would pace around the dorm room nervously for hours and eventually chicken out. Either way, she was grateful.

She wondered what was going on right now. Had Lucas and Tiffany arrived by horse-drawn carriage to the fanfare of a dozen minstrels? Was Tiffany simply the most gorgeous person on the planet at this very moment? If so, would anyone even notice if Sam arrived at all?

There were so many questions, so few answers, but no shortage of worrying.

The only thing that made Sam feel even the slightest bit better was that Tasha had assured her that MTV was not allowed onto school grounds to film the dance. Dean Futuro, being the eccentric weirdo that he was, wouldn't allow camera crews to wander around his campus. Apparently the only reason Sick and Wrong got away with it was that they were idiots and Dean Futuro could have them expelled and discredited in minutes.

She had less than five minutes before Tasha was going to come looking for her. Sam plucked up her courage and reached for the doorknob.

Just then someone knocked on the door.

Sam took a step back.

Tasha wouldn't knock. Zoey wouldn't knock.

Who did she know that would knock?

"Who's there?" she asked.

"Bond, James Bond," a muffled male voice said through the door.

At that exact moment Sam realized her door seriously needed a peephole.

She had no idea who was out there, but considering all of the other weird stuff that she had seen lately, she figured there was at least a ten percent chance that James Bond was, in fact, standing outside her door.

Sam opened the door.

It was official: the world had stopped making sense.

That was the only possible explanation Sam's brain could come up with for the information it was getting from her eyeballs.

Natch was standing in her doorway in a tuxedo with a single rose in his hand.

It was a really nice tux too. It looked too nice to be a rental. And he looked really great in it. His hair was slicked back, and he had a small red carnation pinned to his lapel.

"Miss Hathaway, I respectfully ask if you would do me the great honor of attending the Masquerade Ball with me?" he said in a slow, deliberate manner. He was really pouring on the charm.

"Uh. Huh?" Was all the response Sam could muster.

"Would you like to go to the dance with me?" he asked with a mixture of annoyance and what Sam thought might be fear.

"I thought you weren't going to go to the dance?" Her brain was rebooting.

He slouched a bit and let the rose dangle in his hand.

"Yeah well, about that." He ran his free hand over his hair. "When I take over the world, people are going to write a lot of books about me. I figure it won't look good if I missed my first dance. So I thought I might as well go with one of the prettiest girls in school."

That was easily the weirdest compliment Sam had ever received.

"You want me to go to the dance with you?"

"Yes."

"And why should I believe you?" Sam asked, with the memory of Mountain Dew dripping down the side of her head fresh in her mind.

"Because it will really tick Tiffany off."

"Okay."

"Really?" he asked gratefully.

"Sure, anything to make her mad. Should be fun."

In all honesty she knew there was a good chance he was planning to do something mean to her, but her whole plan to make Lucas think she didn't care that he was with Tiffany was going to work a lot better if she showed up with a date.

"But if this is a trick and you dump a bucket of pig's blood on me or something then I am going to have Tasha beat you up," she added. "I'll even get Sick and Wrong to film it."

He laughed and nodded. "Sounds fair."

He thrust the flower at her. It was very beautiful, but it didn't really go with her costume.

"Do you mind if I leave this here?" she asked as she looked around for a vase, even though she knew she didn't have one.

"That's fine."

In the end she had to set the rose in a tall plastic cup. It looked strangely festive that way.

"Have you seen anyone else?" she asked as she stepped out into the hall.

"Nope."

She was a bit disappointed. Surely he would have seen Lucas in his costume. Maybe he just didn't want to bring up the subject.

"So who are you supposed to be?" he asked. His eyes scanned her from top to bottom.

"My mom," she said proudly.

"Oh, see, that's not fair, I never would have guessed that," he said with a twinkle in his eye.

She explained the whole Anne Bonny thing to him as they walked across campus. He actually listened. Before she knew it, they had reached the dance.

The dance committee had really gone all out with the decorations. Sam figured they must have paid professional decorators to come in and set up everything. It was freakishly similar to those over-the-top high school dances in the movies, except with far better special effects.

Holographic ghosts wailed and moaned as they drifted back and forth across the dance floor, and life-size plastic skeletons hung from the ballroom ceiling, sporadically dancing in midair. Sam swore one of them was doing the robot. A hundred or more jack-o-lanterns lined the edges of the dance floor. Black and orange draperies hung on the walls, and somewhere a fog machine was maintaining a constant six inches of mist on the floor.

Suddenly Sam felt Natch's hand on hers as he led her down the grand staircase.

Two anime schoolgirls (she didn't know exactly which show they were supposed to be from, but they were wearing school uniforms and those contacts that gave people big anime pupils) sneered when they saw her. One whispered something to the other that must have been hilarious, because she couldn't stop laughing.

"Want me to break their knees?" Natch asked quietly.

Sam had to laugh at that.

"No, it's fine. Thanks for offering, though," she said. Sam didn't care what they said.

She didn't.

Really.

The DJ switched over to a slow song, and nearly everyone paired off and started dancing. She was relieved that Natch didn't seem to want to join them.

"Ah, food," he said happily as he let go of her hand and made a beeline for the long tables of snacks by the back wall.

Sam scanned the dancers for anyone familiar. Sabrina and Derek, dressed as Batgirl and Robin, passed by. Sabrina caught her eye and pointed through the crowd to the spot where Zoey, dressed as Albert Einstein, was dancing with Justin Timberlake. Not some guy in a Justin Timberlake costume, the Justin Timberlake.

Sam picked her way through the crowd.

"Zoey! Who's your friend?" she called.

"Hey," Zoey waved her over. "You came after all. I owe Tasha a dollar. And you look awesome."

"Thanks," Sam said with a curtsy. "I don't believe I've met your date."

"That's okay, neither have I," Zoey said. She waved her hand through Justin's head.

"A hologram?"

"Hello, Sam," the Justin Timberlake hologram said.

"How-"

"Esteban," Zoey said cheerfully. "He's a genius."

Zoey pointed at the floor where a small robot was projecting the image of Justin Timberlake into the air. It was a vastly more detailed image than that of Sam's father. He had been transparent, green, and a bit flickery, but Justin appeared solid and completely real, unless you noticed that he was hovering a foot off the ground. Aside from that it easily rivaled the magical glamour she had seen earlier.

"Hi, Esteban." Sam waved at the hologram, not sure if Esteban could see her.

"Nice party, huh?" the hologram asked.

"Sure," she said. "But don't let Tasha hear you calling this a party. She'll hunt you down and delete you."

"You know, I haven't seen her yet," Zoey said, scanning the room on tiptoes.

"Seen who yet?" Natch asked. He had snuck up behind Sam with two drinks in his hands. He handed one to Sam.

Zoey's jaw fell open. She just stood there staring for a moment.

"Wow," she said finally.

"You like the tux?" Natch asked playfully.

"Yeah, actually."

"Ah hmmm," the hologram said, drawing attention back to itself.

"Looking good, Esteban," Natch said.

"Thanks man," the fake Justin said.

"So how do you, you know, dance?" Sam asked.

Zoey held her hand up to Justin/Esteban's hand. "Very carefully for the slow dances." She pushed her hand into the hologram, which rippled a bit. "But we're set for the fast dances."

The holographic Justin busted out a very complicated dance routine. "I programmed over two thousand different dance patterns into this thing. I can even vary the speed."

Suddenly the hologram was popping and locking at superhuman speed.

"Very nifty," Sam said. She couldn't help but wonder what Esteban was actually doing in his room. It seemed kind of sad that he was just in there pushing buttons. Hopefully he at least had some food in there.

She took a sip from her cup. It was remarkably good, not that watery Kool-Aid they had at her old school.

Sam looked around the room. There was an impressively wide range of costumes, from classic ghosts and witches to Ben10s and Lady Gagas. A pack of well-dressed sparkly vampires stood clustered around a classic big-collared Dracula. Still she couldn't find Lucas anywhere. She didn't see Tiffany either, for that matter, although there was a group of about twenty girls dressed as Egyptians huddled together, looking around expectantly. Still, there was no way Tiffany was going to just blend into the crowd, so she must not be here yet.

"Boo."

Tasha popped up in front of Sam. She was dressed completely in green, with a bow and arrow slung on her back and a pointy hat with a long red feather stuck in the side. She looked completely ridiculous. Sam pretended to jump in terror anyway.

"Ahh."

"Nice outfit," Tasha said back. "You make for quite the pirate hottie."

Sam was so embarrassed she could feel her ears burning.

"Did you see the vampires?" Sam asked, pointing.

Tasha rolled her eyes. "Idiots. You know, books like that are the reason teenage girls are the number one victims of vampire attacks. There is nothing romantic about evil bloodsucking monsters."

Sam nodded in agreement, although secretly she had quite the stash of vampire books and movies back home.

"Speaking of which, I have to say I'm a little disappointed in your choice of company," Tasha said eying Natch. "What are you up to, Mr. Bond?"

"Just being a supportive friend," Natch said. "So who are you supposed to be?"

Tasha mocked indignation. "Hello, green tights, green tunic, bow and arrows."

"Don't forget the stupid hat," Natch said.

"Yes, thank you," she said scrunching up her nose. "I'm Robin Hood."

"I was totally unaware that Robin Hood was a girl. Or black," he said playfully.

Tasha stroked the feather in her cap. "Well, records from that period are sketchy at best."

"Fair enough." He raised his cup in salute.

"Where's Dave?" Sam asked.

"I told you I'd be back." Dave's Arnold Schwarzenegger impression was truly horrible. But his leather jacket and fake robot eye added up to a pretty impressive Terminator costume. He had a cup of punch in each hand.

"Isn't that sweet," Tasha said, taking one of the cups from Dave.

"I brought punch," Natch said quietly.

For some strange reason, Sam felt the urge to step closer to him. He was trying, in his weird sort of way.

Suddenly the lights dimmed and a new slow song started.

Dave and Tasha set their cups down on the nearby table.

"We're going to go dance now." Tasha took Dave by the hand and led him out onto the dance floor.

"Yeah, us too," Zoey said. The little hologram-projecting robot had wheels so they headed off to the dance floor leaving Sam and Natch behind.

Sam's breath caught as Natch took her cup out of her hands and set it on the table next to his.

He extended his hand to her. "Would you care to dance?"

She couldn't help but giggle a little. His eyes narrowed at this, so she did her best to fight it.

"Yes, I would." She took his hand.

Natch led her out to the dance floor, somewhere near the middle. She had never been to the middle of a dance floor before. She was more of an edge-of-the-dance-floor kind of girl.

That's when she spotted Doc Frost and Mr. Norton, the chemistry teacher, chaperoning from the sidelines dressed as the

Blues Brothers in matching black suits and sunglasses. Doc Frost tipped his hat to her. She waved back.

Natch placed his hands on her waist. She was so stunned by this that she forgot for a moment what she was supposed to do with her hands. He raised his eyebrows in puzzlement. She could feel him letting go when she remembered to put her hands on his shoulders; his hands settled back on her waist.

She didn't have much in the way of comparison, but Natch was a really good dancer. He seemed to know how to swing with the beat, so she just let him lead her.

Over Natch's shoulder she saw Celestial in some sparkly tutu outfit dancing with a mummy. Celestial gave Natch a once-over while mouthing the word "wow" and gave Sam an approving smile.

Sam blushed but managed to smile back.

"What was that?" Natch looked over his shoulder nervously.

Fortunately, Celestial was cool about it and spun away with her mummy at the last second.

"Nothing. Thought I saw someone dressed as Principal Shepherd." It seemed like a good story to Sam. But she decided to change the subject anyway. "So how did you become such a good dancer?"

"I took lessons," he said matter-of-factly.

"Oh wow, just for little old me." She gave him what she hoped he would understand was a playful smile.

He just shrugged. She switched to a different topic.

"So why James Bond?"

"Irony mostly. I figure one day when I'm about to rule the world and make everything better, some drunk who can't hold a relationship for more than a week will try to stop me."

"Yeah, I heard you plan to take over the world."

"Of course," he said with complete seriousness.

"Why?"

"No one has ever done it before." He spun them around on the dance floor. They wound up dancing next to a couple dressed as Steven Colbert and Wonder Woman. "Look, we only get one chance at life. I figure you should use it to the fullest extent possible. Taking over the world is the greatest challenge I can think of, and it would be a waste of time to do anything less."

"Okay," Sam said politely. She could think of some other, less violent, goals. Like being the first person on Mars, or curing cancer, or stopping global warming.

"I mean, someone has to do it eventually, right?"

Sam hadn't really thought about it before. She figured it might happen some day, hundreds of years from now.

"Do you have any idea what the odds are against you?"

"Sure. Over six billion to one. But I would rather fail at being great than succeed at being mediocre," Natch said happily. "How about you? What do you want to be when you grow up?"

"I have no idea."

"None at all?" he asked with a skeptical look on his face.

"Nope."

He thought that over for a bit.

"That must be nice."

What?

"How is that nice?" she asked slightly more angrily than she intended. "I don't know what I am doing with the rest of my life. How is that a good thing?"

"It means you still have options."

"I guess." She wasn't very reassured. Having a world of options didn't mean a whole lot when you didn't have a direction.

"Okay, look at it this way," he said as he spun them around again. "You are only fourteen. Would you want a fourteen-year-old making important life decisions for you? Do you think anyone out there would trust you to pick a career path for them? No. So don't worry about it. You have plenty of time to pick something."

That actually made sense, even though it was terribly insulting.

"What about you? You're fourteen and you have chosen a career path."

"True. But I am special," he said. "And a little crazy."

"Can't argue with that," Sam said.

The song ended and he let go of her waist.

"You know Lucas-"

He was cut off by a smack to the back of his head from a plastic sword.

"En guard," Zack said, removing the hat of his Zorro costume and taking a bow.

"You want me to feed you that sword?"

He tried to grab it, but Zack constantly kept swinging it out of reach.

"You are too slow, Mr. Bond," Zack said, wiggling his fake mustache.

"Are you here all alone, Zack? That's so sad," Sam said with a pouty lip.

"Not at all. I came with Dorothy over there." He pointed to a tall girl in a dead-on perfect replica of Dorothy's outfit from the original *The Wizard of Oz,* down to the stuffed Toto in her basket. She was making awkward conversation with some of Zack's friends whose names Sam had never bothered to learn. They were dressed up as the Three Musketeers.

Sam suddenly recognized the girl. It was Class President Sherry Hoyle.

"Not bad," Natch said.

Sam elbowed him in the side.

Zack snickered at Natch. "So where's Lucas? Crying in his room?"

"No, he's out. Trick-or-treating," Natch said.

"I'm sure he is."

"What are you talking about? Lucas is coming with Tiffany." Sam didn't like the way the words felt in her mouth, but they were true.

Zack laughed. "Yeah right, like she was going to waste her Halloween at a school dance. She's in Paris right now."

"Really?" Why hadn't anyone told her this before? Poor Lucas.

She had to find Zoey and Tasha right away. She needed advice. Maybe there was still time to find Lucas and get him to come to the dance.

"Before you go," Zack said, sensing her intentions. He beckoned Sherry over. "I want to show you the best part of Sherry's costume."

Sam couldn't have cared less about Sherry's costume, except she could tell by the pure joy in Zack's eyes that he was up to something. Something that was not intended to make Sam happy.

Sherry skipped over to them, her basket swinging in her hand. The Three Musketeers pushed their way through the crowd behind her.

"As soon as the dance is over, we're going to have a special bonfire. You know, roast some marshmallows, make some s'mores, and burn a few effigies." He took the stuffed Toto out of the basket and handed it to Sherry. "Like lions" – he pulled a stuffed lion out of the basket and threw it to Musketeer # 1 who ripped the poor furry toy's head off – "tigers" – he tossed a stuffed tiger to Musketeer # 2 who impaled it on his sword – "and bears."

He pulled Mr. Hopscotch out of the basket.

"Oh my."

Sam lost all connection to the world at that moment. Time stopped. She lost all sense of where she was. Her only thought was to protect Mr. Hopscotch, her oldest and dearest friend, and her last real tangible connection to her parents.

And then one shining lightning bolt of recognition pierced the storm clouds of her mind.

Her oldest friend.

Strength she had never felt before flowed into her arms and puddled in her fingers.

"Give Mr. Hopscotch back," she said slowly and forcefully.

Zack laughed. "Mr. Hopscotch? What a stupid name."

"Give him back." She reached for the teddy bear but Zack held it above his head.

"Why would I do that?" Zack asked with devilish glee. "When I can roast him and post the video on my webpage instead?"

From the look in his eye, Sam was absolutely convinced that Zack would really do it.

She couldn't lose Mr. Hopscotch. She had already lost too much. She fought back her sudden urge to cry. It would only fuel Zack's cruelty.

Natch's hand reached out at lightning speed, pulled the sword from Sam's belt, and held it inches from Zack's face.

"Give her the bear."

Zack's look of surprise was priceless. But he recovered quickly, and with a flick of his wrist he tossed the teddy bear to Musketeer # 3.

Musketeer # 3 immediately gripped Mr. Hopscotch around the neck as if he was about to rip his head off.

"No!" Sam squeaked uncontrollably.

"Stop this now," Sherry said, forcefully. No one paid any attention to her. Sam barely noticed when she huffed and marched away.

Natch waved the pirate sword in Zack's face.

"Anything that happens to the bear will happen to you. Understand?"

Zack tilted his head, looking amused.

Before Sam could say anything Musketeer # 1 and Musketeer #2 had drawn their swords and slashed Natch simultaneously across the back and legs, leaving tears in his tuxedo. Zack slashed Natch's hand, making him drop his sword.

"Idiot," Zack jeered.

Sam reached out to console Natch, but the way he squinted at her told her that was the last thing he wanted.
She rounded on Zack and his friends instead.

"You pathetic little boy," she said. "Give me back my teddy bear."

Zack took Mr. Hopscotch back from his grinning Musketeer friend. He poked the bear's stomach with his sword.

"Say goodbye, Sammy."

"What's going on over here?" Coach Powers' bellowing voice carried over the crowd.

Everyone in the area stopped dancing immediately as Coach Powers made his way through the crowd with Sherry Hoyle bustling along behind him. Coach Powers wore a tattered red leather flight jacket, the kind with the big flap in the front held shut with large gold buttons. A '50s-style ray gun hung from the thick white belt around his waist. Sam had no idea what old science fiction character he was supposed to be, but from the wear and tear and the way it didn't quite fit around his belly she guessed that he had held onto this costume for many years.

"Later," Zach said with a bow.

Zorro and the Three Musketeers took off running through the crowd, laughing and waving their swords.

Sam chased after them, but a pack of students dressed up as life-sized chess pieces blocked her view. She angrily ran around the group looking for any sign of Zack and his friends, but the dancing crowd had come back together erasing their escape path.

There was no chance of her catching them now. Maybe if she got Tasha and Zoey to help they could find Zack and his goons before they burned Mr. Hopscotch.

"The east doors. No, the red ones," Natch said behind her. "Round 'em up."

He was smiling as he hung up his phone.

"What was-"

"Watch this," he said, pointing to the east doors.

Zack and his buddies were still hooting and hollering and waving their swords as they reached the doors and ran outside. A second later they came running back inside, followed by an army of ten Jedi with their lightsabers held high and glowing and ten Klingons waving their weird curved swords.

The swarm of costumed warriors spread out to encircle Zack and his friends. A sword fight broke out, but it turned out that the plastic of the Jedi and Klingon weapons was vastly superior and snapped Zorro and the Musketeers' costume fencing swords off at the hilt.

"Shall we?" Natch said, offering Sam his hand.

"Let's," she said, taking it.

The Klingons and Jedi formed a tight circle. Zack and his friends were standing back-to-back in the middle with their fists up, ready to fight. But Sam noticed that many of these Jedi were quite large. In fact, Mace Windu was Malcolm Harris, the running back who had scored four touchdowns in the latest football game, and the tallest of the three Obi Wan Kenobis was one of Derek's basketball player friends.

Sick and Wrong were standing outside of the circle filming everything.

"Nice going guys," Natch said.

"We're going to have the best blooper reel ever," Sick said, very excited. He tapped Wrong on the shoulder. "Do not stop filming."

Sam stepped through the circle. "How's it going, cousin?"

"Second cousin," Zack snapped.

"And don't you forget it," Sam said. It was amazing how confident she felt with an army of Jedi Masters and Klingon warriors watching her back. "Hand over the bear."

"You'd better do it, Mr. McQueen," Coach Powers said.

Coach Powers, Sherry Hoyle, Tasha, Zoey, and Dave all stood outside the circle, glaring at Zack. Zoey held the holographic projector in her arms, which resulted in the weird image of Zoey holding Justin Timberlake in the air by his feet.

"Oooh," Zack said mockingly as he violently shook Mr. Hopscotch.

"Stop it!" Sam yelled.

"Aw, Sammy wants her dolly back." He pulled a lighter out of his pocket and held it dangerously close to Mr. Hopscotch's foot.

"Please don't. He's my oldest friend."

Out of the corner of her eye she saw Tasha and Zoey nod.

"That's all I needed to hear," someone whispered in her ear.

And that's when everything went black.

Chapter 20

Blackout Bingo

With absolutely no lights and no windows the dance hall was almost completely blacked out. The faint flicker of the jack-o-lanterns lit up the room just enough to turn everyone into faceless silhouettes. At first Sam thought that the power had simply gone out. But that wouldn't explain why the Jedi's swords had stopped glowing, or why the hologram had winked out.

Aside from some shuffling of feet no one made a sound, which made it all the worse when something gigantic roared outside.

The entire room gasped and stared through the darkness in the direction of the roar. Sam wasn't sure if it was some sort of animal or metal being torn apart, but it made her blood run cold.

"Everyone remain calm," Coach Powers yelled commandingly from somewhere in the darkness.

Nothing makes people freak out more than someone telling them to stay calm. The room was awash in worried whispering and then, just as instantly as they had gone out, the lights flickered back on.

"See," Coach Powers said. "The backup generators kicked in."

Sam's eyes readjusted to the light just enough to see a large fireball emblem sown onto the back of Coach Powers' jacket before the room was plunged into darkness again.

Coach Powers cursed loudly.

Rubbing her eyes, Sam reflected on what else she had seen in her half-second of vision. Mr. Hopscotch was missing, and Zack was looking angrily at someone in a white lab coat.

The lights snapped on again.

"And now the backup backup generators," Coach Powers said triumphantly.

"And out they go again," the lab coat wearing figure said, holding up a gold pocket watch in his right hand. Mr. Hopscotch hung limply by the leg in his left.

"He's got Mr. Hopscotch!" Sam yelled as the lights went out again.

Sam felt someone rush past her towards the lab coat guy. She would have bet everything she had that it was Tasha.

She was right. Up ahead in the darkness, she heard Tasha grunt as if she was locked in combat.

Someone hit someone else very hard. And the loser flopped to the floor.

People were shouting around trying to find out who was hurt. A blue beam of light cut through the darkness, casting everyone around it in an eerie glow. Sam squinted into the light to see that it was coming from the head of Dean Futuro's cane.

Dean Futuro casually leaned on the cane, surveying the scene with a sneer. Sam noticed a series of other tiny lights and possibly buttons that twinkled and blinked along the length of the cane like jewels. In the dark she could see faint staticky sparks swirling around Dean Futuro in an organized pattern, making a bell-like shape around him.

He had a force field of some kind.

"Children, be quiet," Dean Futuro said in a very aggravated voice. "Which one of you is messing with my power?"

"That would be me," the lab coat guy said happily.

Tasha was lying on the floor, possibly unconscious, next to the mysterious guy in the lab coat. In the blue glow Sam finally got a clear view of him. He had white hair, made blue by the light, and he had lost a lot of weight, but Sam recognized him immediately.

"Jerry?"

He smiled at her.

"Actually, it's Nero."

"Nero?" That name was coming up too often lately. "Like Alexander Nero?"

"Very good, Sam," he said. "Alexander Nero Sr. was my father."

"The man who bravely built his company on research stolen from his closest friends," Dean Futuro added.

Slowly Nero's smile melted into a scowl.

"Do you really think this is the proper time to make me angry? Especially considering I've just shut down all of your defenses with my electromagnetic pulse generators."

"Oh, I still have defenses at my disposal, dear boy," Dean Futuro said with a devilish glint in his eye.

Sam suddenly noticed that several campus security guards had used the darkness to discreetly mingle into the crowd.

"Please," Nero said disapprovingly. "You're resorting to physical violence already?"

"What can I say, it's a classic." Dean Futuro shrugged.

"Believe me, I'd like nothing better than to beat the snot out of your goons and snap that cane of yours in half, but I have a very tight schedule to keep," Nero said, checking his watch. He idly crammed Mr. Hopscotch into his other pocket as he spoke.

"In, three, two, one."

A bright red glow on the west wall caught Sam's eye. Red flames were licking their way out of the thin crack between the double doors. People backed away.

The doors burst open, and the flames snaked their way into the ballroom, encircling the panicked students and teachers.

"Everyone remain calm," Coach Powers said again. Several of the teachers echoed him.

"This is awesome."

Sam turned to see who had said such an obviously stupid thing.

Sick poked at the flames with one of the Klingons' swords. He pulled it back and examined the places where it had touched the fire. It was completely unharmed.

"These are the most amazing special effects I have ever seen," Sick said to Nero, formerly Jerry. "How do you do it?"

Now that she thought about it, Sam realized that if the fire was real, the room would be filling up with smoke right now, setting off the sprinklers, and the floor would look burnt or something, but it appeared completely fine.

"Ow." Wrong had put his entire hand into the flame. It obviously hurt him, but when he yanked it back out his hand looked fine.

Nero laughed.

"Big C," he shouted. "Come and introduce yourself. You have a fan."

A figure appeared in the doorway. It walked straight through the fire without even flinching. As it emerged from the flames, Sam saw that it was a handsome, tall man with long, red hair. He wore silver armor with a writhing gold dragon on the chest plate. A dozen tiny red sparks flew out of his right hand like a swarm of fireflies buzzing into the crowd. Suddenly all of the security guards slumped to the floor.

Several of the sparks were dive-bombing Dean Futuro's force field, but each one fizzled away as it hit.

"We've got three for pickup Cervantes," Nero said.

So it was Cervantes. Sam had never really bothered to imagine him as anything more than a cartoony vampire before. But seeing him in person, he looked remarkably like a real person--a real person with a strange fashion sense and more magical power than anyone else on the planet.

And his roving eyes had landed on her.

"You." His eyes turned red as they locked onto Sam. He hunched over like a cat ready to pounce.

"Down, boy," Nero ordered. "We have a schedule to keep, remember? There will be time for revenge later."

Cervantes flashed his fangs at Nero, but reluctantly stood up straight again. "Who do you want?"

"We need Mr. McQueen, Dr. Frost, and Miss Dalal," Nero said, pointing at each of them in turn.

"Leave them alone," Sam yelled. "Take me."

She didn't know where that came from, but she stood by it. Nero just laughed.

"The funny thing, this whole thing was actually set up to kidnap you," he said spreading his arms. "Then Cervantes here would tear your mind apart to reveal your oldest friend. But now you are completely useless, so I'll let you keep your brain. Congratulations."

Cervantes snapped his fingers and Zack, Doc Frost, and Zoey vanished in bursts of green light.

"Very cool," a boy in a New York Yankees uniform said as he waved his hand through the air where Zoey had been standing.

People actually started clapping and cheering as if this was all some sort of elaborate Halloween magic act. But Sam was too worried about her friends to bother to correct them. She knelt down to check on Tasha.

"Thank you, thank you," Nero said with a gracious wave. "But we really must be going."

Cervantes ignored Nero, keeping his focus on Sam instead. The smile spreading across his face didn't seem to contain any joy, just teeth.

"Run," Tasha said as she sat up, trying to place her body between Sam and Cervantes.

A burst of lightning crackled over her shoulder, striking Cervantes in the chest. He howled in pain as the force of the blast knocked him backward through the double doors.

Nero snapped his pocket watch shut.

"Later," he yelled as he ran for the door, leaping through the flames along the way.

"Got another one of those?" Tasha asked someone behind Sam.

Sam turned her head to see Coach Powers standing next to her with the ray gun still trained on the double doors. A spark of electricity danced on the tip. It clearly wasn't just for show.

"Just the one," he said. "And I think it just made him mad."

Sam looked back to Tasha. "What happened to Zoey and Doc Frost?"

"They're fine," Tasha said, nursing her head. "It was a teleportation spell. The maximum range is two hundred yards. They didn't go far."

"Then we have to find them."

"We have to get that bear back," Tasha said to Coach Powers.

"The teddy bear?"

"Yes," Tasha said, standing up. "It is a very important present from her parents."

"I see," he said with a weighty nod.

"And we have to save Zoey and Doc Frost," Sam said, just in case either of them forgot. She left out Zack, but they should probably save him too. If they had time.

"I can't just leave all these students," Coach Powers said, clearly torn.

But a quick look around revealed that the students were fine. Most of them seemed to be having a good time. They probably still thought this was all some sort of magic show, anyway. In fact, a crowd had formed near the refreshments table, where laughing students were throwing different bits of food into the red flames. The few students that did seem freaked out were gathered around Mr. Norton and the other chaperones.

No one was standing around Dean Futuro though. Not that Sam was surprised. He seemed to be studying Sam, waiting to see what she was going to do.

"Right, let's go," Coach Powers said.

"Where are we going?" Natch asked.

Sam, Tasha, and Coach Powers turned as one to stare at Natch. In all the excitement Sam had completely forgotten about her date, who had been standing by her side the entire time.

"Uh, I don't think you want to go with us," Sam said as politely as she could muster under the circumstances.

"Stay here with Dave," Tasha said.

"I have absolutely no idea what is going on here," Natch started. "But I'm going with the guy with the laser blaster."

"Fine, come on," Sam said. They didn't have time to argue.

They quickly ran into their first obstacle, the ring of fire.

"Just run through it," Tasha yelled.

"Are you nuts?" Natch asked.

Tasha ran through the fire, screaming in pain the entire way. When she made it to the other side her entire body was shaking and she was breathing heavily, but she looked fine.

"It hurts as much as real fire, but it doesn't do any physical damage," she said.

"Yeah, right," Natch said.

"Just go," Coach Powers bellowed, shoving Natch and Sam through the flames.

The pain was insane. Every inch of Sam's body was instantly fried. She forgot that she even had arms and legs and became nothing more than a ball of pain. It was so intense she just hoped she would pass out.

And then it was over.

Coach Powers had pushed Sam and Natch the entire way through the flames. All three of them were breathing heavily and patting their bodies to put out the non-existent flames.

"What kind of crazy stuff are you people into?" Natch asked, still patting his shoulders.

Tasha rolled her eyes at him.

Coach Powers led them out of the back door of the ballroom and out into the crisp October night. It was a good thing the moon was almost full; without the lights on, Sam could barely see where she was going.

"It's so dark," she said.

"Jerry's EMP fried the circuits of every electronic device on campus," Natch said bitterly. "Except for the Dean's cane and your laser pistol, for some reason."

"That's because they use a crystal-based technology. No circuits," Coach Powers said. "But most of the school still uses old-fashioned circuits and wires."

"Where did-"

The rest of Natch's question was lost in the loud whirring of a helicopter flying overhead. Hanging from the bottom of the helicopter was the prototype hovercar from Doc Frost's lab.

Silently they crept down the side of the Student Union until they reached the corner. From here they could see four large cargo helicopters sitting in the parking lot. Several men in black uniforms were quickly loading computers, robot pieces, and entire filing cabinets into the two helicopters furthest away. A few of the men were trying to figure out how to get the ion cannon to fit in the third helicopter, but Sam was mostly concerned with the fourth and nearest helicopter.

Zoey, Doc Frost, and Zack were being forcibly led into the helicopter, their hands bound by the same blue energy bands Constable Albion had used on Sam. Zoey turned around and pounded on Nero with her bound fists. He swatted her away. Fortunately, Doc Frost was able to catch her before she fell.

Nero pushed both of them into the helicopter ahead of him and closed the door. Sam wanted to rush out and throw open the helicopter door. Tasha must have realized this because she placed her hand on Sam's shoulder to stop her.

"We have to save them," Sam whispered.

"We will. But we have to save the bear first," Tasha whispered back.

But as the helicopter blades began to spin, Sam saw that they had failed on both counts. Nero was sitting in the co-pilot's seat of the helicopter, with Mr. Hopscotch still in his pocket.

"Shoot the helicopter," Tasha ordered Coach Powers.

He looked from her to the ray gun in his hand.

"If I miss I could hurt everyone inside."

"Then don't miss," Tasha said.

"Aim for the back or something," Sam suggested.

Coach Powers took a deep breath and aimed at the helicopter, which was now a foot off the ground and rising quickly.

Bang.

It took Sam a moment to remember that Coach Power's ray gun didn't go bang.

Bang. Bang. Bang.

That was a gun. A real gun.

But Sam thought the campus security guys only carried tasers.

It wasn't a campus guard; it was Agent Rosenberg. She was firing a pistol up at an angry dinosaur the size of a semi truck. Nero must have used the Lantern of the Blue Flame on one of the fossils in the Palentology building.

The only dinosaurs Sam knew by name were Stegosauruses and Tyrannosauruses. This was neither. But it was big and had a mouth three times the size of Sam's head filled with dagger-like teeth.

"Dinosaur!" Natch yelled.

"Zombie dinosaur," Tasha corrected.

"Cool."

In the back of her brain, Sam had to admit that it was extremely cool. Too bad it was seconds away from eating Agent Rosenberg.

A blast from Coach Powers's ray gun knocked the dinosaur backward, giving Agent Rosenberg the opportunity to roll away to safety.

She looked over her shoulder to see her rescuer. Her eyes locked onto Sam. "What are you doing, Powers? Get them out of here."

Coach Powers looked confused and embarrassed for a moment. He looked at Sam and the others as if he was just now realizing he had brought a group of teenagers into a war zone.

"Shoot it down," Tasha commanded, pointing at the rising helicopter.

Coach Powers snapped back into fighting mode. He raised his gun and then immediately lowered it again.

"It's too high," he said reluctantly.

Indeed, the helicopter was already flying over the big glass dome of the Norman Borlaug Agricultural Science building.

"We have to get the bear back from Nero," Tasha protested.

But before they could argue the point any further, Agent Rosenberg shouted at them again. "Get them out of here, Powers!"

Coach Powers looked at Tasha with pleading eyes.

"Fine," she said, grabbing Sam's arm. "Let's go."

Tasha had only dragged Sam ten feet when they heard a pain-soaked scream behind them. They turned around to see Agent Rosenberg writhing on the ground. Her right shoulder was soaked in blood. The dinosaur had clawed her with its giant foot.

"Tasha, get Sam to safety," Coach Powers yelled over his shoulder as he charged at the dinosaur with his ray gun spitting lightning.

"This is nuts," Natch said, watching Coach Powers fire repeated energy blasts at the very angry dinosaur as two campus guards in hockey goalie gear pulled Agent Rosenberg out from beneath the snapping beast.

"Run," Tasha urged.

The three of them ran in silence for several minutes between the blacked-out buildings before coming to a stop near the lake. From here campus looked extremely creepy without any of the lights on. The occasional dinosaur roar didn't help matters either.

"Where are we going?" Sam asked.

"We have to contact someone. The BEA might be able to track the helicopter," Tasha said in a panicky rush. "Otherwise we'll never be able to find him."

"I know where he's going," Sam said.

Tasha looked at her in complete amazement.

Natch just stared at her in complete confusion.

"I cracked the final clue," Sam said with profound joy. "Okay, I guess I didn't, technically it was-"

"Where?" Tasha cut off her rambling.

"Vegas. The Camelot casino."

Tasha slapped her forehead. "Of course. Who would ever think that your parents would hide it with the McQueens? Oh, and that's why Nero took Zack. He probably knows all about the casino's security."

"Cracked the clue? Who talks like that?" Natch asked the night air.

Tasha ignored him. "Okay, how are we getting to Vegas? Think, think, think."

She tapped her left temple and walked in a tiny circle for a few seconds.

"Got it," she said with a snap of her fingers. "The horses."

"What horses?"

"The stables," she said. "Come on."

"Oh, you mean those horses," Natch said pointing over to the horses galloping along the edge of the lake with sword-wielding security guards on their backs.

Tasha swore loudly.

In the distance they saw another helicopter taking off. Sam couldn't tell if it was the one with the computers or the one with the ion cannon. It was probably bad news either way.

"Uh, we got company," Natch said.

Sam and Tasha followed his gaze. There was a light bouncing towards them.

"Get back," Tasha ordered. She drew an arrow from her quiver and took aim at the light.

But as it drew closer, Sam could hear the familiar hum of a moped engine. She recognized Lucas immediately despite his Lone Ranger hat and mask. A half-full trick-or-treating sack hung from the handlebars.

"What's with the arrow?" he asked.

"Sorry," Tasha said lowering her bow.

"And what was with the PG-13 language Tasha?"

Sam stepped forward. "Jerry is Bad Guy, except his real name is Nero. He set off a bomb or something that fried all the electronics on campus, he kidnapped Zoey, Doc Frost, and Zack, and is on his way to Las Vegas to get the Witch Hunter's Gauntlet right now."

She stopped to catch her breath.

"Jerry? Really?"

Sam could have sworn Lucas was actually impressed.

"Wait. The glove is in Vegas?" He slapped his forehead. "Camelot!"

"Yes," Tasha said. "How did you know that?"

"There is a giant replica of Excalibur there. I saw it during the Video Game Finals. I should have figured that out weeks ago."

"Its okay," Sam said, patting him on the shoulder.

"Right now we have to get the word out to somebody who can stop Nero," Tasha said.

"My phone is dead," Natch said angrily shaking his cell phone.

"Wait a minute," Tasha said. "Lucas, you were off campus, right? Gimme your phone."

Lucas had to turn his gun belt a bit to reach the cell phone in his pocket. He handed it to Tasha.

Tasha stared at the phone for several seconds while chewing on her bottom lip.

"Feel free to call long distance. It's covered by my plan."

"It's not that," Tasha said. "I just realized I don't actually know my parents' phone number. Or how to reach the BEA."

"Brilliant," Natch yelled.

"I programmed them into my phone so I wouldn't have to remember."

"Smart."

Tasha sneered at Natch. He sneered back.

"Okay, fine," Lucas said before things could get out of hand. "How about 911?"

"And tell them what? That a teenage billionaire and his pet vampire are on their way to Vegas to steal a magical glove that will let him conquer the world?"

"Vampire?" Natch asked quietly.

"No," Lucas said slowly. "We could say that someone is going to rob the casino or something."

Tasha shook her head. "Even if they checked it out they'd be no match for Cervantes."

"The BEA then. Ask the operator for the number."

Tasha actually laughed. "Right, because all secret government agencies have their numbers listed with the local operators."

"Okay, sarcasm noted. Not helping," Lucas said. "Any other ideas?"

"We have to get to Vegas. We have to stop them," Sam said.

Everyone looked at her in silent surprise.

"Oh come on," she said. "We're all thinking it."

Natch raised his hand. "I wasn't."

She continued. "Okay guys, my parents wanted me to protect the Witch Hunter's Gauntlet. I can't escape that. It's like my job or something, but I honestly can't ask any of you to risk yourselves to-"

"Knock it off, drama queen," Tasha said, shaking her head. "Of course we are going to help. Right, guys?"

Lucas exploded with laughter. "Is that a real question? I've been waiting for something like this my whole life."

"Really?" Sam challenged. "You didn't even know vampires and wizards were real until a few weeks ago."

"True, but I had always really, really hoped."

Boys.

"We still need a way to get to Vegas," Tasha said. "And fast."

"I think I know a way," Lucas said. He patted the back of the moped seat. "Hop on, everybody."

"Yeah, no thanks," Natch said taking a step back. "I really don't feel like running off into battle with the Last Starfighter, Nancy Drew, and Buffy the Vampire Slayer here."

"But this is exciting. And important," Lucas said.

"I've got zombie protocols to follow," Natch said, walking away. "Good luck on your suicide mission, though."

"There are zombies?" Lucas asked, looking around hopefully.

"Zombie dinosaurs, actually," Tasha said.

"Where?" He looked around some more.

"We don't have time for this. We have to save the world now."

"Fine." Lucas slumped forward onto the handlebars. "All aboard."

Tasha gestured for Sam to get on the moped first. It made sense for Tasha to sit on the back so her quiver and bow wouldn't be crushed. That meant, however, that Sam had to sit in the middle, pressed up against Lucas with her arms around his waist.

He didn't seem to mind, though.

If anyone in town knew there was a problem at the school, they hid it well. The town was pretty quiet, but it was after eleven o'clock, so everyone was probably at home gorging on Crackerjacks and fun-sized Kit Kats.

It wasn't until they were a block away that Sam realized Lucas was taking them to Doc Frost's house.

Lucas pulled into the driveway and cut the engine.

"Anyone know how to break into a house?" he asked.

"I don't think that will be necessary," Tasha said. She climbed off the moped, walked up to the front door, and picked up a rock lying next to an empty flowerpot by the door. She turned the rock over and slid the back off, producing a key.

"You would think someone with an arsenal of superweapons in his basement would have a better security system than the old fake rock," Tasha said. "But you know how these brilliant eccentrics work."

Tasha swung the front door open. "This was your idea Lucas. Lead the way."

Lucas led them to the garage where he pulled the canvas off of Doc Frost's candy apple red '66 Mustang with a SALLY1 license plate.

"Ta da."

"We're stealing Doc Frost's car?" Sam asked.

He held up a hand to stop any more questions while he scanned the garage.

"Yes!" He grabbed a set of keys hanging on a nail.

"Lucas," Tasha began as Lucas climbed into the front seat. "This is all well and good. But we'll never catch a helicopter with a car."

"We will if we fly."

He started the engine.

"Oh, hey. What do you suppose will happen if I put it in H?" Lucas asked as he pulled back on the stick shift.

A bright blue light appeared under the car as it lifted an inch or two off the ground.

"That's amazing," Tasha said. Sam remembered that Tasha didn't take physics and so had never seen the hoverboard demonstration. Of course, it was still amazing to Sam and she had seen the demonstration.

"But I thought he was still working on the Model T?"

"He probably is. But the Model T wasn't the first car. It was just the first mass produced car. The first car was the Model A." Lucas grinned proudly.

"Smart thinking," Tasha said, rummaging through Doc Frost's Christmas lawn ornaments. "But we're going to need more than that if we're going to go up against Cervantes."

She yanked the sack right out of the plastic Santa's hand. "Let's go shopping."

They followed Tasha to the basement. They tossed everything that could even remotely be a weapon into Santa's sack.

"Fire or ice?"

Sam dropped the wind-generating gun she had used earlier into the sack and looked up at Lucas. He had the freeze ray in one hand and the heat ray in the other.

"Which do you prefer?" he asked.

She thought about it for a moment. She figured she was less likely to hurt herself or anyone else with the freeze ray.

"Ice."

He handed her the blue ray gun.

Lucas pulled the plastic six-shooters out of the gun belt of his costume, set them on a table, and slid the red ray gun into the holster on his right hip. Sam did the same, replacing her pirate pistol with the freeze ray.

"Hey, maybe we could bring him." Tasha said, pointing at the robot.

"No," Sam and Lucas said together.

"Fine," Tasha said annoyed. "Just a thought."

She picked up the Perma-glue gun and studied it for a moment before setting it aside. It was probably more trouble than it was worth.

"You know we're all going to prison, right?" Tasha said. "Even if we somehow pull this off and save the day, we'll still probably go to jail for exposing a major secret like the hovercar. Not to mention all this other stuff."

It seemed worth it to Sam. They would all probably end up in prison if Nero took over the world, too. At least this way only the three of them would suffer, instead of the whole world.

She looked to see if Lucas agreed.

He was smiling.

"I've already figured that part out." He picked up the Perma-glue gun. "You two just keep loading up on the weaponry. I'm going to go make us a little disguise."

He ran up the stairs.

"How do you disguise a flying car?" Tasha asked.

Sam shrugged.

"So, how are things between you two?" Tasha asked tossing a mechanical spider into the bag.

"I don't know."

Sam wasn't sure if she should be mad at him or if he should be mad at her or if anyone should be mad at anyone.

"We should probably just focus on saving the world right now," she said.

After they tossed everything that looked like a weapon, and several things that really didn't, into the bag, they rushed up stairs.

Lucas stood in the garage proudly admiring his work.

"Wow," Tasha said.

He turned around, startled. Then he gestured to the car like those models on *The Price Is Right*. Sam and Tasha couldn't help but laugh. Lucas had used the glue to attach all eight of Santa's reindeer to the front of the car.

"I'll drive," Tasha volunteered.

"Yeah, no. Believe me, I have experience with this kind of thing," Lucas said very confidently.

"Shotgun then," Tasha yelled, running for the passenger seat and taking her quiver off so she could sit in the car without crushing it.

Sam climbed into the back seat with the bag of weapons.

"Comfortable back there, Sam?" Lucas asked, sliding into the driver's seat.

"I guess," she said. The sack next to her was bulgy and awkward. Plus she had a terrible feeling that more than one of the items inside might blow up.

Once everyone was seated, Lucas turned to Tasha with a mischievous smile. "Ready, Robin?"

"As ready as I'll ever be."

"All right then. Atomic batteries to power, turbines to speed."

And with that they shot up into the night sky.

Chapter 21

The One-armed Bandits Strike

They flew for over an hour in relative silence except for the occasional navigational update.

It turned out that flying off to an epic battle in a far-off city was a lot harder than Superman made it look.

Fortunately they had Lucas' cell phone, which had access to MapQuest.

Sam tried to do anything but think about where they were going and what they were going to have to do, but once they had gotten out of the mountains and out over the boring desert, there was very little to distract her.

"I actually kind of wish we could have brought some of the school's security with us," Sam said out loud for the first time.

"That would ruin the 'surprise' part of our surprise attack," Tasha pointed out. "Turn right. Stick with this highway. It will take us all the way there."

They were on the final stretch now. The cold slab of fear in Sam's stomach was pressing on her chest from the inside.

Mom. Dad. Zoey. Doc Frost. Mr. Hopscotch. Helen and Harold. Johnny Depp. The whole world.

She kept reminding herself of everyone she would be letting down if she didn't do this.

"Remember; when we get there, follow my lead. Don't do anything stupid." Tasha said this last part directly to Lucas.

"Hey. I know you're the boss here. I'm just super-psyched to be a part of the team. I just hope we're going to get there in time," he said, stepping on the gas (or whatever flying cars ran on) a little harder.

"Look."

Sam saw it up ahead, poking out of the endless black desert, a point of light reaching towards heaven. As they got closer, she could see a blanket of lights spread out around the bright beacon.

"That's the light on top of the Luxor pyramid. That's our target," Tasha told Lucas.

The city of Las Vegas rapidly grew larger as they approached. Sam had always wanted to go there someday. Now she wanted nothing more than to pretend she had never heard of it.

Mom. Dad. Zoey...

She closed her eyes and scolded herself for being such a coward.

Lucas took the car higher so it would be harder to see from the ground. Thankfully, not many people were looking up into the sky for a '66 Mustang.

"There's the Strip," Tasha said, pointing to Las Vegas' main road.

From here Sam could see the casinos clearly. The Luxor pyramid was black and shiny, with the Sphinx crouching nearby. The Statue of Liberty was on the next block, and down the road stood the Eiffel Tower.

Sam had never seen so many lights in her life. The street was so bright that the people on the ground probably had no idea that it was even night. One building had so many lights on one side that they formed a twenty-story television screen. The screen switched from some circus act to a giant smiling Sara Berlin. Apparently she was performing live at one of the casinos today. A tiny part of her brain hoped that they could actually save the world in time to catch the show. It would be a Halloween miracle.

"There's the castle. Land us on that flat part of the roof over there."

Sure enough, the Camelot Hotel and Casino was the spitting image of a fairy-tale castle. There were seven tall white towers, each capped with bright red and blue spires, and over the main entrance stood a mechanical statue of Merlin waving his wand over the crowd below. But from their vantage point in the sky she could see that, behind the fancy fake castle walls, there was a patch of normal roof with vents and pipes and all the practical stuff a building needed.

Sam could make out individual people on the ground now. Men in suits and women in evening gowns stepped out of a limo next to a family of four piling out of their SUV. There was no helping it now; people were pointing up at them.

"Wave," Tasha said. "Make it look like we are part of a show."

Sam and Tasha waved to the now-cheering crowd below. Cameras were flashing everywhere.

"Ho ho ho," Lucas yelled over the side of the car.

Lucas swung the car around one of the towers and set it down gently on the roof a few feet away from a maintenance access door.

"Well, we're here," Lucas said with a quiver in his voice.

"I don't see a helipad anywhere. That's good. That means they had to land somewhere else and drive here," Tasha said, doing her best impression of an optimistic leader. "If we are really lucky, we may have actually beaten them here."

"I suppose so," Lucas said, stepping out of the car. "Otherwise they are going to know we're here, now."

"How? All that any of those people down there know is that Santa Claus just landed at the Camelot. Even if Nero hears about it, I don't see why he'd immediately assume it was us," Tasha said, as if saying it out loud would somehow make it true.

Sam handed Santa's Bag o' Superweapons to Lucas so she could climb out of the back seat.

Tasha put her hand on the door. "You two don't need to do this. This is my job. I can-"

"We've been through this," Lucas said sternly. "We're all in this together."

Tasha smiled. "All right. But if you die, promise that you won't come back as a ghost and haunt me."

"Is that really an option?" Lucas asked, a bit too excitedly.

"Just promise."

"Promise."

"Here we go," Tasha said as she turned the knob.

Nothing happened.

Tasha sighed. "The door's locked."

"Well, there goes the world," Lucas said, his shoulders slumped. "Everybody's doomed because some diligent maintenance man did his job properly."

"Just a second," Tasha said with annoyance.

She pulled an arrow out of her quiver and jammed it in the doorframe above the lock. The door hissed and smoked and emitted a horrible burning chemical smell. Something black and bubbly oozed down the door.

"Acid arrow," Tasha explained.

"Awesome." Lucas applauded.

"Let's go," Tasha said as she pulled the door open.

As soon as Tasha stepped through the door, alarms went off throughout the entire building.

"What'd you do, what'd you do?" Lucas yelled.

"That wasn't me," Tasha said calmly. "That's a fire alarm. I think Nero is here."

Sure enough, Sam could hear the panicked screaming of the people below. She ran over to the edge of the building and saw hundreds of people running out of the casino. Huge plumes of familiar red flames erupted from the windows below. In the distance, fire trucks were already fighting their way through the traffic.

"The police and firemen will be here soon," Sam told the others when she got back to the door.

"They won't be able to put that magical fire out. We're on our own for now." Tasha nocked an arrow in her bow and led the way into the casino.

The emergency lighting had kicked in and mixed with the glow of the magical flames to bathe everything in a wavy red light. It turned out that they had snuck into the hotel part of the casino. They found themselves sneaking down hallway after identical hallway of numbered doors.

After ten minutes of running down random hallways, Tasha stopped dead in her tracks. Lucas would have crashed into her if he hadn't grabbed a nearby doorframe at the last minute.

"You're up, Video Game Boy," Tasha said. "Which way?"

Lucas looked up and down the long hallway. "I have no idea. I wasn't in this part of the casino. We need to get to the main floor."

"Fine. This way to the stairs," Tasha said, pointing at a sign with a picture of a staircase next to an arrow.

As they ran down the stairs from the thirtieth floor to the twenty-ninth, Sam felt extremely thankful that they were going down. There was no way she would survive running up all these stairs. The world would be doomed.

They didn't see a single person as they ran down the stairs. The casino had to be mostly evacuated by now, and if Tasha was right, the firefighters were going to be busy outside fighting the magically reproducing flames. They were completely alone.

It didn't help that Lucas was quietly humming the *Mission: Impossible* theme song behind her.

He finally stopped when they reached the main casino floor. Along with the rows and rows of slot machines, black jack tables, and roulette wheels were several tapestries and suits of armor to give the place a medieval feel. In the center of the room stood a fifteen-foot replica of Excalibur stuck in a giant anvil.

Nero was already there.

He wasn't alone. A big military looking guy had Zack in an arm lock. A few feet away stood a very bored Cervantes and floating next to him was a cage made of red magical energy. Doc Frost and Zoey were unhappy but unharmed in the cage.

Sam, Tasha, and Lucas slowly and quietly crawled their way closer to the giant sword, weaving their way through the rows of slot machines and occasionally stopping to take a peek at the situation.

"Okay, Carlson. Break his arm," Nero said to the big guy.

"Go ahead," Zack said calmly. "I already showed you the vault. I don't know what else you want."

"The gauntlet was not in the vault," Nero said angrily. "It has something to do with this sword."

"I can't help you," Zack said.

"Leave him alone," Doc Frost demanded.

"Okay, here is how things are going to go down," Nero announced. "Mr. McQueen is going to show us where the gauntlet is hidden and then Dr. Frost and Miss Dalal are going to come back to my lab and build me a fleet of hovertanks. And do you know why all of these things are going to happen?"

No one responded.

"This is going to happen, because if any of you refuse to do what I ask, then my friend Cervantes over there is going to kill you and then I will bring you back as a zombie and you will do anything I ask anyway. But that is messy and I'd rather not waste the time."

"You're a very disturbed young man," Doc Frost said.

"Come on, Dr. Frost, you especially must appreciate this situation," Nero began. "There is a war coming. You know it and I know it. That is why Dean Futuro is funding your hover research. But I respect you more than he does, which is why I am offering you, and you too Miss Dalal, a chance to join the winning side."

"No offense, kid," Doc Frost said. "But up until an hour ago I didn't even know who you were. You really think you can wage war on magic and science at the same time?"

"No," Nero said with great relish. "I intend to let them fight it out and then pick up the pieces."

He gently set the Lantern of the Blue Flame down on the floor so he could tap the sword. It sounded solid to Sam. She was only a couple rows away now.

"You're up, teddy."

He pulled the bear out of his pocket and held it near the sword. It instantly began to shake and beep in his hand.

"Interesting."

Nero examined the bear. He pulled on a seam, ripping the bear's belly open. Hidden inside the fluffy stuffing was a black box similar to a garage-door opener.

Lucas clamped his hand over Sam's mouth to keep her from screaming out. They were only a couple aisles away now and any noise would have given them away.

"Of course," Nero said. "Dr. Hathaway figured out how to make a tesseract after all. Where better to hide something than nowhere?"

He pushed the button.

And then things got really weird.

A bright pale blue floating dot appeared in front of the giant sword. The dot hung there in midair doing nothing until Nero reached out for it. The dot unfolded into a larger glowing orb that swallowed his arm. Everything beyond his elbow simply disappeared. But apparently this did not freak Nero out.

"This is bad," Tasha whispered. "Are you ready?"

"Ready?" Lucas whispered back while releasing his grip on Sam. "Ready for what? Do we have a plan?"

"No time for a plan. There are three of us and three of them, which one do you want?"

"Between the commando guy, the undead wizard, and not-Jerry? Hmm, let me think," Lucas whispered back sarcastically.

The look he received from Tasha would have made Darth Vader shake in his shiny black boots.

"No time," she repeated.

Tasha rolled across the aisle, putting some distance between herself and Sam and Lucas. She popped up and fired an arrow at Nero's back.

"Sir," the commando guy yelled in alarm. He released his stranglehold on Zack and lunged towards the arrow even though there was no chance of him stopping it from hitting its mark.

But the arrow didn't hit its mark. Somehow Cervantes caught the arrow in mid flight.

He snapped the shaft in half with his right hand and turned to face Tasha just in time to catch a second arrow fired directly at him.

"Ah, a Beaumont, I presume." Cervantes said. "This finally got fun."

He flung a ball of red energy at her. She took off running, dodging and weaving between the rows of slot machines.

"Learn to aim, loser," Tasha called behind her.

With a wild snarl, Cervantes launched himself into the air and charged after Tasha. The chase quickly took them out of Sam's range of vision. But from the rage in Cervantes's growls, Sam could tell Tasha was holding her own.

Suddenly a cardboard display advertising the Camelot Midnight Buffet Special exploded on the other side of the room. Zack had used the distraction to escape. He was running at full speed across the casino with the stun-gun-wielding Commando Guy in hot pursuit.

"I'll get him, sir," Commando Guy yelled as he fired another burst of stun gun energy that sparked harmlessly on a statue of King Arthur.

It was now two on one.

"Not good," Lucas said.

Only now did Sam realize that while she had been watching Zack escape, Nero had somehow pulled the gauntlet out of its invisible hiding place.

"And now the world is mine," Nero announced to whoever may have been listening.

The gauntlet was amazingly elaborate. It was made of gold and silver and some reddish metal Sam couldn't name. Silvery lines twisted their way up the gauntlet toward the fingers like vines wrapped around an old statue. Several different-colored jewels were set along the vines like budding flowers.

"There is still time to call all of this off," Doc Frost pleaded from his cage. "You don't know what that glove will do to you."

"Oh yeah, I'm really falling for that old trick," Nero said mockingly.

He held the gauntlet up appraisingly. The gemstones began to glow, and purple sparks danced between the fingers. There went the slim hope that Nero wouldn't be able to activate it. They just could not catch a break.

"Here." Lucas pushed the bag of weapons over to Sam. "Find something good in there to cover me. I'm going in."

Before she knew what was happening, Lucas had run out from their happy little hiding place and was charging straight for Nero. He collided with Nero, knocking the gauntlet to the floor.

"Lucas, you idiot," Nero yelled as he brought his elbow down on Lucas' back.

Lucas couldn't help but scream in pain. Nero lifted him up by his belt and threw him against the red floating cage. He made a clanging sound as if the bars were made of solid steel.

"Lucas!" Zoey cried.

"Are you okay?" Doc Frost asked, reaching out through the bars of the cage.

"Fine," Lucas said. He was clearly lying.

"What are you doing here?" Zoey asked.

"You know," Lucas said as he rolled over onto his back. "Storming the castle, saving the princess. It's what I do."

Zoey nervously smiled down at him through the bars.

Someone was laughing.

"Okay, I've got Natasha Beaumont running around with a bow and arrow and Lucas the Boy Blunder playing football star.

So, where is Miss Hathaway?" Nero asked. He had already picked up the gauntlet back up and waved it around, practically begging for someone to try and take it from him again.

It was now or never.

"I'm right here, Jerry," Samantha said with a sarcastic flourish.

She aimed her freeze ray right at his smug face.

Chapter 22

Freeze

Sam was willing to admit it; she had no idea what she was doing. Not only did she not have a plan as to what to do next, she couldn't even remember how she got here. Four months ago, she was just another happy nobody working at the Cookie Emporium.

But here she was, pointing a freeze ray at Alexander Nero Jr.

He stared back at her; unfortunately, he seemed far more amused than the shocked or scared she was hoping for. Lucas, Zoey, and Doc Frost certainly seemed shocked, though. Poor Lucas was still sprawled out on the floor, nursing his back.

"So, what's the plan here?" Nero asked with an annoyingly playful tilt of his head.

I run far away and hide in a deep dark hole, she thought to herself. But she said, "You put down the gauntlet, call off your pet vampire zombie wizard, and let my friends out of that cage."

"Yeah," Zoey yelled from the cage.

Nero simply laughed.

On the far side of the room Tasha and Cervantes were still locked in battle.

Sam could see this was not going to be easy.

"A little help would be good about now, Lucas," Sam said through grit teeth.

"Huh? Oh, yeah." Lucas drew the heat ray from his belt. "Please drop the power glove. I don't know what this will do to a person."

"I do," Doc Frost said darkly.

Nero let out a snort of laughter.

"So scary," Nero said as he slipped his fingers into the gauntlet.

Thin tentacles of pulsing dark purple energy sprang from the gauntlet and wrapped themselves around Nero's forearm.

Sam pulled the trigger.

A beam of subzero crackling blue light struck the gauntlet, knocking it out of Nero's grasp. The purple tendrils dissipated into thin air.

"No!" Nero yelled as he groped for the gauntlet.

Sam kept the freeze ray trained on the metal glove, adding more and more layers of ice.

"Ahhh," Nero reached for the gauntlet and the icy beam caught his hand. He recoiled in what Sam hoped was excruciating pain. He tucked his right hand under his left armpit.

With a maniacal laugh, he pulled Mr. Hopscotch out of his left pocket and flung him at Sam. The bear caught the beam and landed at Sam's feet covered in ice.

"Mr. Hopscotch!" Sam cried as she released the trigger and bent down to examine the bear.

"Now give me that heat ray, Lucas," Nero growled.

"Heh, yeah. That's happening," Lucas said with a small, forced laugh.

"It wasn't a request," Nero said. He leapt at Lucas, who fired a shot of red-hot energy at him, but Nero dodged the blast and caught Lucas by the throat, lifting him into the air.

"I'm a lot stronger than I look, huh?" Nero said as he took the heat ray out of Lucas' trembling hand.

"Put him down," Sam yelled loudly, trying to cover up her fear. She trained her freeze ray back onto Nero.

"Catch."

Nero threw Lucas at Sam. She did her best to catch him, but he hit her too fast and the two of them fell in a heap on the floor. The freeze ray slid out of her hand and skittered across the floor.

"Oh, oh, ow," Sam said as Lucas' knee dug into her stomach.

"Sorry," Lucas croaked. He wasn't looking too good as he rolled off of her. "I don't think we're winning."

Sam got to her feet first. She extended a hand to help Lucas up. He was heavier than she expected. While they were just trying to stand up Nero had been using the heat ray to free the gauntlet from the block of ice.

"Hey, look what I've got," Zoey said triumphantly.

Zoey waved a blue computer chip at him from inside the cage.

"How?" Nero checked his lab coat pockets. "Back at the school, right? That's why you attacked me. You little pickpocket."

"Aw, poor you," Zoey said with big, mocking puppy-dog eyes.

"Zoey! Pass me the chip," Lucas yelled as he ran for the cage.

Nero charged toward the cage also. He raised the heat ray, but didn't fire. He was probably afraid of hitting the chip.

Zoey stretched out her arm as far as she could so Lucas could grab it as he ran by.

"Come and get it, Jerry," Lucas said as he ran for the elevators, the chip clenched tightly in his right hand.

"My name isn't Jerry," Nero yelled as he fired a burst of heat at the fleeing Lucas.

Sam saw her chance and took it.

She sprinted toward the ice-covered gauntlet and scooped it up into her arms.

"No!" Nero screamed into the vast empty casino. "Cervantes, get the boy. I need that computer chip back. I'll handle the girl."

Sam took a moment to glance over her shoulder. Nero was racing after her, and he was running nearly twice as fast. She looked forward just in time to see that she was sprinting headlong into a bank of nickel slots. She clipped her hip on the nearest machine, but kept running for the unmarked double doors ahead.

She found herself in a hallway with many doors. She ran past all of them, hoping Nero would assume that she was hiding behind one of them and check them all.

The double doors burst open just as she rounded the corner. She could hear the sounds of him frantically opening doors behind her. There was no telling how much time that would buy her.

"Just give me the gauntlet so I can save the stupid world," he yelled.

Icy cold water dripped down her arms as she ran. The gauntlet was melting quickly. She needed to find a hiding place right now.

Hopefully Lucas was having a better time.

Lucas stuffed the computer chip into his pocket as he sprinted down the hall. The quickly forming stitch in his side made him think that maybe he should have spent a little more time outside and a little less time playing video games. But how could he have ever predicted that someday he would need to outrun a vampire?

Well, okay, he had actually entertained the idea since he was eight. But he never really thought it would happen.

"There is nowhere for you to run, boy," Cervantes called from behind him.

"Oh okay, I guess I'll just take your word on that," Lucas yelled over his shoulder.

It was just ten more steps to the elevator.

But then a vicelike hand gripped him by the shoulder.

"You're mine now," Cervantes said in his creepy vampire voice.

Lucas tried to shake him loose and run, but a cold chill ran from his shoulder to his feet, freezing him in place.

And then the elevator *dinged*.

Before the doors had opened even an inch, an arrow shot out and sailed over Lucas' head. The angry scream behind him told Lucas that the arrow had hit its mark. Cervantes released the grip on his shoulder, and Lucas tumbled forward.

"Come on." Tasha grabbed his hand and pulled him into the elevator with her.

As the doors closed again, Lucas turned in time to see Cervantes pull the arrow out of his forehead.

"Nice shooting," Lucas said.

Tasha pushed the button for the top floor. "Not really. It will only make him mad."

"I'm okay with that."

"Where's Sam?" Tasha asked. Worry etched itself across her face.

"I don't know. She took the gauntlet and ran one way. I took this computer chip from Zoey and ran this way." He showed Tasha the chip as proof.

"What's on it?"

"My brain," he said, gently turning the chip over and over in his hand.

"Kind of small isn't it?" she asked.

He gave her a nasty look and she smiled.

"Why does he want a copy of your brain?" she asked seriously.

"I think he's planning to use it as a control chip for his hovertanks. They would be programmed with all of my moves from Hyper-Urban Assault," he said, sliding the chip back into his pocket. The image of thousands of copies of himself spreading destruction across the world flooded his mind.

"So let's just break it," Tasha said.

"I'd love to," Lucas said. "But as long as Nero wants it, we can use it."

Tasha looked at him appraisingly. "You sound like you have a plan."

"We hop in the car and go somewhere far away and draw Cervantes away from here, giving Sam a chance to escape."

"Sounds like a plan to me."

The elevator finally stopped. Tasha held out her arm to keep Lucas from stepping out first.

She slowly poked her head out of the elevator.

"The coast is clear," she said, waving him to follow her.

They ran up the stairs to the roof, and still no Cervantes.

"Go, go, go," Tasha yelled as they ran across the roof to the car.

A gigantic ball of red flames burst through the skylight, spraying broken glass across the roof.

"Now would be good," Tasha urged as she leapt into the back seat.

Lucas turned the key, clicked his seat belt, and threw it into H.

The car lifted off the roof.

An unearthly roar bellowed from the broken skylight as Cervantes rose into the air atop a great flaming bat.

Lucas spun the car one hundred eighty degrees around and stomped on the gas pedal. He suddenly realized he knew nothing about Las Vegas and had no idea where he was going. But anywhere was better than here, so Lucas pointed the car at anywhere and floored it.

A dozen police cars and fire trucks sat outside the casino below. There was a crowd of nearly a thousand onlookers watching the fire. Except now they were all witnesses to Santa's Mustang tearing across the sky with a giant angry flaming bat in hot pursuit.

"Keep it steady," Tasha yelled at him.

A glance in the mirror revealed that she had her bow and arrow out and was shooting at Cervantes.

"On your right," she yelled.

He looked and saw a burst of lightning crackle two inches away from the car. He leaned hard on the wheel and the car made a ninety-degree turn to the left. But now he was on a collision course with the fake Eiffel Tower. He cranked the wheel just in time to whip around the tower. A burst of flame exploded on the steel beams.

Something exploded behind them.

"What is he doing now?" Lucas asked.

"Oh, that was me," Tasha said cheerfully. "Exploding arrows."

"Awesome."

"Down, down," Tasha yelled.

"But-"

"Down!"

He glanced up and saw hundreds of little red sparks streaking through the sky above them. Lucas aimed the car down, zipping between the casinos.

The neon lights of the Las Vegas Strip whipped by in a blur as they sailed mere feet above the cars. The red sparks were sinking lower. He didn't know what would happen if they touched him, and he didn't want to find out, but they were forcing him down to stoplight height.

Up ahead he saw his only chance. A group of expensive low-profile sports cars sat at the red light. If he did it right, there would be just enough room.

"Heads up," he yelled over his shoulder.

He gunned the engine and lined up all eight reindeer to shoot though the gap between the cars and the stoplights. The NO RIGHT TURN ON RED sign missed his head by just a couple inches.

"We've got to get out of here," Tasha screamed behind him.

As he glanced up he saw that the sparks were getting closer. But on the left side of the road he saw a large gap between the buildings. Large enough that he could risk taking the car and the reindeer in at high speed.

He whipped the car into the gap and came face-to-face with a pirate ship. Dancers in brightly colored pirate costumes screamed and leapt off the riggings into the water below. Lucas pulled back on the wheel, and the car shot up into the sky. One of the front reindeer caught on the crow's nest and snapped off.

"Sorry, Dasher," Lucas said as he leveled off above the casino. The tiny red sparks harmlessly popped on the building below them.

Suddenly the entire world went red as the great flaming bat rose up in front of him. Cervantes' grinning maniacal face was coming straight for them. Lucas instinctively reached for the button to fire his missiles, but then he remembered that he was flying a '66 Mustang, not a hovertank. They were in serious trouble.

Arrows flew past him from the back seat. Two of them bounced harmlessly off of Cervantes' chest. The third stuck in his shoulder. But if it hurt him, he didn't show it.

"Not good," Tasha growled.

"I have an idea," Lucas said. "Hold on tight."

Lucas spun the car completely around while nudging it ever-so-slightly forward. As the car swung around, the reindeer picked up speed and collided with Cervantes at ninety miles per hour. Four more reindeer snapped off, but Cervantes staggered back on his giant bat, nearly falling off. Lucas took the opportunity to fly away at top speed.

Suddenly the unmistakable tones of "The Imperial March" rose from Lucas' pocket. Not only was it a completely bizarre time to be getting a call, Lucas had never even put that ringtone on his phone. He just had to answer it.

"Hello?" he said cautiously into the phone while steering with the other hand.

"Hey, man. How's it going?" Natch asked.

"Kinda busy right now," Lucas said, swerving between some palm trees. "Running away from the love child of Count Dracula and Lord Voldemort, how about you?"

"I'm fine," Natch said joyfully. "He's gaining on you by the way."

Lucas checked his mirror and saw that Cervantes was, in fact, catching up with them again. Tasha fired another arrow at Cervantes. She had to be running low by now.

"Where are you?" Lucas looked around the street for any sign of Natch.

"Esteban's room. The power is back on."

"Really." He couldn't believe it. Esteban finally let someone into his room. "What's it like?"

"You wouldn't believe me."

Natch mumbled something Lucas couldn't understand. It sounded like he was arguing with someone. "Fine. I'm asking, I'm asking. How's Zoey?"

"She's fine. Trapped in a magical cage. But fine."

Natch mumbled again.

"Good," he said finally. "Listen, there are two large shiny black buildings ahead on your right. You should be able to hide between them if you hurry."

"How do you know this?" Lucas asked while slipping the car into the space between the buildings. Cervantes flew past them in a blur of flame.

"Esteban is borrowing one of the Dean's wanderwindows," Natch said.

"What is a wanderwindow?"

"Turn to your left and smile."

Lucas found himself staring at a cloud of shimmering silver gnats. He raised his hand and the gnats followed, vaguely taking the shape of an arm. As he waved, the cloud waved back. It even copied him making the Vulcan hand-signal thing.

"I see you," Natch said slowly. He was clearly having a lot more fun with all of this, probably because he was miles away from the angry undead vampire wizard.

"Okay, that's creepy, but right now we need to keep this doohickey away from Cervantes," he waved the chip at the cloud of gnats.

"Do you have a piece of string?" Natch asked.

Quickly he explained his plan to Lucas, who in turn explained the plan to Tasha.

"That could work," Tasha agreed, ripping a piece of string out of the hem of her costume.

"What about Sam?" Lucas asked simultaneously into the phone and to Tasha.

"The BEA has to be on their way right now." Tasha actually began to laugh. "I mean, there is no way that they could have missed the flying car or the giant flaming bat."

Lucas cracked a smile. "Good point."

"They will save Sam and the others," Tasha added. "We just need to buy them as much time as possible."

"It sounds like a plan," Lucas announced into the phone. "Call us back if you see anything."

He hung up the phone and gunned the engine. The car shot out from its glassy hiding place. He stayed as high as possible, away from the tourists, as he snaked his way through the neon canyons of Las Vegas.

A flash of fire in the rearview mirror caught his attention. "How's our little surprise coming?"

"Finished," Tasha said, holding the modified arrow out for him to see.

"Hold on," he yelled as he pulled the car up and over a twenty-story parking garage.

The car's mirrors were awash in red flame. Two gigantic burning hands were closing in around them. Lucas jammed the accelerator down as far as it would go. They were rocketing through the sky at speeds way beyond reckless, but they still weren't fast enough.

The fingers tightened around the car, pressing on the sides and interlocking in front of the windshield. Lucas had to squat down in the driver's seat to see through the tiny gap between the fingers. It didn't help that he was driving three times faster than he would have liked away from the bright lights of The Strip into the dark unknown industrial side of Las Vegas.

"Lucas." Tasha drew out his name in a long nervous whisper. She kept her bow taut and ready.

"Wait for it, wait for it," he said, wiping the sweat from his forehead.

Lucas could barely see anything, but he could hear the telltale chugging sounds below that let him know that he was exactly where he wanted to be.

He squinted through the three-inch gap left in front of him. It wasn't much, but it was enough.

"There!" he yelled. But the arrow shot through the gap before he could even finish the word.

"Got it," Tasha said triumphantly.

They lurched forward as the hands clasped around the car, forcibly stopping it in mid-air.

Lucas slid out of his seat, doing his best to crouch under the steering wheel, away from the flames. Electrical sparks of pain shot through his arms as he covered his head. There was no escape.

But just like that, the flames receded.

Lucas poked his head up to see the flames retract into Cervantes' hands. The vampire hovered on his great flaming bat next to the car with a smug sneer of victory on his face.

"Hello, children," he said in a silky voice.

"The great Cervantes, reduced to a sad little puppet," Tasha shot back.

Lucas laughed drawing Cervantes' venomous glare.

"That's right, I am a puppet." He brushed his hair back with his ring-laden left hand. "For now. But I am alive, or a near approximation, and if Master Nero's plan succeeds, I will be reunited with the only thing worth living for."

Cervantes held out his right hand.

"Give me the chip," he said flatly. "Or I'll kill you where you stand."

"Yeah, slight snag there Fang Boy," Tasha said. "We don't have it."

His smile mutated into a snarl, exposing more of his fangs.

"You see," Tasha continued with a shrug. "Somehow it got tied to one of my arrows. The arrow I just fired into that freight train below us. Sorry."

Cervantes growled in exasperation as he eyed the high-speed freight train bound for New Hampshire chugging away at over 300 miles per hour.

Please let this slow him down long enough for Samantha to get away, Lucas thought just as he felt the white-hot tingle of one of Cervantes's sparks entering his forehead.

Chapter 23

Victory and Defeat

"Hello, casino patrons," Nero's voice seemed to come from every direction. "We are having a special on hostages on the main floor. These hostages can be saved for the low, low price of just one Witch Hunter's Gauntlet. This is a one-time limited offer. So anyone who would like to keep their friends and favorite teacher from being harmed should hurry on down."

Clearly Nero had found the casino's intercom system. Wonderful.

But what Sam really needed to know was whether or not he was bluffing. He seemed to want Doc Frost and Zoey to work for him, so he probably wouldn't hurt them. But what if he had captured someone else?

She had no idea what had happened to the others while she was hiding in the casino's massive laundry room. Nero hadn't bothered to check the dryers for her, but while he was searching he might have found Tasha and Lucas, or Zack, or just an innocent vacationer who hadn't managed to evacuate in time.

She could be facing Nero, Cervantes, and Nero's bodyguard with nothing more than a frozen metal glove.

A frozen metal glove with amazing magical powers!

Except it clearly didn't have any interest in her. Nero had held the thing for three seconds and it tried to grab his arm; she had spent nearly half an hour huddled in an industrial-sized dryer with the glove and it hadn't done anything except drip water on her.

Maybe the gauntlet didn't think a girl who couldn't even manage to bake idiot-proof fast food cookies was worthy of wielding fantastic power.

Or maybe it just didn't work when frozen.

Sam kicked the dryer door open and crawled out. She figured she could thaw the glove in the dryer in a couple of minutes. The noise would probably give her away, though.

"Don't even think about it," Nero said over the intercom. "Just bring it out to the main floor."

She stood frozen in place. How did he know what she was doing?

"This is a casino, Sam. There are cameras everywhere. I can see everything you do. You have three minutes to hand over the gauntlet."

She couldn't shake the feeling that she should be doing something extremely clever right now. Like in the movies. But she wasn't feeling particularly clever at the moment.

"Get moving, Sam."

She sneered at the nearest camera as she walked by.

"Almost there," Nero boomed from above when she reached the double doors.

"Shut up." She shoved the doors open.

Doc Frost and Zoey were still stuck in their floating cage in the middle of the room. Zoey saw Sam first and made motions for Sam to hide, but it was too late for that. Nero's bodyguard had stepped in behind Sam, blocking her path to the door. Sam kept walking toward Zoey's cage.

The sound of laughter caught her attention.

"You really should have left the building when you had the chance," Nero said as he held the heat ray in one hand and the Lantern of the Blue Flame in the other. "But I am a nice guy and you are useless now. Give me the gauntlet and you can leave. Go. Get out of the way."

"Really? Now, why don't I believe you? Oh yeah, maybe because you sent vampire cheerleaders to kill me."

Nero sighed dramatically. "Which would not have been necessary if you had simply let the whirlybot come to me. No doubt my message would have been a lot more useful than that silly riddle your father gave you."

"Your message? Why would you get a message?"

And then it all finally made sense to her.

"Does your dad's middle name start with an S?"

Nero smiled. He even lowered the heat ray, although he kept it tightly in his grip.

"Very good, Sam. Just as the whirlybot was programmed to find you if your parents were dead, it was programmed to go to my father, Alexander Sebastian Nero Sr., if you were also dead or otherwise unavailable. After my father's death I became the next in line. All I needed to do was initiate an Alpha Level threat. It was really just a happy coincidence that I could frame you for the theft of the Lantern of Blue Flame and then use it to resurrect Cervantes. If Constable Albion had been even the slightest bit capable, you would have been taken away to a nice magical prison somewhere and I would have inherited the whirlybot message and the Witch Hunter's Gauntlet. I sent the vampires because I figured a little mortal danger would give you the incentive to figure out your riddle."

Sam snorted with awkward laughter.

"So I guess I should be grateful you decided to have me sent to jail instead of just killing me, and then attempted to kill me later?"

"Exactly."

A horrible thought occurred to Sam. "You! You disguised yourself as me to rob the vault! Gross!"

She had suffered a lot lately, but being confused with a boy was more than she could take.

"Yes, well. That was humiliating for me too."

He set the Lantern of the Blue Flame down on the floor and held out his now-empty hand.

"Just hand it over and everything will be fine."

"Why don't you tell her the whole story, Nero?" Doc Frost said from his cage.

"What, and give away my entire evil scheme?" Nero yelled in a perfect imitation of an over-the-top cartoon super-villain. "Never!"

Doc Frost continued. "My guess is you weren't completely sure the message would come to you. After all, Samuel could have deleted the message to your father when he discovered he had been stealing Samuel's father's inventions."

"I admit my father was less than perfect. All of you ordinary people are. That is why he spent four hundred and fifty million dollars on my development and training," he said, examining his own hand. "I was tutored by the greatest teachers and masters around the world. My very DNA was perfected to make me stronger, faster, and smarter. I am the ultimate life-form on this planet. And I'm the only one who can save it."

"Blah, blah, blah," Zoey said, making talking motions with her right hand. "Maybe your father should have spent another fifty million on your hair."

Sam noticed that Zoey was very subtly pointing to the left with her other hand. She was pointing at the sack of weapons that was still lying behind the bank of slot machines three rows over. But with Commando Guy watching her, there was no way Sam could make a run for it.

"I had heard rumors that your father had invested large sums of money in genetics research. Genetic manipulation is a messy business; the slightest mistake can have horrifying results. I never would have imagined that he would risk tampering with his own son's life," Doc Frost said dryly. "Still, four hundred and fifty million dollars is mighty impressive. But then, your father was always good at making money. First by selling his father's inventions, then by stealing ideas from his best friend's dead father. It took years for Samuel to finally accept that Alexander had betrayed him. It is just a shame that Alexander never really took the time to understand what he was stealing. Maybe then he, Samuel, and Joanne would still be alive."

Nero's eyes narrowed. Sam was positive that Doc Frost had struck a nerve with that last comment.

Doc Frost turned to Sam. "Your grandfather was a brilliant scientist and a good man. But sometimes his scientific curiosity overrode his better judgment. One of his last inventions turned out to be infinitely more dangerous than he ever could have guessed. It was quite possibly the single most amazing scientific discovery since fire. But like fire, in the wrong hands it could cause untold damage. To his dying day, your grandfather worked to protect the world from what he viewed as the greatest folly in history. It was Alexander Nero Sr.'s attempt to access this technology that resulted in the destruction of Hathaway Manor. The whole incident was classified top secret by the BEA; that's why no one has been able to tell you. I'm terribly sorry."

Doc Frost's eyes were filled with so much pain and remorse Sam could barely look at him without tearing up. She couldn't imagine how difficult it would be to keep a secret like that from someone. Before she could tell him she wasn't upset, Nero started laughing.

"Pathetic," he said, shaking his head at Doc Frost. "Seriously, this is your great plan? Trying to get Samantha so mad that her anger will activate the Gauntlet."

Sam looked at the gauntlet in her arms. It hadn't changed at all, except that more of the ice had melted and dripped down her shirt.

"Not a bad plan," Nero said, as if evaluating a young child's artwork. "Except Samantha here isn't a naturally angry person. She doesn't have the fire of anger in her heart. Do you, Samantha? No. I'm sure if your parents had lived long enough to see the whiny weak mediocre mess you really are they would have entrusted the gauntlet to someone worthy.

"You see, the Witch Hunter's Gauntlet was designed to be worn by heroes, people with strong wills, purity of heart, and clarity of purpose. The more focused the wearer, the stronger the magic. It won't even spark for someone like you. It demands someone worthy; someone who understands power and has the strength of will necessary to feed it and control it. Someone like me."

He took a step forward, his hand still outstretched. She clutched the glove even tighter. Her arms ached from the effort.

"See," he said, taking another step.

It was true, she could feel it, the glove wanted to leap out of her hands.

"Just run, Sam!" Zoey yelled from her cage.

Nero sighed and rolled his eyes at Zoey. "We've done all that already. Please pay attention."

Nero slipped his goggles down over his eyes.

"Sam, we both know I can take that from you at any time. The world is in trouble, Sam, more trouble than you can possibly imagine; it is time for a new hero. So I am asking you nicely to just hand it over."

Sam could feel the gauntlet pulling away from her. For a second she swore she saw a spark of light dancing deep within one of the gauntlet's sapphire flowers, but when she looked closer, it was gone. The gauntlet was waking up, she was sure of it.

It just didn't make sense. Aside from herself, Sam figured Nero was the least heroic person in the room.

"Heroes don't start wars," she said.

"Maybe not, but they do win them," Nero said proudly. His expression quickly turned grave. Sam thought she actually saw fear wash across his face. "And war is coming, with or without me. A war unlike any other in the history of the world."

He pointed an accusing finger at Doc Frost.

"Why do you think they're designing hovertanks, or plasma cannons, or invisibility suits, or magic-detecting satellites? For fun? For the sheer scientific thrill of it all? For education?"

He shook his head and laughed.

"Open your eyes, Sammy. They're preparing for war. The magical community knows that we are only a generation away from surpassing them. They've been happy to live separately from us primitive savages for centuries, comforted by their own superiority. But now that we are on the verge of becoming their equals, they are forced to decide between being overrun by us inferior brutes with our filthy clanking machines or striking first while they still have the advantage."

"No one wants a war!" Doc Frost yelled. His eyes were bloodshot with worry and anger.

"Oh, we both know that's not true," Nero said in a silky-smooth voice. "But don't worry, my way we win with a minimum number of casualties, and the millions that do sadly perish will be reanimated by the Lantern of the Blue Flame as a cheap and obedient workforce."

Sam had never heard anything so horrible in her life.

"You can't do that!"

"Uh, yeah, pretty sure I can," Nero said with a proudly cocked eyebrow and a gleam in his eye.

"If you want to be a hero so badly why don't you try to stop the war?" she asked, hoping to somehow reason with him.

"Oh, the symmetry of it all," Nero said. "My father asked your mother the very same question once. Imagine it, with war on the horizon, the nearly assured destruction of our way of life, and Joanne Hathaway was the first person in hundreds of years to wear the Witch Hunter's Gauntlet, a weapon that finally put us on an even playing field with the most powerful of wizards, and what did she do with it? She used it once to destroy Cervantes and then hid it away just to make those terrified old warlocks happy. To keep the peace."

He practically spat out those last four words.

"And then when my father went looking for weapons to even the odds, your parents killed him. To keep the peace."

He took another step forward. It was unmistakable this time; five of the gemstones facing Nero were clearly glowing.

A sixth gemstone, a golf ball-sized ruby, lit up.

A devilish smile spread across Nero's face.

"See, I told you it was drawn to power and those who know how to use it."

Before Sam could process what was happening, Nero lunged forward, tore the gauntlet from her arms, and shoved her through the air. She flew ten feet before slamming into the marble floor.

Sam sat up gasping for air. Her ribs hurt and her arms were on fire from having frozen metal viciously dragged across them. But none of her physical pains compared with the numb hollow sensation of failure she felt looking up at Nero's triumphant smile.

"Gorgeous, isn't it? Those old mystics really knew how to craft a weapon, didn't they?"

Nero held the gauntlet up like a trophy, turning it slowly.

Every gemstone on the gauntlet was glowing now, spitting out little sparks of reds, and blues, and yellows, and greens that somehow melted together to form a brilliant purple light that flowed around the gauntlet as if it were a liquid, occasionally crackling with violet lightning.

"Still a little frozen."

He fired a quick burst from the heat ray into the gauntlet before tossing the ray gun aside. He poured out the water before slipping the gauntlet on over his right hand. It was like the whole room was suddenly alive with static electricity; Sam could feel the gauntlet's raw power tickling the exposed skin on her arms and face.

Sam watched as the purple light flowed across his skin until it had completely cocooned Nero. No one made a sound.

In a flash the cocoon dissolved into a million little sparks. Nero stood amongst them, smiling, in a dark purple suit of armor with big unnecessary shoulder spikes, a long flowing purple cape, and an N-shaped serpent on the chest plate. And, of course, it glowed faintly, as if it wasn't already amazing enough.

"So cool," Nero said, admiring his new armor.

Bolts of electricity crackled between the spikes of his armor.

"Impressive," a voice boomed from the ceiling. "I suppose I should be flattered."

Cervantes gently floated down next to Nero, making the similarities between his armor and Nero's armor all the more noticeable.

"Ah, Cervantes, I was beginning to worry that Tasha had turned you into a cloud of dust. I believe you have something for me."

Cervantes dropped a computer chip into Nero's waiting hand.

"This is part of a cell phone," Nero said before crushing the chip in his hand.

"They must have swapped it as a last act of defiance," Cervantes said without a trace of concern on his handsome face.

Still, those words hit Sam like a hail of knives.

"What did you do to them?" she asked, slowly rising to her feet.

A thin smile spread across his face. With a snap of his fingers, two green sparks fluttered down from the roof until they hung in the air beside him. With a flash, the sparks turned into Lucas and Tasha.

They instantly crumpled to the floor, unmoving, their eyes closed.

From where she stood Sam couldn't tell if they were breathing, or if they had been… bitten.

"You monster!" Doc Frost yelled from his cage. Tears rolled down his face. "Nero! This is what you are prepared to unleash on the world? This thing! They were children! You soulless monster!"

Sam felt tears running down her face too. If the worst had happened, well, she couldn't let herself believe it.

"Shall I silence him?" Cervantes asked, his right hand already raised and glowing red.

"I need him alive-"

"I'll never help you," Doc Frost spat. "I'll-"

"Oh, don't worry about it," Nero said dismissively. "As soon as I master the necessary spell I'll erase all of your nasty little memories of this ever happening. You'll be more than willing to help me then. Until then I suggest you just calm down; there's no sense in getting all worked up about something you won't ever remember."

Doc Frost lunged at the bars of his cage. The bars crackled as they burned into his clothes and skin, but it didn't stop him. The red energy bars were beginning to bend.

Nero sighed. "I had hoped we could deal with this as adults. Have it your way. You can be my first experiment."

Two blue bands of magic flew out of the gauntlet. One wrapped around Doc Frost's body like a straightjacket while the other wrapped around his mouth, gagging him.

Doc Frost fell backwards. Zoey rushed to his side.

"See, that wasn't so hard," Nero said to Cervantes. "You were a better teacher than I thought. Congratulations. With my superior mind and your tutelage I will master every spell you know by the end of the week."

"You are too kind," Cervantes said, clearly not meaning a single word.

"Now then, there are still hundreds of spells to try. Let's start with something easy." Nero waved his right hand, and a few dozen rose petals appeared and gently floated to the ground.

"Not bad. Let's try something a little bigger."

He raised his left hand, and dark fluffy storm clouds poured out, filling the ceiling. Thunder rolled inside the building, and a warm rain began to fall.

A drop of rain hit Sam right in the eye, shocking her back to her senses. She scanned the room. Everyone else was just as enthralled with Nero's new abilities as she had been. Even Nero's bodyguard was staring in total awe at his boss, completely ignoring Sam--which seemed fair to her, since she was now exactly zero threat, with no weapon, no skills, and no idea what to do.

She figured that at this very moment there had to be literally a billion people on the planet that would be more useful in this situation than her. She really wished a few of those people would show up.

No one came.

Maybe the world was used to having Hathaways save it. Too bad it got the wrong Hathaway this time.

Then she remembered the sack of freaky super weapons just a few rows away.

"Fine," she mumbled to the rest of the world.

It was time to do something stupid.

Chapter 24

Something Stupid

Sam didn't know anything about magic, but she had seen enough movies to know that the only thing stupider than saying "at least it can't get any worse" was standing around while the bad guy reached full power.

Slowly she sidestepped her way to where the bag of weapons sat.

"Abracadabra."

Nero barely twitched his finger and a row of slot machines tore free from the floor and hovered in the air.

"Presto chango."

The slot machines twisted and folded like some giant demented origami, the metal screeching as it rubbed together and tore apart, coins jingling as they sloshed around inside the tangled mess. In seconds, the dozen or so slot machines transformed into a long flying dragon with razor-sharp claws, a line of levers running down its back like spikes, and eyes that constantly kept spinning through images of cherries and lemons and sevens. The metal dragon wagged its tail and looked up at Nero like a loyal dog. It even smiled, if such a thing is possible, revealing long metal teeth while happily chirping and dinging away as if someone had just hit the Mega Million Dollar Jackpot.

"Transfiguration," Cervantes said, gesturing to the dragon. "It takes the average wizard years to master such a feat, but animation, that is a master-level spell. You may actually be as powerful as you claimed."

"Restoration is also a master-level spell," Cervantes said rising an inch into the air like a happy cartoon character. "We must perform the ceremony immediately."

Nero clearly did not share his enthusiasm. As Sam crept closer to the bag, she watched his face closely in case he spotted her, but he was clearly far more interested in his newly created dragon than anything she did or Cervantes said.

Cervantes's eyes narrowed, and his lip curled slightly to reveal a fang beneath.

"Master Nero," he said tersely. "I trust you remember our deal."

"Not now, Cervantes." Nero said offhandedly as if he were addressing an annoying child.

Cervantes floated closer to Nero. "I ask for but this one favor in exchange for an eternity of service."

"First of all, you really have no choice." Nero gestured to the Lantern of the Blue Flame sitting on a slot machine stool three rows away. "And secondly, right now I'm more interested in what exactly Miss Hathaway thinks she's doing."

A ball of green and purple smoke crashed into the floor between Sam and the bag of weapons, spreading across the four feet of marble tile separating them. The floor beneath the smoke bubbled and hissed. Sam stopped dead in her tracks, a mere inch from the vile swirling mess.

"Run, Sam!" Zoey screamed, but Sam was too terrified to process the words.

All she could think about was the triumphant smile on Nero's face. She could see a world war reflected in the lenses of his goggles, millions of people turned to zombie slaves because she was too afraid to do something about it.

She leapt through the writhing smoke.

The right leg of her cheap cotton pirate pants instantly turned black as it came down inside the smoke. She could feel her left leg burn and bubble. Her momentum carried her through the swirling fumes; but, unfortunately, she instinctively bent down to grab her leg. She tumbled forward, landing on the bag. Some sort of dart burst out of the bag an inch from her left arm; she figured she must have landed on a trigger.

Sam grabbed the two frayed ends of the newly rotted hole in her pant leg and pulled, extending the tear up to her knee. A four-inch long green-and-purple blister oozed down her leg. She knew nothing about burns or bruises, and absolutely nothing about magical injuries, but it was numb for now. It was going to hurt like crazy soon, she was sure of that, assuming she lived long enough.

She heard a distant playful voice shout, "Sic her."

Ding. Ding. Ding.

The slot-machine dragon cocked its head and stared at Sam with triple cherries in its eyes. It raised its tail and opened its mouth like an angry cat... or a dragon about to spit fire.

A hail of coins flew out of the dragon's mouth so fast that they embedded themselves into the slot machines next to Sam, and the dragon was swiveling its head toward her. In another second she was going to be shredded by tokens. Sam sprang to her feet, seized the bag with both hands, and ran as fast as she could down the row of slot machines.

Behind her she could hear that the hail of coins had been replaced by the fierce rhythmic scratching of the dragon's metal claws on the marble floor. It was like a dog running across linoleum, only a thousand times worse. It was also getting closer.

She heard the whizzing sound of flying coins just before something sliced across her left forearm just above the wrist.

The instant Sam reached the end of the row, she dropped to the ground and crawled over to the next row. She reached into the bag and pulled out the first thing she found that felt like a gun. It was heavy in her hand and looked very death-raylike to her.

As she waited for the dragon to stop spewing coins, Sam checked her cut. A thin line of blood was slowly trickling down her arm. Just as she thought to apply pressure to the cut, her protective wall of slot machines stopped shaking. The dragon either ran out of coins or was planning something worse.

Sam popped up, took aim at the dragon, and fired.

A four-pronged grappling hook shot out of the gun and hooked onto the metal beast's head. The dragon reared up and pulled the gun out of her hands.

"Stupid Curse," Sam yelled as she ducked back down just in time to miss the next volley of coins. Sam always knew that the Sam Curse loved making her look stupid in public, but she never thought it was actually trying to get her killed.

"You know, if I die you die too," she said to the Curse. "Let's work together here."

Sam dug through the bag for something that looked like a laser gun or a disintegration ray or a metal-dragon melting beam. The pounding sound of coins on metal grew louder and louder, and the slot machine against her back was shaking more and more. Sam slid to the side just in time. The slot machine she had been hiding behind exploded, spraying coins and twisted bits of machinery everywhere.

Without missing a beat, the dragon started pelting her new hiding place. There were only ten more slot machines in this row; she couldn't hide forever. She didn't have time to try every gun in the bag.

A plan formed.

She dug through the bag until she found a gun she recognized, the crazy wind-generating gun. Sam started cranking the gun like mad. In no time it was producing so much wind she could barely hang onto it anymore; it was like trying to hold a hurricane. Next to her sat a pile of coins in the wreckage of the destroyed slot machine.

"Please don't let this be stupid."

In one slick move Sam rolled out from behind her hiding place, landing behind the pile of coins. The dragon opened its jaws and lunged at her. Sam tilted the wind gun up, blasting the pile of coins into the creature's face. One lucky coin went right through the dragon's left eye.

With a sad, painful screech of metal on metal, the dragon slumped to the floor. Its other two eyes stopped spinning. Sam was pretty sure it was dead, or broken, or whatever.

"This is so insane," she whispered to herself.

"So is talking to yourself."

Sam rolled over to see Nero floating above her. Before she could whip the wind gun around, he waved his right hand. The gun flew across the room, shattering against a stone pillar. With his left hand he conjured up a shimmering blue chain that wrapped around Sam, pinning her to the floor.

"You broke my dragon."

"He deserved it," Sam said, staring at the crackling ball of blue and black flame swirling around in Nero's gauntleted palm.

"I'm impressed, truly," Nero said, extinguishing the flame in his hand. "First I was just going to let you leave, then I thought I might turn you to stone, but now that you have proven yourself to be a spunky little fighter, I'm going to erase your memory and have Cervantes turn you into one of my vampire minions.

Personally, I wouldn't want to be stuck at fourteen forever; but then, I hear that vampires are really popular with teenagers these days, so I'm sure you'll be fine."

A white spark appeared at the end of his right index finger. A beautiful tiny point of light that was going to eliminate everything that Sam was or could ever be in less than a second.

Sam struggled against her magical bonds, but it was useless. She wanted to say something witty and defiant, but instead she found herself desperately trying to recall her favorite memories before they were erased forever. Jumbled images of her eighth birthday party when her parents took her to New York City to see the Empire State Building, Tasha threatening to beat up Zack, making homemade pizza with Helen, and Lucas asking her to the Masquerade Ball floated through her brain.

It was such a disorienting sensation that she failed to realize for several seconds that Nero hadn't zapped her brain yet. In fact, he wasn't moving at all. He just floated there pointing at her with a menacing sneer frozen on his face. He wasn't even breathing; he could have been a wax statue of himself.

"Move it, people, nine minutes and counting," a stern voice bellowed. "Clear these civilians-"

"Containment is the priority," a second, even sterner voice yelled. "Restraining and siphoning teams, assemble. Use of lethal spells has been approved."

Sam tried to turn her neck to see who was speaking, but the magical chains around her only tightened more.

An army's worth of footsteps stomped all around Sam. There were so many sounds; yelling, running, the humming of machinery. Sam couldn't make out what was going on. A shimmering blue crystal cage grew around Nero, leaving only his gauntleted right hand exposed.

Finally someone leaned over her. It was Deputy Colver. She hadn't seen him since that day at the mall, but she wasn't likely to ever forget the face of a wizard who tried to arrest her.

"Let's get you out of that chain," he said, waving his hands over the blue chain. He closed his eyes and winced as if he was in great pain, but the chain dissolved into little shapeless globs of light that winked out of existence.

A hand appeared to help her up.

"Great job, kid," Agent Sampson said, pulling Sam to her feet. "We'll take it from here."

Sam finally had a chance to survey the chaotic scene around her. It was easy to tell the wizards and witches from the ISG apart from the agents from the BEA because one group wore long multi-colored robes and the other wore simple black suits. Both groups were scrambling around Nero and Cervantes. Half a dozen wizards were casting the blue crystal prisons around them. Two balls of sunlight orbited Cervantes' prison. The remaining wizards and witches were positioning themselves around the prisons, either casting protective spells or preparing to attack. Three elderly wizards were huddled around Nero's exposed hand either examining or trying to pry off the gauntlet; Sam couldn't quite tell. But she did recognize Constable Albion shouting orders while checking his time-stopping watch.

For their part the BEA agents were also positioning themselves, weapons drawn, around the frozen duo. A few were even setting up huge fancy ray guns on tripods.

Something red exploded on the edge of Sam's vision. Instinctively she clung to Agent Sampson's arm.

He patted her hands gently.

"It's all right," he said, pointing at the scene of the explosion.

Two ISG witches had cracked open the flaming red cage and freed Zoey and Doc Frost. As she watched the witches dissolve the magical bindings around Doc Frost, Sam realized she didn't know what happened to the rest of her friends.

"Where's-"

"We've already evacuated the others," he said answering her unfinished question. But that didn't tell her what she really wanted to know. She needed to know if Tasha and Lucas were going to be okay.

"And now you have to go too," he said, gesturing to the gold-and-glass exit doors. "You've done amazingly well but we've got less than six minutes to-"

He was cut off by the sound of laughter.

"Suckers!" Nero yelled. He either broke free of the time stop spell or had been pretending the whole time.

The crystal prison around him shattered. Pieces flew everywhere. A large piece of cracked blue crystal whizzed over her head.

"Are you all right?" Agent Sampson asked.

Sam nodded.

"Good," he said briskly. "Now get out of here."

He drew his weapon, the same ray gun he had had in Dean Futuro's office, and ran back toward the center of the casino.

But Sam didn't leave. She had lost too much to leave now. She was going to stay and watch them take Nero down.

Unfortunately, that didn't seem to be happening.

Nero was fighting over forty combined wizards, witches, and BEA agents, and he looked as if he was having the time of his life. Not only had Nero shattered his crystal imprisonment, he had turned the three elderly wizards into three shimmering gold statues. He had also summoned up a floating shield that looked like a black hole. It swallowed up most of the spells and ray gun beams that came near him. The few attacks that hit him barely drew his attention.

"You seriously thought I hadn't planned for your little time-stopping trick," Nero yelled. "I'm insulted."

He waved his right arm and unleashed a wave of gold flame that grew into a large glittering snake that coiled and swooped around the room. It passed through two BEA agents manning one of the giant ray guns, turning them to gold. Other agents rushed to take their place; Sam wasn't sure if it was worth it. Whatever the ray gun did, it didn't seem to be working.

A burst of green lightning arced its way around the black hole shield, striking Nero directly in the face. He tumbled backward, ripping his now-broken goggles off and tossing them aside.

"Sneaky!" Nero yelled.

Chief Constable Albion released a second burst of lightning that curved around, striking Nero in the back and shredding his cape.

"That actually hurt," Nero said, sounding a bit impressed.

Deputy Colver summoned a blue hood and shackles around Nero. As Nero thrashed, bound and blinded, two of the large ray guns shot him in the stomach and back, dropping him to the floor.

Albion slowly waved his right hand in a circle, building a ball of bright white energy. Sam could feel the crackle of the energy from several feet away. When the ball was just slightly larger than a bowling ball he hurled it into the floating black hole.

"Abyss begone," Albion yelled.

The black hole swallowed the ball and then sort of burped itself out of existence. Albion collapsed to the ground; the spell must have taken a lot out of him. A red-haired witch ran to his side, projecting a shield around him. Colver stepped up in Albion's place and magically hurled a slot machine at Nero. The machine clanged against his armored chest, knocking the wind out of him.

"That's it," Nero yelled after regaining his breath. The last of his bindings had dissolved away. "Awaken!"

Cervantes' crystal prison exploded in a fury of red flames.

"Shrouds of Tartarus," Cervantes yelled.

Wisps of black smoke flew out of each hand and wrapped around the balls of sunlight like heavy cloth, smothering them until they hung in the air as lightless moons.

"Attack!" Nero yelled as he rose into the air wildly firing orange sparks around the room. Sam narrowly dived behind a suit of armor to avoid one.

She peeked around the armor to see Cervantes toss three BEA agents into the air. They helplessly passed through the glittering snake, turned to gold, and crashed to the marble floor with a great thud.

Meanwhile, Nero was firing green lightning at the shield around Albion when two BEA agents popped up from behind a statue of Lady Guinevere on a horse and hurled grenade-like objects at him. The grenades clung to his shoulder and back, but instead of exploding, they released a blue mist of some sort. He tried to swat the cloud away.

"Gas?" Nero said, a tad woozy. "Haven't you guys ever heard of the Geneva Convention?"

Judging by the way he started tilting sidewise and lazily floating to the ground, Sam figured it must have been some sort of knockout gas.

By the way he was yawning and shaking his head, it was clear the gas was having a far greater effect than the lasers, which just seemed to get absorbed by his magical armor. The agents must have had the same thought, because when they popped back up they each raised dart guns, like the ones used to tranquilize tigers and bears, and fired at the only exposed skin they could find; his head. Three darts bounced off his armor before one caught him in the neck.

"Dirty cheaters," Nero said in a slow, sleepy voice as he pulled the dart out of his neck. He pointed a finger at his face and shot himself in the nose with a spell.

"That's better," he said, shaking the drowsiness away. "I hope you guys like carrots."

Instantly the agents' guns turned into carrots in their hands. Naturally they stared at the carrots in confusion.

"Shazam!" Two bright white bolts of lightning struck the agents.

The agents vanished. Their empty suits crumpled to the floor. Then one of the pant legs started moving. A small fluffy white rabbit poked its nose out of the cuff, sniffing the air.

When Nero laughed, the rabbit scurried back inside the pants.

Sam knew that if they were going to win--and they really had to win--they were going to need more firepower, and she knew where to find some. She was just going to have to run through a volley of spells and fireballs and lasers first.

You've been training for this for years, she told herself as she ran headlong into the maelstrom. *It's just like dodgeball, without the stupid catching and throwing. Just pure dodging. Or you die.*

No pressure.

Sam leapt over one of Cervantes' fireballs, ducked below an airborne roulette table, and swerved her way through a cloud of multicolored sparks. An orange spark caught her in the wrist, and it felt like her left arm had fallen off. She couldn't feel it or move it; she had to look at it to make sure it was still there, but she kept running.

She tried to stay as low to the ground as possible, jumping over the occasional overturned table as she went. The world had become astonishingly simple. She couldn't hear, smell, or even feel anything. She didn't even really think. All of her effort was put into watching the hundreds of objects flying around her and avoiding them all. It was oddly blissful.

A wall of golden fire dropped down in front of her. It was the great glittering snake. She winced as she came to a dead stop. Her momentum tried to carry the top half of her body forward, her leg muscles strained in an effort to keep her from tumbling forward, and her head flopped forward until all she could see was gold. She was too afraid to breathe, just in case she would breathe in some of the glittering dust and turn her lungs to gold.

Just as quickly as it had appeared, the snake flew up into the air clearing her path. Luckily for her, it didn't seem to have a mind of its own; it just randomly twisted and coiled around the room. She saw her prize lying on the ground, half-buried in debris, about three feet away from Cervantes.

He had his back to her, shielding himself from three simultaneous attacks. Sam knew this was going to be her only chance, so she dove for it.

She landed with a crash on top of the slanted felt surface of a broken roulette table. A piece of the wheel slid onto her leg, poking her oozing bruise, opening a floodgate of pain. Sam clamped her hand over her mouth, but it was no use; she couldn't stop herself from screaming.

Cervantes looked down at her, a charming smile across his handsome face.

"Well now, aren't we the brave one? Your mother and father would be so proud. But answer me this: What imaginary sliver of hope could possibly make you risk your life so foolishly?"

"I have a favor to ask you," she said, trying her best to fight her instinct to curl up and cradle her leg, which felt like it was burning from the inside out. Her goal was more important than her leg.

Sam stretched out her good arm as far as she possibly could; she felt the cool metal right at the tip of her middle finger.

"A favor?" he asked with a mixture of curiosity and contempt in his voice. "And why should I grant you a favor?"

Sam's fingers curled around the metal handle.

"Because I have this," she said, pulling the Lantern of the Blue Flame free from the debris.

Understanding flashed in his eyes. He lowered his head in acceptance. All of the little sparks around him instantly fizzled away.

"Well done," he said with genuine appreciation. "What favor do you ask of me?"

"Bring me the Witch Hunter's Gauntlet."

He instantly lit up with delight. His fangs grew an extra quarter inch, and his eyes danced with a joyous, vengeful gleam. A low, beastly, guttural, and disturbingly joyful growl resonated in his throat.

"As you wish."

He spun around and leapt into the air, his cape flapping behind him. With a loud crack, Cervantes tore the fifteen-foot tall Excalibur replica free from the anvil.

Wielding the gigantic blade with one hand he flew straight for Nero. He sliced through the flaming golden snake as it passed by, causing it to instantly dissolve into little puffs of glitter.

Just as Cervantes was about to bring the sword down on Nero's head, Nero summoned a sword of his own to block the attack.

"What are you-," Nero began. He looked from Cervantes to Sam. "You!"

Sam held up the lantern and proudly proclaimed, "Me."

Nero freed up one of his hands for a second to unleash a torrent of green lightning in Sam's direction. It spread out in all directions farther than she could possibly run to escape it. But it turned out she didn't have to; the red-haired witch that she saw protecting Constable Albion earlier rushed in front of her, projecting a shield.

The witch screamed out in pain as the lightning pummeled her shield. The instant the lightning stopped she dropped the shield and collapsed to the floor. Sam was getting really tired of everyone around her getting hurt because of this stupid glove.

"This ought to be fun," Nero said, parrying Cervantes' latest swing. "I've beaten every other teacher I've ever had. But don't worry; I'll bring you back when we're done."

"Silence!" Cervantes hurled a flurry of red sparks at Nero.

Nero deflected the sparks with his free hand, letting them rain down on the people below. Sam rolled the unconscious witch under one of the few blackjack tables that was still standing and crawled in next to her. Thunder cracked directly above the table, rattling her bones.

Only it wasn't thunder; it was the sound of Nero and Cervantes locked in a mid-air duel. But even under the blackjack table she could feel the impact of each and every sword clash. She crawled out from under her hiding place; she couldn't hide forever. Her plan was only half way done.

"Tempest!" Cervantes and Nero yelled at the same time.

"Oh, what now?" Sam yelled as a sudden and powerful gust of wind whipped her hair into her eyes.

She brushed back her hair to see two tornadoes descend from out of the storm clouds above. The tornadoes thrashed against each other, hurling debris around the room at dangerously increasing speeds while Nero and Cervantes continued their epic duel. Random spells and ray beams criss-crossed in the air, endangering everyone.

"Loser," she yelled up at Nero, her words whipped away by the howling wind.

A bolt of lightning struck a slot machine no more than three feet away from her. She wasn't sure if it was a coincidence or a response; but either way, she scurried away as fast she could. If she stood up, the wind would likely pick her up and fling her across the room, so she was forced to crawl through the rubble, dragging the lantern.

Finally she found the sack of weapons lying next to a half-melted suit of armor. It looked to Sam like people had been walking all over it; a few of the ray guns were scattered in pieces across the floor. She prayed that the one she needed wasn't lost or broken.

She sat crossed-legged on the floor, the wounded leg on top, with the lantern in her lap as she dug through the bag with her good arm.

"Samantha!" Nero yelled in a playfully singsong voice over the roar of the wind.

Sam didn't give him the satisfaction of looking up. She could see the handle of the gun she wanted.

"I commend you on your tenacity," Nero continued while slamming his sword down on Cervantes' armored shoulder. "I am seriously impressed here, but you really didn't think this through, did you? I am wearing the one weapon that has already destroyed Cervantes once before, and I know the spell to do it again."

Sam fished the tuning-fork-pronged sonic blaster out of the bag.

"Solarus!"

Instantly the casino lit up like noon on a bright summer day. Nero's sword had transformed into a slice of pure sunlight so bright that Sam couldn't look directly at it for more than a split second. She focused on Cervantes; his skin was rapidly graying from the sunlight.

"Shroud of Tartarus!" Cervantes hissed.

A solid wall of shadow appeared in midair between him and the dazzling blade.

"Nice try," Nero said, slicing through the blackness.

Cervantes threw more shadows at him, but Nero shredded each of them, laughing all the while and getting closer to Cervantes with every swing.

Sam knew she had to act fast.

"Go deaf," she whispered to the lantern.

At that exact moment two very important things happened: Nero stabbed Cervantes in the chest, and Sam pulled the trigger.

A head-splitting screech erupted from the sonic blaster. Sam felt her teeth rattle in her jaw, and her brain threatened to shoot out of her ears, but she kept her finger locked on the trigger. Everywhere she looked, Sam saw people writhing in pain, their hands clamped over their ears. For the one hundredth time in less than ten minutes, she really wished her left arm still worked.

Most importantly, Nero had been forced to release his sword to protect his ears.

The only person not writhing in pain was the person with the most cause. Cervantes hung in the air with the sun sword run through his heart and sticking out his back, gray ash spread out from the wound consuming his body.

But in his eyes Sam saw neither fear nor pain, but simple determination and anger.

As his body deteriorated into nothingness, he brought his gigantic sword down on Nero. At the last second Nero must have noticed this, because he instinctively raised his hand to defend himself. The sword sliced through his arm just below the Witch Hunter's Gauntlet. The sword, gauntlet, and the rest of Nero crashed to the ground followed by the fluttering ashes of Cervantes' body.

Cervantes was little more than a floating head, but Sam saw that he was yelling something. She suddenly found that she wanted to know what he had to say in is final moments so she released the trigger.

"-eth!"

And then he was gone, his ashes blown away by the dying winds of the shrinking tornadoes.

"My hand!"

Nero crawled forward, his right arm tucked into his lab coat; his armor had vanished the moment his hand was severed, and he had crashed to the floor cradling his bleeding stump. But he was still the closest person to the gauntlet. If he reached it, Sam knew that this whole battle would start all over again.

Sam limped forward as fast as she could. Every step made her leg burn more than the last. But Nero was only inches away from the bloody gauntlet. She wasn't going to make it.

"Ow! Ow! What the-?" Nero screamed. Two rabbits were biting his ankles.

As he stopped to kick the rabbits away, Sam dove for the gauntlet grabbing it by the fingers. To her surprise several of the gemstones lit up. Then she saw the reason: Nero had reached the base of the gauntlet. The stones on his end had lit up, but the ones on her end were still dark.

He laughed a deep maniacal laugh. His eyes were sunken and tired but fueled by pain and rage. More gemstones lit up on his side. Thin tendrils of magic reached for him.

At that moment, Sam realized she was about to become a rabbit or a statue or worse.

I'm going to die. I'm going to die without saving the world. Without making the slightest difference.

The longest second ever ticked by and she was still alive. Nero seemed to be just as surprised and confused as she was.

"You've just doomed us all," he spat at her.

The gauntlet exploded in a burst of blinding green light.

When she opened her eyes, Sam saw that Nero had disappeared, leaving her with half a gauntlet, twisted and broken. And his severed hand.

She threw up.

:

Chapter 25

What Just Happened?

"-an unexpected Halloween treat last night in Las Vegas as thousands of tourists witnessed an unscheduled special effects spectacle."

"Brilliant."

Lucas' head felt like it was about to explode. When he opened his eyes, the sensation only got worse.

"This amateur video was shot by a Tucson man in town for an electronics convention."

His eyes refused to focus; it was like he hadn't used them for years.

"Hey, look at that. You are alive."

Lucas sat up. The blurry image in front of him finally congealed. It was Natch holding a TV remote.

Confused, Lucas scanned the room. He was in some sort of hospital.

And then it all came rushing back to him.

"Jerry is a genetically altered super-bad guy! Cervantes! The gauntlet!" he blurted out. "Did Sam get it? Is she okay? Am I a vampire?"

"Are you a what?" Natch shook his head like he thought Lucas was completely nuts. "Dude, calm down. You are rambling. You passed out in your virtual reality game pod and they brought you to the Student Health Center."

"What?" Lucas couldn't believe what he was hearing. "No, you were there. Sort of. Remember, you called me when I was flying away from-"

He was interrupted by Natch's laughter.

"It happened, it happened. I'm just messing with you," he said, making calming gestures with his hands. "The gauntlet was broken and everyone is fine. And you are not a vampire. You should be so lucky."

"Jerk!" Lucas pulled one of the pillows out from behind his head and hurled it at Natch. He missed by over a foot, which just made Natch laugh even more.

"Check it out, you're on TV."

Lucas hadn't paid any attention to the TV on the wall. Apparently Natch had muted it when he saw Lucas was waking up, but up on the screen he saw shaky handheld camera footage of himself flying Santa's sleigh up over the pirate ship with Cervantes on his trail. The image was too blurry to see who was in the car. Even Lucas couldn't tell it was him.

"The BEA covered up the whole thing by telling people it was all a part of Sara Berlin's stage show," Natch explained. "Apparently weirder things have happened in Vegas."

It was terrifying to watch. At the time Lucas hadn't really realized just how close he had come to being caught. But seeing it now, he was surprised he was alive.

Instinctively his hand reached for his forehead. There was a small bandage taped over the spot where he had felt the little spark of magic enter his head--the spark that should have killed him.

"Oh, yeah, you're welcome for that, by the way," Natch said. "Free of charge."

"Huh?"

"I saved your life, genius. Well, technically Esteban did, but it was my idea." Natch got up and opened the room's tiny closet. "You remember the wanderwindow I used to watch you? It is actually made up of thousands of tiny little flying cameras. We clustered a bunch of them on your forehead right where the spark was going to go. They absorbed most of the magic or whatever, but they did leave a nasty scar. By the way, you'll probably want to get dressed before the nurse gets back."

Natch tossed him a set of clothes someone must have taken from his room. Lucas realized, to his embarrassment, that he was only wearing a hospital gown under his blankets. He quickly scooped up the clothes.

"What about Tasha?" Lucas asked, reaching for his pants.

"She'll have a scar too. You'll be like twins." Natch turned around and covered his eyes. "Now hurry up and get dressed."

"So where are we?" Lucas asked as he crawled out of bed and started getting dressed.

"The Student Health Center, like I said. Since I was pretty much the only person involved smart enough to not get hurt, I got the fun job of sitting here waiting for you to wake up."

"Sorry about that," Lucas said, tugging on a sock.

"Whatever," Natch said. "By the way, your ex-date, Tiffany, was seen making out with some TV star in Paris last night. So I think you two might be officially over."

"Pfft! You know, with everything going on I had completely forgotten about her."

"And after all the work I did to get you two crazy kids together," Natch said with fake indignation.

"What are you talking about?" Lucas pulled his shirt down over his head.

"It was pretty clear that you were going to need help with the whole Sam thing, so while I was busy infiltrating the A crowd-"

"Infiltrating?" Lucas asked.

"Yeah," Natch said, looking at Lucas like he was a sad, naïve child. "This might not be normal high school, but it is still a high school, and high school is war. If I'm going to be stuck with these people for the next four years I want to know everything about them; their strengths, their weaknesses, their secrets. So I spent the last several weeks getting to know the enemy."

"But wouldn't they have learned your secrets and weaknesses?" Lucas asked.

"My secrets are fake and I have no weaknesses," Natch said with a shrug and a smile. "Besides, they were far more interested in your secrets and Sam's secrets. It was the only way I was able to earn their trust. Tiffany really doesn't like me. Fortunately, Tiffany hates Sam more, so after my little documentary at the football game when Tiffany tried to have me thrown out of the group, I offered to prove my loyalty by destroying Sam. I told her that you were Sam's best friend or maybe a little more and it would completely devastate Sam if Tiffany asked you to the dance first. She jumped at the idea. Then I made sure she would find you at the exact time and place Sick and Wrong were going to be filming."

Lucas could not believe what he was hearing. Honestly, who thought like that?

"Why would you do that?"

"To help you, duh," Natch said, opening the door. "It was a win-win situation. If you said yes, you would be world-famous as the guy Tiffany Summers asked out, which would make Sam pretty jealous. If you said no, you would have been even more famous as the guy who turned Tiffany Summers down, and you would have scored major points with Sam by choosing to support your friend rather than go out with her enemy even though she is beautiful and famous."

"Or she could stand me up and fly off to Paris," Lucas added.

Natch rubbed his chin. "Yeah, that was a shocker. Who knew she was that smart? Still, it bought you sympathy points didn't it?"

"You could have told me this plan," Lucas said, slipping on his last shoe.

"This is true," Natch said. "But I didn't trust your acting ability, so it was better to let you make the choice yourself. You chose poorly, by the way."

"I know." Lucas didn't want to think about that, though. "Did you ever figure out why she hates Sam so much?"

Natch waved the question away. "Ah, Princess Tiffany doesn't like anyone who doesn't immediately grovel at her feet. Plus Zack is always filling her head with stories. He has her convinced that Sam runs one of the many Tiffany Summers Sucks websites. The more he can keep her insecure and angry, the easier it is for him to control their clique."

Sadly that sort of made sense to Lucas.

Not that Lucas was any better. Hadn't he agreed to go to the dance with Tiffany to make Sam jealous, angry, and as sad as he was after she said no to him? Was that any way to treat a friend?

He wouldn't blame her if she never spoke to him again.

"Okay, happy face on, we've got to see the others. The BEA guys want to debrief us before they let us go."

Lucas followed Natch out the door.

"Look who's alive," Natch announced as they stepped into the hallway.

A nurse rushed to Lucas's side, checking him over. She shot Natch an angry look. "I told you to alert me the minute he woke up."

"I'm fine," Lucas said politely, trying to keep her away. He didn't particularly feel like being poked and prodded right now.

"He's fine," Natch said with a shrug.

"Then he won't mind answering a few questions," a stern-looking man in a black suit said, clasping Lucas by the shoulder and ushering him into another room.

It turned out to be a doctor's office, which made Lucas even more uncomfortable. A young man in a long brown robe stood behind the desk. Before today Lucas would have pegged him as one of those weird role-playing guys, but now he knew there was a good chance he was an actual wizard.

"Sit," the man in the suit commanded as he sat down behind the desk.

Lucas sat down.

"I am Agent Sampson with the Bureau of Extraordinary Affairs," the man said, laying his badge on the table. "This is Deputy Colver from the International Sorcerers Guild."

The young man in the robe held up a silver medallion Lucas assumed was his badge.

"You are a remarkable young man," Deputy Colver said with an appreciative nod.

"Uh, thanks," Lucas said awkwardly. "I try."

Agent Sampson pulled a computer chip out of his vest pocket and set it down on the table. They must have found it in the car. Tasha had hidden it somewhere in the back.

"Let's talk about your brain."

"It was Dr. Zhang," Lucas blurted out. "He copied our brains to use in robot hovertanks. He's probably working for Jer-, Nero."

"No. I assure you Dr. Zhang is working for the BEA," Agent Sampson said. "And now that his research has fallen into unfriendly hands, we are going to have to redouble our efforts. It looks like you are going to be playing a lot more video games, young man."

"Great."

Sam hurt everywhere. Her adrenaline high had completely worn off, and she wanted nothing more than to sleep for the next week and a half. The orange glow of the morning sun in the Student Health Center's waiting room windows wasn't helping either.

It turned out that, when it wasn't getting beaten down by Nero and Cervantes, the BEA was a highly efficient organization.

They had whisked her out of the casino and into a helicopter bound for Miller's Grove in less than four minutes. In those four minutes, she had to make some very important decisions. As the last Hathaway and the current possessor of both the Lantern of the Blue Flame and the remains of the Witch Hunter's Gauntlet, it was up to her to decide what to do with the magical artifacts. She decided to continue with her family's wishes, so she returned the Lantern of the Blue Flame to the ISG and kept the gauntlet for herself. This decision seemed to make both the BEA and the ISG very unhappy, so she figured it was a good one.

Along the way, BEA nurses and ISG healers argued over how best to treat Sam's cuts and burn. They even fussed over her hair, which she thought was pretty rude. In the end the healers won. Their special bandages could not only heal Sam's injuries in an hour, but do it without leaving big, nasty telltale scars behind. They also assured Sam that Nero's spell would wear off and she would regain full use of her left arm in a few hours. She was looking forward to that.

Shortly after getting back to campus, Agent Sampson and Deputy Colver made her tell them everything that had happened. In turn they had interviewed everyone else, a process that took several boring hours. While Zoey was being interviewed, a pair of sullen ISG witches approached Sam telling her that they were unable to save her hair. Apparently she hadn't done as good a job of avoiding the great golden snake as she thought. A few strands of her bangs had turned to gold, and the witches had no idea how to turn them back. Considering the other things that could have happened to her, Sam figured she could live with it.

Sam was twisting the golden strands, which flexed and curled like normal hair, between her fingers when Natch strode back into the room and took a seat in the corner all by himself. That had to mean that Lucas had finally woken up. He was the last person to be interviewed, so as soon as he was done they could go.

Tasha and her parents sat on one side of the waiting room, discussing what had happened. They were very proud of their daughter and not nearly as angry or worried as Sam imagined Helen and Harold would be in their places. That was one reason Sam wasn't going to tell them.

Zack and his mother sat on the other side of the room, away from everyone else. It took Sam a few minutes to remember where she had seen Zack's mother before. Sam was forced to watch a movie about her in fourth-grade gym; she was Swiss athlete Astrid Luhner, now Astrid McQueen, the first woman to win gold medals in both the Summer and Winter Olympics. Apparently Zack's father was too busy taking care of things at the casino to come check on his son.

Sam sat in the middle of the room with Zoey. Neither of them had much to say; Zoey looked nearly as tired as Sam felt. None of them were supposed to leave. Amy, Agent Rosenberg, stood guard at the door just to make sure. Sam was glad to see that she had survived her tussle with the dinosaur in one piece.

From what Sam had pieced together, the zombie dinosaur was about to eat Coach Powers when it suddenly turned back into a fossilized femur. That was probably at the exact moment Sam handed the Lantern of the Blue Flame over to Deputy Colver and he commanded the lantern to undo all of Nero's resurrections. Sam wished she had thought of that.

She caught Zack eyeing the remains of the Witch Hunter's Gauntlet in her lap.

"What?" she yelled loudly across the room.

"Oh, nothing," Zack said innocently. "We're just discussing how the gauntlet survived for thousands of years only to be destroyed by one touch from you."

"Be polite," his mother scolded. Although judging by the half-smile on her face, she didn't really mean it.

Sam looked away.

She didn't know how she had broken the priceless ancient magical artifact. She just did. It didn't necessarily mean anything, or so she told herself repeatedly.

"Couldn't get the gems to light up, huh?" Mr. Beaumont said, taking a seat near her. "Me either. Neither could your father."

"What?" Sam asked in total shock.

"I was there, at Baldorag Castle, when your parents found the gauntlet," he said proudly. "I'm not surprised you don't know. We swore never to bring it up unless it was absolutely necessary."

Sam didn't know what to say. So many questions were competing for attention in her brain. She tried her best to pick the right one.

"What? How? When?" she blurted.

"It was years ago. A couple years before your parents got married," he said with a far-off look in eye as the memories came flooding back. "Cervantes was on a rampage and your father got it into his head that he was going to be the one to stop him. Against your grandfather's wishes I might add. Your mother was bound and determined to go with him. And since they were about to do battle with the most powerful vampire of our time, they came to my father for help. When he said no, I said yes. I was young, stupid, and ready to prove myself.

"So there we were, three college kids out to show the world how it was supposed to be done. Cervantes had let it slip that he was looking for the Witch Hunter's Gauntlet. Your father tracked it down to Baldorag Castle, and we rushed to claim it before Cervantes could." Mr. Beaumont shook his head. "It just goes to show how naïve we really were. Cervantes had let it slip on purpose and was using us to find the gauntlet for him. We led him straight to it."

That was a lot to take in all of a sudden. But something in his story stuck out as wrong to her.

"Why did Cervantes want it?" she asked. "I thought it only worked for non-magical people."

Mr. Beaumont nodded enthusiastically. "It does. We figured either he was going to give it to someone, someone he could control, or he just wanted to eliminate the only weapon that could stop him. We never found out which."

"Because you got there first," she guessed.

"Right, but we couldn't get it to work," he said. He still sounded a little embarrassed about it. "It turned out we weren't the big heroes we thought we were, until Cervantes was about to kill your father. I can still remember it like it happened yesterday. He had Samuel by the throat, dangling in the air. My left leg was shattered; there was nothing I could do. And then suddenly the whole room lit up like the sun itself had fallen into the castle. When the light finally faded Cervantes had turned to ash, Samuel was gasping for air on the ground, and there stood your mother, wearing the gauntlet. And then just as suddenly, the gems went out and the gauntlet was useless again. None of us were ever able to get it to light up ever again, so your parents decided to hide it."

"But how did she get it to work?"

"None of us knew for sure," he said, shaking his head. "But I think it worked because your mother was trying to save someone she loved. I think that gave her the power, the pure emotional strength, to activate it."

"But if it wouldn't work for three heroes like you, why did it work for Nero?"

Mr. Beaumont laughed and then sighed. "I don't know if you should go and throw the H-word around like that, although we certainly tried our best. But you have to consider the culture that created the gauntlet; back then their heroes were conquering kings, fearless warriors who challenged the gods themselves, men and women who made history with the tip of a sword. They were passionate, fearless, and ready to fight for what they believed in. Those qualities could apply to a hero or a villain. It all depends on how they choose to act on them."

That wasn't a comforting thought at all. Those ancient mystics should have put a little more thought into the design of their awesome magical weapon. Maybe they could have taken the time to teach it that people who want to save their friends and destroy vampires are good and people who want to start wars and turn people into zombies are bad.

"You know, I had the gauntlet in my hands before Nero even put it on," Sam confessed. It was like admitting that she had set a church on fire or something equally horrible. "If I had been braver, I could have stopped all of this from happening."

"But you did stop him, Sam," Mr. Beaumont said, resting his hand reassuringly on her shoulder. Mrs. Beaumont and Tasha nodded in agreement.

"Yeah," Zack spoke up from his side of the room, where he had clearly been eavesdropping. "Your patheticness was stronger than his courage. You beat him by being the world's biggest loser. Way to go."

The Beaumonts and Zoey gave him nasty looks. Natch just laughed. Zack's mother cracked a tight little half-smile.

"That's it!" Tasha sprung to her feet, fire in her eyes.

"It's okay," Sam said to everyone. "He's sort of right."

Sam might have been mad at him if the thought hadn't already occurred to her.

"My patheticness was like kryptonite to the gauntlet," she said, patting the twisted metal in her lap.

Mr. Beaumont winced. "I don't know if I'd phrase it like that-"

"Hey, at least I did better than hiding in a broom closet waiting for the BEA to show up." Okay, so she did have to get in at least one little dig on Zack. It wasn't like he didn't deserve it.

Mr. Beaumont chuckled softly. "Yes, you did. In fact, if you hadn't been draining power away from the gauntlet at the time, I'm positive he would have teleported away with the entire gauntlet."

"Do you think his half still works?" It was the million-dollar question. If his piece still worked, all of this could just start all over again.

"I don't think so," Mr. Beaumont said. From the tone in his voice, she could tell he had been thinking about it for quite a while now. "I also don't think he knew that teleporting away at half power would splinter it. Wherever he is, he isn't happy."

Something was still nagging at her.

"Do you think this means there won't be another Heroic Age?" she asked softly, afraid of the answer.

"What do you mean?"

"The Witch Hunter's Gauntlet is also called the Hero's Glove because whenever it is discovered it ushers in a new Heroic Age, right? But this time it was broken. There might never be another Heroic Age."

"Hmm, you make a good point," Mr. Beaumont said slowly rubbing his chin. "It may be for the best."

She hadn't expected that answer. "How?"

"Well, for one, we don't need a powerful weapon floating around that could fall into the hands of someone like Alex Nero Jr. Besides it seems like each Heroic Age has been shorter than the one before it. Ours didn't amount to much. It could be that we no longer need them as much anymore. Or maybe we just need a new kind of hero. Look at how much more has been accomplished in the last few centuries without the gauntlet's influence. Louis Pasteur; Mother Teresa; Mahatma Gandhi; Martin Luther King Jr.; and so many others have improved the world in ways far greater than most of those old sword-swinging warriors ever did. Maybe it is time that we look to ourselves to be the heroes we need, not some magical device."

Mr. Beaumont got up from his seat.

"But just in case," he said, patting her on the shoulder. "Maybe you should keep that thing in a safe place."

"I'll try," she answered. She really had no idea what she was going to do with the stupid thing.

"I know that Samuel and Joanne would be very proud," he said warmly.

"Thank you. But I have so many more-"

Mr. Beaumont shook his head ever so slightly and glanced quickly at Agent Rosenberg. It was a clear sign that any other questions Sam had would have to wait until they were away from the prying ears of the BEA. Sam had the feeling that a lot of their adventures were not exactly the kind that the BEA would have approved of.

She nodded in agreement.

"You have inherited a very heavy burden. It is completely unfair but completely inescapable," he said with the air of someone who knows. "But then again, nothing beats the feeling of saving the day, right?"

"It certainly feels… different."

Mr. Beaumont burst out laughing, a real gut-busting laugh. It was bordering on insulting. When he finally got himself under control, he looked her right in the eye.

"That is exactly what your mom said."

Chapter 26

The Last Age

Even the rush from Mr. Beaumont comparing Sam to her mother, easily the best compliment she had ever received in her life, couldn't stop Sam from thinking about the things Nero had said. Was Miller's Grove just a training ground for some super-teen army? Were they here to become the best they could be or to fight a war? Was her grandfather Professor Xavier or Magneto?

At that exact moment, the one person who could answer her questions entered the room. Doc Frost had changed back into his usual lab coat. He looked extremely tired, but also quite relieved.

"Ah, Lucas must be awake, finally," he said as he took the seat across from Sam.

"Yes," she answered flatly, trying to hide her own overwhelming relief, but judging by the way Zoey smiled at her she had failed.

Sam shot her a quick "knock it off" look.

Doc Frost didn't notice any of this; he was more interested in the piece of gauntlet in her hands.

"It seems like you have been given a rather large responsibility there," he said.

"Yeah," she said unenthusiastically. She didn't know if her piece of the gauntlet could still do, well, anything, or if the two pieces could be put back together somehow. But she was pretty sure someone would come looking for it.

"You made clever use of it tonight," Doc Frost said. "Draining the gauntlet's power."

"I didn't do anything."

"Didn't you? I saw the whole thing," he said. "The first time it practically leapt into his arms, but the second time it resisted."

"Maybe it was because he was distracted from getting his hand cut off."

Doc Frost nodded. "Maybe. But what were you thinking at the time?"

"Nothing. I just didn't want him to get it."

Doc Frost smiled and tilted his head.

Sam didn't believe it. But there was that one tiny spark...

"Anyway, I found this after you left." Doc Frost pulled Mr. Hopscotch out of his coat pocket.

Instantly her eyes welled up. It was embarrassing, but she couldn't help it. She didn't want to help it.

"Mr. Hopscotch!" She took the bear with both hands and gave him the biggest hug ever.

"I think you'll find that he's as good as new," Doc Frost said softly. His left pointer finger wiggled ever so slightly--so slightly, in fact, she wasn't sure if she had seen it correctly, but next to his finger was a loose thread on the bear's belly.

Sam inspected the bear. Aside from the loose thread Mr. Hopscotch was looking better than he had in years. He had been dried and restuffed, and now a small, smooth black stone hung from a silver chain around his neck. It looked strangely familiar. And then she realized it was a piece of the anvil that had broken off when Cervantes pulled out the sword.

"A funny thing about tesseracts," Doc Frost said quietly. "When they're closed it is next to impossible to find the darn things again. So you have to bind them, by just one single tiny atom perhaps, to an object so you know where it is at all times."

He sat back and looked around the room briefly as if to say that he would not speak about it any further with all of these people around. But that was okay, because Sam was pretty sure she understood. She had other pressing questions that she just had to ask at the moment.

"Doctor Frost, you knew my grandfather really well, right?" Sam asked.

He smiled at her in a kind, resigned sort of way that made Sam think he knew what she was about to ask.

"I had the honor of working with him for many, many years. A brilliant man."

"Why did he help establish this school?" She was too tired to beat around the bush.

"You're concerned about the things young Mr. Nero said," Doc Frost said in a soft tone. "You think your grandfather conspired to build a school to train some sort of private army?"

"But what about the hovertanks? And copying Lucas's brain? And Dean Futuro-"

Doc Frost waved his hand to cut her off. "All valid points. I admit Alistair Futuro has always been a little more eccentric than the rest of us. In fact, Dr. Hathaway was the only one who could get him to tone it down a bit. During the early planning stages of the university, Alistair wanted the school to focus solely on science and technology. It was Samuel who talked him into opening up the school to the full range of academics, athletics, and the arts. He understood that not all of the universe's mysteries could be unlocked with circuits and electrodes alone, and that inspiration can come from the most unlikely of sources.

"It was your grandfather's idea to open an academy where a wide range of the best, brightest, and most dedicated young people of all fields, especially those commonly overlooked by traditional schools, could come together and hone their skills, pursue their passions, and share their ideas for the betterment of all mankind. In his absence we have all done our best to uphold his ideals--even Dean Futuro, in his own way," Doc Frost said.

That sounded like a nice snippet to put in a brochure, but considering she wasn't the best, brightest, or the most dedicated at anything, it just made her remember that if it weren't for her last name she wouldn't even be here. Plus, it didn't really answer her question.

"But, what about-?" she started to ask.

"The point of all of this," Doc Frost answered, "Is to make the world a better place. It was his way of making amends for his one terrible mistake. That is why he spent so much of his fortune and time campaigning to have this place built and outfitted with the most state-of-the-art technologies. And part of making of the world a better place is defense. It is a cruel fact of life, but there are other threats out there besides Alex Nero. Some are far worse."

His face grew dark as if he had just thought of some terrible thing he tried very hard not to think about. And then, just as instantly, he perked back up again.

"Good to see you, Mr. Fry."

Sam turned to see Lucas walk into the waiting room flanked on either side by Agent Sampson and Deputy Colver.

"About time you woke up, Sleeping Beauty," Tasha said jokingly.

"Thanks a lot," he said as he sat down next to Natch.

He sheepishly cast his eyes at Sam and quickly looked away before she could smile or speak or anything.

"So," he said, turning toward Natch and away from her. "What was Esteban's room like?"

"Like I'm going to tell you a juicy bit of information like that for free," Natch said, holding his hand out. "Fifty bucks."

"Ahem," Agent Sampson said loudly.

The boys stopped talking.

Agent Sampson stood in the middle of the room like a very annoyed statue while Amy passed out thick documents and pens.

"Well, congratulations," Agent Sampson announced. "Your stories match up. And apparently, for about the hundredth time the world owes its safety yet again to the Beaumonts, Hathaways, and McQueens. And their friends, of course."

That wasn't a very accurate dispersal of credit. Sam and her friends pulled off some pretty amazing stuff, but according to his own story, all Zack did was set off a secret alarm that alerted the BEA and ISG to rush to the casino. As if they wouldn't have figured that out on their own when they heard about the big flaming bat chasing Santa's sleigh around Las Vegas, but whatever.

Deputy Colver stepped forward. "The ISG thanks you all for your assistance as well." He looked directly at Sam, his hands crossed in front of him. "I have also been charged with extending a sincere apology to you, Samantha Hathaway, on behalf of Constable Albion. He would have preferred to apologize in person, of course, but he is still recovering from the recent ordeal. He sacrificed several years' worth of his own life force to destroy Nero's Abyss Shield."

Sam got the feeling he added that last part to make sure she felt guilty enough to accept the apology. It worked.

"Tell him I accept," she said. "And that I hope he gets better soon."

"I will," he said with a happy nod.

"Yes, well, we were all played for suckers on this one," Agent Sampson said. "He knew exactly how to play on our old mistrusts and fears."

The not-too-subtle dig was not lost on Deputy Colver, who shifted awkwardly on his feet.

"You don't honestly expect us to sign this, do you?" Natch asked, holding up the papers Amy had given them. "You want a group of minors to sign a confidentiality agreement without legal counsel or our parents' knowledge?"

Agent Sampson took a deep breath and smiled.

"I expected that reaction from you, Mr.-"

"I'm sure you did," Natch blurted out quickly, cutting Agent Sampson off. Lucas looked particularly disappointed.

"The BEA would like to count on your support in the future. But for everyone's safety we must preserve certain secrets from the general public, for the time being, of course." He gestured to Deputy Colver. "However, if any of you should choose not to sign the agreement, then I believe Deputy Colver has been authorized by his superiors to perform memory-erasing spells on all of you."

"It is quite painless," Deputy Colver said reassuringly. "Not that you would remember anyway."

Natch did not look happy, but he signed the papers anyway, as did everyone else. Lucas leaned over to try to see Natch's real name, but Natch twisted away from him and covered the paper with his left arm.

"Thank you for your support," Agent Sampson said as Amy went around the room collecting the signed documents. "Now for your cover story. The rest of the school is under the impression that last night's fire and commotion was all part of an elaborate Halloween show to create a properly spooky atmosphere. Tragically, the show was cut short when one of Doctor Frost's experiments, left unattended in the excitement of the holiday festivities, accidentally exploded, releasing an electromagnetic wave that fried everyone's cell phones, computers, and other electronic equipment."

It didn't seem fair for Doc Frost to take the blame, but he nodded in agreement.

Agent Sampson continued. "You all were supposed to be part of the show, but since it was abruptly ended due to technical difficulties, you all just simply returned to your rooms and watched scary movies when the power came back on. That is where you found Mr. Fry home from a night of trick-or-treating. If anyone asks about your scars, tell them it was a hilarious but embarrassing apple-bobbing accident. As for your little escapade in Las Vegas, fortunately, the McQueens have graciously agreed to go along with the cover story that the casino suffered minor fire damage due to a gas leak."

"The Camelot was due for a remodel anyway," Zack's mom said.

Agent Sampson continued. "And our friends at the ISG have altered the memories of key personnel in Las Vegas to believe that the flaming bat and Santa Claus bit was actually some pop star's stage show gone wrong."

"And you expect everyone to believe all this?" Natch asked, reluctantly handing his signed form to Amy.

"It doesn't matter if they believe it. That is what happened," he answered sternly.

Personally, Sam thought it sounded like a pretty believable story. She would have been really happy with a night like that. In fact, part of her would rather think that was what happened.

"What about 'Jerry'?" Zack asked.

"Ah, yes. The official story is that 'Jerry' simply cracked under the pressure and returned home," Agent Sampson said with a shrug.

"What about his roommate?" Lucas asked with his hand raised as if this was just another class.

"Turns out he didn't exist," Agent Sampson said.

Lucas lowered his hand. "Oh."

"All we found in his room was the fat suit and hair dye he used to disguise himself," Amy added.

Sam was the last person to hand her signed confidentially agreement to Amy. Amy handed the forms to Agent Sampson, who shuffled through them quickly, undoubtedly making sure they had all been properly signed. Satisfied, he slipped the papers into a shiny black folder.

"Okay," he said in a deep, serious tone as he placed the folder into a metal box. "Remember, what happened tonight never happened. Now I think it is best that everyone gets some rest."

That sounded wonderful to Sam, but Zack apparently still had more to say.

"What about Nero?" he asked. "Have you found him yet? Or is it up to us to finish that job for you too?"

From the way he motioned to his mother, Sam was pretty sure the 'us' he was referring to was the McQueens.

Agent Sampson slapped a clearly fake smile on his face. "As much as the BEA has enjoyed the assistance of certain independent parties in the past, I must assure you that we have the situation under control."

"So you found him?" Zack pressed.

The fake smile disappeared from Agent Sampson's face.

"Actually," he said slowly. "He found us."

Sam couldn't believe it. She looked from Agent Sampson to Amy to see if this was true. For a second they locked eyes, and Sam could tell that it was true; but then Amy looked away, almost ashamed.

"A couple months ago-," Agent Sampson said, breaking the stunned silence. "Victoria Nero contacted our agency to report that her son had been kidnapped from his English boarding school by his bodyguard. She was afraid that he had been brainwashed. We've been looking for him ever since."

"No way-," Zack and Tasha yelled at the same time. They gave each other nasty looks as if they couldn't believe the other had dared to have the same exact reaction.

Agent Sampson ignored them. "We were all quite surprised to see him in the casino tonight. According to the reports I've recently received, Alexander woke up from his brainwashed state when his hand was cut off. Scared and confused, he used the gauntlet to teleport to the only place he thought was safe, his mother's estate in New York, where she found him bleeding and unconscious a mere three hours ago. After calling her private physicians to stabilize his condition she alerted the BEA."

"Do not tell me you're falling for this?" Tasha yelled. Mr. Beaumont held her shoulders to keep her calm.

Sam felt Doc Frost's reassuring hand on her shoulder as well.

"Right now, the BEA is looking into all possible explanations," Agent Sampson said in his official government-agent voice. "The bodyguard we arrested backed up the story. He claimed he found out about the gauntlet from Alexander Nero Sr. and used a combination of medication and psychological manipulation to brainwash Alex into stealing the item for him."

"Wow, that's a pretty brilliant lie," Zack said as if he was actually impressed.

"Agreed," Deputy Colver said coldly.

Sam was certainly glad to see that at least someone in authority knew a lie when they heard one.

Then Zack brought up another important question. "What about all the technology he stole?"

"We don't know. The official story is that, due to the severity of the brainwashing technique used on Alexander Nero Jr., he has no memories of what happened. And unfortunately, shortly after confessing the bodyguard ingested a memory-wiping pill he had hidden in one of his teeth," Agent Sampson said.

"Oh, what a load-," Tasha started but Mrs. Beaumont gave her a warning look.

Agent Sampson cleared his throat loudly.

"Possibly," he said. "However, fortunately for us, most of the technology that was stolen would have been damaged by the very same EMP that was used to take down the school's security systems. It would take months for someone to recover all the damaged data and a considerable fortune for them to begin production on anything they discovered."

"A fortune? Well it is a good thing that Nero is dirt poor then isn't it? Oh wait, his family owns a giant billion-dollar international corporation," Zack said with a cocky bob of his head.

Agent Sampson nodded. "A company which the BEA will be monitoring closely."

"As will the ISG," Deputy Colver added.

Agent Sampson looked directly at Sam. "I must remind you all that, while the BEA has overlooked freelance investigations in the past, we cannot allow anyone to interfere with our investigation. Anyone found harassing the Nero family will be arrested."

He looked away before Sam could decide if he was warning her, or challenging her.

"Agent Rosenberg, I believe it is time to escort our young heroes back to their rooms."

And with that, the meeting was clearly over. It was decided that Amy would escort Sam, Tasha, Zoey, and the Beaumonts back to Cooper Hall, Agent Sampson would escort Zack and his mother back to his dorm, and Doc Frost would escort Lucas and Natch back to their dorm. Sam waved at Lucas as they parted company. He waved back, but it was a short, half-hearted wave.

Campus was cold and empty in the wee early hours of the morning. Everyone was either too angry or too tired to talk. Sam placed herself solidly in the too-tired category.

As they reached the dorm, they caught the sound of voices approaching from behind a cluster of frosted spruce trees. Everyone but Sam snapped into action. Tasha and her parents formed a protective triangle around Sam and Zoey while Amy stepped in front of the entire group, her hand in her suit jacket, ready to draw her gun on whoever came around the corner. Even Zoey had taken some sort of karate stance.

Sam imagined they all looked pretty foolish to Dean Futuro and the tall, thin man in the fancy suit and bowler hat walking with him. From his posture and expensive briefcase, Sam was not only positive that this man was a lawyer, but she suspected that he could have been the real-life lawyer that all cartoon lawyers were based on. He gave her a passing glance, as if appraising how much money she could be worth as a client and deciding she wasn't worth the precious seconds it took to evaluate her.

"May I introduce, Mr. Ellis," Dean Futuro said with a feeble wave of his hand.

"Hello," the lawyer said. "I represent the interests of Nero Industries and the Nero family."

Sam instantly tensed up. She did not like the way he was smiling; it looked like a kid who had just eaten the last cookie while no one was looking.

"This is Samantha Hathaway, and a bunch of other people," Dean Futuro said, pointing at Sam with a long crooked finger.

"Ah, yes, I have been personally charged by Veronica Nero herself to thank for your help in locating her son Alexander," the lawyer said in a very polite New England accent. "And to assure you that she will not be pressing any charges over the unfortunate loss of limb."

He pursed his lips and chuckled to himself over what he must have thought was a funny joke.

"In fact," the lawyer continued, "Mrs. Nero is so grateful that she has agreed to cover the expenses to repair all of the damages and replace all of the personal belongings destroyed by Carlson's horrific and regrettable assault on your lovely academy."

"That is very generous," Dean Futuro said, laying it on a bit thick. "While she is in such a generous mode you may want to mention to Mrs. Nero that Miller's Grove could benefit greatly from the addition of a new genetics laboratory."

Without even excusing himself, Dean Futuro walked straight through their little group with the lawyer trailing him.

"Come this way. I'll show you the perfect place for Nero Hall."

Mr. Ellis tipped his hat. "A pleasure meeting you all."

Nero Hall?

If Sam needed another reason why she should leave Miller's Grove, that was it. She could put up with her token underachiever status at the school, with the irrationally vindictive pop star, and even with the occasional zombie dinosaur, but living near a building named in honor of a family that had done so much to ruin her life was surely more than anyone could expect from her. If she was leaving anyway, she might as well give Dean Futuro a piece of her mind. She found herself marching toward Futuro and the lawyer with no idea what she was going to say when she reached them.

"Stop, Sam," Tasha urged, grabbing her hand and pulling her back.

"I know how angry you are," Mr. Beaumont said, stepping in Sam's way. "But yelling at Dean Futuro will only make things worse."

"You do not want to be on Futuro's bad side. He could expel you without a second thought," Mrs. Beaumont added in that stern-but-sympathetic mom tone. It was exactly like the tone Sam's mom had used on her.

"Fine, let him." Sam yanked her arm out of Tasha's grip. "First Nero gets off scot-free for trying to take over the world, and now he is getting his own building? Why would I want to stay here?"

"Believe me Sam, no one believes Alex is innocent," Mr. Beaumont said calmly. "But claims of brainwashing and mind control are very difficult to disprove. I've encountered at least four types of mind control in my life, and two of them are untraceable. It will take time for the BEA to determine what really happened."

"But-"

"Just give it time, Samantha," Mrs. Beaumont said. "There's no need to make any rash decisions. Sleep on it."

"You can't leave," Tasha pleaded, fear and loss in her eyes.

"Yeah, you can't leave now," Zoey chimed in. "We have that English test on Monday. I need someone to study with."

The truth was, Sam was very tempted to just go home. Getting expelled for standing up to the Dean would be a great way to do it. She could feel good about it, and Helen and Harold would understand.

It certainly would be nice to go back to her nice quiet life in Presley; but that was not what Samuel Hathaway Jr., would do; it wasn't what Joanne Hathaway would do; and it was not what Samantha Hathaway was going to do. She had to stay. If she ran, Nero would win.

It was as simple as that.

"I'm not going anywhere," Sam reassured everyone. Tasha in particular looked relieved. "I'm not giving Nero the satisfaction. He can't chase me away from my friends or my rightful place at the school my grandfather founded just by buying some silly building. Besides, if I went home, how would I stop the stupid thing from being built?"

Tasha's hand shot up in the air, waiting for a high five. "Yes!"

Sam slapped her hand. Before she could lower her arm, Zoey rushed forward and pinned her in a tight bear hug. Sam awkwardly bent down her free arm to pat Zoey's shoulder.

"Thank you for not leaving me alone in this crazy place," Zoey said, clinging to Sam like she was a life preserver on the Titanic.

"Never," Sam said. "We're in this together. Whether we like it or not."

The Beaumonts offered to buy the girls breakfast, but all they wanted to do was sleep. Sam had already decided against changing out of her costume. That was just precious sleep time that she would be wasting. But she had one more task to perform before she could go to bed.

She slipped into the bathroom, telling everyone that she needed to examine her new lock of golden hair for a minute. In reality she just needed a few minutes alone. But she was going to have to work fast; girls were going to be waking up and staggering in at any minute. She could not risk letting anyone see what she was about to do.

Pulling on the loose thread on Mr. Hopscotch's belly released the flap of fur on his right side just the way she hoped it would. Doc Frost had returned Mr. Hopscotch to his original condition, including the tesseract controller hidden inside of him. Gently she retrieved the controller, making sure not to remove any of the bear's stuffing. She then took the necklace from the bear's neck and set it on the counter next to the sink.

When she hit the button, she saw a tiny spark of light wink into existence right above the anvil piece. Without hesitation she put her hand into the light, which expanded to the size of her arm, forming a glowing bracelet. Everything past the bracelet had vanished. It was quite disconcerting to look down and not see her hand, but she could still feel her fingers wiggling inside the tesseract.

For some reason she had expected the inside of the tesseract to be cold, but it wasn't. It wasn't warm either. Aside from the movement of her skin over the tendons in her hand as she wiggled her fingers, she couldn't feel anything.

Once she removed her hand and gave it a quick inspection to make sure it hadn't been damaged somehow, she retrieved the remains of the gauntlet from her pocket and slid it into the light. She pulled her hand back out and hit the button to close the tesseract.

After putting the controller back inside Mr. Hopscotch's belly and doing her best to close up his side, she slipped the anvil necklace over her head. From now on, the most powerful weapon in the world was going to be near her at all times. If Nero was going to come looking for the other half, he was going to have to go through her first.

Sam returned to her room to find Zoey already asleep. She hadn't changed out of her costume either; in fact, she hadn't even managed to get under the covers; she had just sprawled out on her bedspread. She was even drooling onto her pillow already. Sam wished she had a camera.

After yanking off her boots and nestling Mr. Hopscotch into a comfy nest between the pillows, Sam curled up on her bed beside him. But before letting her heavy eyelids close, she took one last look at her new necklace. It would serve as the perfect reminder of her brand-new responsibility.

Despite Mr. Beaumont's kind words, Sam knew the truth. There might never be another Heroic Age because of her. Somehow she was going to make this one count.

But first she was going to sleep for the next day and a half.

Printed in Great Britain
by Amazon.co.uk, Ltd.,
Marston Gate.